MECHANICAL HEART

May your voice be heard.

Sarah Pennington

SARAH PENNINGTON

Mechanical Heart

Cover design by Dragonpen Designs (www.dragonpenpress.com)

Published 2019

Printed in the United States of America

ISBN: 9781075485183

This book is dedicated to Alana and Rachel because without good friends and little sisters, nothing in it would get done.

CHAPTER 1

Her heart beat on, as it always did.

Breen waited, eyes shut, trying to ignore the pain of her bones knitting back together. The crystal in her chest burned with an almost unbearable heat as it fed magical energy into her body. Yet the clockwork of her heart pumped on, unperturbed.

She'd fallen. Again. That seemed to be happening more and more lately. She wondered how many stories it had been this time. Just one? Two? Three? She opened her eyes and stared at the machinery crisscrossed with wooden walkways above her. Only two floors this time. Not so bad, all things considered.

The heat from the crystal slowly faded as the last fractures healed. Breen flexed her fingers; wiggled her toes inside her worn shoes; bent her elbows and knees, making sure everything had healed. She almost hoped that something *wouldn't* work. Perhaps if she were broken enough, Madame Gottling would take her somewhere other than the clock tower. But, no, all her limbs seemed functional once again, if a bit sore.

With a sigh, she sat up and gathered the tools that had scattered from her belt. Of course such a short fall wouldn't break her irreparably. She still remembered the time she'd dropped down four of the clock tower's ten stories — more accurately, she remembered the pain *after* she'd fallen. Her injuries had healed in a mere fifteen minutes, but for the rest of that day, every movement made her wince.

Today, however, the pain was already as good as gone, and there was nothing to stop her from continuing her work. Breen headed for the nearest flight of narrow iron stairs and climbed up, passing weights and counterweights and massive gears set with sparkling gems. Everything shone bronze or copper or, in the case of the gems, various shades of red, blue, and white. Of course it shone — she had to clean it all while she checked for wear and breakage. As if magic *could* wear down.

The clock struck two just as she reached the second-to-top level where she'd been working. The sound made the floor vibrate beneath her feet and up through her bones, and all the gems on the gears flashed like sudden stars. Breen stood still and savored the moment.

Then the gems faded, and the tower stilled, and she had to go back to work. Breen stepped off the wooden walkway and straddled a long beam of grey steel. She slid herself along with careless speed — after all, it wasn't as if falling again *mattered.*

[2]

She reached the spot where she'd been before her most recent tumble, locked her legs around the beam, and grabbed her polishing cloth from where it had snagged on the tooth of a gear. Then she inspected the nearest gears one by one and inch by inch, wiping away dust and dirt, occasionally scraping away specks of corrosion with a thin scrap of metal. Thankfully, Breen found no serious damage on that level, nor the two above.

At last, she reached the very top of the tower. Up here, the great glass clock faces let the afternoon sunlight stream in. Breen carefully checked and cleaned the smaller gears and the massive rods that turned the clock hands, then tucked her tools back in her belt and stretched. When Madame Gottling came tonight, she would surely be satisfied with Breen's work.

Breen unbuckled her toolbelt and dropped it to the wooden walkway. Until Madame arrived, she could relax. Then she sat down by the western clock face and rested an elbow on the frame. From here, she could stare out and watch the whole city spread out below her.

Years ago, when she'd first been brought to the clock tower, she'd feared to look outside. She had been warned again and again that she must never let others see her. That anyone who found her would call her an abomination. But people never seemed to look *up*, and with the tower's height and the afternoon sun glinting off the clock face, Breen doubted anyone would notice her.

She, however, noticed them.

Here, high above almost every other building in the city, she sat and watched life go by. The streets bustled with boxy black carriages, most horse-drawn, others horseless and puffing steam from pipes attached to the backs of the passenger boxes. On the sidewalks, men in black or brown suits and ladies in bright dresses strolled together, chatting and laughing merrily, or hurried along, faces hidden by their hat brims, weaving alone through the crowds. Smoke flowed in ribbons and streamers above them and around the tower, pulled from the chimneys of homes and factories alike.

Over the slums and factory districts across the river, the smoke hung black and heavy as a bank of thunderclouds. But Breen only glanced that way for the briefest of moments. Thinking about the part of the city she'd once called home always made her uncomfortably aware of the clockwork in her chest and the loneliness that lurked in the back of her mind. It was better for her to be up here instead of down there. At least up here, she had the view — better than being choked by smoke in a factory or locked away in a laboratory. Still, she'd gladly trade the sights of the city for a hug from her parents or an evening of chatter with the others like her in the lab.

Instead of looking at the factory district, Breen watched the palace. Though far older than almost any other building in the city, it was still grand, with its cone-topped towers and sturdy red stone walls and the golden dome in the center that shone in the afternoon sunshine. Chania's Senate met under that dome every week. And the royal family lived in the east wing, the one nearer her tower, while the west wing was filled with government offices.

Once, before the accident, her father had brought her and all her siblings across the river. He'd led them up to the edge of the palace grounds, as close as anyone could go without being nobility. There, while they stared, he told them all about the palace and those within it as proudly as if he were one of the senators or nobles.

Breen had often wondered since then why he'd been so proud. Neither the king nor the government seemed to have helped her family much. Not when they'd nearly starved one winter because food cost more than her family made. Not when they'd nearly been turned out of their house two summers before that because the factory owners cut Breen's father's pay. Not when the accident had nearly killed Breen and *had* killed Lily. But she remembered his words all the same.

Breen stayed in the tower-top, watching, until darkness covered the sky and streetlamps flickered on, casting white alchemical light over the sidewalks and streets. Her stomach pinched with hunger, but she'd eaten the last of her bread and porridge the day before. She'd have no more until Madame Gottling arrived.

At last, Breen's pocket vibrated with Madame's signal device. Breen leaped to her feet, scrambled back down to the next level, and dashed to the cut-out corner of the floor where a thin chain looped through a series of pulleys. She grabbed the chain and pulled, grunting with the effort.

Soon, a railed platform rose to floor level, its edges bumping against the wall. On it stood Madame Gottling, straight and unyielding as the tower itself. Madame stepped off the lift, set down her large carpetbag, and turned to Breen. She signed with sharp hand motions: "You were slow."

She'd moved as fast as she could. What more did Madame expect? But Breen just bowed her head and circled her fist over her heart. "Sorry."

Madame gave a little shake of her head and headed for the stairs. Breen followed as Madame walked through the tower, inspecting gears and cogs and rods, running her fingers across the metal and frowning at any minuscule specks of wear she found. But, as Breen had expected, Madame found nothing to criticize, and so she started back up the stairs without a word to Breen.

On the top level, Madame picked her bag up and stalked across to the cupboard against the wall where Breen kept her food. A ruby pendant bounced on her chest with each step. Breen stood still, waiting and watching as Madame Gottling unloaded hard bread, porridge oats, and small potatoes into the cupboard. No tea, Breen noted with a frown, but that was to be expected. It was only early autumn, and she'd not receive tea until midwinter.

Madame shut the cupboard and pulled on a pair of gloves from her pocket. She removed a clear glass flask and several vials of liquid from the bag. She set the flask on the single gas burner of Breen's tiny stove, turned the burner on, and poured the contents of several vials into the flask. The clear liquid bubbled as she stirred the chemicals together with a glass rod. Then, from the smallest vial, she added a tiny bit of thick liquid that turned the concoction an angry crimson. She stirred the mixture for a few more minutes. Then she turned around and faced Breen, signing: "Sit."

Breen sat down on her hard cot. Anticipating the next order, she unbuttoned the top of her rough work shirt to reveal the brass socket at the top of her ribcage. A miazen crystal shone faintly in the socket, clear save for the red glow at its very center.

Madame nodded brusque approval, stalked over, and twisted the crystal out of its socket. Breen felt the loss of its magic immediately. Her body became heavier; her heartbeat slowed; all her weariness rushed on her at once. She watched Madame's lips as the woman inspected the crystal and muttered to herself, but her brain worked too slowly for her to interpret any of her words.

Madame's lips hadn't stopped moving when she returned to her flask and dropped the crystal into the boiling solution. Breen counted the seconds and minutes silently. One, two, three minutes since the crystal's removal, and her heartbeat continued to slow, the ticking and whirring gears louder than usual in her ears. Four, five, six, and her fingers and toes grew numb. Seven, eight, nine, and grey crept into the corners of her vision. Ten . . . eleven . . . twelve . . . focusing enough to count became difficult.

On the stove, Madame's solution slowly faded from red to clear as the miazen crystal soaked in the crimson hue. By the time Breen counted thirteen minutes, the crystal glowed like the sunset.

Madame withdrew the crystal out of the flask. Without a word, she returned to Breen and twisted the crystal back into place.

Renewed magic spread through Breen's body like warmth from a fire. Her head cleared, and her vision snapped back into focus. The tick of her heartbeat sped back to normal, and her fingers and toes tingled. For a moment, she felt actually alive. Then the magic quieted, and everything faded into dull normalcy.

Breen stood, murmuring words she couldn't hear, accompanied by signs: "Thank you, Madame." Then, at the woman's command, she carefully lowered her mistress back down the lift to the bottom floor of the tower.

She slumped against the wall, staring down the shaft of the lift. Would her heart fail if she fell that far? Or would the magic and the clockwork keep working even then? And if she couldn't die, was she really alive? Or had she died when her mangled heart was replaced with gears and crystal like the clockwork of the tower? Perhaps she was just a . . . a not-dead shell. An automaton like she'd seen at a long-ago fair.

Breen shook her head. It didn't matter. She was what she was, and she couldn't change that. So, she turned away from the shaft and tore off a chunk of bread from Madame's provision. Then she climbed back up to her seat by the clock face, where she sat and stared and wondered.

And her heart beat on.

CHAPTER 2

"Powerless!" Josiah waved his hand in the air, pacing up and down the rich red carpet of the royal library. "That's what we are. What we've become. Powerless!"

He spread his arms, gesturing towards the windows that looked out over the city. "Children starve; men and women work days without sleep to buy week-old bread; orphans scavenge the streets and turn to thieving in order to survive. The wealthy grow fat on the sweat of the lower classes and demand their lives' work in return for even the smallest debts. Smoke chokes the city day by day. Politicians and nobility scheme and lie and plot to serve their own interests, forgetting those whom they are sworn to represent and serve. In the midst of it all, blood alchemists steal the life from our subjects to fuel their dirty excuse for science. All this in the greatest city in the greatest empire in this world. And we, the established rulers of that empire, can do nothing about it! Nothing!"

Josiah's father, King Stephen, barely glanced up from his papers, reports of conditions all through the Chanian empire. "If you must exaggerate to make your point, Josiah, either your information is lacking, or your point is not worth making. Do not stretch the truth even for a good cause." He set down one page and picked up the next. "Is our work upholding the laws nothing? Do we not speak in the Senate whenever our voice may do good? Do the charities we fund and run provide no sustenance or shelter for those in need? Does our support of the Inventors' and Alchemists' Guilds lead to no innovations that better our peoples' lives? If nothing else, do the people not benefit from the fact that we have maintained friendly terms with other lands far and wide?"

"Very well." Josiah inclined his head slightly. "Perhaps I overstate — but not by much. Those reports in your hand will affirm my words. All our work only makes the present situation easier to bear; it does nothing to eliminate society's problems. And yet we cannot — or will not — do more! We, the royal family of the greatest empire since the golden days of the Helethians!"

"Boastfulness, even in the guise of patriotism, is no more fitting to a prince than is exaggeration, Josiah." This time, King Stephen did look up, raising an eyebrow. "In any case, I seem to recall that not so long ago, you were proud of how our government had changed in recent generations. What was it you said?" The king adopted a mock-thoughtful look. "Ah, yes. 'The developments of this past century will put the power of government solidly in the hands of the people, to whom it belongs! No more will those not blessed with land, titles, and wealth be at the mercy of those who know not their struggles, for the common man will, at last, have a say in his own fate!' Was that not it?"

"I did say that, yes." Josiah stopped pacing and faced his father. "And I stand by what I said, in theory, just as I stand by our government, in theory. Yet, when I spoke those words, I was younger, and I foolishly ignored the reality of the world and the nature of mankind. I now see that the common man has no more say in his life than he did ten, twenty, thirty years ago. The only difference is that his plight is ignored not only by his aristocratic lord but also by his more fortunate brother. Can you deny that? No. And what can we do about it?"

"Nothing. So you have said already." The king sighed, raising his eyes to the high ceiling as if it might sympathize with his plight. "Sometimes, Josiah, I wish that you didn't see fit to practice your speech-making on me. And what would you do about the situation that has not already been done? The Senate has as many common representatives as it does noble. All have the same opportunity to speak and the same power to make and change the laws. If change is to be had, the Senate will effect it, not us."

"The noble and common representatives have the same power only in theory." Josiah shook his head. "Too often, the wealthy and influential find ways to silence those lower in rank than they, and so society stays the same as it has been — or grows worse. Surely there must be something we can do to set things right!"

"We use our influence and our resources to guide others in the right direction." King Stephen set down his papers to look directly at Josiah. "We protect our people from outside threats and offer them relief from internal ones, and we give them someone to look up to and emulate."

"Give them someone to emulate — oh, yes!" Josiah couldn't hold back the bitterness from his voice. He turned and resumed pacing to hide his expression. "By sitting passively while the nobles, the rich, and the factory owners slowly kill our subjects through overwork and starvation. Such an example we set! No wonder the state of our nation grows worse by the day."

"Josiah, that is hardly proper speech for any young man of influence, a prince least of all!" King Stephen snapped, picking up his papers again. "We do what we can to alleviate the situation, as you well know. And as far as change goes, you have spoken well as our representative in the Senate and used our two High Council votes wisely. Is that not enough?"

"I apologize, Father." Josiah took several deep breaths, forcing himself to calm down. Passion was the lifeblood of change, but letting passion overtake him, whether in a conversation or, worse, before an audience, was a trap. "But speaking is not always enough. Just think of what happened with the indenturement bill a few months ago. I did everything I could to speak and fight against it, but it still passed — and when it did, it brought back debt-slavery in all but name, less than a decade after it had been abolished. Surely we can do more than just speak!"

"We do what we can, and we pray to Jeros for the rest. He will set all to right in the end."

"And if we are the people He will use to set things right? What then?" Josiah demanded.

"Then He will make that clear," the king replied, unruffled.

"I believe that He already has." Josiah turned on his heel. "Good night, Father."

His father's sigh followed Josiah out of the library and down the dark-paneled halls to his bedroom. Josiah huffed a sigh of his own as he walked. The king was a noble man in every sense of the word — yet he refused to *act*. Refused to do anything that might push the boundaries of what was accepted. And always he insisted that Josiah do the same, that he accept the place given to him and not try to step outside its boundaries.

And yet, Josiah had to wonder, was what he wanted truly beyond his place? He was the crown prince. One day he would be king. Surely Jeros had given him his position and his passion for good reason!

Of course, Josiah would be the last to argue for the old concept of divine right to rule. That foolish idea well deserved the revolutions it had caused. But divine *responsibility*, that was another thing altogether. The duty of royalty was to watch over the people and to protect them from threats both outward and inward. Surely that duty had not been nullified with the rise of democracy! Yet that same change seemed to have robbed Josiah of the means to carry out his responsibility to his people.

Josiah pushed open the entrance to his temporary rooms. A botched assassination attempt last week had significantly damaged his usual quarters. Though the would-be assassin had been caught, Josiah had been forced to move to different rooms until his own could be fixed.

He passed through the anteroom into his bedroom proper and shut both doors behind him harder than was strictly necessary. He paused by his bed to turn up the gaslight and pull off his cravat. Then, loosening his cuffs, crossed to the window and stared out.

The darkened palace grounds extended below him. Beyond those, the city fairly glowed with light. Josiah could still faintly remember a time when the city would have been nearly as dark as the sky at this hour. Yet now the glow of gaslights filled every window, and white alchemical lights shone from streetlamps and marked the passage of carriages. Rivenford, it seemed, was becoming a city that never slept.

Josiah's gaze rose from the streets near the palace to the slums across the river, still dark save for occasional spots of light. A bank of smoke hung over the region, its boundaries marked by the absence of the stars it hid. For all the wonders of invention, only the nobility and middle classes seemed to truly benefit from them. The lower classes were, if anything, worse off than before — but what could he do to help them?

He raised his gaze still more to the nearest and grandest of the city's seven clock towers. Tiny alchemical lights in blue, white, and gold ran up the sides and along the corners of the roof, while the face itself shone golden as the harvest moon. Josiah had seen it a thousand times before, usually from other angles, yet he never failed to appreciate its beauty. Yet tonight, he noticed something unusual: silhouetted between the five and the six was a dark, almost human-looking form.

Josiah shook his head and shut his eyes in disbelief. He was imagining things. Perhaps he'd lost so much sleep on so many successive nights that he was hallucinating. But when he opened his eyes again, there it still was. As he watched, the person stood and stretched, then moved out of the circle of the clock.

Why is there a person in the clock tower? The clock towers were closed to the public, and as far as Josiah knew, they had no keepers.

Could whoever it was be hiding in the clock tower? No. If the person — Josiah thought it was a girl; the shape looked too slender for a man — if she was hiding in the tower, she wouldn't sit in the clock face where she could be seen. But what if someone else was hiding her there? What if she was trapped and this was her attempt to attract help?

There was no guarantee that the girl's presence was connected to any significant wrongdoing, of course. There was always the chance that she was simply a homeless beggar taking advantage of somewhere warm and dry to sleep for the night. But just in case . . . it wouldn't hurt to do a little investigation.

CHAPTER 3

The next afternoon found Josiah neither in the palace nor at the clock tower but rather in the cramped back room of Kronos Clocks and Gadgetry, gesturing wildly as he ranted to the owner's son: "But *why* is there a girl in the clock tower?"

"Haven't the foggiest." Luis flicked a new lens down over his magnifying goggles and peered at the device on the table before him. "Hand me the smallest screwdriver, please.

Josiah searched the back wall of the workroom until he found the requested screwdriver and handed it to his friend. "It doesn't make sense, Luis. No one goes into the clock towers. *No one.* According to every alchemist and engineer in the city, the towers are – and I quote – 'self-sustaining and self-maintaining.' They don't even need a keeper to check the mechanisms once a year. They're expressly forbidden to the public. And yet – *and yet* – there she sat, real as the tower itself, at an hour when any sensible person should've been in bed."

"Not counting yourself as sensible, I see." Luis grinned at his own joke as he tightened a screw on the complicated assemblage of gears, wire, and crystal. "She probably snuck in on a dare. Nothing so unusual about that."

"I don't think so." The back workroom of Kronos Clocks and Gadgetry barely had room to pace, but Josiah managed anyway, squeezing between the worktable and tool bench, weaving through baskets of broken clockwork and half-finished inventions, narrowly avoiding racks of parts. "If she were there on a dare, would she have merely been *sitting*? I think not. She would have been signaling to her friends below, trying to catch their attention and escape again before she was seen by anyone else."

"She snuck in for solitude, then." Luis's smile faded as he inspected the machinery before him. "Not so hard to imagine, in a city this large. If I didn't have the workroom here, I'd consider it myself. Why do you have to make everything so complicated, Your Highness?"

"You're one to talk." Josiah laughed and shook his head at Luis's mess of machinery. "I would agree with your theory, save for one thing. I tried to get into the clock tower myself this morning to see if she had left behind any clues to her identity. However, the door is at the bottom is locked not once, not twice, but *thrice*."

Luis glanced up, raising an eyebrow. "Really? Someone's worried about security. What, are they using the clock tower as spare storage for state secrets now?"

[18]

"That's exactly what I'd like to know." Josiah stopped pacing in front of Luis's bench. "There are windows, of course, but they're glass-covered and too small for any human to squeeze through. So, then, how could this mysterious young woman get inside?"

"She somehow got the keys?" Luis flicked up a lens on his goggles and grabbed a different screwdriver. "I still think you're overthinking this."

"It is a mystery to be solved, Luis. Not unlike your . . ." Josiah paused, frowning at the assemblage before Luis. "What exactly is that?"

"If all goes well, and if I don't run out of money for parts, my ticket into the Inventors' Guild. If all goes as it's currently going, nothing." Luis shook his head. "You said you went to the tower to look around inside. Did you find anything?"

"No. And do you know why?" Josiah started pacing again, frustration driving his steps. "Because, despite the fact that the towers are government property, and the royal family is *theoretically* still part of the government, I'm as unable to enter the clock tower as this young woman should have been! I don't have the keys, of course. But I asked everyone who *might* – ten people, in fact! And what did they say?"

Luis sighed and tried to turn one of the gears on the device. When it wouldn't turn, he picked up his screwdriver again, this time to loosen some screws. "Since you're ranting in my workshop, I suspect they said *no*."

"Wrong! Five people said they had no keys whatsoever and sent me to someone else. Two had keys to one of the locks, one had a key to the other lock, and one had keys to both of those two but not the third. And the tenth very snippily said that I had no need to concern myself about the clock tower because the presence of a person untouched by magic would undoubtedly cause the magic running the machinery to stop working." Josiah scowled, recalling the pinch-faced woman. "Even if I can't properly work in my own government, one might think that I could at least look around in my own clock tower!"

"What a tragedy." Luis leaned back in his seat and pushed his goggles off his face. "Though if I were them, I'd let you have full control of the government sooner than I'd let you in the tower unsupervised. At least in the government, you have a hundred other people to moderate whatever trouble you cause."

"Very funny." Josiah rounded a rack of parts yet again. "I have yet to break any of *your* inventions."

"My inventions are unfinished and not likely to cause city-wide calamities, given that I'm not trying to find new ways to distill the innate magic of the world into a usable power source or whatever else the Alchemist Guild does with its time." Luis pointed his screwdriver at Josiah. "Mark my words, if you go into that clock tower, something will break. I'd bet money on it."

"Your lack of faith wounds me." Josiah stopped pacing to face his friend directly. "Wait and see. I *will* find a way into the clock tower, and when I do, I *will* find answers." He paused. "Of course, it might be easier if I had some help."

Luis's brow furrowed in confusion, which quickly turned to disbelief. He pulled his goggles back down and started flicking through lenses as if a different magnification would turn Josiah's words into sense. "Are you implying what I think you're implying, Your Highness? You're asking me to help you break into your own clock tower? Are you *mad?*"

"The answer is no, just as it was the last time you asked." Josiah gave his friend a hopeful smile. "As you said, it's *my* clock tower. It's hardly illegal. Or, for that matter, breaking and entering."

Luis ran out of lenses and settled for giving Josiah a look of bug-eyed incredulity. "You want me to help you break into your own clock tower."

"Weren't you just listening? Of course not." Josiah shook his head. "The last time I checked, locksmithing is one of the services that you and your father offer. That's all I need. I've lost my keys, and I need a locksmith. I'd pay you, obviously."

Luis pulled off the goggles, unmoved. "A locksmith. For a lock on a government building which someone doesn't want anyone to enter, which contains delicate machinery that will probably break the moment you set foot inside."

"It will *not.*" Honestly, why was Luis so reluctant? True, he sometimes needed convincing before he would help with any of Josiah's more . . . unique plans. That was one of the reasons Josiah liked Luis; he forced Josiah to think through all the details of a new idea. But usually, he wasn't this resistant. "If someone doesn't want me in the building, that clearly means they're hiding a secret that needs to be exposed. You'd be doing your country a service."

"I'm honestly not sure I would." Luis hesitated a moment longer, then sighed. "Oh, very well. I suppose it's your risk to take. I'll tell Father about your order and come out – but I'm not coming inside the tower with you. Tomorrow afternoon?"

Josiah shook his head. "Tomorrow evening. This evening, if you can, near dark. I'd rather avoid notice if at all possible."

"This evening, then. I'll meet you at the corner of Castle and Cross." Luis paused. "But, Your Highness, do me a favor and be careful. I'd like you and the tower both to make it through this with all parts attached."

Josiah grinned. "Don't worry. No one and nothing will be unnecessarily damaged because of my investigation. You have my word for it."

CHAPTER 4

The signal button in Breen's pocket vibrated, pulling her out of a dreamless sleep. She blinked groggily. *What . . . ?*

Realization pushed her up and out of her cot in alarm. *Madame will be furious!* She dashed to the lift, bare feet skidding on the smooth floorboards, and grabbed the chain as high as she could reach. What could Madame Gottling *want?* She pulled the chain downwards and shifted her grip. Certainly nothing good at this hour. She'd just been here yesterday, which was why Breen had felt she could safely go to bed this early . . .

A final pull brought the person on the lift halfway above floor level. Breen let out a soundless yelp and jumped back, dropping the chain. *That's not Madame!*

The young man grabbed the edge of the floor just in time as the lift fell away beneath him. His hat flew off his head and landed several feet away. Breen scrambled back and grabbed a wrench from her toolbelt. She lifted it uncertainly, staring at the man as he struggled to pull himself up. From his clothes and the cut of his brown hair, she guessed he was upper-class.

Oh no. What if he's a messenger from Madame? But, no, that couldn't be. Madame rarely sent messengers, and when she did, she always sent women. And there was something else about him that seemed different from Madame and her messengers, though Breen couldn't figure out what. So who was this person?

The man managed to haul his upper body onto the floor. With another heave, he rolled himself all the way out of the lift hole. He lay there for a moment, breathing hard, and then sat up, picked up his hat from where it had fallen, and looked around. As he spotted Breen, his face lit up with triumph. He scrambled to his feet, speaking too fast for Breen to even try to read his lips. She took a step backward, still holding up the wrench defensively, and stared him down.

The young man's speech slowed, then stopped, and he looked at her expectantly. Breen swallowed, her mouth suddenly dry. What had he said? She tightened her grip on the wrench, hoping she looked frightening and not frightened.

The young man just frowned at her, puzzled. He held up his hands in a gesture of . . . confusion? Surrender? Goodwill? At least he didn't seem hostile, and she had no doubt now that he wasn't from Madame. Anyone Madame sent would know she couldn't hear. But in that case . . . *He shouldn't be here.* She had to get rid of him somehow, but how? Would waving her wrench more scare him off? *Maybe. It's worth a try. Isn't it?*

Then the clock struck.

As the vibrations from the first stroke shivered up Breen's body, the man clapped his hands over his ears, mouth bursting open. With the second stroke, he fell to his knees as if the sound were a weight pressing him down. He huddled there, his hands and arms clasped against his head.

Breen considered him a moment, recalling her own pain in the months before her hearing faded and let her appreciate the tower's silent beauty. Without setting down the wrench, she pulled the thin blanket from her bed and offered it to him.

He released his grip on his head just long enough to take the blanket and wrap it so it covered both ears with multiple layers of cloth. Then he pressed hard, shutting his eyes as if that would somehow soften the sound. Breen waited, watching the glowing lights in the machinery in the tower's center.

Then the vibrations died away, and the lights faded, and the young man hesitantly removed his hands from his ears, looking dazed. He unwrapped the blanket and offered it back to Breen, smiling weakly, his mouth moving in what Breen guessed was "Thank you." Hoping she'd interpreted correctly, she nodded and set the blanket back on her bed in a lump.

When she turned to the man again, he was on his feet and staring at her with a thoughtful, questioning expression. He pointed to her with one finger, then pulled his hand back to just in front of his ear with his hand cupped and index finger and thumb touching.

Turning his head slightly so she could see his motion, he flicked his finger upwards, then raised his eyebrows and pointed at himself.

Breen blinked. That . . . that was the same sign language she knew. Was this man from Madame after all, then? But he hadn't known to use the signs at first, so perhaps he wasn't.

Either way, he'd asked if she understood him, and this time she had. And now he was waiting for a response. She nodded and signed back: "How do you know sign?"

"My sister is deaf." Breen had to think a moment to parse his words; he signed in the wrong order — like speech instead of sign. "My name is—" his fingers slowed as he spelled the name — "Josiah Chambers. What is your name?"

"Breen." She paused, then added as an afterthought, "sir." Why did she know the name Josiah Chambers? She felt as if she'd heard it, or part of it, before. But where? And when?

Josiah furrowed his brow and spelled her name back, ending with an outward sweep of his hands. "Breen what?"

Breen just shook her head and changed the subject: "Why are you here?"

"I saw you in the clock. I was curious. No one is supposed to be here." Josiah raised his eyebrows slightly. "Why are you here?"

No one? But didn't the clock need a keeper? Breen frowned. "I live here. I keep the clock."

Josiah's expression puckered in clear confusion. He glanced around, then signed, "The clock is magic. It doesn't need a keeper."

Didn't it? Perhaps there was more than one reason Madame Gottling demanded that Breen kept out of sight. *But then* . . . Breen's breath caught. What if Josiah tried to force her out of the clock tower since she wasn't supposed to be here?

Then again, would that be so bad? If Josiah threw her out of the tower and then let her go from there, perhaps she could stow away on a ship or a train and get far away from Madame and the rest. She'd be free. Surely Madame wouldn't hunt her that far . . .

But it wouldn't last long. Breen's hopes fell, cut off by the crystal in her chest. If she left tonight with her heart freshly refueled, she might last as long as two or three weeks — assuming she didn't get injured, and that she could find enough food. But after that, her heart would stop. And even if that weren't so, Madame and the others would force one of her family to pay the rest of her debt, and . . . no. That would be too much. So, Breen simply shrugged. "Maybe I'm no one."

Josiah let out a short laugh. "I doubt that." He sat down in the center of the floor, taking off his hat and setting it beside him. "Are you trapped here? Can you leave?"

Breen blinked at him. She couldn't *lie*. That would be wrong. But she had a suspicion that if she told him the truth, he wouldn't leave, and she *needed* him to leave. So, she folded her hands and stared at him, hoping he'd take the hint and go away.

Unfortunately, he didn't, only nodded as if she'd answered anyway. "I take that as a yes. Who trapped you here?"

Breen, for lack of a better idea, kept staring at him, adopting the dullest, blankest expression she could. Josiah smiled at her — was that supposed to encourage her to talk to him? She shoved her hands in her pockets, trying to make her point clear.

They faced each other like that for several long minutes. At last, Josiah signed: "If you aren't trapped, say so, and I'll leave. But if you are trapped, I want to help you."

Breen pulled her hands out of her pockets so she could sign, "I don't need help." That wasn't a lie. She was fine, really. Better off than most. And it wasn't as if he could help her.

Josiah raised an eyebrow. "Your refusal to answer my questions says otherwise."

Breen groaned. Maybe it would be better to answer. "I owe a debt. If I leave, my family pays."

Josiah huffed angrily and muttered something. It didn't seem to be directed at her, though. "I could pay your debt."

"No, you can't." Breen hardened her expression to emphasize her statement. "You should go. Please. Find someone who needs you. Thank you, good night." To further drive home her point, she went to the lift and pulled the platform up so he could step on it.

Josiah reluctantly did as she wished. "I'll come back another time. Think about my offer."

Breen didn't respond, just slowly let the lift down. She felt the chain go slack when he reached the ground, and she hooked it in place so it wouldn't drop further. Then she returned to her bed.

CHAPTER 5

Problem:

Josiah tapped his pen against a corner of his paper, trying to figure out how to most succinctly state the problem of the clock tower. The hum of discussion filled the Senate room around him as senators found their seats in the half-circle of desks that radiated up the sloped floor of the room. The Senate meeting would begin soon, but for once, Josiah had other things on his mind.

He finally decided on the best wording and jotted it down in his notebook. *Problem: Hidden indentured servant kept on off-limits government property.* That was all fact. He circled that, then added other ideas around it. *Trapped. Poorly treated. Illegal? Refused help.*

The *tap-tap* of a gavel drew Josiah's attention away from his notebook and quieted the room. Prime Minister Wentworth cleared his throat. "Thank you. This session of the Chania National Senate will now begin. Secretary Morrows, please review the minutes from last week's meeting."

Secretary Morrows stood, nearly dropping his pages, and began to read. Josiah returned his attention to the notebook. He circled each of the new ideas he'd written, then added further notes on each of them. *Trapped.* There could be no doubt of that. Breen had said that she couldn't leave and that a family member would take her place if she did. In addition, Josiah had noticed that the clock tower door had keyholes on both sides, and he suspected that Breen *didn't* have the keys.

Prime Minister Wentworth's voice interrupted his thoughts again. "Thank you, Secretary Morrows. Now, our first order of business for the day: a call for a greater police force in the Rivenford slums. Arguing for is Lord-Senator Caraway of the Loyalist Party; arguing against, Senator Thompsons of the Workers' Party."

Josiah sighed as the two men took their places behind podiums on the Senate floor. He'd heard this issue many times before. The Loyalists claimed that more police would deter crime and protect the honest inhabitants of the slums; the Workers' Party insisted that if conditions were improved, there'd be no need for more police; and the Progressives were split between the two sides. They'd argued over the issue for the last hour of the last meeting, and they seemed ready to debate another hour now.

Instead, Josiah turned his attention back to his notebook. *Poorly treated.* Admittedly, her living quarters had looked well-kept, and her clothes, though worn and much-mended, had been in better shape than those of many factory workers and slum-dwellers. She could clearly do with better meals, though, and her manner suggested that she'd suffered ill-use of other kinds. Then again, his unexpected appearance probably caused some of her nervousness.

Illegal? Josiah tapped his pen on the paper again, wishing he'd thought to ask when she'd first come to the clock tower. Indenturing people hadn't been legal until a few months ago, but Josiah guessed she'd been there at least a year. Had she been deaf before she entered the clock tower? Or had living beneath the bells destroyed her hearing?

Refused help. Josiah grimaced, both at the page and at the raised voices from the floor. Apparently, Senator Thompsons had lost his temper again. That was unfortunate — especially since the man was up for reelection this year. If he didn't learn to control himself better, he would lose his hard-won Senate seat, and the Workers' Party would lose one of their most passionate senators.

Josiah was half-tempted to speak up and warn both debating senators to calm down, but he knew from experience that such an action would do no good. Instead, he refocused on his notebook. Breen hadn't just said she didn't need help. She'd said he *couldn't* help her. What had she meant by that? Simply that she wouldn't let him help? Or did she believe that he was literally unable to pay off her debt?

That seemed unlikely. Even if she owed someone a life debt, most men would accept a sufficiently large amount of money in place of someone's service for life. And if she'd been indentured before the indenturement bill passed, Josiah could easily have her contract declared illegal. He'd have to return tonight and make sure she understood the type of help she was turning down. He hated the idea of her, or anyone, remaining trapped when freedom would be so easy to win. And this was a problem he *could* solve, unlike so many other issues.

The question still remained, though: why was she in the clock tower in the first place? A factory, a plantation, a mine, even an airship — those locations would make sense. But the *clock tower?*

Josiah flipped the page in his notebook, jotting down a list of thoughts. The clocks didn't need a keeper. Their magic was enough. *Although . . .*

The clocks were magic, yes. But magic items all shared a common trait: their magic leaked. Anything alchemically charged would eventually need to be *re*charged. The alchemists claimed that normal people somehow leached the power away, though they were tight-lipped as to how or why. The clocks, however, were so large, and the magic bits so isolated that the magic mostly stayed contained. The little that did leak out was recaptured almost immediately. But what if that wasn't the case? And if it wasn't, who would profit from that lie? The alchemists, perhaps?

Below Josiah, the debate died to a close without any real resolution, and both senators returned to their seats. Prime Minister Wentworth shuffled through his papers. "Next on the agenda: a petition to legalize blood alchemy.

Whispers of surprise, horror, and anger rippled through the room. Josiah paused, ink from his pen soaking into the page, trying

[32]

to process what he'd just heard. Or had he imagined it? He knew such petitions existed — people would try to legalize *anything*. But for such an idea to reach the Senate? He had to have misheard.

Yet the prime minister went on, "Arguing in favor of legalization is the Lord-Senator Weston, Independent, of the High Council. Arguing against is Senator Aaronson of the Workers' Party. Lord-Senator Weston, you have the floor."

Weston rose. Like the other High Council members, he sat not in the main half-circle of desks but in the reserved seats to either side of the prime minister's box. Gold glittered in the gaslights as he strode to one of the podiums: gold on his cane, on his waistcoat, on the chain around his neck and the ruby medallion pinned to his lapel. Josiah scowled at him. Weston had been the chief architect and supporter of the indenturement bill; it had largely been his influence that pushed it through the Senate.

Weston set his hands on either side of the podium and addressed the room. "Gentlemen of the Senate, we live in an age of progress and discovery, an age of science and intelligence, an age in which we cast off the shadows of ignorant superstition and move boldly forward towards a better world."

His deep voice rolled through the room, confident as that of a king. "And so, in the spirit of the age, I believe that it is time we open our eyes to the possibilities which blood alchemy offers to us. My associates have interviewed many leading alchemists, and all agree that this path would lead to a new era of innovation, particularly in the realm of medicine and healing. There is power in blood, gentlemen, the power to cure disease, to heal injury, and even to stave off the effects of old age. Yet we will achieve none of this if we continue to cower as we have, to act as children afraid of shadows instead of men with the courage to do what we must in order to move forward."

Prime Minister Wentworth nodded. "Thank you, Lord-Senator Weston. Senator Aaronson, your response?"

Aaronson stood and walked down the aisle between desks to the podium, his steps brisk, his gaze blazing with righteous anger. "Lord-Senator Weston speaks boldly of progress, innovation, and so-called healing — fine words from someone who asks us to legalize *murder* to achieve them. Blood alchemy requires man's blood, and where will it come from?

"How many of us have already heard of the crimes committed by illegal blood alchemists hungry for power? The alchemists and their hired murderers slit the throats of honest men and women in back alleyways and bleed their bodies dry. They steal children from their parents and buy them out of orphanages as the subjects of their experiments. Is *this* what we should legalize?" Aaronson glared at his opponent. "Blood alchemy is and always has been outlawed for a reason: because in its desire for power and so-called progress, it throws human lives away like trash!"

Lord-Senator Weston shook his head, smiling indulgently. "Are you so desperate to convince others of your view that you resort to urban legend, Senator Aaronson? I fear I must correct you on certain points which you have evidently forgotten." *If you knew them in the first place*, his tone seemed to add.

Weston widened his attention once more to include the whole room. "As I said already, my associates and I have interviewed several leading alchemists on the topic of blood alchemy and its exact requirements. It is not such an evil practice as Senator Aaronson's stories suggest, gentlemen. Yes, blood alchemy requires the blood of men, but so do many noble causes. And based on the research of the alchemists I interviewed, even the most potent applications of blood alchemy would require little actual blood — a few drops a week at most, no more."

"But what about the source of those few drops?" Senator Aaronson leaned forward, gripping the edges of his podium. "If any blood could be used in blood alchemy, none of us would oppose it. Who among us wouldn't gladly give a pint of his own blood to save a loved one, if that were the only thing necessary? But we all know that blood alchemy requires deathblood — not just the blood of a dying man, but blood taken in such a way that the taking kills the man. Would you demand that in order to save one man, we kill another?"

"Certainly not. But I would give those who will die anyway the opportunity to save others through their deaths," Lord-Senator Weston replied. "Consider a criminal, a murderer, condemned to die. Let that man pay for his crimes with the means to give others new life. Or what of the many men and women who, at any moment, lie dying with no hope in hospitals and homes across the city? Blood alchemy could cure many of these, true. But for those whom it cannot save, at least the blood alchemists could give them peaceful, painless passage and the knowledge that they, in their dying, did some good.

"And what may we gain from all this?" Lord-Senator Weston's smile grew broad. "Broken bones and bodies healed rapidly with few side effects. Prosthetic limbs affordable enough for even the lower classes. Devices to give life and breath and vigor to failing bodies. Any of these things, gentlemen, would require only a few drops of blood, perhaps a few ounces at most for the most powerful cures. Are such benefits not worth a bit of blood fairly bought? Is that not worth the painless death of a few criminals?"

Great Jeros, what if he's right? If blood alchemy could do all that Weston claimed at so little cost, perhaps it would be worthwhile. How many lives could one unavoidable death save? *But it's been outlawed all this time; surely there's a reason for that.* Then again, maybe not. Normal alchemy had been forbidden for nearly five hundred years before Josiah's great-grandfather overturned that law, and look how far they'd come since.

But that law had only been overturned after significant investigation into potential benefits and consequences — after every connected law and text had been examined and everyone with relevant knowledge had been questioned on the topic a dozen times. So far, Weston had provided none of that. The question was: could he?

[36]

On the floor, Senator Aaronson pointed out that, yes, letting criminals pay back their debt to society with their blood was all well and good, but what happened when judges started sentencing more people to death, believing they were doing good? Or when doctors gave up on the potentially-dying too soon in hopes that their blood could save other patients? "Is that what you want, Weston?" he demanded. "Another way for the rich and powerful to gain at the expense of the defenseless?"

Josiah cleared his throat before Weston could answer. "Another question, if I may speak?" He waited for the nod from the Prime Minister before going on, "How certain are your alchemists of the potential benefits of blood alchemy, Lord-Senator Weston? And from where does that certainty come? I believe it would be difficult to pursue and draw reliable conclusions in a field of study that is currently forbidden."

Lord-Senator Weston smiled thinly. "To answer Senator Aaronson's concerns, that seems to be a very pessimistic view of the matter. Doctors are sworn to save lives as best they can; judges to dispense justice to the best of their ability. If you are concerned with how they choose to do that, you would be better off to take it up with them, not us."

He turned to face Josiah. "As for your question, Your Highness, it is a fair one. However, my alchemists have done a great deal of purely theoretical research on the topic based on notes, records, and prototypes seized from exposed blood alchemists. Based on their findings, one man's blood could save three, four, or even more people from death or serious disability. The only way they could be more certain would be to actually test their theories. Is Your Highness suggesting such an experiment?"

"I am *not*." Josiah just managed to keep his indignation from his tone. "But I trust that your alchemists will be glad to share their research with others, appointed by the Senate, to verify their words."

"Of course, Your Highness." Lord-Senator Weston bowed his head slightly, then addressed the room as a whole. "Now, what other objections are there?"

The debate went on for hours. Senator Aaronson and other senators of the Workers' party peppered Weston with demands about the potential social effects of introducing blood alchemy, interspersing their questions with heated words about how the plight of the lower classes was bad enough; would Weston see their very lives stolen for the benefit of the rich?

Lord-Senator Caraway of the Loyalist party chimed in as well with questions about the logistics of legalizing blood alchemy: how would it be regulated? Who would be allowed to practice it? Who would control the supply of blood, and what situations would permit its use? Josiah broke in every so often with more questions about what evidence Weston had to back up his claims and about how he would go about testing them.

Lord-Senator Weston replied smoothly to every demand with careful suggestions and promises of proof. Again and again, he emphasized the potential benefits — "Benefit for *all* classes," he added, smiling, "the lower classes perhaps most of all. Surely anything that puts good health and effective treatment within their grasp is worthwhile?"

Eventually, the debate stretched to noontide, and Prime Minister Wentworth called for a two-hour recess. The senators filed out of the room, grumbling and discussing this new turn of events with their comrades. Josiah tucked his notebook into his pocket, stretched, and hurried to the end of the aisle between Weston's seat and the door.

He intercepted Weston just in time. "Lord-Senator Weston, a moment?"

"Of course." Weston bowed, not deeply. "You wish to speak about the blood alchemy bill, I assume?"

"You assume correctly." Josiah chose his words carefully. "It seems like a bold move, even for you. If it fails — if blood alchemy is proved as harmful as everyone believes — you'll lose considerable respect, perhaps even more. This is a High Council reassessment year, is it not?"

Weston raised an eyebrow. "Are you threatening me, Your Highness?"

"No. Only stating facts." Josiah shook his head. "And I wonder what you see in the idea that would drive you to risk so much. Until today, I have heard nothing good about it — but if it truly is all that you claim, I would be interested to learn more."

"Ah. Perhaps we will understand each other after all." Weston smiled faintly. "Are you free the day after tomorrow, Your

Highness? Perhaps at two o'clock? I would be pleased to discuss the matter with you privately."

"That would be acceptable. Have your secretary contact us to set up the appointment." Josiah nodded once. "Good day, Lord-Senator."

Weston returned the nod. "I look forward to it. Good day, Your Highness."

They parted ways, Weston joining with a group of other senators caught in animated discussion and Josiah slipping out the door into a hallway. *First the girl, now this.* He'd be busy in the next few weeks. The Senate would no doubt put together an official committee to look into Weston's claims, but Josiah fully intended to do some investigation of his own. He'd need to talk to alchemists not affiliated with Weston, interview any clergy members he could find with special knowledge of the topic, research the history of blood alchemy . . . Excitement quickened Josiah's steps. Threat or not, at least this meant he had something useful to do!

Chapter 6

Josiah's thoughts were still tumbling over each other when he stepped out of the hallway into a large public anteroom. He made for the great locked doors on the far side of the room that would let him into the royal wing of the palace. Two hours wasn't much time, especially when at least half an hour of it would be taken up by lunch, but it *might* be just long enough for him to do some preliminary research on blood alchemy. One of the royal archivists might have information — hopefully Johnson was on duty; he specialized in the history of science and alchemy. Simms would do nearly as well, though; she was the leading non-practicing expert on alchemical theory. Barring that, there should be a priest on duty in the royal family's private chapel; he could at least clarify the Church of Chania's official position on blood alchemy. And, if all else failed, Josiah could find a book, though that would be slower . . .

He'd only made it halfway across the room when a slim hand grabbed his and tugged. He turned to find his sister standing there. She released his hand and signed, "You walked right past me!"

Josiah blinked and smiled distractedly. He signed back, "Hello, Grace. Sorry; I'm a bit busy . . ."

Grace pulled a face at him. "I need to talk to you, though, and Luis does as well." She leaned in slightly. "I saw you leave last night. What are you up to?"

Blast it! That was right; he had arranged to meet with Luis now. And of course, Grace would've seen him slip out . . . Josiah stuffed his frustration behind his smile. "Thank you, Grace," he signed, touching the fingers of one hand to his lips and then extending them downwards towards her. Then he turned, scanning the room for Luis.

He spotted him hanging back a few steps, near the end of a row of chairs. Now speaking aloud, he said, "I apologize. There was something of a shock in the Senate. You're here about our business yesterday?"

Luis nodded and pulled a ring with three keys on it from his pocket. "Spare keys for the lock, as you requested. All well inside?"

"Hard to say. Come with me, and I'll tell you what happened." Josiah waved Luis towards one of the smaller meeting rooms off the main anteroom.

Grace grabbed his arm again and pulled him around to face her. With sharp motions, she signed, "Josiah!" Scowling at him, she added, "Don't ignore me. I want answers. Where did you go last night?"

Josiah sighed and signed back, "Come with Luis and me and I'll tell you about it. Will that do?" He supposed there would be no harm in her knowing the full secret. In fact, now that he thought about it, she could be quite useful . . .

She nodded cheerfully and linked her arm around his. Josiah led the way to the nearest meeting room, then shut and locked the door once everyone was inside. While he did, Luis turned on the gaslamps. "I take it that the girl wasn't just a vagrant?"

"I don't believe so." Josiah sat down at the head of the room's rectangular table. "One moment; let me catch Grace up on the details." He turned to Grace and signed, "Two nights ago, I noticed a girl in the nearest of the clock towers. I thought it was suspicious, so I decided to look inside and investigate. However, someone doesn't want others inside, so I had to enlist Luis's help." He switched to speaking and signing at the same time, a trick he'd taught himself so he could more easily include Grace in conversations with other hearing people, and described what had happened when he'd entered the clock tower the previous night. He finished with, "I intend to return tonight and make my offer again, this time clarifying my ability to help her."

Luis nodded. "And what happens if she says no?"

"Then I find out what help she *will* accept, offer that, and learn all I can about who put her in the tower and why they put her there. To that end, Grace . . ." Josiah offered her his brightest smile.

"How would you like to come with me tonight? Or tomorrow, if that becomes necessary?"

Grace gave him a look of sisterly suspicion. "Why?"

"I hope that Miss Breen will see you as less threatening. If that's the case, she may be more likely to either accept help or offer information." Josiah tilted his head slightly, eyebrows raised. "If you're interested?"

Grace considered, the tip of one finger pressed against her lip. "Not tonight. The Society of Women in Sciences is hosting an event, and they invited Mother and me. I can't cancel now, even if I wanted to — which I don't. I go to too many society events where I'm ignored to miss one of the few where I'm actually welcomed. If you still need me tomorrow, though, I'll come." She paused a moment, then added, "Just *ask* if we can come back first." She emphasized her statement with a fierce glare.

Josiah frowned in mock offense. "Of course I'll ask. I'm not rude."

Grace raised an eyebrow meaningfully. "No. But you always want to help people, and you don't always consider how they feel about it."

"I will be perfectly considerate, Grace. Thank you." Josiah sat back in his seat, once again speaking and signing at the same time. "Something else came up in the Senate today." He quickly explained the blood alchemy bill. Then, letting his hands rest and focusing his attention on Luis, he continued, "I plan to do research of my own, but it occurred to me earlier that you might have more luck than I will on certain fronts. You are friends with many members of the Inventors' and Alchemists' Guilds, correct?"

Luis nodded slowly. "Yes. But with all due respect, Your Highness, don't you have people for this sort of things? Spies and such? Or couldn't you just call people in and order them to tell you what they know?"

"I could, yes." Josiah nodded. "And I will conduct official interviews with experts on the topic of blood alchemy. However, I would appreciate it if you could get a more . . . casual opinion. For some reason, many people don't feel as comfortable as you do with speaking openly in front of me." He managed a laugh to hide his frustration. "There's something else that I want you to look into as well, unrelated to the bill. Miss Breen claims she keeps the clock, but you and the Inventors' Guild claim that any human contact with the inner workings of the clock would harm it. Someone is hiding something, and I need your help to figure out the who and the what.

"I can't officially investigate that yet — there's too much risk that whoever put Miss Breen in the tower will get wind of my questions and quietly disappear, along with anyone else involved. You, on the other hand? The alchemists and inventors know you, and I suspect they'll be willing to talk to you."

"Hmm." Luis toyed with a small screwdriver that he'd pulled from a pocket. "I suppose that if someone's trapping people in towers, I'd like to see them stopped — especially if they've found a way to prevent miazen crystals from draining around people and haven't seen fit to share that discovery. And of course I'd rather not see blood alchemy legalized; if the rumors are true, the bleeders do enough damage already." He frowned. "I'd need you to cover my expenses, though. Right now, all my spare money is going straight into my prototypes."

Josiah nodded. "Naturally. I'll cover whatever you need — and a little extra, if you want. I'd like to see one of your inventions finished someday."

Luis snorted. "So would I, Your Highness. So would I." He stood. "I can't stay much longer; Father will expect me back at the shop. Anything else I need to know?"

Josiah shook his head. "Not that I'm aware of. But if you're gathering information for me, I'll give you an advance on those expenses. Will . . ." He peered into his pocketbook. "Will forty marks be enough?"

Luis rolled his eyes. "I'm buying drinks and occasional dinner, not funding someone else's entire prototype. Half that will be more than enough."

"Twenty, then, and ten towards your inventions." Josiah passed the three ten-mark notes to Luis. "Let me know if you need more."

"Naturally." Luis nodded and headed towards the door. "I'll see myself out. Good day, Your Highnesses. Keep me updated with the girl in the tower." He paused at the door with a grin. "Maybe you'll have to let me meet her sometime too."

"I just might. Best of luck with your work." As Luis left, Josiah turned back to Grace. "Where do you need to be?"

"With Mother. There's a formal luncheon soon." Grace scowled. "Can you give me an excuse not to go? I *hate* these luncheons; they're nothing like the Society of Women in Science dinners. Everyone acts as if I'm stupid simply because I can't hear, but if they'd just look at me when they talked, or if they'd learn some signs, we wouldn't have a problem. And it's so awkward to bring an interpreter; people keep trying to talk to her instead of me."

"I'm sorry, but I can't help you. I'll be in a Senate meeting for most of today, and I have people to meet before it reconvenes." Josiah stood, offering his sister a wry smile. "But if you need to, I give you full permission to claim you have plans with me and slip out early."

"Thank you." Grace stood as well. "I might. Let me know what happens in the tower tonight."

"I will." Josiah opened the door so she could sweep out, then followed her. He glanced at the great clock above the door into the Senate room. A little over an hour remained before the meeting would reconvene; perhaps if he hurried — and skipped lunch — he could have a brief meeting with an archivist like he'd hoped earlier. With that thought in mind, he headed once again for the double doors and the library beyond.

CHAPTER 7

Josiah returned to the tower that night, this time alone. He clicked the locks open one by one; Luis had done his work well making the keys. As he finished, he glanced around. No one near, at least not that he could see — but a part of him half wished that he'd brought a guard or two for protection instead of slipping away from the retinue that usually accompanied him. If anyone knew he was sneaking in here . . .

It was too late now to do anything. And in any case, the fewer who knew about this, the fewer who could draw attention or let slip information to whoever was behind Breen's presence in the tower. And he had a revolver; he could defend himself if need be.

Josiah slipped into the shadows of the clock tower and crossed to the lift. He'd been lucky to stumble across it last night, shrouded in darkness as it was on the far side of the tower. The only thing that betrayed its presence was a single dark blue gem on the wall, lit from within by a faint glow of magic. Josiah pressed his finger against it and waited.

The lift rose more rapidly this time than last night. Apparently, Miss Breen had been expecting someone. And since she didn't drop him this time when he reached the top, Josiah dared suppose it might be *him* she'd been waiting for.

He stepped off the lift, touching his fingers to his lips in thanks and bringing his hand outward in a wave of greeting. She nodded back and replied, "You're here again. Why?"

Well, if she'd been expecting him, she wasn't happy about it. "I still want to help you." Josiah found the stool he'd used last night. "May I sit?"

Breen shrugged and sat down on the floor next to her bed. Taking this as a yes, Josiah took his seat on the stool. "To whom do you owe your debt?"

Breen just looked blankly at him, her expression full of pretended ignorance. But Josiah had learned to read a face long ago, and he pressed on, "Last time, you said you owed someone a debt and that they're keeping you here so you can pay it off. Who do you owe that debt to? Is it a factory owner?"

Breen continued to stare. Josiah tried again: "One of the nobles?" That would be unusual, but not unheard of.

Still, Breen refused to respond. Josiah sighed and changed tactics. "Why do you owe these people a debt?"

Breen pursed her lips slightly as if debating whether or not to answer. With slow motions, she signed, "They saved my life."

Josiah nodded. "And they claimed it as payment. How did they save your life, if I may ask?"

A spark of *something* — mischief? rebellion? — flickered in Breen's eyes. "You can ask."

Josiah waited. Breen's hands remained still. Gradual realization dawned on him, slow enough to be embarrassing. "How did someone save your life?"

She just looked at him, less blank than before but still unspeaking. Josiah sighed. "Ah. So I can ask questions, but you might not answer them?"

Breen nodded. She seemed almost cheerful about it. Well, at least that was a step in the right direction — certainly better than her earlier dead-eyed disengagement. Josiah smiled in return. "I suppose that's fair. You said you keep the clock. What do you mean by that?"

She gave him another look — as if he'd asked, "Is water wet" or something equally obtuse. "I clean the pieces. Make sure nothing is broken or stuck. Fix it if it is." Almost as an afterthought, she added, "It usually isn't."

"I see." Josiah nodded slowly. "Everyone says the clock doesn't need keeping."

Breen shrugged. Josiah sighed, unsurprised. "Does anyone else besides the person keeping you captive know you're here?"

Breen's lips pursed, but her hands remained still and silent for several minutes. Around and above them, the giant clock ticked on relentlessly. The sound grated on Josiah's nerves in a way he couldn't explain. It was too loud, too echoing, too like and yet

[51]

unlike the clocks he knew. Between that and the bells every hour, no wonder Breen was deaf.

Finally, she replied, "My family knows. Some of them."

Ah! This could be helpful. "How long since you since last saw your family?"

Breen tilted her head thoughtfully. "Years."

Years? They'd kept her here for *years?* He would have the scum who'd done this thrown in prison for *life* — even if what they'd done to Breen was technically legal now, it hadn't been then. And even now, the bill ensured a certain standard of treatment for indentured workers, and keeping someone from their family for years on end did *not* fit that standard. "When was the last time you left the clock tower at all?"

Breen's rough laugh burst the quiet of the tower. Her hands flew: "I never leave. My place is here."

Never left? Great Jeros . . . Josiah felt claustrophobic enough when he had to stay in the *palace* for more than a few days. And yet Breen was content to stay in one *tower* for years?

He forced himself to tamp down his anger, to unclench his hands and relax his expression. There was a place for passion and anger, but it wasn't here. Breen didn't need him to rant to her about how bad her situation was — she certainly knew that already. "Would you like to leave now?"

Breen's expression hardened again. "I owe a debt."

"I could pay your debt!" Josiah forced himself to sign clearly, to not let his emotions make his motions sloppy. "Whatever it is, I can afford it, and I will pay it gladly enough." Then he would see the man responsible taken to court, but better to make sure Breen was free first.

Breen shook her head. "You can't. It's mine to pay."

"I said I could afford it. I am . . ." Josiah paused, hesitating. Debating. She would talk to him at the moment, at least a little. But would she talk to the prince? Likely not. "I am a noble of no small means. Even if you owe a life debt, most men who trade in lives can put a price on them willingly enough."

"You can't." Breen pressed her lips together. "You should go. Find someone else who needs you more than I do."

"No, I shouldn't." A hundred grand speeches flooded Josiah's mind, but somehow, he suspected Breen would believe none of them. So, he settled on the most honest answer he could manage: "Even if others suffer more than you do, your suffering matters too. Besides, I'm already doing all I can to help those others. I can't solve their problems on my own, though. I can solve yours if you'll let me."

Breen looked at him for a long moment. Then she signed back: "You can't solve my problem either. You don't have all the information."

As if he didn't know that! As if she wasn't *keeping* that information from him! "Then tell me what I need to know."

She just stared at him, her expression unrelentingly blank. They sat like that for what seemed like an eternity. At last, she said, "The clock will strike soon. You should go."

Josiah checked his pocket watch. She was right; he had ten minutes 'til the hour. He'd have to leave soon or else suffer through the bells again, and he still needed to find a way to block out the sound. "Very well. You don't want me to pay your debt. I'll accept that. But whoever has imprisoned you here has broken the law. Will you give me some information I could use to find him and take him to court so you could be free that way?"

Breen raised an eyebrow, her meaning clear enough.

Josiah sighed. "If you insist. One last request, then: I would like to return tomorrow and talk to you again. You don't have to answer my questions, and we don't have to talk about this. We can discuss something else, anything you choose. And I'd like to bring my sister with me. She's deaf like you. I think you'd like her. If nothing else, let us offer you some company since you have none."

Breen contemplated the floorboards for several minutes before she replied, "You can come back."

"Thank you." Josiah stood, offering her a brilliant smile. "Until tomorrow. Don't worry about the lift; I'll take the stairs. Do you get a signal when someone presses the gem by the lift?"

Breen nodded and pulled out the signal device to show him. Good! Josiah nodded, satisfied. "Tomorrow, I'll press the gem to let you know we're here, then come up the stairs with Grace. That'll save you some trouble. Is that agreeable?"

"Yes. Goodnight." She punctuated her statement with meaningful glances towards the clock machinery.

Ah, yes. He was undoubtedly running low on time before the hour struck. Josiah tipped his hat and waved farewell. Then he hurried down the stairs. He reached the street just as the bells started to ring.

CHAPTER 8

Breen didn't tend the clock the next morning — not properly, anyway. Madame wouldn't return for another three or four days, and the clock never accumulated much grime in a day. Normally, she'd clean it anyway — but right now, she needed something that would occupy her thoughts as well as her hands. So, instead of going through her usual routine, she worked her way downwards through the machinery, quickly checking for serious damage. As usual, she found none.

The machinery ended on the fourth floor, though the weights at the end of the four massive clock chains reached just past the floor and into the third level. Breen didn't bother taking the stairs down to level three. Instead, she jumped and caught the lowest of the weights. From there, she could drop to the ground with minimal damage. The force of the landing jarred her ankles and knees, and she stumbled but ignored the brief pain. After all, she'd suffered worse.

On this level, crates, barrels, and shelves full of boxes of all sizes and shapes lined the walls and sat in rows down the center of the room. Breen made her way to one of the smaller crates near the stairs and dug through the tiny gears until her fingers found cloth. Then, she pulled the cloth-wrapped item out, shaking it slightly to dislodge any gears that had gotten stuck.

She tucked the bundle under her arm, then retreated to a spot near the middle of the level, where crates shielded her from the view of anyone who might happen to come up the stairs. There, she unwrapped her bundle, tugging the cloth free where it had snagged on gears.

The roughly rectangular assemblage of gears, rods, pulleys, rope, and wire inside didn't look like much. But Breen examined it carefully, making sure no loose parts had made their way inside the mechanisms. Once she was satisfied, she set it on the floor in front of her and laid out all her tools around it.

She'd been working on this device for almost a year now, on and off. She knew how it *ought* to function. But pieces were still missing — and not just the miazen crystals that she would need to power it if she ever made it work. At least she knew she needed the crystals, even if she had no way to acquire them. Though she'd found a few boxes filled with roughly-cut miazen crystals of various sizes, they were too small for her needs, and almost all were uncharged. The rest of the pieces . . . she still hadn't figured out what she was missing.

Breen studied the device for several minutes, reminding herself of the problems she needed to solve. After some thought, she dissembled half the device, then made her way around the storeroom, collecting what she thought she'd need. Then, she set to work in earnest.

Hours passed as Breen worked, removing and adding pieces, testing one configuration and then another. By noon, she'd almost completely disassembled the device and started rebuilding it in a larger form, mentally grumbling about her foolishness in not having realized sooner that of *course* it would have to be bigger; it was supposed to replace her own effort in manning the lift. And of course if it were larger, the rope wouldn't keep getting caught on gears . . .

As the day wore on and afternoon turned towards evening, however, Breen's progress on the device slowed. More problems appeared for which she didn't have solutions: how to make sure she had just enough force to work the pulleys and raise the lift, why particular gears kept jamming even though they should turn freely, and more. Finally, her frustration and her growling stomach forced her to a stop. She reluctantly wrapped up the device and hid it on a bottom shelf behind several boxes of parts, as it was now too big to fit in its former hiding place. Hopefully, even if someone discovered it, they wouldn't think she'd made it. Then, she climbed back up the stairs to her quarters.

As she climbed, the clock struck six o'clock. Breen thought back to the last two nights. Josiah had arrived around seven-thirty both times. That gave her an hour and a half to figure out how to deal with his return tonight.

On the top floor, she filled her pot with water from the tap and put it on the burner. She dropped a few small potatoes and a pinch of salt into the water, then sat down to wait.

Why had she told Josiah he could come back? She should've told him to leave and never think about her again. Then again, she'd tried that. She'd told him she didn't need his help. That was *true*. She was safe here; she had food and shelter and work, and, if Madame Gottling told the truth, she was helping to provide for her family. Josiah would only put them both in danger; what if someone saw him coming or going or realized he'd been here? She could only guess how Madame Gottling would punish her for that, but one thing was certain: she wouldn't see the sky again, if ever. But Josiah hadn't listened; he'd just kept asking things until it was easier just to say yes.

Breen huffed. Why couldn't he realize that she had *reasons* for not wanting his help? Why couldn't he see that even if she wanted to accept his offer to pay her debts and set her free, she might have other ties holding her here, ones that couldn't be severed so easily?

Then again, even if he saw those, he'd probably try to cut them anyway.

She had to admit, though; it had been nice to *talk* to someone again, even if he kept asking questions she couldn't answer the way he wanted her to. It had been so long since someone treated her like a real person instead of a not-dead machine — since someone acted like she *mattered*.

Then again, she probably didn't matter to him either — not really. She was a problem to be solved, a jammed gear to be worked free as he put together the machine of his perfect world. Nothing more.

Breen walked over to the burner and checked the potatoes. They seemed tender enough when she poked them with a knife, so she turned off the burner and poured out the water. As she waited for the potatoes to cool enough to eat, she fetched a hunk of hard, dark bread from the cupboard and started on that.

She had to put a stop to this tonight. She almost wished Josiah hadn't said he and his sister would take the stairs. If they were using the lift, she could simply ignore the signal and refuse to bring them up. But since that wouldn't work . . . when they arrived, she'd say hello and then ignore them completely. Eventually, they'd have to get tired of asking her questions and receiving no answers. They'd realize she was a lost cause and go help someone else who needed them, someone who deserved their aid.

Breen finished off her bread and started on her potatoes. She knew her plan wasn't really much of a plan, but it would have to do. Who knew? Maybe Josiah would have changed his mind between last night and now, or maybe he would've found another problem to solve and forgotten about her. She could always hope. And she'd find out for sure in an hour.

CHAPTER 9

The signal buzzed earlier than Breen expected: seven o'clock instead of seven-thirty. So much for Josiah forgetting about her. She sat on her bed and stared at the steps and waited for her visitors to appear.

Josiah reached the top of the stairs first. He tipped his hat and smiled, then signed, "Good evening."

Breen returned his greeting with a nod. Then her gaze flicked back to the stairs as a girl about her own age came into view, hurrying up the last few steps. As the girl reached the top, she waved to Breen, then put a hand on Josiah's shoulder to steady herself as she caught her breath.

Breen nodded back again, studying the girl. This was certainly Josiah's sister. They had the same rounded nose and brown hair, though the girl's hair was pulled up in an elaborate twist. They carried themselves with the same easy confidence as well, but the sister's blue eyes sparkled with a steady cheerfulness quite unlike her brother's intensity.

Once the girl could breathe normally again, Josiah stepped forward and signed, "Breen, this is my sister, Grace. Grace, this is Breen."

Breen stood and replied in the same fashion, "Nice to meet you."

"It's nice to meet you too." Grace tilted her head, still smiling. "May I give you a hug?"

Breen blinked and nodded uncertainly. Grace, apparently requiring no further prompting, sprang forward and wrapped her arms tightly around Breen. Breen awkwardly returned the gesture; after so long in the tower, it felt strange to be touched in a non-threatening way. Was this a normal greeting among the rich?

Grace released her and took a step back, already signing as fast as Breen could follow. "My brother told me about you. I thought you might need a hug."

"Thank you?" Despite her best attempt at politeness, Breen couldn't keep her expression from puckering into a question. What had Josiah said about her? A spark of pride burned her thoughts: did they see her as that pitiable? She wasn't — she shouldn't be.

Grace tilted her head, her own brow wrinkling slightly. "What's wrong? Was the hug too much?"

Breen shrugged, glancing away. Josiah stepped forward. "Don't let Grace scare you. She's very enthusiastic about people."

Grace nodded. "He's right. If I'm overwhelming, tell me. I'll give you space." She flashed another smile. "Thank you for letting me come, by the way."

Again, Breen shrugged and glanced away. She hadn't exactly had much of a choice — not that she was going to say so. In fact, she should probably get on with her plan of ignoring the siblings . . . though that seemed much harder now than it had earlier.

Grace's expression darkened slightly, and she turned to Josiah, her skirts swirling with the motion. She signed to him, her motions much sharper than they'd been a moment before, "You did *ask* if I could come? If we could come back?"

"Yes." Josiah frowned back at her. "Of course I did." He looked at Breen. "I asked you, did I not? We talked about this."

"Yes, you asked." Breen finally managed to school her face into flat neutrality.

Grace glanced from Breen to Josiah a few times. She pursed her lips, her cheerfulness slowly morphing into quiet, fierce disapproval. "Did he pressure you into saying yes?"

Breen hesitated, uncertain what the consequences would be if she said *yes*. But even that hesitation seemed to be answer enough.

Grace huffed. "I'm sorry. Excuse us; I need to talk to my brother." She caught his arm and pulled him halfway down the staircase.

What was *that?* Breen blinked a few times. She'd expected Grace to be a female version of Josiah, but she'd seemed to genuinely care about whether or not Breen wanted them there. Or had Breen just misread that whole exchange? She had to have misunderstood *something* . . .

Grace and Josiah reappeared a few moments later. Josiah's face was flushed red, and he looked as embarrassed as if he'd been caught claiming the sky was green and the ocean red. As they approached Breen, Grace nudged him.

He stopped and squared his shoulders before circling a fist over his heart. "I'm sorry. I might have unintentionally forced you into saying we could come back. I only wished to help, but I should have paid better attention to whether or not I actually was helping."

He'd actually *apologized*. A noble had apologized to *her*. Breen almost felt as if she ought to say "It's all right" and welcome him to stay anyway — but what would that accomplish? Nothing. So she just shrugged yet again and replied, "I forgive you."

"Do you actually want us here?" Grace asked, head tilted and eyes serious. "If not, say so, and we'll leave. I promise."

She *meant* it. Either that or she was an excellent faker. Breen hesitated. Here was her chance; she could tell them to leave, and they'd be gone for — how long? Long enough for Josiah to forget about her, perhaps? Surely she should take that opportunity.

Grace seemed to sense her uncertainty. "We really will go. I'll drag Josiah home by the ear if I need to. I can't promise that he'll give up on your situation, but I'll try to make sure he doesn't come back and bother you without your permission. I would've made him stay home tonight if I'd known you didn't want us here." With a half-smile, she added, "If you want us to stay, we'd be happy to, but we don't *need* to."

Breen hesitated only a moment longer before snapping to a decision. Perhaps it was still a bit risky — but this time, the risk might be worth it. She pointed at Grace and signed, "You can stay." She switched her point to Josiah. "Not you."

Josiah stared at her, disbelief rapidly replacing his embarrassment. "What?"

Grace's mouth formed an *O*, and her eyes widened slightly. "Are you sure? We really will go if you want us to."

Breen nodded. "Please, just you stay." She couldn't trust Josiah not to focus just on his desire to help her whether she wanted it or not, but Grace . . . Grace seemed to genuinely *care* enough that maybe giving her a chance was worthwhile.

Josiah's fingers twitched as if he wanted to sign but couldn't figure out what to say. Grace glanced from him to Breen and then shrugged. Her expression seemed to say "Well, then, this is happening." She turned to Josiah. "You know what she said."

"But . . ." Josiah managed the one word before he let his hands drop to his sides again. He gave his sister a pleading look.

Grace raised an eyebrow at him. "You can't say you want to help people and then ignore what they want. Go. Wait for me downstairs. Don't worry; I'll try not to be too long."

Josiah looked as if he might protest. Then he sighed. "Very well. Good night, Miss Breen." With another tip of his hat, he headed down the stairs.

Both girls waited a few moments. Breen watched the steps until she was certain he wasn't coming back. Then she turned back to Grace, not certain what to do now.

Grace smiled apologetically. "I really am sorry about him. Josiah is full of plans, and he forgets that other people need to have a say in them. Thank you for letting me stay."

Breen managed a smile back. "Thank you for standing up for me." She paused. "Why did you?"

Grace blinked, brows furrowing in confusion. "Why wouldn't I?"

Breen shrugged. "Most people wouldn't care."

"Most people are fools." Grace wrinkled her nose. "They think *I'm* an idiot simply because I can't hear them, but we both know that's not true. I'm just doing what's right." She gave a little shiver as if shaking the topic free. "Now, tell me, what sorts of things do you like?"

What did she like? Breen thought. What could she say that wouldn't sound foolish? The clock? People-watching? She could mention her work with inventions, but she didn't quite feel comfortable enough for that . . .

Grace must've picked up on her uncertainty. "Do you like working on the clock?"

Breen brightened. "Yes. It's beautiful. You should be here when it chimes. The whole tower vibrates, and the gems glow."

"It sounds lovely." Grace glanced back towards the machinery. "I'm sure you know all about how it works too."

[68]

"I know a lot." Not everything, unfortunately, but all the gaps were alchemical, not mechanical, and Breen knew she couldn't teach herself that — not here.

Grace stepped forward, leaning in slightly. "Tell me about the clock and the tower? Please? I'd like to learn more about how it works."

Grace wanted to know about the clock? Breen tilted her head and studied the other girl. She seemed genuine enough — and at least that would be something to talk about. She nodded towards the stairs. "Come with me. It'll be easier to show than tell."

"Lead the way." Grace looped her arm through Breen's as Breen started towards the stairs. It felt odd — but not in a bad way. For the first time that evening, Breen allowed herself to relax a little. She knew this wouldn't last; eventually, someone would find out, or Grace would reveal that she had her own plans, or Josiah would push back in. But she would enjoy it for tonight — or perhaps even longer.

Much to Breen's surprise, Grace proved an extraordinarily attentive listener. She followed Breen from one level to another, glancing between Breen's hands and the mechanism as Breen explained the workings of the clock. She talked about how the gears and chains and weights and rods all worked together to turn the hands and toll the bells, powered by the force of the rising and falling weights combined with the alchemically charged miazen crystals embedded in most of the gears. She described how the backup machinery intertwined with the normal structure, waiting for a main gear or rod to fail and ensuring that the clock would never fall a minute or two behind, at least in theory. As long as Breen had lived in the tower, she'd never seen anything break down. She even explained how the four great chains in the center of the tower could be used to set the clock faces either individually or all at once and how the bells would be triggered whenever any of the clock faces struck an hour, which was why all four had to remain as close to perfectly synchronized as possible.

She wasn't sure how much of her explanation Grace had understood. Machinery was a complicated thing to explain in sign, and a few times she had to resort to charades to get an idea across. But whenever she started to lose steam, Grace would sign a question about what she'd just said or about another piece of clockwork that she hadn't yet explained.

By the time they reached the third floor, the eight o'clock chime had come and gone. Breen had grinned at the surprise and awe on Grace's face when the sound set the tower vibrating and the gems glowing. Somehow, the fact that Grace loved the experience as she did made her seem even less like a noble and more like a normal girl.

On the third level, Grace surveyed the assortment of containers. "What's all this?"

"Spare parts." Breen opened one of the smaller boxes and held up a handful of gears to show her. "I don't know what they're for. They're too small for the clock." She opened another box. "There are uncharged miazen crystals as well."

Grace peeked inside several other boxes before replying: "With all this and how much you know about the clock, you could probably make anything."

Breen just shrugged. She didn't quite feel comfortable getting out her inventions yet; they'd been her secret for so long. Maybe she'd show them to Grace eventually, but not today.

Grace looked around a few more moments, then sighed. "Josiah and I should go. I enjoyed talking to you, though. May I come again another night?"

This time, Breen didn't hesitate. "Yes. I'd like that. Tomorrow night?"

"Yes!" Grace paused, then her face fell. "No. Not tomorrow. There's an event, and Mother wants me with her, and I won't be able to leave until late at night. The night after?"

Breen shrugged. It was all the same to her; she'd be here either way. And perhaps in two days, she could figure out how to make actual conversation that didn't revolve around the clock. After a moment, she realized that she needed to give a proper answer. "The night after tomorrow is fine."

"Good." Grace headed towards the stairs. "I'll tell Josiah, then. Will you come down to say goodbye?"

Breen shook her head. "No." Even if Josiah had apologized, she still had the nagging suspicion that if she saw him again, he'd try to push her for permission to visit too next time. She watched Grace, waiting for pushback.

Grace, however, just gave a little shrug. "Then I'll say it here. Good night, and thank you again. I'll see you soon."

"Good night." Breen waved. Grace waved back, and then she disappeared down the stairs. Breen didn't wait, but headed up the steps, back to her bed.

CHAPTER 10

Josiah fiddled with the keys in his pocket, watching the street outside the window of his carriage as it rolled towards Lord-Senator Weston's city residence. He'd spent the entire morning in the library, interrogating Archivist Johnson on the history of blood alchemy and past generations' arguments against it. Unfortunately, the interview had been far less helpful than Josiah had hoped. As Johnson explained, blood alchemy didn't have a clear starting point; it seemed to have just always been. He showed Josiah references to it under other names appearing all the way back to the earliest days of the Chanian kingdom, even before people started practicing normal alchemy. The only consistent details were that it was always practiced by people on the fringes on society, and always practiced in secret — and beyond that, details varied from source to source.

As for arguments against it, those were even more disappointing. For most of Chania's history, Johnson explained, no one really needed a reason to be against blood alchemy; the fact that blood alchemy derived its power exclusively from death was deterrent enough. But what was that today, when so many died even without blood alchemy as a motive for their demise? No, the modern era demanded a better answer.

Still, some information was better than no information. And perhaps Weston was right, though thinking that made Josiah feel as if he'd betrayed his own principles. If Weston argued correctly, if blood alchemy really could save lives at no moral or ethical cost, it would be foolish to reject the idea simply because of the person who suggested it.

The carriage pulled into Weston's circular courtyard and stopped before the grand front doors. The two guards riding on the back of the carriage jumped down, and one opened the door for Josiah.

Josiah stepped out and strode to the double doors of the house. Before he could knock, it swung open. A man — a butler, by the look of him — bowed. "Your Highness. Lord-Senator Weston has been expecting you. Please come in."

"Thank you, sir." Josiah entered. His guards fell in behind him.

The butler led Josiah and his men up to Weston's office on the second floor. There, he opened the carved wooden door and announced, "His Royal Highness Prince Josiah to see you, my lord."

"Welcome, Your Highness." Inside, Weston stood up, pushing his heavy chair back from his desk. "Please, come in."

"Thank you, Lord-Senator." Josiah nodded to his guards, who saluted and took up positions on either side of the door. Then he walked in, letting the butler shut the door behind him. "I appreciate your willingness to speak with me on such short notice."

"I appreciate your interest in speaking with me, Your Highness. I feared the royal family would be resistant to my proposed changes. I am glad to find you so open-minded." Weston took a set of wineglasses and a dark glass bottle from the sidebar. "Something to drink to help our discussion? I recently acquired a Ventian red of a particularly excellent vintage."

Josiah shook his head and sat down in one of the fine leather chairs near the desk. "No thank you, Lord-Senator. I doubt that our discussion will need much assistance."

"As you wish." Weston replaced the glasses and wine bottle and returned to his seat. Behind him, floor-to-ceiling shelves held a mixture of books and rare items from around the world. "I feel I should inform you that I have invited one of my associates to join us a little later on. She is something of an expert on blood alchemy and has been heavily involved with the research on which the bill is based. I thought you might appreciate hearing her perspective as well as mine."

"An excellent idea. I look forward to hearing what she has to say." Josiah had hoped for an entirely private meeting; it was easier to take people off their guard when they believed there was no one else to hear them. Still, as his official purpose for the meeting was to learn more about what benefits and negatives blood alchemy might offer, bringing in one of Weston's experts made sense. "While we wait, I would like to ask you a few questions about your personal thoughts on the bill."

"My thoughts?" Weston raised an eyebrow. "You will have to explain yourself, Your Highness."

"Naturally." Josiah nodded. "With due respect, Lord-Senator, blood alchemy has been outlawed, either implicitly or explicitly, since the very dawn of Chania. Suggesting that we change that, regardless of whether or not such a change is due, is a bold, risky move. I am curious what would inspire you to take such a step."

Weston spread his hands in a "come now" gesture. "We both serve the interests of the people, Your Highness. You have heard me describe the benefits for the Chanian people, your subjects, multiple times by now."

"I have, and I am not speaking of the benefits for the people." Josiah leaned forward slightly. "Shall we be honest with each other, Lord-Senator? You and I both know that you are a cunning man. You do nothing if it will not somehow support your own goals. So, what do you hope to gain from this?"

"Ah. I see now." Weston nodded slowly, his eyes never leaving Josiah. "So you admit openly that this meeting was never about learning about blood alchemy, only discerning if I am a threat or not?"

"I never said that." If Weston was trying to get a rise out of him, it wouldn't work; Josiah had long been immune against that particular tactic. "As I pointed out already, Lord-Senator, you are a cunning man, and I would be a fool not to recognize that fact. I wish to understand both blood alchemy *and* your plans regarding it. After all, as *you* said, we both serve the interests of the people. For me, that means doing all I can to ensure that systems instituted to help them are not going to be abused by anyone, be they rich or poor."

"So, you are only doing your duty. Is that it? Not trying to ensure that your own position remains secure?" Weston smiled thinly. "Don't be shocked, Your Highness. As you said, I am a cunning man. I can see that you enjoy your own position as I enjoy mine, and I can tell that you at times chafe against its limits. You speak as if the Chanian people were your primary motivation, and you have claimed before that you would like nothing more than to see the common people in charge of the land. But I imagine that if such an event occurred, if the rule of the land were turned over to the lower-born and you were shut out, you would be even more ill-pleased than you are now. You believe you know what is best for the country, and you do what you must to see it done, save when you are thwarted by someone stronger."

This was not the conversation Josiah had come here expecting. He forced himself to keep his expression neutral, though Weston's comments struck at his mind like darts. "I desire power only to protect my people." That was *true*. He didn't seek power for himself. He never had. "I do not claim to always know best, but Jeros does, and I know what is and is not in line with his principles." He straightened. "In any case, Lord-Senator, you seem to be avoiding my questions. What do you hope to gain from the blood alchemy bill?"

"I seek the potential, Your Highness." Weston rested his elbows on the arms of his chair and pressed his fingertips together. "My alchemists are certain that blood alchemy can save lives. But they are also confident that it could extend life as well by warding off the effects of old age and sickness. With time and research, we may be able to use blood alchemy to double or triple man's lifespan — or perhaps evade death altogether.

"And there are other potential applications as well. Any alchemist can tell you that blood alchemy has far more power than normal alchemy does. If we were to begin to draw on what it offers, who knows what we might accomplish? Transportation, production, warfare, all would be revolutionized." He leaned forward slightly. "What would you say if there were no more factory deaths, Your Highness? No more accidents for railway workers, no more souls lost in storms at sea, no more men killed in wars? What if there were no more need for child workers in any industry? What if we could create machines that would take the places of all these people? Would that not be a better world, Your Highness? Ordinary alchemy cannot achieve it, but my alchemists believe that blood alchemy could make these things reality."

A world with no death. A world in which men and women were no longer forced into dangerous occupations to fill a rich man's pockets. A world in which children were free to learn and play and enjoy life instead of slaving sunup to sundown to provide for their families. It sounded like paradise, like what the priests said would come when Jeros fully healed the break between the heavens and the mortal realm and reigned directly over humans once again. Could blood alchemy truly put such a world in their grasp before then?

And if it could . . . there was a bigger question on the line. "What of the cost?" Josiah asked, leaning forward himself. "Blood alchemy demands death. Would you build paradise by the blood of innocents, Lord-Senator? Would you kill to create a society with no death?"

"Bettering any society requires sacrifice, Your Highness. You of all people should know that. As for what that sacrifice might be . . ." Weston glanced at the clock that hung on the wall by the door, its golden pendulum swinging gently. "I believe the person who can answer that question will be here momentarily."

Josiah raised an eyebrow. "Your blood alchemy expert?"

"One and the same." Weston nodded. "I believe you will find what she has to say interesting, to say the least. Perhaps even attractive, if you are truly willing to let go of your prejudices in order to create a better world for your people."

Blast Weston and his taunts. Josiah met his gaze squarely. "I will do what is best for the people according to Jeros's principles."

Before Weston could answer, someone knocked on the door. He sat up and turned towards it. "Ah. This must be my expert now. Perhaps she will be able to clear away some of your doubts." Louder, he called, "Come in."

CHAPTER 11

The door opened. Josiah turned to see a woman walk in carrying a bulky black carpetbag. A ruby pendant hung halfway down her breast, and she wore a pin with Lord-Senator Weston's crest on it pinned to the lapel of her fitted blue jacket. With her cold expression and her tight brown bun, she put Josiah in mind of some of his and Grace's harsher tutors. She seemed familiar for some reason, though Josiah couldn't place where he'd seen her.

The woman made a half-bow towards Weston and Josiah both. "Your message said you needed my expertise, Lord-Senator?" She spoke with a faint accent, not Chanian. Josiah guessed it was from one of the Mountain Kingdoms on the mainland.

"Indeed." Weston beckoned. "His Highness wishes to understand what blood alchemy might have to offer. Your Highness, this is my associate and one of my leading alchemical researchers, Madame Gottling."

"A pleasure to meet you." Josiah's memory finally clicked. "Lord-Senator, I thought this woman was one of your aides. She was with you in the last Senate meeting."

"I have acted as his aide in the Senate on occasion." Gottling walked over to Josiah and Weston and set her bag on the floor beside Weston's desk. "It is convenient to do so when the my lord may need to call on my knowledge. However, my true work is with alchemy." She knelt and opened her bag. "I will not waste your time, Your Highness. You wish to know what blood alchemy may create? Very well, I will show you."

From the bag, she took several devices. A few, Josiah could recognize as a mechanical version of an arm, leg, or hand. The others, however, he could only guess at, though they seemed to involve an unusual number of leather-like sacs.

Gottling laid the devices out on Weston's desk. "I am certain you can recognize some of these. No doubt you have seen or heard that the common alchemists are working with the Inventors Guild to develop some of the same technology, such as a prosthetic hand or foot. However, with blood alchemy, we could create deeper-level parts. This, for example —" she indicated one of the devices — "is a mechanical heart, and this —" she gestured to another — "is an artificial lung. All that we require to make them functional is the proper power source: blood alchemy."

"Very interesting." Josiah studied the devices, though he couldn't see how they would work. "But how do you know they will function as you intend when you cannot legally test them?"

"We based these devices on the notes of illegal blood alchemists. They reported success with similar creations," Gottling replied. "And we have consulted with medical experts who agree that these should be effective replacements for lost or damaged body parts."

"I see." Josiah wished he knew more about these things; right now, he had no one's word but Gottling's to go on. Eventually, he'd be able to meet with reputable alchemists, but at the moment, they kept putting him off. "And is there any reason why these devices would not function under the power of ordinary alchemy?"

"There are, in fact, two such reasons." Gottling pulled a pen and a pad of paper from her bag. "First, ordinary alchemically charged gems are far less powerful than those charged by blood alchemy. Second, blood alchemy is required to properly maintain a connection between machine and man."

Josiah pulled out his own pen and notebook. "Interesting. And how do you know that blood alchemy is the only way to maintain this connection? Do you have a reason why blood alchemy will create this connection and normal alchemy will not?"

"To answer your first question, we have tested these devices with an ordinary charged miazen crystals for power." As if anticipating Josiah's next question, she added, "There are an abundance of people in the slums who will gladly take a slim chance if it might save their lives. We had no trouble finding willing volunteers. However, the devices would either desync with the patient's body after a minute or two or would simply never connect at all. And as the device must be integrated into the patient's nervous system to be of any use or value, you can imagine how this would be a problem.

"As for why only blood alchemy will maintain the connection . . ." Gottling paused, one eyebrow slightly raised. "How much do you know about the source of alchemy's power, Your Highness?"

"Very little." Josiah leaned forward. "Would you care to educate me?"

"If you do not know, I am limited in what I can say. We alchemists have our trade secrets just as any other guild does, and we have a right not to reveal those unless it is absolutely necessary." Gottling pressed her lips together for a moment. "Suffice it to say that the power of any kind of alchemy comes from man. Ordinary alchemy uses what is cast off; blood alchemy takes the power directly from the source. That makes it more powerful, and it more readily integrates with another source of the same power."

Alchemical magic came from living things as well? Josiah made a mental note to ask an alchemist about that later. He suspected that plying Gottling for further details would be a lost cause, and he'd rather get the information from a more trustworthy source anyway. "I understand your reticence, Ms. Gottling. Another question, then. No doubt you are aware of Lord-Senator Weston's plans. Tell me, how many men and women would have to die every year to make them a reality?"

Gottling smiled, her lips tight. "No more than die every year now, Your Highness."

"But you claim that you can save many of those people through blood alchemy." Josiah raised an eyebrow. "An estimate, please."

Again Gottling pressed her lips together, annoyance flickering over her face. "As you insist." She indicated the mechanical heart again. "This is our most resource-intensive device. We estimate that it would require fifteen to twenty drops of blood to power it per week. For comparison, the average human male has roughly ninety-five *thousand* drops of blood in his body. That means that one man's blood could theoretically power mechanical hearts for two to three people for the duration of their natural lives."

"And what about the lord-senator's other plans?" Josiah demanded. "Extended lifespans, mechanical workers, and so on? How much more blood would those require?"

"I am afraid I do not have an estimate on that yet, Your Highness." Gottling smiled coolly. "Perhaps by the time we can make those plans reality, we will have found a more efficient method of pulling power from the blood. Perhaps we will have even found a method that requires only blood, not death. But even if we do not, we cannot stop people dying of natural causes. If all else fails, we use what will occur anyway."

Josiah turned to Weston. "Do you agree with her?"

Weston raised an eyebrow. "Do you not, Your Highness? Consider it. Why should we not use the inevitable to build Paradise? In doing so, we may give meaning to tragedy and turn evil to good purpose."

"It sounds disrespectful of the dead if you ask me, Lord-Senator." Josiah stood. "I thank you both for your time. You have given me much to consider. However, I have other meetings, and I would not want to keep either of you from your work."

Weston stood and made a partial bow. "Good day, Your Highness. Think on what we have said here. And keep this last thing in mind: change will come whether you like it or not. Better to be prepared for it and shape that change while you still can than to fight until it knocks you down and drowns you."

"Change may be inevitable, Lord-Senator, but specific changes are not. My aim is to choose which ones succeed and which ones do not," Josiah replied. "Good day, Lord-Senator, Ms. Gottling."

He stepped out the door and beckoned to his guards. They followed him obediently as he strode quickly out of the house and back to his carriage. There, he gave the order to return to the palace.

As the carriage rolled away, he leaned back in his seat with a sigh. He still felt as if he had more doubts and questions than answers. Weston's arguments for using blood alchemy to save lives were compelling, especially if one man could save two or three others — or more. It *would* be a good way for the worst criminals to pay back their debt to society. Yet his other suggestions — using the blood of those who died of terminal illness or natural causes to create a new world of longer lives and strange new machinery — made Josiah feel as unsettled as if they were speaking of cannibalism as the solution to the starving masses.

The worst of it was that he couldn't give a good reason *why* their suggestions unsettled him. After all, even the non-medical innovations Weston suggested would, at least in theory, make people's lives better. One could even make the argument that it was in line with Jeros's principles; Jeros did delight in turning evil to good and death to life. But it still *felt* wrong.

Josiah shook himself. He'd arranged a meeting with a high-ranking priest for tomorrow; perhaps then he'd figure out some answers. Until then, he'd continue to think on the matter himself in between additional meetings.

Now, what was next for the day? Ah, yes. A meeting with his father, who had requested that Josiah update him on his investigations regularly. Josiah reached into his pocket to pull out his notebook and review what he'd learned, but as he did, his fingers brushed the keys to the clock tower.

He drew those out instead and considered them. If Weston's plan were enacted, if blood alchemy were legalized, perhaps Breen wouldn't be in the clock tower. Perhaps she wouldn't have owed the debt in the first place, or if she had, she would have been allowed to pay it off working somewhere more pleasant and less prison-like. Or perhaps she'd be there anyway; he had no idea what had caused her debt — and, at this rate, not much chance of asking any time soon.

Josiah pressed his thumb against the teeth of one of the keys, scowling. The clock tower had been his investigation! His work! And then Grace had literally pushed him aside and taken over.

True, she'd told him afterward what had gone on and what she'd learned — which had been very little about Breen and quite a lot about the tower — but the rejection still stung.

Then again . . . Josiah grimaced. Grace did have a point. He'd pushed his way into Breen's life and expected her to welcome him and his help. He hadn't considered that she might not be emotionally ready for freedom, or that even if she wanted companionship, she might not be comfortable with *his* companionship. And if she already owed a debt to one person, she might be afraid that he'd take advantage of her in the same way if she left on his terms . . .

Josiah paused, staring at the keys in his hand. *I'm a fool.* If all he wanted was for her to be free, he could've given her that the second day he visited her. The same keys that let him in would let her out even if they weren't in his hands. He should've just left the keys with her and told her she could choose whether or not to use them — but he'd kept them so he could be the hero. No wonder she'd chosen Grace over him.

Josiah tucked the keys back in his pocket. He'd give them to Breen tomorrow night when he and Grace returned to the tower. Perhaps that would put him a little closer to Breen's good graces, enough that she'd talk to him and he could learn something about how she ended up in the tower in the first place. And even if she didn't, at least he would have technically accomplished his purpose.

That, however, was tomorrow night. Between now and then, he had considerably more investigating to do, a dinner to attend tonight celebrating the revised trade agreement his mother had worked out with the Ventian ambassadors, and, of course, the meeting with his father. With that thought in mind, Josiah pulled out his notebook and started reminding himself of all he'd learned so far.

CHAPTER 12

Breen sat cross-legged on top of one of the largest crates on the third floor of the tower, fiddling with what had been a clock — albeit one without a face or casing. She'd figured out how to make a normal-sized clock after a month of studying the tower's mechanism. Since then, she'd put together and taken apart so many that she could almost do it in her sleep.

She kept alert for the vibrations of the signal device. Grace should have arrived fifteen minutes ago, based on her last visit and Josiah's visits before then. Breen hoped she hadn't forgotten.

That probably was what had happened, though. Breen sighed and pulled apart another section of gears from the remains of the clock. Josiah had come because he wanted to save her. Grace had come because of Josiah and stayed the one time because Breen asked her to, or perhaps because she also wanted to save Breen but in a different way. But now that Breen had asserted herself and let them know that she couldn't be saved, they'd probably lost interest.

Odds were, she'd see neither of them again. That was good; she didn't need them. It was better that they stayed away.

Still, it had been nice to talk to Grace. She'd genuinely seemed to care. Perhaps that had all been an act — but the feeling of being wanted had brought the old ache of loneliness back as sharp pain, even fiercer than it had been during her first year in the tower. And this was one of the few types of hurt that her mechanical heart couldn't heal.

Breen had nearly decided to go back upstairs when she felt the signal device vibrate in her pocket. Out of habit, she hurried over to the lift and peered down. No one was on the platform, which meant this had to be Grace. *So she didn't forget.*

Grace appeared at the top of the stairs a few moments later and signed a cheerful hello. "I'm sorry we're late. Josiah was talking to Mother and Father about politics."

Breen just shrugged. Then, feeling that wasn't enough, added, "I'm glad you came back. I thought you might not."

"Why?" Grace sat down on the nearest of the crates, fighting with her skirts until she found a comfortable position. "I said I would, didn't I?"

"You're rich." Breen climbed onto another crate, not the one she'd been sitting on earlier; that was too far away for a good conversation. "I'm no one. You don't have to care about me."

"I want to care." Grace's handsigns were breezy and careless, yet her smile was somehow serious. "I choose to. That means keeping my word."

"Why do you care?" Breen hadn't intended to ask the question, but her hands formed the words before she could consider them. "There are others who need you more than I do. Josiah said I'm a problem he can solve and that's why he comes back. Is that what you think too?"

Grace clapped a hand to her forehead and let her head flop forward in exasperation. She held the position only a moment before signing, "I'm sorry. I'll talk to him. You're not a problem to solve. You're a person. He ought to know that."

Breen shrugged. Whether or not she was a person wasn't the point. "What about you, though? Why are you here?"

"I'm here because I was asked." Grace's smile had faded fully into seriousness now. "Josiah asked me to come the first time. He thought I could set you at ease. Then you asked me to come back, so I did."

Breen's brow furrowed. "Is that the only reason?"

"No. Not the only one." Grace shook her head. "Josiah wants to be the white knight in the storybook, the one who slays giants and rescues princesses from wizards and stands between people and pain. That's not a bad thing. I just don't think it's everything. I think sometimes, people need someone who'll stand beside them and listen and bear their hurts with them just as much as they need someone who'll stand and fight on their behalf. Maybe they even need that more than a rescuer."

Breen considered this. "But why me?"

"Why not you? You need a friend, and being friends with you doesn't stop me from standing by others too. If Jeros put us in each other's lives, he must have done so for a reason." Grace's grin returned. "Besides, girls like us should stick together."

Girls like us? Breen blinked several times, trying to find the place where she and Grace became *us*. "What?"

Grace tapped her cheek just under her ear and again by the corner of her mouth. "Deaf."

Oh. That was what she meant. Breen supposed she couldn't argue with that — nor could she argue with Grace's reasoning. She *didn't* need a rescuer. But what Grace offered, a friend and a listening ear, she at least *wanted*.

So, she returned Grace's grin with a smile of her own and touched her fingertips to her lips, then moved them outward. "Thank you."

Grace returned the gesture, then added, "Of course." She slid off her crate. "Is there somewhere in the tower that has a good view of the city? I'd like to see what it looks like from up here if you don't mind."

Breen shook her head and beckoned for Grace to follow her. She led the way up the stairs, all the way to the very top of the clock tower, where the lights that lit the clock faces from behind cast the whole area in a golden glow, save for the deep shadows among the machinery in the center of the room. Just above that machinery hung the four great bells of the tower, silent and waiting.

Grace stopped at the top of the stairs and leaned against the wall, catching her breath. Then she looked around, taking in the scene. "This is lovely." She hurried to the glass clock face and stared out for several minutes, then turned to face Breen. "You can see for miles from up here!"

Breen nodded and joined her at the clock face. It wasn't her favorite; this one looked out to the south and faced the slums directly. But if she looked down, she could still see the lights of the city and the carriages moving along the streets, and she could ignore the starless blackness that hung above her former home.

She sat down on the wooden floor and gestured for Grace to do the same. Grace did, once again fighting her skirts and petticoats. When she finally sat, a rippled puddle of fine fabric surrounded her. Breen felt a momentary pang; surely such lovely clothes ought to be kept off her dirty floors.

Grace, however, seemed unbothered. She watched out the clock a little longer, then turned to Breen. "I'd love to have a view like this. Do you spend much time up here?"

Breen nodded. "I sit up here when I'm not busy with the clock. It's my favorite place in the tower."

"I'm sure! Thank you for sharing it with me." Grace peered out the window again for a moment, then signed, "Do you ever try to look for your home, wherever you lived before you came to the tower?"

Breen bit her lip. "Not anymore." She pointed towards the dark expanse across the river. "It's somewhere over there. Too far away to see."

Grace tilted her head slightly, studying Breen's face. "I'm sorry. You probably don't like to talk about it."

Breen just shrugged, keeping her expression neutral. "What about your home? Can you see it from here?"

Grace rose onto her knees, leaning close to the glass and looking first to one side, then the other. She sank back down after a moment and shook her head. "Not quite. It's in that direction." She pointed between the eastern and northern clock faces. "It's a little too far out of view of the window."

Breen nodded. That wasn't really surprising; many nobles had their homes fairly close to the palace. "Do you have siblings other than Josiah?"

Grace shook her head. "No. Josiah is my only brother. Can I ask about your siblings?"

Could she? Breen considered the question. Talking about her family seemed risky, and thinking about them always made her feel more hollow and lonely more than ever. But there were so many people in the city; surely as long as she didn't say her family name, Grace couldn't tell Josiah anything that would let him interfere. And talking about her family with the others in the laboratory never hurt as much as thinking about them alone.

"I have four brothers and —" she paused, stopping herself before she could sign *three*. "Two sisters."

"Sisters! I would love to have a sister." Grace wrinkled her nose. "Instead I just get a brother who talks too much and drags me into his schemes. Did your brothers do the same thing?"

Breen thought back to the time before the factory, when she and her brothers and the neighborhood children had been free to do as they wished as soon as their chores were done. "Yes. But I got them into as much trouble as they did me." Lily had been the sensible, responsible one, but even she could be persuaded. And once she was persuaded, she'd come up with the best plans. Not that they'd had much time for such things once they started working.

Grace laughed, throwing her head back and clasping her hands together in glee. Once she'd calmed down, she signed, "I like you. Tell me about what you did? I'll trade you a story for a story, and then we'll get to know each other well."

Again, Breen hesitated — but every child on the street surely had stories just like her own before the accident, and Grace seemed to want to know. So, she nodded and began: "My younger brother, Jack, and I always played jokes on my older brothers . . ."

Though Breen started out hesitantly, Grace again proved herself an attentive listener, and Breen found herself sharing first one story, then another and another. She recalled pranks on her siblings and games with the other children who'd lived on the street and the disappointment whenever one of their playmates had to start working to help support their families. Not that the rest of them didn't have work at home, but it could be finished quickly

[97]

and even made enjoyable if there was someone else to do it with. Not like the factories, where you weren't allowed to talk except as absolutely necessary.

In between her accounts, Grace shared her own stories of her and Josiah's childhood. She talked about escaping their nursemaids and governesses and, eventually, tutors to play hide and seek in the upper levels of their home, of sneaking out of bed to peer at their parents' parties and galas, of making fun of their lessons and competing to see who could pry the best stories out of their teachers. She described everything casually, yet Breen could imagine the life of luxury she and Josiah must have led. Did they know how lucky they were, to have rooms upon rooms to explore and private tutors as soon as they were old enough to be taught? Did they realize how much they'd been blessed?

Yet for all that, Breen noticed another thread running through Grace's stories. While Grace frequently referenced Josiah enjoying spending time with other boys of the same age, she rarely referred to friends of her own except very early in her childhood. When Breen asked about it, Grace frowned, and her hands slowed. "It's hard to be friends with people whom you can't understand and who won't learn to talk to you. Didn't you ever have that problem?"

Breen shook her head and pointed to the bells above. "I wasn't deaf before I came here."

"That makes sense." Grace sighed. "I was five when I lost my hearing. I got sick, and the sickness settled in my ears. I got better, but my hearing didn't come back. After that, no one outside my family bothered much with me." She managed a smile. "At least Josiah learned sign language along with me so we could still talk. I learned how to read lips too, but it's difficult, and most people forget that they need to face me." She shivered as if trying to shake off the bad memories. "Who taught you sign language if you didn't need it until you lived here?"

How could she answer that safely? After a moment's thought, Breen signed, "The people I owe my debt to taught me before I came to the tower. I think they knew I would go deaf."

"And they still sent you here?" Grace wrinkled her nose. "That was rotten of them."

Breen shrugged. "The clock needs a keeper. I don't mind so much anymore."

At that moment, a shadow fell over them from the direction of the stairs. Breen turned to see Josiah standing there. "I don't mean to interrupt, but Grace and I need to go before we're missed. I'm sorry."

Grace glanced in surprise at the clock beside her. "I didn't realize how long we'd been here. Help me up?"

Josiah walked over and pulled her to her feet. He turned to Breen. "Thank you for letting Grace come back."

Breen stood and nodded awkwardly. How was she supposed to respond to this? Why was he up *here*? Why hadn't they kept an eye on the time so he wouldn't have to come get Grace?

"Yes, thank you." Grace echoed Josiah's signs. "I enjoyed our conversation. May I come back another time?"

This Breen knew how to answer. She nodded again, this time eagerly. "Yes. In two nights again?"

"I look forward to it." Grace darted in for a quick hug, then dipped back just as swiftly. "Good night! I'll see you then."

With a wave, she disappeared down the stairs. Breen expected Josiah to follow, but instead, he signed, "I have something for you." He seemed more ill-at-ease than she'd ever seen him. His hands were stiff, his signs oddly formal, and he kept shifting his weight from one foot to the other and back again.

Breen gave him a wary look. Josiah stuffed a hand into his pocket and pulled out a ring of three keys, which he held out to Breen.

Were these what she thought they were? Breen held out her hand and let him drop the keys into it. They were lighter than she'd expected, yet they had a weight to them that had nothing to do with their size.

Josiah started signing again, now so quickly that Breen almost couldn't catch his words. "These are the keys to the tower door. I should have given them to you the first night I came, but I was selfish and thoughtless. I apologize. I had another set made so Grace can continue to visit, but I'll hand those over as well if you decide you would rather she not come back. I hope you will let her continue to visit, though, and that you will think slightly more kindly of me in the future. I know I can be blind, but I am trying."

Breen stared first at him, then at the keys in her hand. What was she supposed to do with these? It wasn't as if she could leave on her own any more than she could with him.

But he was trying to do the right thing. He still wanted to be the rescuer, but at least he'd found a way to do that without forcing her to leave the tower. She could appreciate that. So, she tucked the keys in her pocket and signed, "Thank you."

"You're welcome." Josiah nodded gravely. "If you need anything else, tell me or Grace, and I'll see that you get it. If you decide to use the keys and you need a place to hide, go to the palace and ask the guards if you can speak with Captain Douglas. Show them this if they won't listen." He pulled a letter sealed in wax from his pocket and handed it to Breen as well. From the feel of it and the slight bulge in one spot, Breen could tell that there was something hard and circular inside. Another seal, maybe? "Once you reach Captain Douglas, give him the letter. He knows me well. He'll tell me that you're here and make sure you're safe and protected."

He was sending her to the *palace* for protection? What kind of power did Josiah have? Then again, no doubt Josiah and Grace spent considerable time at the palace since they were nobles. And Josiah seemed like the type of person who'd befriend the guards gladly, given the chance.

"Thank you," Breen signed again. "I'll remember that."

"Good." Josiah glanced around as if searching for something else to say, then settled for, "Good night" and hurried after his sister.

Breen waited until they had undoubtedly left, then stared at the letter in her hands. If she ever needed a way out, she had one. It was just too bad she'd never have a chance to use it.

CHAPTER 13

Josiah tapped his pen against the corner of his paper, each tap adding another drop of ink to the growing dot there. "Would you say, in your professional opinion, that blood alchemy is or has the potential to be more powerful than normal alchemy?"

Doctor Zachariah Sterling, the alchemist on the other side of Josiah's desk, kept his expression carefully, pointedly neutral. "That would depend on what you mean by *power*, Your Highness. Please be more specific."

Note to self: if at all possible, avoid engaging Dr. Sterling as an interview subject in future. Not that Josiah had much of a choice. The good doctor was the Alchemist Guild's leading expert in potential biomedical applications of alchemy. If anyone would know how feasible Weston's proposals were, it was Dr. Sterling. Unfortunately, he'd also spent the entire interview hedging his answers and evading the most useful questions.

Josiah suppressed a sigh. By now, he'd figured out that his only option was to play Dr. Sterling's game and hope he could pry some helpful information out of the man. "Power, the capacity to enable particular actions for an extended length of time. Or any other definition you might consider relevant."

Dr. Sterling cleared his throat and adjusted his round spectacles. "Well, Your Highness, in alchemy, there *are* several different ways to measure how powerful a particular method or charged crystal is."

"In that case, enlighten me on what those are, Doctor," Josiah replied, unable to keep the weariness from his voice. "Please keep in mind the goal of this discussion. The Senate must have all possible details in order to make an informed decision on the blood alchemy bill. It would be in everyone's best interests if you shared what you know on the topic."

Dr. Sterling raised an eyebrow. "If I may say, Your Highness, I do not believe you are on the committee established to investigate Lord-Senator Weston's claims about the capabilities of blood alchemy."

"No, I am not, but I do represent the interests of the royal family and our two votes on the High Council. And I am as able to speak in the Senate as any other man there." Josiah pressed his pen to the page. "Please, Doctor, answer the question."

"Very well." Dr. Sterling huffed. "As I said, we have several different measurements of power, some which apply to the method used to charge crystals and some which apply to the charged crystal itself. Of the latter there are three: how much energy the crystal is able to hold, how much energy the crystal is able to output, and how long the crystal is able to maintain that output without draining itself dry. To our understanding, crystals charged via blood alchemy are able to hold and output more energy, but they seem to drain more rapidly."

Josiah held up a hand. "Another question before you go on. It would seem to me that the first two measurements would largely determine the third. A crystal would drain more rapidly if it could hold less energy, and so on."

"An easy mistake to make." Dr. Sterling pulled a mid-sized crystal from his pocket, the sort used in carriage lights. "Energy put into a crystal and energy output from a crystal are only equal if the alchemist has done his job very poorly. You are aware of how placing mirrors around a candle can increase the apparent light it releases?"

Josiah nodded. "I am. The light is reflected and thereby increased."

"Exactly. A properly cut miazen crystal, charged by the correct methods, will, in a sense, reflect and magnify the energy within. The very best of our alchemical methods result in crystals that output approximately ten or twenty times the energy with which they were originally charged and can recharge themselves to some degree by recapturing excess output energy. Of course, methods used to produce such crystals are both expensive and time-consuming, so the standard alchemical crystal only outputs about four or five times as much energy as it originally holds. On the other hand, if the captured records of blood alchemists are to be believed, their crystals can output up to forty times the energy with which they were originally charged, but they seem to lack the capacity to recharge themselves as effectively, and thus they drain more quickly."

Again Josiah nodded, jotting down Dr. Sterling's words in his notebook. "I see. I have always been told, though, that crystals drain faster in the presence of people. How does this affect your measurements?"

"It does affect them slightly, yes." Dr. Sterling took off his spectacles and polished them with a handkerchief. "We believe that crystals charged by blood alchemy are less prone to being drained by the presence of people. However, they still drain more quickly overall."

"Do you have a theory about why the one holds its charge longer and the other does not?" Josiah asked.

"We do, but it's not relevant to this discussion." Dr. Sterling put his spectacles back on. "Suffice it to say that it has to do with the source of the energy and the way in which that energy is used."

"Anything could be relevant, Dr. Sterling. Please expound."

Dr. Sterling coughed slightly. "Your Highness, trust me when I say that it is not relevant. Even if it were, that information, like the methods we use to charge crystals, is a secret known only to those in the Alchemists' Guild. I would not reveal it even if to do otherwise would mean my death."

Josiah again stifled a sigh. He understood why the Alchemists' Guild wanted to keep some things secret; after all, if all alchemy were public knowledge, there would be little to stop people from doing it improperly and accidentally blowing themselves or others to bits. But in this case, the secrecy seemed a bit much.

Still, he knew he wouldn't learn anything by pushing Dr. Sterling, not unless he could somehow prove that the fate of Chania rested on this particular piece of information — perhaps not even then. "Very well. You said there were other ways of measuring power as well, ones that had to do with the method?"

"Indeed." Dr. Sterling nodded. "Certain methods are able to put more energy into a crystal than others; certain methods are also able to charge a crystal more efficiently or quickly than others. The more energy with which a method can safely charge a crystal or the more efficiently it can do so, the more power it has. In this respect, blood alchemy and normal alchemy seem to be on roughly level ground."

Josiah nodded. "What about the versatility of the energy in the crystal? How does that play into the measure of power? And does blood alchemy or normal alchemy produce more versatile results?"

"Blood alchemy would seem to be more versatile, assuming the records can be believed," Dr. Sterling replied. "If it is, I expect that property has to do with the source of the energy again more than the methods used. However, I am confident that with enough research and development, we will be able to use normal alchemy for as many purposes as the blood alchemists can use their craft.

Perhaps the Senate might consider providing the Guild with additional funding for such research?"

"Perhaps. Such a proposal would be much more readily accepted if you could show that you are close to achieving the same ends that the blood alchemists promise." If they could, Josiah would champion the request himself. Of course, anything normal alchemy could create would likely be prohibitively expensive for the lower classes, but maybe Josiah could work with his mother and the Guild and set up some form of charity . . . Josiah shook the thoughts away. He had too much to do at the moment to entertain pleasant fantasies. "You keep implying that the records kept by the blood alchemists are untrustworthy. Why do you believe this?"

Dr. Sterling raised an eyebrow. "You are not aware yourself, Your Highness? I expected those would have been among the first sources you investigated."

"I am in the process of studying those which are available to me, but I have many duties to attend to, and I find it more helpful to interview current experts than to rely primarily on older sources." That much was true, though not the whole truth; Josiah had spent quite a bit of time squashing the voice in the back of his mind that said he ought to spend more time slogging through the copies of the blood alchemists' records that he'd requested. But reading took intolerably long even at the best of times, and the complicated technical language of the blood alchemists' notes didn't help. It was so much easier to have one of the Archivists talk him through what he needed to know; he got far more information that way than he would on his own.

He did recall Archivist Simms mentioning that there were unusual irregularities in the blood alchemists' notes, but he hadn't pursued the topic. She'd implied it was unimportant. But if the irregularities were significant enough that the blood alchemists' notes could be dismissed altogether as a source of proof... "Please, Doctor, describe to me what makes you think the records are untrustworthy."

"Simply put, what the records claim changes over time. I don't mean the ordinary changes that you'd find over time as theories are proved and disproved, Your Highness. You'll find those in any scientific text. I mean significant changes with no explanation — one that particularly stands out is what sort of blood the alchemists have to use." Dr. Sterling pulled a notebook out of his own pocket and drew a line across a page, then marked it into three unequal sections: one long and two short. "This line represents the whole of time since blood alchemists started recording what they did in a form that's survived to today."

He tapped the longest section of the line. "Now, this piece is most of that history. All along this line, most blood alchemists were convinced that only royal or noble blood would suit their purposes. They claimed that royal blood worked best, but lesser nobles would do in a pinch. Even royal blood didn't work every time, though, or so the records seem to say, but if we want to be forgiving, we can chalk it up to human error. Alchemy's a delicate process, and they seemed to get results about ninety percent of the time."

Dr. Sterling moved his pen to the first of the shorter sections. "Here's where things become, shall we say, messy. Around here — I don't recall the exact dates, but I believe it's a few generations before our civil war — records suggest that blood alchemy just stopped working consistently. A blood alchemist apparently had a fifty-fifty chance of his alchemy working at all, and another fifty-fifty chance of it working as intended. All our worst horror stories about blood alchemy come from this era. They were trying to do some of the same things Lord-Senator Weston claims blood alchemy could do now, but when their alchemy went wrong, it went *badly* wrong. People turned to ravening beasts, abominations of stitched-together parts, people like walking dead men, the like."

Dr. Sterling shook his head sadly. "That only added to the chaos of the civil war, I'd guess. In any case, at some point after the war, the records change again." He indicated the final section of the line. "That would be our modern era, during which the blood alchemists suddenly discovered that they can use the blood of any man, woman, or child for their dark arts. But what brought about the change, no one can say for sure."

Josiah nodded slowly. He'd copied the chart in his own notebook, along with an explanation of what each section meant. "If you had to guess, what would be your hypothesis?"

"That is a hard question to answer." Dr. Sterling tapped the middle section again. "If not for this and some of the records from the first era, I could explain the discrepancy easily enough. After all, in those days people used to claim that nobility and particularly royalty had magical powers because they were descended from angels or specially blessed by Jeros or other such nonsense. The blood alchemists might've believed those stories and thought they were tapping into the magical energy that already existed in their victims. Then, when the stories were disproved, the alchemists woke up and realized that ordinary people might do just as well."

"But the middle section disproves it." Josiah glanced over his notes again, putting the facts together. "The noble blood didn't always work then, but neither did the blood of the lower classes."

"Exactly. In addition, some early blood alchemists did experiment with the blood of lower class people, but they claim they were unsuccessful. Yet I can see no scientific reason why there should be a shift from some blood working to all blood working." Dr. Sterling shook his head. "And until I find that reason, I hesitate to trust the blood alchemists' records."

"Thank you, Doctor." Josiah jotted down a last few notes. "Do I have your permission to bring that issue up in the next Senate meeting if given the opportunity?"

"By all means." Dr. Sterling stood. "Now, Your Highness, if you'll excuse me, I need to go. I have two apprentices whom I promised a lesson this afternoon, as you yourself said you wouldn't keep me too long."

"Of course." Josiah stood as well. "Thank you for your help. You are dismissed. May I call on you again if necessary as more details are revealed?"

"As you will. Good day, Your Highness." Dr. Sterling bowed and departed.

Josiah sat again, glancing over the pages he'd filled in his notebook. Despite Dr. Sterling's frequent caginess earlier in the interview, a trait he'd shared with almost every other alchemist Josiah had spoken with thus far, he had been reasonably helpful. At the very least, he'd given Josiah a few points to press Weston on at the next Senate meeting. *Hopefully, Luis is having better luck.* But, on the other hand, Luis had been at work less than a week. It was probably too soon to call on him for information.

Josiah sighed. The pieces were coming together all too slowly. He could only hope he'd be able to get a complete picture before it was too late.

CHAPTER 14

Breen stood atop a narrow beam of steel in the center of the clock tower, balancing carefully as she inspected the bottom of a massive gear. Below her, more gears and rods and beams waited to break her should she fall. Above her, rays of sunshine that had snuck in through the clock faces reflected down off more of the same machinery to where she was.

She ran her fingers along the surface of the gear, trusting touch to reveal what sight might not, though she made sure to avoid the sharp edges of the metal. Though a cut finger wouldn't bother her, it would mean she'd have to clean the blood off the gear.

Satisfied as to the gear's level of cleanliness, Breen shuffled to the side along the beam and checked the next piece of the machinery. Now more than ever, she couldn't afford to displease Madame. If Madame stayed here any longer than necessary, or if Josiah and Grace arrived early . . . Breen could predict a half-dozen outcomes, and none of them were good.

Why hadn't she *thought* before saying Grace could visit again tonight? Why hadn't she remembered that today was inspection day? Breen pulled a polishing cloth from her belt and rubbed furiously at a spot on a gear, growling silently at herself. She was a fool, that's why. A fool who was going to get herself and Grace both in trouble — and Josiah as well, but Josiah could most likely get himself *out* of trouble as well. He seemed that type of person.

But it was too late now to do anything about it. She had no way to communicate with Grace or Josiah, no way to forestall Madame's inspection. Her only option was to do her duty the best she could and hope it would be enough.

On an ordinary day, cleaning the clock took the better part of the daylight hours. Occasionally, when Breen allowed herself to be a little less careful and only tend what really *needed* tending, she could finish her work in only half a day or less and have the other half free to do as she pleased. Today, as she was taking extra care, she didn't finish until after five o'clock.

Her stomach growled as she reached the top of the tower, and she thought of the last of the food in her cupboard: one potato and a quarter of a small loaf of bread. She'd managed to make her food stretch so she could have dinner this week, but now . . . Madame Gottling could arrive at any moment, and she would be displeased if she found Breen eating. Better to let her stomach growl until Madame departed.

Still, as time stretched on and Madame didn't appear, Breen found herself wondering if she shouldn't have eaten after all. Surely she could've crammed down some bread by now; surely she could've boiled the potato and scarfed that down if she didn't mind burning her mouth . . . She stared at the machinery, trying to reassure herself that it hadn't somehow slowed down and, in doing so, slowed time itself.

Breen very nearly made up her mind to eat something anyway and risk Madame's displeasure when the signal vibrated in her pocket. She leaped to her feet and dashed to the lift. A glance down confirmed that yes, Madame was here.

She pulled the chain hand-over-hand until Madame could step off onto the main floor. As usual, Madame set down her carpetbag beside the lift and turned to Breen. "Slow again. Are you becoming lazy?"

"I'm sorry." Breen bowed her head, just barely keeping Madame's hands in view. "It won't happen again."

"Make sure it doesn't." With that, Madame turned on her heel and stalked towards the machinery in the center of the tower to begin her inspection.

As always, Breen followed, lagging behind a step or two so as to not risk rousing Madame's wrath. Madame peered at gears and ran her fingers along the metal and seemed to study every *atom* of every piece of the clockwork. But Breen's effort seemed to have paid off anyway, and she found nothing about which to complain. At last, she turned and stalked back up the stairs.

Breen followed, noting that the set of Madame's shoulders seemed slightly less stiff than usual and that her steps were not quite as sharp as they often were. That was good; Madame was as close to pleased as Breen could hope for her to be. That meant she'd leave sooner, and perhaps she'd even bring tea next time as a sort of not-quite-reward. She had done that once or twice, though not in a long time.

They reached the top of the stairs. Madame picked up her carpetbag and went to the cupboard. A sharp frown darted across her face as she looked inside, and she turned to Breen. "I see I left you too much food last time."

Oh no, no, no, please no . . . Breen shook her head, unable to hide her desperation. "I worked extra hard on the clock today. I didn't have time to eat dinner before you came." Her stomach growled — she could feel it; surely Madame had heard that? *Madame* wasn't deaf . . .

"If you can work so well without food, you must have eaten more than enough the rest of this week. Or perhaps you simply work better when you have not stuffed yourself." Madame's shoulders were stiff again, and she stood intimidatingly straight. "I will adjust your rations."

Breen slumped. She knew arguing would do no good. This sort of thing had happened before on occasion. Madame knew the minimum amount of food on which Breen could survive, and she would give Breen no more than that for several weeks. Eventually, if Breen behaved and did her work well enough, Madame would increase her rations back to their usual level. Breen would just have to bear the hunger until then.

So, she watched miserably as Madame stocked the cupboard with her thin provisions and then heated the solution for her crystal. She sat meekly on the bed and allowed Madame to remove the crystal, and she counted off the thirteen minutes as her mind and body grew numb.

Then Madame snapped the crystal back in place, and the rush of *life* that flooded back into Breen along with the magical energy almost drove out her despair. The feeling lingered just long enough for Breen to lower Madame down the lift. Then she slumped. Would even her best efforts never be enough?

She knew the answer. They wouldn't be.

With a sigh, she went to the cupboard and got out the quarter-loaf of bread she'd planned to eat for dinner. Tomorrow morning, she'd go over her food stocks and figure out how to ration her meals to last her through the week.

I could ask Josiah and Grace for help. If she said she didn't have enough food for the week, they would probably be willing to bring her something to make up the difference — maybe even make sure she had more than she needed. Maybe they'd even bring her tea.

Breen nibbled her stale loaf, trying to make it last. Was it worth asking, though? Josiah would use it as an excuse to try to convince her to leave the tower, and he might be offended if she refused the help he wanted to give and asked for something else. And Grace . . . Grace would pity her, if nothing else. And Breen didn't want her pity; not when she found such relief in being treated as someone's equal.

Anyway, it wasn't as if this were a major problem. She had dealt with it herself before. She'd deal with it herself again. She'd be careful about how much she ate and find ways to distract herself from her hunger. And if she went to bed hungry a few nights, well, that was hardly unusual.

The signal buzzed again in her pocket. Josiah and Grace were here. Breen finished off the last of her bread and headed for the stairs. No, she wouldn't tell them. She'd enjoy Grace's conversation, tolerate Josiah's presence, and handle her own problems on her own. And she'd be fine, just like she always had.

CHAPTER 15

Josiah clicked open the last lock on the tower door, glancing up and down the darkened street as he did. So far, his and Grace's visits to the tower seemed to have gone unnoticed, but he was starting to wonder how long his luck would last. As he hurried Grace inside, he made a mental note to tell her and Breen to switch up how often they visited. Better not to give anyone watching a pattern to rely upon.

Inside the tower, he locked the doors again while Grace crossed the room and pushed the lift button. He rejoined her at the bottom of the stairs.

She glanced at him and tilted her head to the side. "You're coming up?"

She spoke aloud; the lowest level of the tower was too dark for either of them to see signs clearly. Josiah nodded, then found her hand and squeezed once in case she'd missed his motion. After all, the only way he could test whether or not he'd successfully made a step towards Breen's good graces was to go up, say hello, and see if she did anything more than stare at him.

Grace shrugged and started up the stairs. Josiah followed, staying two steps behind. They reached the third level and found Breen coming down the stairs on the far side of the room. She waved at Grace, then froze when she saw Josiah.

Not a good sign. Josiah hung back as Grace fairly flew across the room to hug Breen. She might just be surprised to see him, but if so, she wasn't particularly happy about that surprise. Then again, he supposed he couldn't blame her.

Nonetheless, as Grace released Breen from her hug, he stepped forward and signed, "Good evening, Miss Breen."

She nodded, eying him with . . . well, it wasn't quite suspicion. That was something. With efficient motions, she added, "I didn't expect you to come up."

"I wanted to say hello." Josiah gave her the most non-threatening smile he could. "I didn't mean to bother you."

Breen blinked at him. "You're not." She paused, thinking, then added, "Yet."

Josiah forced a laugh, not that she'd be able to hear it. "Will that change if I remain up here while you and Grace talk rather than going back downstairs?"

Grace, who had turned so she could watch both sides of the conversation, shot him a look that said "What are you *doing*?" as clearly as her hands would have. Josiah just raised an eyebrow at her. But, when her expression didn't fade, he added, "You need not say yes, and I'll leave at any time if you ask."

Breen pursed her lips, then nodded. "You can stay."

"Thank you. I won't disturb you two further." Josiah sat down on a nearby crate with his back against the wall. This was certainly an improvement over sitting downstairs in the dark — especially since Grace had told him that she and Breen hadn't even stayed on this level last time. If he'd have known that, he would've come up so he wouldn't have to listen to the endless, eerie ticking of the clock and strain his eyes peering at shadows.

Breen and Grace settled themselves on other crates on the far side of the room and started talking, their hands fairly flying through the signs. Josiah watched, but from the side, he couldn't pick out more than one word in three.

Instead, he studied the room, wondering what the various crates, barrels, and boxes contained. Spare clock parts, perhaps? But surely the clock couldn't break down often enough to make all this necessary — and surely someone would notice if it did. Perhaps, then, the same person who had imprisoned Breen here was using it as a storage space.

Josiah inspected the crate he was sitting on, searching for any kind of marking to indicate ownership. He found none — not on his crate, nor on those on either side of his. So much for that idea. He made a mental note to ask Breen later if she knew what was inside all these. He could go look in some of the smaller boxes on the shelves himself, of course, but he didn't want to put Breen too much on edge.

Something on one of the top shelves caught his attention: half-formed devices, their shape indistinct in shadow. From what Josiah could see, they somewhat resembled the half-assembled clocks he often saw in the back workroom of Kronos Clocks and Gadgetry, but they seemed . . . off. The shapes seemed wrong, somehow.

He pulled out his notebook and started jotting down thoughts in webs of connecting words, occasionally glancing up to check on Grace and Breen. Grace seemed to be sharing stories of her recent frustrations with the Ventian ambassador's daughters — both decent enough girls, in their way, but even more ignorant than most Chanians about how to interact with a deaf person.

Did Breen know that he and Grace were royalty? Josiah added the question in another circle on the page. After a moment's thought, he wrote down another question: *Should we tell her if she doesn't know?* He hadn't told her; he knew that. Had Grace? He made a mental note to ask later, but he guessed the answer was no. Breen seemed too comfortable with Grace, if not with him, to know the truth.

Josiah looked up again, studying the two. Breen seemed to be doing most of the talking now, gesturing every now and then to the clockwork overhead. Perhaps, once she was more comfortable with him, he should ask her about the clock. From what Grace had said, she knew the tower's mechanisms well; there was a chance she could clear up some of the mystery of why her presence didn't cause the calamity that everyone said humans in the tower would.

Had his and Grace's presence in the tower caused problems? Or would it? Josiah jotted the thought down along the edge of one page, along with a few names of people who might have the answer. They couldn't have had a significant effect yet — he would have noticed if the clock had stopped altogether or if it was off by a large margin — but there were others better suited than he was to noticing small issues. In fact, Breen was probably one of them. He'd have to ask her that as well.

Across the room, Breen leaned forward slightly as she described something to Grace. Josiah didn't bother to try to make out the words; his attention was arrested by a pinkish-red spot that had appeared just under the top button of Breen's oversized work shirt. Was it a stain? Was she bleeding? But it didn't look like blood; it looked more like there was a small, faint light behind her shirt. The spot's position on the shirt moved as she moved, eliminating the possibility that it was a stain of some kind.

Josiah frowned, thinking back to the previous times he'd seen Breen. He hadn't noticed a light or spot last time or the two times before. The first night, though . . . had it been there then? *Maybe.* He hadn't noticed or at least hadn't registered it as any odder than the fact that she was here at all.

The light reminded him of something, though he couldn't put his finger on what. He flipped the page in his notebook and wrote "Light under shirt" in the center, intending to start another web of possibilities. However, before he could get any further, movement drew his attention. Breen hopped off her crate and pushed the lid to the side. She bent over, dug through whatever was within, and then drew out a cloth-wrapped bundle.

With surprisingly little effort, she replaced the crate lid and unwrapped the bundle to reveal something mechanical — no, several somethings. Josiah tucked his notebook into his pocket and slid off his seat, his curiosity piqued. He wouldn't disturb them, of course, but surely he could get a little closer and figure out what was going on . . .

He hadn't taken three steps before Breen looked up sharply at him. Josiah smiled apologetically at her and held up his hands in a gesture of peace, then signed, "I apologize. I saw clockwork, and I was curious. Are these things you've made?"

Breen pressed her lips together as if debating whether or not to answer. She glanced at Grace, who signed something rapidly; Josiah caught the words *safe* and *if you want*. The angle made the rest of what she'd said impossible to identify.

Breen gave two slow nods before looking back at Josiah. "Yes." She thought a moment more, then beckoned him over.

Josiah joined the two by the crate where Breen had spread her creations. Two clearly were clocks, minus their wooden housing — yet the way Breen had designed the clockwork was almost a thing of beauty itself. Their faces were not the ivory white Josiah was accustomed to seeing; rather, Breen had fixed in place large gears — too big for an ordinary clock — with teeth to represent the numbers: twelve on one clock; twenty-four on the other. Josiah guessed from the rough, shiny spots between the teeth that Breen had cut or broken off the extra teeth from each gear.

As Josiah and Grace watched, Breen set the twenty-four-hour clock and turned a key at the bottom to wind it. Its sudden tick-tock echoed that of the tower itself.

Grace had picked up another object, a small box with a dull, barely-lit miazen crystal at its top. She turned it over several times, then tried and failed to open it. She gave Breen a quizzical look, gesturing at the box with one hand.

Breen took the box from Grace and set it on the top of the crate. She touched the miazen crystal, and Josiah heard the whirr of something mechanical. The box suddenly folded outwards and reassembled itself into a squarish, humanoid figure. Grace let out a laugh. "You made this?"

Breen nodded and ducked her head. "I did. There are boxes of uncharged miazen crystals on the shelves. I found a half-charged one and decided to do something with it." Her fingers darted through the signs as if she was embarrassed to talk about her own accomplishments.

"Impressive." Josiah picked up another of the creations, a mechanical creature of some kind with a crank in its back. Josiah turned the crank, and the creature's legs began to move. He set the thing down, and it ran jerkily across the top of the crate until it hit a crack and fell over.

Josiah surveyed the various other mechanical creations spread out on the crate. "Did someone teach you to do this?"

Breen shook her head. "I studied the tower and figured out how it worked. Then I made a miniature version of it. And then I started making other things and experimented until I got them right."

"You taught yourself. Impressive." And she'd started with clocks — complicated pieces, according to Luis — rather than something simple. "How long did it take you to learn?"

Breen thought for a moment. "Not very long. Four months for the first clock. I could've done it faster, but I had to keep up my work."

Four months. She'd taken four months to teach herself something that many apprentices spent years learning from their masters. Of course, Breen had no one to tell her that she couldn't do it — but it was still an impressive feat. "That's amazing."

And with skills like those . . . Josiah thought of the keys he'd handed to Breen and his assumption that a door was all that really stood between her and freedom. "You never needed the keys. With your skills, you could figure out how to pick the locks or make a device to break them. Why didn't you?"

Breen stared at him for a long moment. Grace frowned at him. "You shouldn't ask that." She turned to Breen. "You don't need to answer."

Breen shook her head. "It's fine. I did make something. It was a . . ." She thought for a moment as if trying to figure out how to describe what she meant. "An adjustable key. Each tooth was its own piece, and I could raise and lower them until the lock would turn. It wasn't hard to make once I thought of it. I left, and I went to my family. Then my . . ."

Again, she paused, hands still as she tried to think of the word. "My masters found me. They told me I'd die if I didn't come back. That one of my siblings would take my place. So I came back, and I didn't try to leave again."

"I'm sorry." Grace patted Breen's shoulder. "That's terrible."

"It is." Josiah studied Breen's expression. She was carefully blank as she had been the first few nights he'd talked to her, but having seen her interact with Grace, he could now more clearly see the dull sadness in the depths of her eyes. "I apologize for my presumptions earlier. May I ask another question?"

She nodded. Josiah chose his words carefully. "Is the threat to your family the only thing keeping you here?"

For a moment, Josiah thought Breen wouldn't respond. Then she slowly signed, "No. But it is one of the things."

"I see. And the other things are what keep you here even after I offered help?"

She nodded once. "You might be able to protect my family and me. You can't solve the other problems."

Perhaps not, but he could try — and he would, if only so he'd be solving *something*, if only so he could right one wrong. But he wouldn't push; not tonight. "I understand. Thank you." He thought of the light he'd noticed earlier. Did that have something to do with whatever kept her here?

"I still think what you've done is impressive." Grace tilted her head slightly as she brought the conversation back to a safer topic. "Are you working on anything else?"

Once again, Breen hesitated. Then she nodded and hurried to a shelf. She pushed boxes out of the way and pulled from behind them a boxy mass of metal and gears. She set it on another crate next to the first one. "This is what I'm working on now."

Josiah looked it over, frowning slightly as he tried to puzzle out its purpose, comparing it to the things he'd seen Luis work on — not that he'd known what half of those are. Grace seemed as mystified as he. "What is it?"

"It's for the lift." Breen gestured at the corner where the chain ran from top to bottom of the tower. "To make it go up on its own without my having to pull it. I've been working on it for months now, but I can't get it right."

A machine to work a lift? And she'd gotten this far on her own? Josiah studied the device with new interest. Then, an idea occurred to him — a risky one, but perhaps worth trying. "I have a friend who is an inventor and clockmaker. Maybe he could help. May I bring him sometime? If you would prefer I didn't, say so."

Breen glanced again at Grace. "What is he like?"

Grace answered first. "He's nice. He's less pushy than Josiah. He can keep secrets; Josiah and I both trust him. He's smart, and he's clever with tools, and he tells Josiah when he's being foolish."

The corners of Breen's mouth quirked upwards in a smile. "He sounds nice." She turned back to Josiah. "If he wants to come once, he can."

"I am surrounded by people who tell me when I'm being foolish." Josiah made a face at Grace. "Thank you all the same. I'll ask him if he's willing and when. I expect it'll be near the end of the week. Is that acceptable?"

Breen nodded again. Josiah smiled, unable to hide his triumph. "Excellent." He took a step backward. "I'll let you two talk a while longer now and stop disturbing you."

He turned, intending to return to his previous seat, but Breen tapped his arm before he could take a step. He faced her again, raising an eyebrow in question.

Breen signed swiftly, as if she wanted to get the words out before she could second-guess herself. "You don't need to go all the way back over there. You can stay closer if you want. I don't mind."

Josiah's smile grew. "Thank you, Miss Breen." He moved to a nearby crate and sat down, close enough that he could be a part of the conversation if Breen and Grace decided to include him, but far enough that they wouldn't feel forced to do so. This night had been an even bigger success than he expected — and he could hardly wait to see what happened when he brought Luis.

CHAPTER 16

Josiah left the tower that night well-satisfied with the past hours' events. By the time he and Grace left, Breen had grown comfortable enough with his presence to occasionally address comments to him as she and Grace chatted. And she'd seemed . . . well, she hadn't been outright excited about the idea of Luis visiting, but she'd smiled. That was more than she'd done when he ever asked to visit.

Better still, he knew a few more fragments about her. She was clever in the ways Luis was, for one. That told him something about how to reach her, how to connect with her so she'd see him as an ally and not a threat. He'd caught several snatches of her past from her conversation with Grace as well: that she'd worked in a factory before she lived in the tower, and that she'd been involved in an accident of some kind there. More significantly, he knew a little more about what held her in the tower — she'd said it wasn't just the threat to her family, and he guessed it was more than a threat to her own life too. After all, he could protect her as easily as he could protect her family, perhaps more so.

And then there was the strange light he'd noticed, assuming he hadn't been imagining it. Was that connected to the forces preventing her from accepting his help or leaving the tower on her own? He'd have to think about it more.

The next day, however, left him little time to consider Breen's situation. A meeting with several senators opposed to blood alchemy took up most of his morning; the rest was eaten by an attempt to push through the records of the previous blood alchemists. What should have been a few free hours in the afternoon turned into an impromptu conference with both parents on how the countries on the mainland had handled their problems with blood alchemy and how legalizing blood alchemy might affect diplomatic relationships with those countries.

Josiah's mother, Queen Lillian, expressed particular concern over this last matter. Several of their most powerful allies were staunchly opposed to blood alchemy, and the queen predicted that some of those alliances would break if the alchemy bill went through. Josiah promised to bring her concerns up in the Senate the next day; perhaps the potential threat of war would be enough to make the bill drop.

Josiah left his unexpected conference just in time to make a last meeting with the Archivists and finally sent Luis a note asking about a visit to the clock tower later that week. Then he had to rush off to the last event of the day: a dinner and a dance hosted by the younger Lord Caraway. While the threat of the blood alchemy bill had allowed Josiah to set aside many social duties over the last week, he couldn't afford to ignore them entirely — this least of all. If Lord Caraway inherited his father's place and prestige in the Senate as well as his lands and estates, he would make a valuable ally in years to come. And if men like Lord-Senator Weston continued to have their way, Josiah would need every ally he could get.

The party lasted late into the night, and Josiah fairly had to drag himself out of bed the next morning in time for the Senate meeting. Still, he managed to arrive well before the meeting would start. That left him with nearly twenty minutes in which he could review his notes and sip strong black tea. The official committee researching blood alchemy would be near the beginning of the day's agenda, and Josiah planned to follow their report up with one of his own that would cover any areas they might have missed.

At eight o'clock sharp, Prime Minister Wentworth called the meeting to order with a sharp rap of his gavel. "First on the agenda," he announced, once the minutes had been read and the room had quieted, "the findings thus far of the committee to investigate Lord-Senator Weston's claims regarding the potential of blood alchemy and the merits of the blood alchemy bill. The committee has informed me that Senator Martin Frederichs, Independent, will be their spokesperson. Senator Frederichs, you have the floor."

Senator Frederichs strode forward with quick, purposeful steps, a black leather folder under one arm. Josiah studied him with interest. This was the first time he'd seen or heard anything from the man, who'd just been elected last spring. Josiah would've expected the committee to send a more well-known and respected man to represent them, but perhaps the man had some hidden merits — or the committee might just hope that another Independent would be able to argue better with Weston than someone of another party could.

Senator Frederichs reached the floor, set down his folder on a podium, and cleared his throat. "The chief finding of the committee, my fellow Senators, is that the matter of blood alchemy is far more complicated than many of us believed. There are many factors at play, and many more elements which must be investigated before any decisions should be made. However, we are currently able to suggest answers to a few questions raised last week, even as we bring more questions to the table."

Direct and to the point. Excellent. Josiah turned to a new page in his notebook, pen poised to record what the senator had to say. The first ten minutes, however, were all a review of information Josiah had already learned: relative power levels of blood alchemy versus normal alchemy, the unclear history of blood alchemy, and the fact that many alchemists thought that Weston suggested was possible in theory. "And, in theory," he added, "Lord-Senator Weston's plan could be carried out without more deaths than currently occur each year. However, whether or not theory translates to reality is impossible to tell at this time.

"If we had practical proof that any of this would work, that would be another matter," Senator Frederichs continued. "The problem, of course, is that we cannot test any of this ourselves without breaking the current laws. Therefore, the committee recommends that the military and police forces increase their efforts in uncovering blood alchemists and in doing so before those blood alchemists realize. In this way, we might find some of their experimental subjects still living and be able to learn what exactly the blood alchemists are able to do."

Senator Frederichs turned over a paper on the podium in front of him and glanced down at it. "Our second concern is this: who exactly will be permitted to practice blood alchemy, and who will oversee that practice? Will it be limited to those specially chosen by the state? Or will private alchemists be able to gain a license, as doctors can now, in order to practice the craft? Will policing it fall to the purview of a noble house? A new department of the government? The ordinary law enforcement? Lord-Senator Weston's proposed bill answers none of these questions, but we cannot legalize this until we know that it will be practiced and overseen responsibly."

A ripple of approving murmurs spread through the room. Frederichs continued, "At the moment, these are our two primary concerns regarding blood alchemy. However, our committee is investigating several other aspects of the practice, and so we recommend that the Senate refrain from any decision to pass or not pass the proposed bill until we have had more time to fully examine all involved elements."

"Thank you, Senator Frederichs," Prime Minister Wentworth said. "Lord-Senator Weston, have you any response to the committee's questions?"

Weston stood and took his place behind the other podium. "I recognize that the committee has valid concerns. Regarding the first issue that Senator Frederichs raised, if the Senate deems that his suggestion to strengthen the pursuit of illegal blood alchemists is the best option, I will, of course, offer my full support of that effort. However, I would remind my fellow senators that such tactics may be counter-productive if those alchemists learn of the search. They may well destroy their test subjects and flee the country. Instead, I suggest that the Senate make a way for individuals involved with blood alchemy to anonymously provide information or evidence relating to its effectiveness.

"Regarding the second issue, that of how to regulate blood alchemy: my eventual vision for the bill is that it would result in a guild like any other city guild, one that will both support and regulate its members. Private alchemists would practice as doctors do now and would take the same vows that those doctors do. However, if the Senate deems it necessary, there is no reason why the practice could not be initially limited to certain individuals overseen by one of the noble houses.

"I am fully willing to discuss at length either of these matters or any other objections that anyone in this room might raise." Lord-Senator Weston gazed around the room, including everyone in his statement. "As I have stated before, the goal of this bill is to achieve progress and secure a better future for Chania, and I am ready to do what must be done in order to achieve those goals."

Josiah stood. "If that is so, Lord-Senator, I have some concerns that I would like to add to those of Senator Frederichs and the committee. With your permission, Minister Wentworth?"

The prime minister nodded. "As you will, Your Highness."

Weston turned to face Josiah. "I would have been surprised if you had not spoken, Your Highness. What have you to say?"

Josiah flipped to the correct page in his notes and cleared his throat. "First of all, I would concur with the committee's uncertainty about how well alchemical theory will translate to reality. I am particularly concerned about the unreliability of the blood alchemists' records. To my understanding, these records demonstrate dramatic and unexplained shifts in what they claim does and does not work. Are you aware of this irregularity,?"

Weston allowed himself a small chuckle. "Your Highness, I expected a more compelling argument from you. Yes, the writings of the early blood alchemists are incorrect on some significant points. However, I might point out that ordinary alchemy and even the non-alchemical sciences were full of similar misconceptions. And alchemy of any kind is a delicate process. It would be unsurprising to learn an alchemist had measured something inaccurately, heated it a few moments too long, or made a similar mistake, then blamed it on an unrelated factor because he was unaware of some essential fact."

"You raise a fair point, but I wonder if you comprehend the severity of the shifts in the records. Today, when we expose a misconception in the sciences, the real explanation will fit with the information we had before. Blood alchemy, on the other hand?" Josiah paused for just a moment. "Four hundred years ago, the blood alchemists believed that only blood from members of a certain family or social class would power their work, and their records seem to back that claim up. Yet more recent records suggest that the blood from any man, woman, or child can be used in blood alchemy — even if that man, woman, or child would not have been qualified four centuries ago. Without knowing the reason for this shift, we cannot safely legalize blood alchemy."

"His Highness has a point." Senator Frederichs nodded emphatically. "What happens if we allow people to practice blood alchemy only to discover that only the blood of certain people is usable? People within that category may feel pressured to give their lives so others can be saved through blood alchemy, or others may begin to treat those people differently because of the peculiar power in their blood. Even if blood alchemy can save lives, we cannot afford to create those kinds of cracks in our society."

"Certainly not." Weston smiled thinly. "It would be foolish to do something to better society only to destabilize it. I will have my scientists, alchemists, and archivists investigate reasons for the shift in collaboration with whoever the Senate selects to assist them. I am confident, however, that there will be a rational and reasonable explanation for the change." He turned to face Josiah again. "Have you additional concerns, Your Highness?"

"I do." Josiah nodded. "I was speaking about this topic with the queen the other day, and she raised an interesting point. We can control nothing but our own country, yet many countries other than our own will make decisions based on what we decide here. Many of our allies are opposed to blood alchemy even more strongly than we traditionally have been. How will they react if we choose to legalize this practice? Perhaps some, even all, will accept it and cautiously continue to treat and trade with us. But some may not; some may see our decision as a sign of moral degeneracy or a cover for building up our own power. What happens when enough countries with which we are currently at peace decide that an empire practicing blood alchemy is too great a threat? What happens when they decide to go to war?"

"We would crush them, naturally," Senator Frederichs scoffed. "No power in the world, not even the combined powers of multiple nations, could defeat our empire."

Josiah bit back a dozen historical anecdotes about other empires that had thought the same way. Even if Senator Frederichs could use a dose of reality, there were better ways to give it to him. "Perhaps so, perhaps not. But if so, at what cost? Our goal is to preserve and save lives; how many men would die in such a war, even if we do win? Perhaps blood alchemy could save some, but not all. Would you risk sending the men and women of Chania to die in bloody battles over scientific progress? Would you risk making Chania an empire of widows and orphans? Is blood alchemy worth that risk?"

"You take a particularly pessimistic view of the matter, Your Highness." Lord-Senator Weston raised an eyebrow at him. "What if the opposite occurs? Our neighbors and allies are, as you said, influenced by our choices. Why should they not be? We are powerful and prosperous above all other nations and empires currently existent. And if we legalize blood alchemy successfully, many may rethink their views and do the same. Our grandchildren, perhaps even our children, may live in a world where blood alchemy can cure all but the worst of wounds and diseases."

"Perhaps they may, or they may live in a world torn asunder by our decision to legalize blood alchemy. Either is possible, Lord-Senator. I do not claim that one is more likely than the other, only that we cannot know which will happen." Josiah paused to let his words sink in. "Whatever we decide, we must decide it with eyes open to the risks in that decision. For now, Chania is great. Let us not squander that greatness by making poor decisions."

He bowed slightly, then sat. The Prime Minister tapped his gavel on the desk in front of him. "Thank you, Your Highness. Do any other members of this body have useful perspectives to add at this time?" He waited a moment, but when no voices rose above the general murmur, he continued, "Very well. One item of action has been proposed: to try to locate a working example of blood

[140]

alchemy's capabilities, either by increasing the search for illegal blood alchemists or by accepting anonymous submissions of information and evidence. All in favor of increasing the search efforts, say yea."

"Yea," Josiah called out, along with what sounded like a majority of the other senators. No surprise there. Deepening the search for blood alchemists would benefit both those in favor of the bill and those not in favor of it.

Prime Minister Wentworth made a note on a sheet of paper. "Next, all in favor of anonymous information, say yea."

A slightly smaller chorus of yeas rang out. Most of them seemed to come from those who had been Weston's staunchest supporters in previous matters. Once again, that was no surprise.

Wentworth made another note. "All against either option, say nay."

Scattered nays came from around the room. Prime Minister Wentworth gave a short nod. "The issue is decided. The order will be given for the police and guard forces to increase their efforts in finding and capturing illegal blood alchemists. Any significant findings will be examined by qualified Senate members as evidence to help decide the fate of the blood alchemy bill." He shuffled through his papers. "The next issue on the agenda: the lapse or renewal of the Science and Alchemy Fund."

The senators on the floor returned to their chairs, and Josiah sat back in his seat. He already knew how this next issue would go; the day the Senate refused to renew the Science and Alchemy Fund would be the day the sun fell out of the sky — and then only because they'd all be dead, scientists and senators alike. If anything, they might increase funding in hopes that the alchemists would discover a less morally ambiguous alternative to blood alchemy. Josiah made a mental note to propose such a change if no one else did. He knew the odds of such a discovery were slim — but any chance was better than none, especially on an issue like this that could very well tear the whole world apart.

CHAPTER 17

Later that week, Breen knelt on the third floor of the tower, her lift mechanism before her and miscellaneous other parts and pieces strewn on the floor around her. The last of the late afternoon sunshine filtered in the small slits that served for windows, casting stripes of light and shadow over her work. Since she started working earlier that day, she'd adjusted the position of herself and the lift mechanism multiple times to take the best advantage of the light as it shifted. At this point, however, moving again wasn't worth it; soon, the sunlight would fade altogether and leave her with the steady glow of the alchemical lights in the walls.

And then Josiah and Luis would come.

Breen frowned at a gear as she compared it to a slightly larger one already in place, trying to decide whether or not to switch the two. Josiah had confirmed during his and Grace's last visit that Luis would indeed come and was excited to do so. *Excited.* Breen couldn't imagine why. True, Josiah and Grace had been impressed with her inventions, but surely they were just being nice, Grace for the sake of kindness and Josiah to try to win her over. There was no chance that anything she could make would truly astonish them that much. Odds were, Josiah had exaggerated Luis's enthusiasm too.

Still, even if Luis wasn't as thrilled as Josiah had claimed he was, the idea of showing her work to someone else, someone who knew what he was doing, had consumed Breen's thoughts all that week. More than once, she'd ended up doing the bare minimum of her duties and spending most of the day working on her invention in preparation for Luis's visit. True, he was supposedly coming to help — but she wanted to have something worth his time when he arrived.

Breen's stomach rumbled, interrupting her train of thought. She set down her screwdriver and glanced up through the layers of machinery, trying to decide if it was worth going upstairs and getting dinner. Even with careful rationing, she just barely had enough to last the week, and she'd hoped to save enough for a slightly more substantial noon meal tomorrow before Madame arrived.

But if she was hungry while Josiah and Luis were here, she wouldn't be able to think as well, and then she'd seem even more foolish than she really was. And if her stomach continued to growl, Josiah would likely use it as an excuse to push her to leave the tower. She couldn't have that.

With a sigh, Breen stood and made the long trek up to the topmost level. She fetched a now-stale hunk of bread from the cupboard, tore it in half, and nibbled on one piece, trying to make it last. She wished she had cheese, honey, anything to make the bread a little more palatable. Then again, she should be thankful. Stale as it was, the bread was more than most people had and more than she deserved.

She finished her meal and returned to the lower level. By now, the sunlight had nearly given way to the alchemical lights. The clock struck seven as she walked down the stairs. *Almost time.* Josiah had said that he and Luis hoped to come a bit early, but how early?

Her answer came ten minutes later when the vibrating signal device in her pocket announced Josiah's arrival. Breen looked up from her lift device and sat back, watching the stairs.

Josiah appeared first and greeted her with a tip of his hat and a signed, "Hello." After him came another young man, this one half a head shorter and olive-skinned and dark-haired instead of pale. *Luis. It must be.* Breen tilted her head, studying him. He certainly had less of a *presence* than Josiah did, and he dressed more plainly. In fact, he looked rather like a cleaner, better-fed version of the kind of people Breen had grown up with.

He caught her look and doffed his flat cap to her. Then, with shaky hands, he signed, "Hello. I'm Luis."

"He doesn't know signs as well as I do," Josiah interjected. His lips moved as he signed; Breen guessed he was repeating himself for Luis's benefit. "I can translate if necessary."

"Thank you." Breen smoothly moved her hand from her lips into a wave at Luis. "I'm Breen."

[145]

Luis nodded, then stepped forward eagerly, his gaze fixing on the device before Breen. "This . . ." he gestured at the device, then at the lift in the corner, a questioning look on his face.

"Yes." Breen hesitated. What else could she say? What other signs did he know?

Luis knelt on the other side of the device, setting down his worn leather bag. He inspected the mechanisms, turning it over onto its various sides so he could study it from all angles. Then he looked up at Breen and grinned. "Good." He frowned at his hands a moment, then addressed a series of comments to Josiah.

Josiah nodded, then addressed Breen in sign. "Your overall idea and execution are excellent. Your . . ." Now he paused, evidently trying to find the right word. "Your method of transferring power to the motor mechanism needs work. He wants to know if you have trouble with other areas."

Luis said something else. Josiah nodded and added, "And he wants to know if you can read and write."

Breen nodded. Then, she cleared her throat and said, "I can read and write some. I can talk to you out loud, too, if it helps."

Luis nodded eagerly. He pulled a half-dozen sheets of well-folded drafting paper and a pencil from his bag and jotted down a message on the top page: "All that helps. Less for Josiah to translate. Where do we start?"

Breen chewed on her lip, then slowly explained the issues she'd been trying to solve: making the mechanisms more efficient, fixing a section of machinery that always seemed to get stuck, and so on.

As she finished, she added, "What about the power mechanism needs fixed?"

"I'll show you." This Luis managed to sign without Josiah's help. He pulled more tools and a pair of jeweler's goggles from his bag, then grinned at Breen. Signs or not, his message was clear: *Let's get to work.*

Breen quickly realized why Josiah had wanted to bring Luis to the tower. She'd never met anyone as clever — well, perhaps one or two people, but certainly not many. Even with the language barrier between them, she rarely had to explain anything more than once. And once he knew what she was getting at, he analyzed the idea from every side and built on it, shoring up the weak spots and improving what was already strong.

Before long, Breen and Luis had disassembled almost half the lift device with the intent to put it back together in even better ways. But they'd barely begun to reconfigure the mechanism before Breen remembered the time. She glanced up, noted the position of the clock's machinery above her. *Almost eight!*

She tapped Luis's shoulder and cleared her throat. When he looked at her, she said aloud, "You need to go."

Luis frowned, his brow wrinkling. In sign, he answered, "Why?"

Breen pointed at the clock above, then tapped her ear several times. Luis nodded, but instead of packing up to leave, he dug again in his bag. He pulled out what looked like a band of cloth, then held it up so Breen could see the thick, multi-layered squares of cotton sewn on either side of the cloth. This he fitted over his head, so the squares were over his ears. He pulled out a second and tossed it to Josiah, who put it on and then signed, "Luis thought of the bells. He thinks we're not likely to suffer much down here, but these will help muffle the noise."

Breen nodded. If only Madame had given her similar protection — but, then again, it would only have delayed the inevitable. "Good idea." She picked up the screwdriver she'd been using earlier. "What now?"

With the bells no longer a concern, Breen was free to devote her full attention to Luis and the lift device. As they worked, the minutes turned to hours, which flew away like sparrows from the chime. Breen and Luis tested one configuration of parts, then another, trying to find the strongest and most efficient arrangement. Josiah watched and occasionally interjected questions or translated comments — though this last was a rarity. Luis's signing skills were shaky, true, but machinery was a language he and Breen both knew well. With gestures and taps on pieces and occasional questions or diagrams scribbled on paper, they made themselves understood to each other.

But as the eleven o'clock chimes came and went, Breen's eyelids grew heavy, and her hands fumbled with the parts as often as not. Luis's eager quickness had worn away into lethargy. Finally, he shook himself and jotted another note down for her: *'Late. Do we keep going? Or stop?"*

Breen considered. Her body said *stop, please, let me sleep*. But her mind, her heart — these felt awake and alive like they hadn't in years, even when Grace was here. "What do you want?"

Luis shrugged and wrote his answer: "Either. I think we're close to done. I wouldn't mind finishing, even if it takes another hour or two."

Breen thought of the work she had to do tomorrow, of how she'd need to make up for her distraction these last few days, of how tired she'd be in the morning. And then she thought of how it would feel to be finally done with this, and about how she had no guarantee that Luis would come back, but she could guarantee that he'd stay a little longer. "Let's finish."

Luis grinned. He dug in his bag again and this time pulled out a jar of ground coffee. He tossed it to Josiah, who barely caught it, and said something — Breen guessed it was something along the lines of "Go make some of this." Then he turned his attention back to the lift device.

Josiah stood and headed for the stairs. Breen hesitated, wondering if she should help and if her mugs were clean. But then Luis tapped her knee and gestured to the device, and Josiah slipped from her mind. She barely noticed when he returned and pressed a mug of coffee into her hands — but she did notice the pleasant warmth that spread through her when she took a sip. And she certainly noticed the way the warmth transformed her weariness into alertness, allowing her and Luis to attack the lift machinery with renewed vigor.

Breen soon gave thanks for that new energy. She and Luis had left the hardest part for last: fixing the power connections for the crystals. Breen had thought that she'd done fairly well wiring in the connections, especially given that she had no prior experience with the art. Luis, however, said there was a better way, and so they took out all she'd done and reworked the whole system.

Only when they'd nearly finished the process did Breen realize why Luis's idea had meant redoing so much. She sat up straight and tapped Luis's shoulder. "You're rewiring it for the wrong crystals."

Luis stopped and set down his pliers so he could face her. "What?" he signed, brow furrowed.

"I wired it for many small crystals." Breen made a circle with her fingers to show him the size she was thinking — the same size as those on the clock gears or the one that powered her heart. "You're wiring it for two big crystals." Again, she showed the size, but this time she had to use both hands with the tips of her fingers and the bottoms of her palms touching.

Luis nodded as if what she'd said was obvious. "Small crystals are less efficient," he wrote. "Larger crystals are better."

"I don't have large crystals." Breen made the smaller circle again. "I have little ones." Even those mostly weren't charged, but she'd hoped she could figure out a way to wire them into the tower itself so that whatever kept the clock gems charged could power the lift's crystals as well.

Luis frowned, tapping his pencil against his paper. Breen sighed and waited for him to ask why she'd wasted his time on a project she didn't have the materials to properly finish.

But instead, he reached into his bag once more and pulled out a pair of miazen crystals, just the size for the connections he'd set up. He set them by the device and picked up his pliers again.

Breen gaped. He couldn't be serious, could he? "I can't take these."

Luis raised an eyebrow at her. Even without signs, she could read the question, *why not?* in his look.

"I can't." Breen shook her head. She could only guess how much such crystals would cost. And Luis was no noble, not like Josiah. "They're too much. You can't afford to give them up."

Luis grinned and gestured to Josiah and rubbed his fingers together like there was a coin between them. On paper, he added, *"They were a gift. I'm passing it on."*

Still, Breen hesitated. Josiah waved a hand to get her attention, then signed, "Go ahead. I'll pay for new ones. It would be a shame for you not to finish your project after all this work."

Well, if Josiah wanted to spend his money that way, Breen supposed she couldn't argue with him. So, she shrugged and smiled at Luis, then handed him his pliers so they could get back to work.

Half-past two found them almost finished at last. Breen balanced precariously on the stool at the edge of the lift hole in the uppermost floor as she secured the lift device in place and threaded the lift chains through the pulley. The two miazen crystals glowed on top, their light mostly blocked by the machinery. Breen had positioned the device in a shadowy spot atop a beam where she hoped that it would go unnoticed by Madame or anyone else. As long as she made sure that she was by the lift when Madame arrived, it should work.

Josiah steadied her as she stepped off the stool and gave her a once-over as if to make sure she was all right. Then he leaned out and called down the hole to Luis, who waited at the bottom to test their creation.

The lift signal buzzed in Breen's pocket. Breen held her breath, praying they'd put everything together correctly, that Luis had successfully connected the crystals on the signal and the lift mechanism, that their work wouldn't be in vain.

On the device, the crystals' glow intensified. Then the gears began to move, and the chain slowly wound through the pulleys and the machinery that turned them. Gradually, the lift rose higher and higher until the chain ran out, and Luis stood safely before them. He stepped off the lift and grinned almost giddily at Breen. Then he turned to Josiah and spoke so quickly that Breen couldn't even guess what he was saying.

Josiah translated a moment later. "He — and I — say well-done. Luis thinks you could get into the Inventor's Guild with this if you chose."

Breen ducked her head, her cheeks growing warm. As if she'd ever be able to leave this tower, let alone join a guild! And even if she could, would they let her in if they realized what she was? But all she said was, "He helped." And then, to Luis, "Thank you."

Luis nodded and returned the gesture, then said something to Josiah. Again Josiah translated: "The idea was yours, and most of the execution. All he did was help you work through the last few issues and get you the resources you needed. He'll vouch for you, once he's in. And I'll sponsor you if you need it."

How could they talk about this as if it were a possibility? As if she weren't trapped here forever? Then again, in their minds, she wasn't. Josiah was still set on getting her out, even if he was more subtle about it than he had been at first, and she guessed Luis felt the same. But in this moment, she didn't want to argue. So, she just said "Thank you" again and smiled as if they were right.

"Can I bring Grace to see?" Josiah gestured at the lift. "Tomorrow night? I know it's sooner than usual, but we have to be somewhere the night after."

Breen thought for a moment. She'd certainly be tired tomorrow night — *to*night at this point. But Grace would be excited to see the lift, surely — genuinely excited, not just pretending out of kindness. "Yes. A short visit is fine."

"Excellent. I'll see you then. And now I'll let you sleep." Josiah bowed his head slightly. "Good night."

Luis said something to Josiah, which Josiah translated: "Luis says goodnight as well, and thank you for letting him work with you. He enjoyed it."

Breen smiled at him. "I enjoyed it too. If you want to come back sometime, you can. Good night."

Luis's smile was answer enough. He signed another thank-you, then waved and headed for the steps. Josiah followed.

As soon as they were gone, Breen pulled off her toolbelt and goggles and collapsed into bed. Was this what friendship meant when you were grown and not poor? Late nights sharing projects and ideas and dreams and possibilities? Choosing to stay awake to spend time with others, rather than forcing your body to work long after your mind had failed so you could be sure your family would eat the next day? Looking at the future as if it held potential and not just more of what already was?

If it was, she wanted more.

As soon as she had the thought, something in her heart twinged. Was it selfish, this wanting? Was it wrong? Shouldn't she want only what she really needed? She thought she remembered someone — a minister, a parent, one of *them*, she wasn't sure which — saying as much.

But for the first time in ages, she felt alive. Her heart felt like a heart, not like gears and wire and gems. So maybe this was something she needed after all, and she just hadn't realized it before. Maybe this wasn't selfish.

With that thought in mind, she fell asleep smiling.

CHAPTER 18

"So, what do you think about Miss Breen?" Josiah sat back in his chair, careful not to bump his head against the rack of parts and tools behind him. "Now that you've met her in person, I mean?"

"She's wasted in that tower." Luis carefully unscrewed a gear from the clock on the workbench in front of him. "She knows her way around clockwork and gears and machinery as well as I do, and that's without anyone to teach her. And I stand by what I said; if she went to the Inventors' Guild with her lift engine, they'd probably let her in."

Josiah nodded slowly. "Don't lift engines already exist, though?"

"Large, bulky, expensive ones, yes. Hers?" Luis raised an eyebrow. "She made it out of spare parts, and it's small enough that I can pick it up with no trouble — that's the definition of small and inexpensive. But it's still powerful enough to lift . . . I'd say two or three people. Make it a little larger, use sturdier parts and a stronger chain or cable, and add an extra crystal and some kind of safety mechanism, and it could carry eight, maybe even a dozen people at a go. The large crystals do drive up the cost of parts, but it's still better than what's currently available."

"I'll take your word for it." Josiah watched as Luis removed more gears from the clock. "That was quite generous of you to offer her those crystals, especially since they were meant for your own invention."

"It was your money I was spending, not mine, and it seemed like something you'd do. I'll get another set eventually." Luis shrugged. "And if she does use her lift engine to join the Inventor's Guild after you get her out of the tower, she can put in a good word for me."

Now it was Josiah's turn to raise an eyebrow. "You're so certain that I'll find a way to get her out of the tower before you join the guild?"

Luis picked up a screwdriver and pointed it at Josiah. "I know you. You won't give up until you figure out a way to convince her to leave the tower. And as soon as you do that, you'll find her a good job or a university scholarship, and we'll both convince her to join the Inventors' Guild, and then you'll have *another* person to help you on your next project. I, meanwhile, will probably be working on my entrance piece for the guild for the next three years."

"I thought you were getting close. You seemed to be the last time I checked." Josiah picked up his mug of tea from the desk and took a sip. "But you are correct that I still intend to get her out of the tower as soon as possible — or, at the very least, remove whatever force is keeping her there. Speaking of which, any thoughts on the who, what, or why?"

"You'd know better than I would. But if I had to guess . . ." Luis set the screwdriver aside and picked up a pair of tweezers. "I'd say there are two possible reasons why she's still there. Option one: she's afraid of something." He inserted the tweezers between the gears of the clock and began carefully feeling around with them. "Option two: she is, in fact, there by her own choice and doesn't actually need to be rescued."

Luis pulled a dull, cracked crystal from the clock with a small noise of triumph. "There it is! As I was saying, she's clever enough that she could have figured out a way to escape the tower by now if she tried. So, I'd say that she hasn't tried, either because she doesn't want to leave or because she's too afraid of what will happen if she succeeds."

"She has tried and, from what I understand, succeeded for a time, but then she was caught again. I asked earlier this week." Josiah picked up a spare gear from the table and started running his finger along the edge. His inability to pace in this space left him fidgety. "She insists I cannot protect her and her family from whomever or whatever keeps her in the tower, even though she knows I am nobility with enough power that I can tell her to go to the palace for help if she ever does escape. And I've made it clear that if she wants to leave, I'll help her do so."

[157]

"She may be too proud to accept help. A lot of people, their dignity is all they have." In the socket where the cracked crystal should have been, Luis placed a clear one with a white glow in its center. He pressed it until it clicked. "Or she may believe that whatever force is keeping her in the tower is more powerful than any noble."

He paused and glanced up at Josiah, his eyes large behind his goggles. "If we're being honest, you might not be able to shelter her as well as you think you can. What if she's in the tower because she or someone in her family committed a crime, and the people keeping her there will expose that crime if she leaves? A lesser nobleman could skirt the law and ignore whatever she did. You don't have that liberty unless you can justify a royal pardon."

"I'm well aware of that, thank you." Josiah squeezed the gear so tightly that the edge of one of its teeth drew blood. He wiped it away and scowled at the cut. *Please, Jeros. Do not allow this to be another situation where my ability to help another is cut off by my rank.* "Putting that aside, let's assume Miss Breen believes that I'm a nobleman of significant rank and power. Who might have a reason for holding her there and enough power to make her believe I couldn't protect her?"

"Anyone with less honor than you, Your Highness." Luis sighed. "But, most likely . . . a higher-ranking noble house, or someone who claims to be attached to a high-ranking noble house. Any secret criminal organization with enough money to hire a good assassin."

Josiah set the gear down and picked up a screwdriver to toy with instead. "That doesn't narrow our search down much. What about anyone involved with the tower or its construction?"

"You'd know that better than I would. And please give me my screwdriver back." Luis held out his hand for the tool. "If you're that restless, get up and pace."

Josiah handed the screwdriver back but stayed where he was. With the extra chair in the back room, he didn't have enough of a path to pace. "The government sponsored the towers, of course, and the Alchemists' Guild and Architects' Guild were involved with the building. The Inventors' Guild did as well, though they didn't officially exist until midway through the project. The whole thing was overseen by a mid-ranking noble family, the Torwoods, but they fell on hard times shortly after the towers were completed. The family itself went bankrupt, their son died, and their daughter married into another family, which absorbed the Torwoods' lands and responsibilities."

"Hmm." Luis frowned absently, whether at the corroded gear in his hand or at Josiah's words, Josiah couldn't tell. "Which noble family?"

"I'm not sure. The books didn't say, and I didn't think it significant enough to look up," Josiah replied. "What about the guilds?"

"Why would the guilds want to keep a girl locked in a clock tower?" Luis scoffed. "The architects have no reason to do it. The alchemists are secretive enough, but their magic doesn't work on people. In fact, keeping her there should be detrimental to their guild's reputation since she'll eventually cause the clock to run down. The Inventors' Guild . . . as clever as she is, I could see a particularly desperate member trying to keep her a secret and then passing her inventions off as his own, but if that were the motivation, they'd give her access to all the parts and tools she needed. They wouldn't limit her to buckets of spare parts from who-knows-what."

He paused, staring at the half-assembled clock in front of him. "That is an odd thing, though. All those parts being stored there – most of them are too small to be used for the tower's machinery. Even the largest ones, like what we were working with last night, are sized for a much smaller machine than the tower."

Josiah nodded slowly, recalling the boxes and barrels of gears and screws and miazen crystals. "You have a good point. Do you think that the parts are from whoever's holding Miss Breen there, though? Or were they left behind by someone else?"

"Some of the pieces we used last night were made within the last five years. At the very least, whoever is storing the parts there has to know she's there too." Luis unscrewed a cracked gear and replaced it with a new one. "But I'd put my money on the people storing the parts being the same as the people keeping her there."

"Hmm." Josiah pursed his lips, shifting in his seat and almost knocking his head on a half-finished piece of clockwork. "A noble wouldn't need to hide a stock of parts in a clock tower. Could she be connected to an inventor's experiment? Or some new project of the Alchemists' Guild? Or . . ." He hesitated. "Could blood alchemy be involved somehow? Miazen crystals are used in both."

Luis was silent so long that Josiah began to wonder if he'd heard the question. With deft fingers, he replaced the rest of the gears in the clock and screwed the back on once again. At last, he said, "I don't think it's any of those. No single inventor would have that many spare pieces at once, and the whole guild couldn't be involved in something like this. The alchemists wouldn't need the mechanical parts, and they don't work with people, just magic and crystal and chemicals. The only exception would be if they were looking for ways to keep crystals from leaking magic, but they wouldn't keep a project like that secret this long."

"And blood alchemy?" Josiah asked.

"It's a stretch." Luis shook his head and turned the clock over. Glancing at his own watch, he set the hands to the correct time. "How would they get that kind of control over the clock tower? And Miss Breen doesn't look like she's been involved in blood alchemy on either end. I think you just have it on your mind because of the Senate bill."

"That's probable." Over the past week, Josiah had talked to many of the major party leaders and recognized thinkers among the Senate, trying to understand their perspectives on the blood alchemy bill. Lord-Senator Weston remained its staunchest supporter, but other senators were drifting over to his side. Even some members of the Workers' Party who typically argued with anything Weston proposed on principle were giving the idea serious consideration. "In any case, have you learned anything from your investigations?"

"Not yet." Luis shook his head. "I'm close. I've convinced one of the younger members of the Alchemists' Guild that I want to invent a device to automate the creation of charged miazen crystals —"

"*Do* you want to invent that?" Josiah interrupted. He immediately regretted it. The answer shouldn't matter; Luis was doing his best to do what Josiah had asked him to do.

But Luis just shrugged. "I've considered it before, but I dropped the idea because I didn't know what would be involved. If I know what I need, I'll most likely try. And this fellow seems like he'll be willing to give me information soon. I'm talking to some of the members of the Inventors' and Architects' Guilds as well. They all agree that having anyone around the miazen crystals should cause them to drain faster, but no one agrees about how much faster. I think I'll have to talk to an alchemist to figure that out for certain."

"I'm not surprised. Thank you for doing all this for me; I appreciate it." Josiah fished in his jacket pocket. "And, just in case you need them any time soon . . ." He pulled out the miazen crystals he'd picked up that morning, twins to those Luis had donated to Breen's lift the night before, and set them on Luis's worktable. "Here you go. Let me know if you need anything else for the inventions or the investigation."

Luis gave a short laugh. "Why am I not surprised? Thank you, Your Highness."

"You're welcome." Josiah stood. "As I said, I appreciate your help. And now, I'll leave you to your work. I've probably distracted you long enough."

"Thank you." Luis inserted a brass key into the side of the clock and wound it until the key would turn no further. "I suspect you have other people besides me who you want to talk to as well."

"You're correct. I have several more meetings with individual senators, and I hope to talk to the committee investigating the possibilities of blood alchemy at some point before the Senate meeting in a few days as well. And I've heard some odd rumors that I want to look into, but that may be a problem for another day." Josiah picked up his hat from a shelf. "Good luck with your work."

"Same to you." Luis waved absently, already turning his attention to the next clock to be fixed. Josiah nodded back and then headed out the door.

CHAPTER 19

Breen woke the next morning to a sunbeam shining directly in her eyes. She cracked one eye open, then shut it again. Why was the light so *bright?*

The tower vibrated with the tolling bells as the clock struck the hour. Breen rolled over so she could open her eyes without being blinded and watched the gems glow. Their light and the vibrations lasted far longer than she expected. Breen frowned. *That was more than six chimes. What time is it?* If she'd slept late, that would explain why everything was so much brighter than usual . . .

Breen peered at the gears, but reading the time by their position was harder on this level. So, she rolled out of bed and stumbled up the narrow steps to the level with the clock faces. She blinked, letting her eyes adjust to the increased light, and then checked the nearest clock face. There was one hand on the twelve, of course; the clock had just struck. And there was the other . . . on the ten. Not the six as it should be. Not the eight, which would be have been tolerable.

Ten o'clock. She'd slept until ten o'clock. *And today is an inspection, and I haven't been cleaning the clock properly all week. Madame will be furious!* Panic burned through Breen's veins at the thought. She fairly hurled herself back down the stairs, grabbed her toolbelt, and scrambled down to the lowest level of machinery.

Why had she stayed awake so late last night? Why had she not thought to keep track of the time? Why had she not insisted on finishing the project another night? *I'm such a fool . . .* Josiah wouldn't have known better, of course. He was probably used to staying up until dawn at galas and dances and events, then sleeping until noon. And Luis . . . he was an artisan, not a common laborer. No doubt he could afford to sleep later than many in the city.

Breen fairly flung herself over the railing onto a beam and scanned the nearest gears for any sign of wear. *Why was I so stupid?* She should've known better, even if Josiah and Luis didn't. She should've said something; stopped earlier. Now, even if she rushed, she would be lucky to work back up to the top floor before Madame arrived. And when Madame saw her poor work . . .

Breen shied away from the thought, scooting further along the beam. *I knew this was going to happen.* Sooner or later, letting Josiah and the others back would lead to trouble. She should've told him to leave and not come back the very first night. Why had she said he could return, let alone bring others?

It didn't matter. She couldn't change what she'd done before. All she could do was work as fast as she could now and hope it would be enough.

[166]

But as the day wore on, Breen's frantic pace slowed to a crawl — not out of decreased panic, but out of necessity. Her head ached as if the weight of the whole tower rested upon it, and the pain gradually spread down her neck and into her shoulders. She frequently found herself staring at a gear or a rod or another part for precious minutes, somehow unable to process what was before her, even though she'd seen it hundreds of times. She fumbled with tasks she could've done in her sleep — if only she *could* do them in her sleep!

She stopped at mid-afternoon for lunch. She knew she was wasting time, but she hoped that food would wake her up, give her enough alertness and energy to finish her work before Madame arrived. Luis's coffee would've done the trick, but he hadn't left any of that behind.

Thankfully, food did help — for a little while, long enough for her to finish a level at *almost* her normal speed. But as afternoon turned towards evening, her thoughts and movements grew slow and clumsy once again.

And then she fell.

She didn't even know how it happened. One moment, she sat on a beam, leaning back as she inspected a gear. The next moment, she toppled down, down, down, flailing for a handhold, until she hit a walkway and felt her ribs *crack*.

Breen lay still, trying and failing not to breathe too deeply as the gem in her chest warmed. She should've been more careful; she didn't have time for a fall . . . She sucked in a sharp breath as the pain in her ribs and at the back of her head and shoulders increased. Was she healing more slowly than usual? Or was she merely imagining things?

The heat and the worst of the pain gradually faded. Breen scrambled back to her feet, grabbing her scattered tools. One of the wrenches had fallen further than she had, forcing her to walk all the way to the third level to retrieve it. She hoped it hadn't hit anything important as it fell.

She hurried back up to where she'd left off as quickly as she could. That level only took another ten minutes to clean — but even ten minutes was more than she could afford. The clock had struck seven not long ago, and the light that filtered in through the windows was steadily fading. She only had three levels left, though; perhaps if she rushed, she could have them passably clean before Madame arrived . . .

Breen managed to finish the next level more quickly, though she knew Madame wouldn't be fully satisfied. There were far too many small imperfections that would add up to overall displeasure. But if she could get through the rest of the tower, however imperfectly, that would be better than the alternative.

Then the signal in her pocket vibrated. Breen's heart leaped into her throat — or would've if the mechanical beat didn't just keep stolidly ticking despite her panic. *She's early! Oh no . . .*

She had to make it to the top now. Breen wasn't sure how Madame would react to the lift device, but it would be better if she didn't know. At best, Madame would accuse her of stealing. At worst . . . Breen didn't want to think about that.

Breen scrambled to the center of the tower, jumped, and grabbed one of the clock chains. She clawed her way upwards, switching from one chain to another so her weight wouldn't significantly change the time. She reached the top level and swung onto a beam, then scooted along it as fast as she could. She reached the edge and leaped onto the solid floor —

Only to see Madame rise to floor level and step off the lift. She turned towards where Breen should be, then froze when she saw only the chain coiling on the floor. She turned slowly towards the center of the tower where Breen stood, her expression settling into something as deadly and cutting as the February wind. When she signed, her motions were sharp as glass shards. "What is the meaning of this?"

Perhaps she could salvage this. Perhaps she could placate her. Just in case Jeros happened to be listening, Breen sent up a swift and silent prayer. "I'm sorry. I was awake late last night working, and then I slept late today. I only have this top level left; please, just give me more time."

Madame Gottling crossed the floor in five long strides and slapped Breen across the face. Breen stumbled and nearly fell backward into the machinery, but Madame grabbed her shirt front and yanked her back to solid ground. As Breen tried to recover her balance, Madame signed, "Do not confuse me with an idiot, girl."

Breen bowed her head low enough that she could see only Madame's hands, not her face. "I'm sorry. Please forgive me. I was wrong. I'm ready for your inspection now."

Madame slapped the other side of Breen's face so hard Breen nearly fell again. "Do not instruct me." She pointed at the lift device. "What is this?"

There was nothing for it but the truth, or part of the truth. "I made it." Breen kept her gaze low. "I thought it would help. I'm sorry."

Madame slapped Breen a third time, then grabbed Breen's chin and jerked her head up. "Look at me!" Her hands flew so fast they were nearly unreadable. "Did we save your life so you could toy with gears rather than work? Did we give you shelter and food so you could steal from us?"

"I didn't steal; it was all in the tower." The words slipped out before Breen could stop herself. She stiffened, then hastily added, "I'm sorry. I shouldn't have done it. I didn't let it get in the way of my work, I promise." That was a lie, but only a small one. "I hoped it would help."

Madame huffed and unhooked a riding crop from her belt. The gem on the end of the handle flashed red, and flickers of something like red lightning ran up its length. Breen cringed away, dreading its sting. But instead, Madame turned and stalked towards the lift. She stopped at its edge and struck the screws fastening the lift device to the rafters.

The gem's light flared. The device fell, the screws broken in half. Both it and the lift plummeted down the shaft. Breen cringed, imagining the crash at the end and all her work shattered on the ground.

Madame turned back to her, hooking the crop back in its place. "Now, show me your real work."

"Yes, ma'am." Breen obeyed, leading the way down the stairs as far as she could go. Then she trailed after Madame as she inspected the machinery, peering at gears and rods and gems and running her fingers along them to check for grease and dust. Breen prayed that what she'd done would be good enough, but the way Madame's scowl grew with every level, she knew that it wouldn't be.

At last, they reached the top floor. Here, Madame didn't even bother to inspect Breen's work. "So you steal from us, and you refuse to do the work we set you. Do you think you are above us somehow? Do you forget the gift you were given? Should we take it back? Tell your family their daughter threw away their sacrifice? Tell them not to depend any longer on your support to survive?"

"No. No. No. Please." Breen shook her head, cowering. A voice in her head that sounded rather like Josiah whispered that she shouldn't be cowering. That she should speak up and defend herself. But Josiah didn't know what it was like to stand before someone who held your life, your family's lives, in her hands. "Please, don't. I won't do it again. Please."

"You live only because we choose to let you. If we were not merciful, you would have been left to die long ago. Now you waste what we gave you." Madame stated it as a fact, her hands and face sharp. "Do you think you should escape punishment?"

Please. Yes, please. But saying that would only make her inevitable punishment worse. Slowly, Breen shook her head. "No, Madame."

"At least you recognize what you deserve." Madame unhooked her riding crop once more. The gem glowed red as blood. "Kneel."

No. Please, no. But Breen obeyed woodenly, kneeling with her head on her mattress and her arms over her head and neck. She bit down on her blanket, tensing as she waited for the first blow to fall. She knew what was coming. She remembered last time all too well.

This time would be worse.

As always, the first fall of the crop came as a shock. The stroke stung as any blow would, but the wound it left burned like fire. The second stroke was worse. Madame had a knack for overlapping her strikes so each blow hit both already-suffering skin and previously undamaged areas. And with every blow, the fiery pain increased. Within minutes, Breen's back and arms burned so much that she wondered if she really were burning. Perhaps that was some new property of Madame's alchemy-enhanced weapon.

But she couldn't be truly on fire. If she were, Madame would have stopped after a minute or two. But instead, the crop fell and fell and fell again. Every inch of Breen's back and arms was bruised and burned and, in some cases, bleeding. And unlike other injuries, these did not heal instantly, though the crystal in Breen's chest grew almost unbearably hot, and its magic pulsed through her body.

The part of Breen's mind that sounded like Josiah whispered that she shouldn't let herself be beaten. That she should get up and fight back. She had a wrench in her belt still, and there was a heavy pan on the stove. One, maybe two hits and then Madame Gottling would never hurt her again.

The crop fell again, harder than the last time, and struck a particularly tender spot. Breen whimpered, shutting her eyes to keep her tears in. She couldn't hit back, no matter how much she wanted to. That would be wrong. She belonged to Madame and Madame's people, and so they had a right to punish her, no matter what the Josiah-voice said. You beat a donkey if it refused to walk; you beat a dog if it disobeyed; you beat a slave if she failed to do the work set to her. And if the slave wasn't properly alive at all, well, there was no reason why she should receive better treatment than even the lowest of animals . . .

At last, Madame's crop rose and didn't fall again. Breen remained still. Tears of pain leaked past her eyelids. She felt the faint tremors in the floor as Madame stalked away towards the stairs, and she silently gave thanks that the lift was broken. At least that meant Madame couldn't force her to operate it. Once she was certain Madame wouldn't return, she pushed off her shoes and her tool belt. Then she crawled onto her cot, curled up, and prayed that sleep would come and bring her relief.

It did not. She'd already slept too late today.

CHAPTER 20

Josiah pushed open the door of the clock tower and stepped inside. Far above, the clock tolled the hour: nine o'clock. Hopefully, Breen wouldn't mind that he and Grace were late. They'd have to make sure they kept their visit short; no doubt she was tired after their long night last night.

With Grace in tow, he crossed to the lift. However, as he stepped onto the platform, his foot bumped something. It rattled faintly. Josiah knelt and felt about until he found the item: a chain the same size and weight as the one that should be attached to the lift.

Something in Josiah's chest squeezed into a knot. He looked up. The higher levels were illuminated slightly more than this one, and in that dim light, he could tell that there was no chain leading up to the top floor. *Did the lift engine break?* And if it had, was Breen all right?

Grace tapped Josiah's shoulder and spoke aloud: "What's wrong?"

Josiah turned to face her and signed: "It's broken. Do you have a light?"

He had to repeat the signs several more time before she could read them through the shadows. Finally, she nodded and reached into a hidden pocket of her dress and pulled something out. She tapped it, and the white light of a high-quality miazen crystal illuminated the area around their feet.

The crystal in question hung from a silver chain with a ring of metal on one end. Grace pulled the chain partway through the ring, making a loop, and then hung the gem from her wrist. "What's broken?"

Josiah gestured to the lift as a whole, then added, "Hold the light." He knelt again and inspected the lift platform and the ground around the lift. Aside from the chain and a few small gears, he found nothing that shouldn't be there. Perhaps the chain had simply come loose from the mechanism somehow.

Josiah stood. "I want to check on Miss Breen. She could be hurt." Admittedly, if she had fallen with the lift, he would expect her to be down here as well. But she could have fallen off partway down, or . . . something else. He wasn't sure about the logistics.

He took a step towards the stairs, then thought better of it and pressed the lift button so he wouldn't accidentally sneak up on her without warning. To Grace, he added, "Stay behind me." With that, he started for the stairs.

They slowly made their way up the tower level by level, checking each carefully for any sign of Breen. They found none, and by the time they reached the topmost floor, Josiah had convinced himself that she was fine. The chain had pulled free while the platform was on the ground floor; nothing more had occurred. He'd offer to help her fix it and then let her get some rest.

Then they reached the top floor. Josiah half-expected to see Breen sitting on her cot or her stool, watching and waiting for them as she had on the first nights they'd visited. Instead, he found her curled up on her cot with her thin blanket pulled up about her shoulders. Odd; the night was relatively warm. Was she sick?

Josiah glanced back to Grace and signed, "Stay over here." Then he approached Breen's cot, stepping heavily so the floorboards would tremble and possibly warn Breen of his approach. She didn't stir, so when he reached her, he put a hand on her shoulder.

His palm touched something sticky and faintly warm. Josiah pulled his hand back in surprise and looked at it, then at Breen's shoulder. There, a dark red stain spread across the dirty white of her shirt. *Blood.*

Breen stirred, then partially turned and peered up at him with one eye. "What?" she mumbled.

"What happened?" Josiah couldn't sign fast enough; he needed to know. If this was somehow his fault . . . "Are you all right?"

Silence. Breen stared at him, then nodded once, shut her eye, and rolled over so her face was half-pressed into her pillow. As she did, she let out a quiet, pained whimper.

Josiah knelt and tapped the back of her hand to get her attention. He waited until she opened her eyes again and then signed, "Tell me what happened."

Breen groaned, but then cleared her throat. "I fell behind on my work because I stayed up too late, and Madame didn't approve of the lift."

Josiah tensed. For once, he wanted nothing more than to punch whoever this *Madame* was in the teeth. But instead, he signed, "Madame is the one who keeps you here? She hurt you? Beat you?"

"Yes." Breen shut her eyes again. "I'll heal. Everything just hurts right now."

And he'd let it happen. Caused it, even. He should've known better — but since he couldn't change the past, he had to try to fix the present. Josiah stood so quickly he almost overbalanced. Just in case Breen happened to be watching, he signed, "I'll be back." Then, with steps as sharp as any soldier's, he crossed back to the stairs.

Grace's hands flew as he approached. "What's happening?"

"Breen is injured." Josiah thought for a moment. He didn't want to leave Breen alone, but he also couldn't carry her through the streets without drawing too much attention, and she didn't seem in any condition to walk. Grace could stay and keep watch, but he also didn't want to leave the girls unprotected. As a compromise, he pulled out his pistol and offered it to Grace, grip-first.

She took it and gave him a questioning look. "I need you to stay here. Make sure nothing changes, but don't disturb Breen if you don't need to. You remember how to use the pistol?" He waited for her nod, then continued, "Keep it ready, just in case. I'm going to go back to the palace and fetch one of the medical staff. I'll be back soon."

Grace nodded again, gripping the pistol tightly. Josiah hurried back down the stairs and out onto the street. Once he'd gone a block away from the tower, he didn't even bother to try to blend in with the crowds but simply rushed along, weaving between people and occasionally shoving through the largest groups. He needed a nurse for Breen, and then . . .

Well, then he'd have to have a talk with her about the future. Surely now she'd see sense and tell him what he needed to know so he could free her from the tower. If he had to lay all his cards on the table and tell her who he was in order to convince her, so be it. He couldn't leave her there to face more unjust beatings, and she couldn't possibly believe that staying was in her best interests.

Of course, if he rescued Breen, whoever kept her in the tower would know that something was wrong. That might make them desperate and therefore careless — but, more likely, it would mean they'd go underground and be more careful than ever. He might never catch them, might never bring them to justice. Well, so be it. He'd accept that risk if it meant saving a life.

Josiah reached the palace and stepped inside with a nod to the guards. Once within, he made his way through the halls to the castle infirmary and the medical staff quarters alongside it.

The infirmary was, as always, open. Josiah slipped inside and glanced around until he spotted the nurse on duty dozing in an armchair in a back corner of the room. "Ma'am, I require your services."

The nurse shook herself, blinked once, and then shot to her feet and into a bow. "Your Highness, what can I do for you?"

"There is a person who requires medical assistance from someone discreet and trustworthy. Pack what you need to treat wounds and come with me at once." Josiah paused, studying the woman's face to remind himself of her name. "Do not waste time, Nurse Turner."

"I understand, Your Highness." Nurse Turner stepped into a back room and reappeared a moment later carrying a black bag. She set this on a low table. "I will go wake someone to take my place, then I will be ready."

Josiah nodded. "As I said, hurry."

She returned the nod and left the room. She returned a few minutes afterward and picked up her bag from the table. "Where is this patient?"

"You will see. Follow me, please." Josiah led the way out of the infirmary and down the halls. "Please keep your questions to a minimum, and do not speak of this to anyone else unless I tell you otherwise."

Again, she bowed her head slightly. "I understand, Your Highness."

He knew she did. A staff member who couldn't hold her tongue wouldn't last long in the palace or any other noble house. Granted, the type of secrecy Josiah was insisting on was usually reserved for royal emergencies, but Josiah didn't want to risk anyone hearing about this who didn't need to know — not yet, anyway.

Nurse Turner followed him silently through the streets to the clock tower. She took in their destination with a raised brow, but she kept her tongue as they made their way up the stairs.

They found Grace sitting on the stool by Breen's bed, still clutching Josiah's pistol. She relaxed and set the gun on the floor when she saw them. "No change," she signed.

Josiah nodded. He addressed Nurse Turner. "Your patient is on the cot. Her name is Breen. I will introduce you and explain your presence to her, then leave you to your work. Is that agreeable?"

"Of course, Your Highness." Nurse Turner hefted her bag and undid the clasp. "I may need to ask her some questions in order to treat her properly, though."

"Understood. Keep what she says to yourself, though. In addition, be aware that she is deaf. You understand sign, I assume?" He didn't wait for a response; all medical staff learned sign just in case they needed to communicate with Grace. "Come."

[181]

He crossed the room to Breen's cot and again tapped her shoulder, avoiding the bloody spot. Breen shifted and opened her eyes, staring dully at him.

Josiah knelt so he was on eye-level with her. "This is Miss Turner. She is a nurse who works for my family. She is going to take a look at your injuries. Is that all right?"

Breen pressed her lips together, hesitation clear on her face. Josiah quickly added, "She will not tell anyone that you're here or anything about you. She knows how to be discreet. Don't worry."

Breen sighed, then nodded. Josiah chose to take that as acceptance. "I'll leave you to your work, Miss Turner."

With a last glance at Breen, he returned with Grace to the steps and descended two levels down: far enough to ensure Breen's privacy, but close enough that either Breen or Nurse Turner could call him back up. There, he sat on a step and scowled. "I should have forced Breen to leave in the first place. Then this wouldn't have happened."

Grace shook her head at him. "You did the right thing to let her stay. You didn't know this would happen. And now that it has, we just have to figure out how to make it right."

CHAPTER 21

The minutes seemed to stretch on as Josiah and Grace waited for news of Breen's condition. Grace attempted conversation once or twice, but worry eventually stilled her hands. Josiah, for his part, sat on his step and stewed, reviewing what he had done, what he should've done instead, and what he could do now.

He would get Breen out of this tower and out of danger; that much was certain. He'd find a home for her in the palace, somewhere where she could be safe and comfortable and unnoticed. If she wanted to work, he'd find something for her to do; if not, she'd earned her rest. He'd locate her family and bring them in as well; make a place for them among the palace's live-in staff. And then, with Breen and her family all safe, perhaps one of them or all of them together would be able and willing to tell him enough that he could find the person who'd enslaved Breen.

And if she refused to leave . . . well, he could still force her to go. It would be well within his power. But she'd insisted that she had a reason to stay beyond the threat to her family. He would learn that reason and prove he could deal with it — or else find some other way to protect her. Guards, spies, something. And if her keepers, if this *Madame* person, beat her, how else might they mistreat her? He'd have to find ways to remedy that as well . . .

The stairs creaked. Josiah stood and turned as Nurse Turner approached, her bag in hand. "She will recover in time. I do not think this is not the first time she's been beaten. I cleaned and bandaged her injuries, then gave her a small dose of laudanum for her pain. I left the ointment for the wounds and the laudanum with her with instructions on how to use them."

She paused as if mentally wrestling with herself. "Your Highness, you said not to ask questions, and I respect your commands. But may I make one inquiry?"

Josiah nodded. "You may."

"Do you know why this girl is here?" Nurse Turner didn't quite meet his gaze, but she came as close as she could without being impolite. "As a medical professional, I have concerns."

"I understand." Now it was Josiah's turn to debate with himself about what to say. "She is not here by my will, nor entirely by her own. I am doing my best to liberate her from this place, and I hope that I will be successful after tonight."

"I see." The nurse hesitated a moment longer, looking almost as if she wished to say something more, then shook her head slightly. "I understand. I assume you wish to speak with her, then?"

"Yes, I do." Josiah glanced up the steps. "Is that possible?"

"It is." Nurse Turner nodded. "With your permission, I will wait here until you are done so I do not intrude."

"Thank you." Josiah beckoned for Grace to follow him and then headed up the steps. He found Breen still on her cot, now sitting up and looking a little less pained. "I am sorry," Josiah signed as soon as they were close enough. "This is my fault."

Breen shook her head, then winced slightly. "No. My fault. I fell behind. I disobeyed."

"You fell behind because of me." In part, anyway, and that was enough for him to take responsibility, as a good leader should. "I didn't realize this would happen."

Breen just shrugged, then winced. "I made my choice."

"You were punished because you took the time to do something good." How could she stand to take unjust treatment so passively? "How often does this happen?"

"Not often." Breen smile weakly. "I'm used to it."

"You shouldn't be," Grace signed before Josiah could say anything. "Do you want us to help you leave the tower? We'll protect you and your family." She glanced at Josiah. "Won't we?"

Breen's expression flattened. "I can't. I know you want to help, but I can't leave. I've told you before. Nothing has changed."

"Nothing has changed for you. We didn't know you were being beaten as well as imprisoned." Josiah shifted, resisting the urge to pace and rant. "You said that you and your family are in danger if you leave, but you're in danger if you stay as well, and I have a responsibility to protect you."

[185]

"Why?" Breen's motions were sharp, her eyes hard. "You may want to help, but that doesn't mean you're responsible for me."

"No, but the royal family — myself in particular — are responsible to protect the people of Chania," Josiah shot back. "That includes you and your family."

Breen stared at him, her eyes growing wide. "You . . ." She just let her hand hang there, pointing at Josiah as if she wasn't sure how to finish her sentence.

"I am the prince, yes." Josiah nodded. "And so when I say that I can and have to protect you and your family, I mean it. We'll bring you to the palace. We'll employ your father and anyone else in your family who wants to work. We already have live-in staff, so it won't attract attention. You can all stay until we find out who's threatening them and hurting you. Perhaps even longer."

Breen pressed her lips together. "You can protect them. But you can't protect me. You don't have all the facts."

"Then give me the facts!" Josiah snapped. "Earlier, you said that your keepers had threatened you and your family to make sure you stayed here. We can make sure their threats don't happen. What else is there to keep you here?"

Breen hesitated, trembling — whether out of fear or frustration, Josiah couldn't tell. Finally, she signed, "They won't kill me if I go. They don't have to. I'll die if I leave the tower for too long. I can't tell you more than that. Please, trust me."

Grace responded before Josiah could. "Then what can we do? We don't want to leave you here where you'll be in danger."

[186]

"You have to." Panic suddenly flooded Breen's face, and she stiffened, then winced. "I'm sorry. Your . . ." she struggled for the next sign.

Josiah held up a hand. "You don't need to act towards us any differently than you did before."

"Thank you." Breen still bowed her head slightly as she touched her fingers to her lips and then moved them outwards. "I'll be fine. I just have to be more careful in the future." She slumped, signing with tiny motions, "Beatings are better than death."

"I understand." Grace nodded. "We both do. We'd still like to protect your family; will you let us do that?"

Bless you, Grace! Josiah had to keep from exclaiming aloud. If Breen would tell them how to find her family, perhaps they could give Josiah more answers than Breen — and that would mean he could, at last, get a lead on whoever was keeping her here.

Breen hesitated, then nodded. "My father is Matthew Wellens. He worked in the textile factory nearest the river, and we lived in a house a few blocks from there. That's all I can tell you."

Scant information, but hopefully it would be enough. "Thank you." Josiah gave her an encouraging smile. "Once we find them, would you like me to bring your father or any of your other family members to see you?"

Breen looked down at her hands. "Maybe. I don't know yet. I don't want them to see me hurt."

That was understandable. "I'll ask again later," Josiah replied. "Is there anything else we can do to help? Anything at all?"

Breen thought for several moments. Then, with tentative hands, she signed, "Madame didn't restock my food when she came today. I'll be fine without, but if you don't mind . . ."

Grace looked indignant. "Is she trying to starve you?"

Breen shook her head hastily. "She will be back in a few days. She knows I'll survive that long. But if it's no trouble . . ."

"I'll return tomorrow and bring you something." Already a list formed in Josiah's mind of what he'd need to do and acquire. "Don't worry. Anything else?"

She shook her head. Grace patted her uninjured shoulder. "Then we'll go and let you rest. Good night."

Breen managed a smile. "Good night. Thank you."

"You're welcome." Josiah bowed his head, then headed for the stairs. Tomorrow, he'd have a talk with the royal intelligence forces. If anyone could find a man based on as little information as he had, they could. And he'd have to have them set a surveillance roster on the tower as well; in fact, he should've done that weeks ago, when he first discovered Breen. He doubted that the person ultimately responsible for Breen's imprisonment was the same as the one who Breen called Madame, but the latter might lead him back to the former.

They reached the bottom of the tower, where Nurse Turner waited. Josiah led the way out onto the street and locked the tower behind them. It was unfortunate that progress had to come at the price of Breen's pain — but at least he'd now have a better chance of bringing those who hurt her to justice.

CHAPTER 22

By the next morning, the pain in Breen's back and shoulders had subsided enough that she could force herself off her cot and move around. Another dose of the medicine Nurse Turner had left her eased it still more, and she took advantage of this by checking on the machinery nearest to the walkways on the upper few levels. She cleaned what she could without straining herself too much, hoping to reduce what she'd need to do later on. She thought once or twice about going up to the level of the clock faces, but she didn't dare. Instead, she napped whenever she wasn't working, hoping that sleep would help her ignore the empty ache in her stomach.

At last, as the glow of alchemical lights replaced the sunshine, the signal in her pocket pulled her out of her doze. *Josiah.* It had to be; Madame would know that the lift was still broken, and she wouldn't have the courtesy to signal otherwise. She sat up on her bed, watching the stairs.

Sure enough, Josiah appeared, carrying a bundle under one arm. He smiled cheerfully at her and waved with his free hand.

Then he crossed the room and set the bundle down on her cot. "You look better," he signed.

Breen nodded. "The medicine helped. Thank you."

"Good." Josiah gestured to the package. "Food, as you requested. You can open it now or later, whatever you prefer. Do you mind if I stay a few minutes?"

"Thank you. You can stay." Breen accompanied the motion with a grateful smile. "Do you mind if I eat?"

"Go ahead," Josiah nodded and fetched the stool so he could sit next to her cot.

While he did, Breen pulled open the bundle. Here were a half-dozen small loaves of bread — not the coarse, hard, dark variety she was used to, but light, golden-crusted rounds, some speckled with what looked like cranberries. Here was a packet of large tea leaves, which Breen smelled eagerly — even their faint scent was delicious — and a jar full of coffee, at which Breen let out an cry of delight. Here were round, red-cheeked apples, and a small wheel of hard, white cheese, and a metal tin of porridge oats and another small jar of — oh, delight! *Honey!* And at the very bottom of the bundle, she found a small box wrapped in gold paper, tied with a white ribbon, and stamped with the words *Düetschin Confectionary.*

She glanced up at Josiah. "Chocolates," he signed before she could ask. "That's how Grace usually likes me to apologize for things. As for the rest — I wasn't sure what you'd want, so I guessed. I hope it's all right."

"It's good. Thank you." With this much food . . . it could last weeks if Breen was careful. One week, if she wasn't. *Either way, I can afford to be full tonight.* She removed a loaf of bread, an apple, and, on another moment's thought, the chocolates, then wrapped the rest of the food back up to hide later. "You didn't need to do this much."

"I wanted to. You're my friend, and you were hurt because of me, whatever you say. I want to make it right," Josiah replied. "And you work hard here. You deserve to be treated well. 'The worker is worth his hire,' after all."

The worker is worth his hire. Where was that from? The preacher's book, wasn't it? Jeros's words? Breen considered this, biting into the apple. Could she argue with that, even if all she was doing was trying to pay off some measure of a debt she could never fully fulfill?

Perhaps. She allowed herself to be persuaded, to enjoy the apple without feeling guilty about it. In any case, she had it whether or not she deserved it, so she might as well make the most of it.

Josiah adjusted his position on the stool so he could face her better. "Were you able to rest at all today?"

Breen nodded, setting down her apple. "Madame won't be back for a few days. She knows I can't work much after a beating." She hesitated, then asked, "Could you find my family?"

"I'm working on it. I think we'll know where they are in a day or two." Josiah paused, then added, "I ordered people to watch the tower. They'll let me know who comes and goes. I thought you should know."

Breen considered this. That wasn't a bad idea, really. She couldn't be blamed for telling anyone anything, and Josiah would find out what he wanted to know. "Thank you for telling me."

"You're welcome." Josiah fell silent, his hands still in his lap.

Breen finished off her apple and started on one of the rounds of bread. Normally, she would have split each into two or three meals, but she was so hungry, and, just once, she wanted to enjoy what she had while it was freshest. And this bread was truly *fresh*, light and fluffy and soft. She'd never had anything so wonderful.

She glanced at Josiah again and, on impulse, signed, "What did you do today?"

Josiah's eyebrows rose. "Me?"

"You." Breen straightened, gaining confidence. "You always just ask me about me. But I never ask about you. So I'm asking. Is that all right?" She added the last bit with an uncertain smile, not certain how Josiah would take it.

But he smiled. "Yes. It is." He paused, thinking, as Breen went back to eating her apple. "I met with people, mostly. Some of them were senators or nobles, some were alchemists, and some were the people who are going to look for your family and watch the tower. Grace and I attended lunch with nobles from the —" he fingerspelled something that Breen didn't quite catch. "I did research and prepared for the Senate meeting tomorrow. Father

[192]

and I attended a formal dinner with the Guild leaders. Then I came here."

"Oh." Breen searched for another question. "The nobles. What were they like? Where did you say they're from?"

"Interesting enough. Less stuffy than some here." Josiah smiled slightly. "They live on the Selitan Islands." This time, she paid closer attention when he spelled the name. "One told me much about the voyage here, his ships, and his sailing excursions. It sounded pleasant. What do you think? Would you enjoy sailing if you could try it?"

Would she? Breen frowned thoughtfully. Until this moment, her world and thoughts had been restricted to the tower and the city. What would it be like to stand on a ship's deck, to have the ground shift beneath you with the waves? "I would try it. But I don't think I'd like it."

She hoped Josiah wouldn't be offended. He didn't seem to be; he just nodded. "Why not?"

"I like solidness." Breen gestured to the tower around them. "This doesn't move."

Josiah laughed, head back and eyes closed. "I see. You'd like mountains, then. They're solid. Still. Peaceful. Like the top room of your tower, but better. You can see for miles."

"That sounds nice."

"It is." Josiah and Breen both fell silent again. Breen finished her loaf and contemplated the cheese. She shouldn't eat more, she knew. But everything else had been so good . . .

Thankfully, Josiah asked another question before she could give in. "Are there others like you? In other clock towers? Or are you the only one?"

Breen hesitated. Did she dare answer that question? *If Madame finds out . . .*

But Madame hadn't found out yet. Or maybe she already knew. If she hadn't found out yet, saying this couldn't hurt. And if she already knew, then it would be better to tell Josiah more while she could. Either way, if Josiah really wanted to help, it would be selfish to keep that all for herself.

So, she set down her bread and nodded. "Yes. Probably. In some. I don't know which. They aren't just in clock towers; they're in other places too. I don't know where. We . . . When we were younger, we served Madame's people in the place where they do their work. When we got older, Madame's people took some of us away, like me, to work in other places."

Josiah nodded. "Did they take everyone away?"

Breen shook her head. "No. There were always people older than me. And sometimes, Madame's people would let the cleverest of us join them and work with them."

Josiah raised an eyebrow. "I would think you'd be one of the cleverest ones."

Breen blushed, but for once, she couldn't argue. "I might have been. Madame's people hinted that they wanted me to work with them. They let me serve longer in better jobs, and they'd have me help in more secret rooms. But I didn't like what they were doing

— it was wrong. So I disobeyed sometimes. A lot of times. And then they sent me here."

"I see." Josiah nodded slowly, and Breen half-expected him to press for more details. But instead, he asked, "If I went to other towers, how could I convince those there that I want to help them?"

Oh. This was a harder question. Breen frowned thoughtfully, chewing the last of her bread. "Be kind, like you were to me. Tell them you know Breen, but say it like this." Breen formed the sign for B with her right hand and a half-circle with the fingers of her other hand, then slid her right hand through the circle of her left, extending her fingers outward as she finished the sign. "We didn't show name-signs to Madame's people, so they'll know you know me, not Madame."

Josiah imitated the sign. "This?"

"Yes." Breen thought a moment more. "Be careful. Some might tell Madame's people you were there because they want to go back where we were or think they'll get a reward. Or they might attack you."

"I'll be careful. Thank you for the warning."

Breen nodded. She gave the chocolates a hard look, then picked them up and tugged at the ribbon until the bow came undone before asking, "You aren't going to ask more about where I came from?"

Josiah tilted his head and raised an eyebrow. "Do you want to tell me?"

Breen shook her head.

Josiah made a "Well, there" expression. "Then I won't push you. I learned my lesson. And you've told me quite a bit already."

"Thank you." Breen unwrapped the paper and lifted the lid off the box. Stiff paper rectangles divided balls of chocolate, some darker than others. "Do you want one?"

"If you'll share, but they're yours." Nonetheless, when she held out the box to him, Josiah took a dark chocolate. "Thank you."

Breen smiled and tasted one of the lighter chocolates. She shut her eyes and savored it, knowing she'd probably never taste these again once the box was gone. Once the piece was gone, she signed, "These are a good apology."

"I'm glad." Josiah resettled himself on the stool. "If there's anything else I can do to help you, just ask."

"I know." Breen smiled. "But . . . you've already done so much, and just coming back helps. So, thank you for that too."

CHAPTER 23

Josiah tapped his pen on his note-filled page, only half-listening as the Senate discussed its latest distraction from the blood alchemy bill, a petition for the government to sponsor a coalition of Guilds researching air travel. The coalition members, drawn from the Inventors, Engineers, Mechanics, and Alchemists Guilds, claimed their work would expedite trade with Shanfey and other eastern lands and would give Chania tactical advantage in the event of war. Josiah suspected that most of them really just wanted to see if the government would pay them to do another thing that had never been done before — and he knew that the government *would*. Support for new innovation was the one thing every party could agree on, even if they differed on its uses. And so, Josiah had to wonder why they even bothered to debate the matter, especially since there were so much more interesting topics close at hand.

For example, the rumors that had been spreading the last few days about Lord-Senator Weston. Josiah glanced downwards, but the High Council seats were immediately below his own, and so he couldn't quite see the man. If what Josiah had heard could be believed, Weston's forces had uncovered a small blood alchemist hideout and had made a significant discovery, though the rumors were inconsistent as to what that discovery might be. Several, however, speculated that he'd captured the results of the alchemists' human experiments.

Josiah knew better than to believe everything he heard. But he also knew better than to wholly discount information because it started in a rumor, especially one of which his intelligence force had made a point of informing him. Every rumor, after all, revealed a tiny bit of truth, either about its source or its subject. In this case, the story had been leaked by someone in Weston's own household — and Weston knew how to keep secrets. That meant that he was likely not only aware of the rumors but was in fact behind them.

The research fund discussion finally wound down, and Prime Minister Wentworth called for a vote. Josiah absently called out "Yea" in chorus with almost everyone else in the room, his mind still fixed on the problem of Lord-Senator Weston. Clearly, Weston wanted others to believe that he had gained some kind of inside information, perhaps even definitive proof for his position. And that most likely meant that he was preparing to reveal some new argument for the blood alchemy bill — or intending to strengthen a previous argument — today or in the near future.

Prime Minister Wentworth turned over a new page on his desk. "Next on the agenda, further discussion of the issue of blood alchemy. The investigative committee has not approached me with any new findings. Do any other senators have new information which they wish to share?

Silence. Josiah waited for Weston to stand and speak but — nothing. Josiah frowned, his pen pressed to his paper. Had he interpreted the rumors incorrectly? Or was Weston just biding his time?

Prime Minister Wentworth cleared his throat. "If there are no additions to the topic —"

Movement drew everyone's eyes to the side of the room. A page hurried down one of the smaller aisles towards the High Council seats. Josiah had to resist from leaning over the edge of his own box so he could track the boy's passage, but he had a guess all the same.

Sure enough, a few moments later, Weston spoke. "A moment, Minister. It seems I do have something to add."

He strode forward towards the middle of the room and took his place at his usual podium. Josiah leaned forward slightly. Had that whole scene been purposeful? He wouldn't put it past Weston to manufacture a last-minute arrival of evidence to make his news seem more exciting.

"Gentlemen of the Senate, I am sure that many of you have heard that my forces recently discovered and raided the laboratory of a group of blood alchemists. This is true." Weston paused, allowing people to react to this confirmation of the rumor. The room remained silent, waiting, so he went on, "Unfortunately, the blood alchemists fled, but we were able to capture a significant amount of their notes and their work — including a still-living specimen of their experiments, a boy with alchemically-powered implants of the type I have advocated for. My scientists and alchemists studied the modifications made on the boy, then turned him over to a group of neutral scientists and alchemists so they could do the same. They confirmed that the implants do what we expect them to do with no ill effects on the subject."

Again he paused. This time, murmurs spread through the room. Josiah turned to a fresh page in his notebook but didn't write anything down yet. He should've seen this move coming, especially with the events of the last Senate meeting. Weston couldn't get the bill passed without proving that blood alchemy did what he claimed, and, naturally, he'd want to be the one to provide and control that proof. Still, it was rather convenient that he managed to find such evidence so quickly . . .

Senator Aaronson stood. "That's convenient for you, Weston. Tell us, how did you come upon this nest of blood alchemists so soon?"

"Careful observation and a bit of luck, senator. I suggest you speak to my guardsmen if you wish to know further details. Captain Taylor led the force; I will instruct him to make himself and his squadron available to any members of the Senate who wish to hear details of the event." Weston surveyed the room again. "My alchemists have provided me with a full report of what they learned from studying the boy and the other captured items. I would be glad to share that report with you now. Or, if other senators prefer,

I have taken the liberty of including several of my scientists and alchemists and the boy in question in my retinue. They are currently waiting outside, but I can easily call them in and let them speak to you themselves."

Clever move. Weston knew that the most influential senators would rather get their information firsthand, and so he gave them just that — yet he still controlled access to that knowledge. Josiah made a mental note to find out which supposedly-neutral scientists and alchemists checked the work of Weston's people; he'd have to investigate and make sure they *were* actually neutral, then interview them personally. And if he could find a way to interview Weston's people too without Weston looking over his shoulder . . .

Prime Minister Wentworth stilled the murmuring senators with a rap of his gavel. "Thank you, Lord-Senator Weston. Senators, what do you say to this?"

Lord-Senator Caraway rose. "I move that we allow Weston to call his alchemists and the captured boy in so we may hear their reports for ourselves."

"Seconded," several senators called, almost at the same time.

"All in favor?" Prime Minister Wentworth asked.

A chorus of ayes rose around the room. Prime Minister Wentworth nodded. "The motion passes. Lord-Senator Weston, call in your people, but keep their number small."

Weston bowed his head slightly. "Thank you, Prime Minister." He beckoned to the page who'd brought him the note and said something Josiah couldn't hear. The page dashed out and returned a few minutes later at a slower pace, leading three people. Josiah recognized one as Madame Gottling, Weston's alchemical expert — no surprise there. The second was a tall, thin man whom Josiah didn't recognize. The last was a boy of twelve or thirteen dressed in a white shirt and black pants, neither of which seemed to fit him particularly well. Both the man and the boy seemed ill at ease; the man hunched his shoulders and neck and kept his hands shoved into his pockets as if trying to make himself appear shorter, while the boy glanced around with wide, wary eyes. Gottling, by contrast, walked as if she owned the place — but, then again, she'd been here before.

They stopped just behind Weston. Weston swept a hand towards them. "These are Madame Gottling and Doctor Baumann, two of my leading researchers in alchemy and the medical sciences, respectively. Both of them have been heavily involved in the research behind the blood alchemy bill. And this —" he indicated the boy — "Is Stephen, also known until recently as Subject 25, an orphan currently kept alive by an artificial lung created and powered through blood alchemy."

On the far side of the room, Senator Frederichs and Senator Aaronson seemed to be having a whispered argument. After a few moments, Aaronson bowed his head slightly. Senator Frederichs turned to the prime minister. "Minister Wentworth, Senator Aaronson and I request that we lead the questioning as the chief opponent to the bill and the leader of the investigative committee, respectively."

"Granted." Prime Minister Wentworth nodded to them. "Begin, please."

Both senators stood and crossed to the other podium. Senator Aaronson cleared his throat. "We will begin by interviewing the boy if that is acceptable."

"Entirely." Weston nodded. "I must inform you, however, that the boy is mute and speaks through sign language. Do either of you gentlemen know signs?"

Both men shook their head. "As I expected." Weston beckoned Gottling forward. "In that case, Madame Gottling will serve as an interpreter, unless anyone else has an aide present who is able to translate?"

Silence. Josiah squeezed his pen so tightly he nearly snapped it in half. Of *course* none of the other senators had aides who could sign. Why would they? No one expected the deaf and mute to appear in the Senate, even though a few senators and nobles, not to mention Josiah himself, had family members who fit those categories and could choose to come if they wanted. And Josiah could've brought someone, but he never brought aides; he didn't need them. He could call for someone . . .

But Senator Frederichs was already speaking. "Acceptable. The boy is able to hear, correct?"

Both Weston and Gottling nodded. "You may address your questions directly to the boy," Weston added. "Madame Gottling will translate his answers."

[203]

"Very well." Senator Frederichs looked at the boy. "We will begin with something simple. Please tell us, for the record, your full name and age."

The boy signed slowly, "Stephen Tanner. Thirteen." Gottling translated verbally a moment after he finished, though Josiah only half-listened to her.

"Thank you." Senator Frederichs made a note on a piece of paper. "Do you have any family, Stephen?"

Stephen shook his head. Again, Gottling translated as he signed. "All dead. Years ago."

"We are sorry for your loss," Senator Aaronson said, sounding genuinely sorry. "Please tell us how you encountered the blood alchemists."

"I was sick. The bleeders found me. Said they could make me better." Stephen screwed up his face. "They made me sleep. I woke up, and I could breathe."

Josiah frowned, narrowing his eyes at Gottling as she related what Stephen had said. Besides switching Stephen's slang, *bleeders*, for the more formal *blood alchemists*, she'd translated *sick* as *dying*. The two words were similar; had it been an innocent mistake? Or something else?

Gottling spoke, though Stephen hadn't signed anything. "If I may clarify, gentlemen, we have investigated the boy's case through the blood alchemists' notes. It seems that he was suffering from an illness of the lungs. The illness, if caught sooner, could have been treated by non-alchemical means, but had advanced such that one of his lungs was essentially non-functioning and would not heal properly. The blood alchemists replaced this lung and increased the activity of the boy's immune system such that the remainder of the illness could be purged."

"Thank you, Madame." Senator Aaronson again addressed Stephen. "How long ago did this occur?"

Stephen considered, then signed, "Two years."

"Interesting." Senator Frederichs made another note on his page. "Have you been with the blood alchemists ever since?"

Stephen nodded but did not offer additional information. Senator Aaronson asked, "Did the blood alchemists do additional experiments on you after they replaced your lung?"

Again, Stephen nodded. "The first lung didn't work long. They changed it. They changed other things too."

Gottling translated, then added, "We have been unable to identify these other changes so far, and the boy has not been forthcoming about what they are. We will continue research, but we currently believe that the other changes were simply further modifications on his lung."

Behind Gottling, Stephen frowned slightly. Josiah raised an eyebrow. Perhaps it was nothing, but perhaps Stephen knew something Gottling wasn't saying . . . Even more reason to try to talk to the boy alone at some point.

Senator Aaronson frowned. "Madame, while we appreciate your clarifications, you'll have your turn to speak." He again addressed Stephen. "Were you forced to stay with the blood alchemists, or did you choose to stay with them?"

Stephen hesitated, glancing first at Gottling, then at Weston, and finally back at Aaronson and Frederichs. "They told me I'd die if I left. So I couldn't leave."

There it was again — the mistranslation. Stephen had said *couldn't* leave. Gottling said *didn't*. Another innocent mistake? Or was Gottling deliberately adjusting what Stephen said to put the blood alchemists in a better light?

"I see." Senator Frederichs made another note. "Do you understand how your artificial lung works?"

Stephen started to shake his head, then stopped. "A little." He touched the front of his shirt, just above the second button, where Josiah could see a very faint red spot. "There's a crystal here. The bleeders put magic in it, and then it makes my lung work like my normal one."

"And how do they put the magic in it?" Frederichs asked.

Stephen screwed up his face, frowning at his hands. His signs slowed as if he were trying to figure out how to say what he wanted to say. "They take the crystal out of me. Then they put it in a glass with blood and other things and heat it. Then they put the crystal back in me."

"Does the process hurt?" Senator Aaronson asked. "Or is it painless?"

Stephen blinked at him as if that were a silly question. "It's hard to breathe. My lung doesn't work while they fix the crystal."

[206]

"Naturally." Senator Aaronson nodded. "But is it painful in other ways as well?"

Stephen just shrugged. "I don't notice."

"Would you show us the crystal?" Senator Frederichs interjected, leaning forward slightly.

Stephen shrugged again and undid the top two buttons of his shirt. Something shone with a dim, red light on his chest. Josiah had to lean forward and peer at the boy to see clearly: a small, clear crystal with a red glowing core, set in a metal socket in the boy's sternum.

Other senators stared as well, muttering among themselves. Stephen stood there, shoulders slumped, head drooping. After only a moment, Aaronson made a gesture. "That will do. Thank you." As Stephen buttoned his shirt back up, Aaronson went on. "I have two more questions for you. First, if you had been given a choice about whether or not the blood alchemists replaced your lung, would you have chosen the replacement?"

Stephen again glanced at Gottling and Weston, drooping as he had before. His hands shook slightly as he signed, "I don't know." Then, with a moment more of hesitation, "Yes."

"Hmm." Senator Aaronson stared at the boy for a long moment. "My last question is this: why are you mute?"

The boy's eyes widened. His hands flew, still shaking, but almost desperate in their hurry. Gottling translated almost as fast: "The illness took his voice."

What? Josiah stiffened, mentally replaying the boy's signs. *That's not what he said.* It wasn't even close. Small wonder, though, that she'd want to hide it — the boy had signed clearly: *"They cut out my tongue."*

CHAPTER 24

They cut out my tongue. Who were "they"? The blood alchemists? Or someone else? Josiah opened his mouth to interrupt the proceedings and ask —

But Senator Frederichs was already speaking. "Thank you. There are no more questions for the boy at this time. At a later time, Lord-Senator, members of the investigative committee may call on you to further speak with Stephen. Now, however, I would like to hear from Madame Gottling and Doctor Baumann on what they learned from the boy and the items found in the blood alchemists' laboratory.

"Naturally." Madame Gottling waved a hand at Stephen, who scurried behind Weston as if glad someone else was now occupying the room's attention. "Shall we summarize our findings and allow you to ask questions afterward?"

"That would be acceptable, yes." Senator Frederichs turned to a new page. "Begin whenever you are ready."

Doctor Baumann stepped up beside Gottling. "Well, er, we shall start with the boy, I suppose . . ."

What followed might have been a summary, if one used the term loosely — but Josiah had never heard a summary that involved such technical language. Doctor Baumann, in particular, seemed determined to use the most obscure possible terms for everything, interspersed with an abundance of "*er*"'s and "*so to speak*"'s. Gottling managed to keep her terminology to an almost-understandable level, but she hedged every statement and softened every would-be solid fact. To make matters worse, both constantly alluded to theories and concepts of which Josiah had never heard — but neither bothered to clarify.

Josiah did his best to keep up, filling three whole pages with a web of connecting terms. Yet by the time they finished, he was only somewhat confident that they had said that Stephen had lived with a blood-alchemy-powered organ for four years with no ill effects; that they could see no reason why there would be complications in the future; and that the design of the lung matched what they already had. There had been something about energy transfer as well, and he thought Gottling had said that the blood alchemists' notes suggested a way to make the crystal-charging process more efficient — or perhaps it was the crystal's output that would be more efficient. Josiah couldn't tell. All he knew for sure was that both considered Stephen's case indisputable proof that blood alchemy was both feasible and reasonable.

Silence fell after they finished. Gottling smiled thinly. "There you have it, sirs. Can we answer any questions?"

"Yes . . . one moment." Senator Frederichs stared at the page on which he'd been taking notes as if trying to decipher something written in a foreign language. Josiah sympathized — but, unfortunately, asking them to repeat the whole thing again, but slower and more clearly wasn't an option.

Josiah glanced at his own notes again, then gave up — he'd need to review them again and rewrite them before they'd be any use for at-a-glance understanding. Instead, he fell back on a question that could apply to any situation. "If I may interject, how certain are you that this boy's case is representative of all potential cases? I imagine that the medical situation for an older man or a woman would be significantly different from his."

Doctor Baumann cleared his throat. "It would, er, not differ such that it would, er, significantly impact the method or success of the, er, transplant. The chief, er, difficulty would be ensuring that the patient's body did not start, er, attacking the organ, er, so to speak. However, the unique, er, properties of alchemical transplants make this unlikely, as they, er, supplement the patient's immune and, er, nervous systems."

"Ah, good. No real concerns in that area, then?" Senator Frederichs made a valiant effort to reclaim control of the conversation. "And could the connection between the implant and the patient's body be lost?"

"Unlikely," Gottling said before Baumann could speak. "We believe that, over time, the alchemical transplant will become more and more integrated with the patient's body. Eventually, there should be no practical difference between the transplant and the patient's original body parts, save that one would take its power from a different source. Furthermore, we believe it likely that, if further, non-theoretical research into blood alchemy is made possible, we may discover a method of blood alchemy that does not require deathblood. If so, we may be able to make alchemical transplants that are semi-self-sustaining in much the same way that many large devices powered by common alchemy are."

"Interesting. And how far in the future would such developments be, Madame?" Senator Frederichs asked, fiddling with his pen.

"That is uncertain. They could take a year or ten years, depending on the number of researchers, among other factors. However, it would not be unreasonable to expect such a discovery within our lifetime." Gottling smiled thinly. "That is, if such research is legalized. If not, then our knowledge will remain largely at its current level."

"Yes, we're aware of that, thank you." A hint of annoyance crept into Senator Frederich's tone. "How certain are you that your results will hold for other transplanted or prosthetic parts? A heart, for instance, or an arm? Would those not present unique difficulties of their own?"

"Certainly they would," Gottling replied crisply. "But, as any doctor will confirm, every medical procedure has its own challenges. No two are exactly the same, even if they treat the same issue in similar people. But, just as treating a wound in a man's leg is different from treating an injury to his chest but both are possible, so also replacing a man's heart or arm would be different from replacing his lung but should be equally possible."

That, at least, made sense. Perhaps he *should* ask Gottling to explain her whole speech more slowly, though not in those words. At this rate, she might actually give useful information. But before Josiah could ask anything, let alone that, Stephen caught his attention again.

The boy had made his way behind Weston, Gottling, and Baumann and sat on the ground, huddled into himself. The red gem glowed behind his shirt, creating a reddish spot almost like a stain. It seemed familiar, though Josiah couldn't place why. More importantly, however, the boy was signing something, repeating the same letters over and over: *H-E-L-P-M-E. Help me.*

Josiah focused on the boy, momentarily distracted from Frederich's questioning of Gottling. Interesting that he should call for help *now* when Weston had ostensibly rescued him from a bad situation. Then again, Weston probably had no qualms about threatening Stephen with bodily harm if he said anything that would counter Weston's claims. And the *they* that he had mentioned . . . Josiah had assumed that Stephen meant the blood alchemists. Could he mean someone connected to Weston instead?

[213]

But, no; Stephen knew sign too well to have learned it only recently. So, either Josiah's first guess had been correct, or the boy had learned sign for a different reason . . . Or Weston had possessed Stephen far longer than he claimed. But if that were the case, why had he not presented the boy as evidence in the first place?

Josiah sighed and turned to a fresh page in his notebook. He began jotting down questions to ask after he convinced Weston to let him speak with the boy privately. The list, however, quickly turned from "questions to ask Stephen" to "questions that need to be answered" — and the latter list grew depressingly fast. For all his work, all his research, he still didn't know half as much as he'd like to.

He flipped back a page and refocused his attention on the Senate floor in time to hear Frederichs ask. "How will the situation change as the boy grows?" Frederichs made a general upwards gesture as if to indicate a child getting taller. "Certainly the same lung made for an eight-year-old will not still be suitable when he is sixteen or thirty or sixty!"

Baumann shook his head. "You are, er, correct. But we do not believe that the, er, alchemists failed to consider that, er, issue. The construction of the, er, lung is designed so that an alchemist or surgeon would be able to do a small additional operation to, er, expand the organ, so to speak. Of course, if the case were different, if the boy had an, er, artificial arm or leg, the, er, alchemist could easily adjust it as he grows."

"In addition, the issue of growth naturally ceases to be an issue after a person reaches a certain age," Gottling added, "And in the future, we may be able to develop artificial organs that *will* grow with a child. Of course, such developments would be years away even if we were able to start research this very day, but they are not impossible."

"I see." Senator Frederichs made one more note on his page. "I believe that is sufficient for now. Again, the investigative committee will wish to speak with you more on this topic at a later time. Thank you for your assistance."

Baumann nodded. Gottling smiled. "Naturally. Are there any further questions from anyone else?"

"Anyone else who wishes to ask additional questions can do so outside of an official Senate meeting." The barest hint of exhausted exasperation laced Prime Minister Wentworth's tone. "The issue of the blood alchemy bill is important, but not so important that we cannot spend time on other topics." He tapped his gavel on his desk. "The Senate will now break for a brief recess. We will reconvene in an hour. Thank you."

Josiah stood and stretched. He blotted his last page, then tucked his notebook in a pocket. In theory, he knew he ought to use this time to get lunch and see to some other small duties. But, on the other hand, he should speak to Weston before he left . . .

He spotted Weston striding up one of the aisles, followed by a group of other senators. Decision time, then, and Josiah barely had to think. A dozen steps took him to the top of the aisle.

Weston slowed slightly as he approached. "Good day, Your Highness. I take it you are looking for me?"

"Yes." Josiah nodded. "You presented some interesting developments today, Lord-Senator. I would be interested in learning more about what you discovered in a more appropriate setting. In particular, I would like to speak directly with the boy you found — Stephen, the one on whom the blood alchemists experimented. I think that hearing the perspective of someone who has experienced the blood alchemist's work would be quite illuminating."

"Naturally." Weston bowed his head slightly. "I would be surprised if you did not, Your Highness. You never are content with a thing until you have done it for yourself." Was that a hint of sarcasm in Weston's tone? Perhaps, but it was too subtle to be insulting. "Shall I have my secretary arrange a meeting?"

"Please do." Josiah nodded. "I look forward to seeing what you've discovered, Lord-Senator, and to interviewing the boy. I do prefer speaking to people myself when I can, particularly when the alternative involves an intermediary. After all, some things do get lost in translation."

To his credit, Weston didn't react to Josiah's jab — but that meant nothing. The man was used to hiding his thoughts and feelings from others. Instead, Weston just smiled tightly. "Understandable, Your Highness. Good day."

He pushed past, and Josiah let him go. Perhaps he shouldn't have reminded Weston that he knew sign and given away that advantage — but he'd rather have Weston on edge any day. People, even Weston, made mistakes when they were nervous, after all.

But for now . . . Josiah checked his pocket watch. *Lunchtime.* And then he'd see what else he could accomplish before he returned to the Senate meeting this afternoon — though he doubted anything to come could compete with the morning's revelations.

CHAPTER 25

This was a bad idea.

Breen lay on her stomach on a beam, hugging it with her arms and legs as her back protested every movement. Why had she been so *stupid?* She knew she was never well enough to work, really work, two days after a beating. But the medicine had made her feel so much better — not good as new, but still. So, after she finished tending to the parts of the clock she could easily reach, she'd thought maybe she'd healed enough to risk the harder areas.

And now here she was, clinging to a beam as pain lanced up and down her back and shoulders, regretting every decision that had led to this moment.

Grimacing, she managed to push herself into a sitting position and scoot slowly along the beam, pausing every few moments so the pain in her back would subside. Once she reached the walkway, she gave herself one last push and tumbled onto the wooden floor. There, she lay on her back, wincing. Why, oh *why*, had she been such an idiot?

What now? She couldn't lay here forever. Theoretically, she supposed she should go rest more. But she didn't want to go lay on her cot and pretend she was going to get to sleep before night. And she couldn't go up and watch the city like she might any other day. Well, realistically, that left only one option . . .

Eventually, the pain her back eased enough for her to stand up and head for the stairs. She wandered down through the levels until she reached the third floor. There, she carefully sorted through boxes and shelves, gathering up armloads of parts and spreading them out in the center of the room.

There, she sat down and surveyed what she'd gathered. Slowly, she picked out pieces from the spread and started to fit them together. At first, she worked almost aimlessly, creating connections simply to see how they would grow. However, as she continued to work, she recognized the configuration. She'd worked on it just days before: the central portion of her lift mechanism.

As the realization dawned, she set down her parts and tools and stared at the assemblage of gears and rods. The last version of the device had brought her nothing but trouble. If she hadn't told Josiah about it, if he hadn't brought Luis, if she and Luis hadn't stayed up so late, if she hadn't been so caught up working on the lift device instead of doing her real work . . . If not for all that, she wouldn't have been beaten; she wouldn't be in trouble with Madame now.

Was it worth recreating what had caused her so much strife? Breen picked up the next piece of the device and turned it over in her hands. What good would it do, really? She couldn't use the device in the tower; Madame had made that much clear. And this wasn't like her other creations; she wanted to do more with it than just wrap it up and set it on a shelf. If that was all she was working for, what was the point?

But *was* it all she was working for? Breen recalled what Josiah and Luis had said that night. They'd both been confident that, if she ever left the tower, the lift device would get her into the Inventors' Guild. That was something — *if* she left the tower.

She *couldn't* leave, though. Not if she wanted to live. She'd learned that already. Sooner rather than later, the crystal in her chest would run out of power, and her heart would stop for good. She needed Madame to recharge it, and she only had Madame if she stayed in the tower.

For a fleeting moment, Breen wished she'd paid better attention before she'd come to the tower. Maybe then she'd know how to keep herself alive. Maybe then she could try to survive outside the tower — an illegal survival, true, but she was already illegal. The only difference would be more people to try to hide it from.

Almost as soon as the thought crossed her mind, Breen squashed it, clenching her hand around the gear so the teeth bit into her palm. Even if she had the knowledge, she'd need materials — and those she couldn't get, one in particular. *Every heart requires blood*, Madame had said once, back when Breen could still hear.

Some require more blood than others. That was certainly true in Breen's case.

And that was the sticking point. Enough people's lives had already been spent to keep Breen alive. She couldn't — *wouldn't* — make anyone else die for her, no matter what. Who was she to judge her own life more valuable than someone else's when she knew it wasn't? What gave her any right to make that decision? Nothing. Nothing at all.

With a sigh, Breen set aside the gear and started to dismantle what she'd built. Better not to waste her time; better to make something insignificant, something that could just sit on a shelf and be taken out occasionally. Better to leave the lift device and the trouble it had caused behind entirely.

Except . . . Breen paused before taking apart the last few pieces. Perhaps it *wasn't* pointless. After all, *she* didn't have to get use out of a thing for it to be worth something.

Breen stared at her device without really seeing it, unable to shake the idea running through her head. She could remake her lift device, make it even better than before. Then, she'd ask Josiah or Luis to sell it for her. Probably not Josiah, not now that she knew he was the prince, but maybe Luis would be willing. And whatever profit the device made, Luis could send to her family. True, Josiah said he'd give them work and board at the palace, and she trusted that he'd do as he said. But the extra money from her device might be enough to give some of her siblings a better education or a chance at an apprenticeship. That was worth doing.

With that thought in mind, Breen started reassembling what she'd just taken apart. She would have to be more careful about her work this time around so she wouldn't get in trouble with Madame again. But that was nothing really new; she always had to be careful. And if it worked . . . well, maybe she could sell other inventions too.

Of course, then she really would be stealing from Madame. Breen chewed on her lip, considering. She couldn't put herself in more debt to Madame and Madame's people. She couldn't give them any greater hold over her. But she couldn't build anything with no parts . . .

Perhaps she could ask Josiah to bring her what she needed and pay him back out of what she earned on the device. She'd recreate the device with what she had here, then do it again with parts she wouldn't be stealing. That would still put her in debt to Josiah, but it would be a different sort than her debt to Madame and the others. And, despite all his flaws, she trusted that Josiah wouldn't try to collect more than he was owed. In fact, she might have the opposite problem: would he accept payment?

She could cross that bridge when she came to it, though. For now, she would focus on actually remaking the device — this time without getting a beating over it. And so, she set to work.

Breen kept working until the light outside began to fade. Then she cleaned up the level, moving stiffly and slowly to keep her back from hurting too much. She hid her partially-finished lift device in the same spot she'd hid the previous one; if Madame hadn't found the first, she probably wouldn't find this one.

She double-checked the whole level, then returned to the top floor. Her stomach grumbled, but she didn't retrieve her bundle from its hiding place on the clock face level. Madame might return tonight, and she'd expect Breen to be starving and in pain.

And not bandaged. Breen carefully unbuttoned her shirt and slipped it off. That, at least, she could do with minimal pain. Then she untied the first of the bandages wrapped around her and tugged it off. She let out a hiss of pain as the cloth pulled free of the cut beneath it. Did she really need to remove *all* these bandages?

Yes. Yes, she did. She couldn't risk Madame finding out that anyone else had been here. And she'd have to change the bandages later anyway. Breen untied and unwrapped another strip of cloth, wincing. Why did it have to *hurt* so much?

Breen finished undoing the bandages and put her shirt back on. She'd have to hide the bandages somewhere; upstairs seemed the best option. She hurried up the stairway, bundling the cloth together as she went. Once up there, she crept to the southeast corner, keeping low and as much out of the view of the clock faces as possible. In that far corner, she stood, steeled herself, and then jumped.

Her back screamed in pain, but she just managed to wedge the bundle in the corner atop a beam. Then she landed, stumbled, and dropped to her knees. *Ow.* Breen pushed herself back to her feet, only for another burst of pain to shoot up her back. She stumbled into the wall, smacking her head against the stone.

Stars burst in front of her eyes. The crystal in her chest warmed ever so slightly. The spot on her head tingled, pain and heat mingling as the damage reversed — slowly. The feeling lingered too long, almost as long as it did when she fell all the way down the tower. And when it faded, it left her dizzy and gasping for breath.

This wasn't good. Breen lowered herself to her knees and crawled over to the stairs. She went down them backward, moving as unsteadily as a child who hadn't yet learned to walk. Once on the next level down, she made her way over to her bed and pulled herself in. She lay atop the blanket, trying to keep her eyes from drifting shut. She had a vague idea that she shouldn't fall asleep when she felt like this . . .

But she couldn't help it.

CHAPTER 26

Breen's chest *burned*. Every cut and bruise on her back flared with pain, and every nerve tingled like she'd been struck by lightning. She woke gasping, heart as close to pounding as it ever came.

She blinked. Madame Gottling stood over her bed, scowling. With sharp hands, she signed, "Your crystal was drained almost to the last drop. What were you thinking?"

Breen sat up. Her head spun, and she swayed for a moment before steadying herself enough to reply. "I'm sorry. I knew you were angry with me. I knew I had failed you. I wanted to fix my mistake. I thought I could get up and really work, but I hurt myself. I'm sorry."

Madame gave a slight toss of her head. "Foolish. But your attempt to make up for your mistake is something." Without another word, she turned on her heel and went to the cupboard. There, she started unloading provisions of dark, dry bread and small potatoes into the cupboard.

Breen glanced around. The first thing she noticed was that the lift was fixed; someone had mounted the pulley back on the beam and threaded the chain through it. Madame hadn't done that; certainly.

She turned towards the stairs. A boy sat on the top step. He couldn't have been more than thirteen; too young for even a trace of stubble or facial hair, with arms and legs that looked too long for his body — save for his left arm, which was made of copper and steel. He stared at her, silent and wide-eyed.

Breen glanced at Gottling. She was still busy, but not for much longer. Could she risk a smile? A few signs? Her fingers twitched. She couldn't get in trouble again so soon; she couldn't get someone else in trouble; but the boy looked scared . . .

She only had a few moments left to say anything. Keeping one eye on Madame, Breen made a few quick signs: "You'll be all right. Don't be afraid."

Hollow comfort, she knew, given why he was probably here. Madame wouldn't have brought him solely to fix the pulley. More than likely, she meant the visit as a warning for the boy: *This is what happens when you defy me too often. This is what happens when you fail me.* For many, simply visiting the tower — or the other, worse, places where one might be forced to work — was reason enough to fall in line. But if the threat of isolated imprisonment wasn't enough, the results of the brutal beatings usually were.

She only had a moment more. Breen's hands flew with one last small encouragement. "The pain always fades."

[228]

That was a bit of a lie, maybe. Sometimes, the pain didn't fade. Sometimes you just grew so used to it that you didn't care anymore. But it was the closest thing to true that she could tell him.

The boy's expression didn't change. Perhaps he didn't know sign yet, or perhaps he just hadn't learned enough to understand her. Or maybe he understood her, and he had already learned that the best way to keep Madame and the others happy was to act as scared and submissive as possible. Breen hoped it was the last.

Madame turned and faced Breen. "Have you learned your lesson now about wasting your time and stealing from us?"

Breen nodded once, keeping her eyes downcast. "Yes, Madame. I won't do it again." Except, of course, she would. She'd just be more careful this time.

"Good." Madame picked up her bag and walked to the lift. She faced the boy. "Meet me downstairs." Then she looked expectantly at Breen.

Oh no. Breen's back ached just at the thought of operating the lift. But if she protested, Madame would just say that if she was well enough to try to work, she was well enough for this. Stiffly, she slid off her cot and pulled the lift back up so it was level with the floor.

Madame stepped into the center of the platform and stood, arms crossed. Breen took a deep breath, then slowly lowered the platform, inch by inch. She clutched the chain with a white-knuckled grip as tiny jets of pain arced up and down her back.

Her grip slipped. The lift dropped. Breen grabbed the chain and stopped it again just in time, but the movement set her muscles screaming. She couldn't let the lift fall. She couldn't. She'd done so before — on purpose that time — and she remembered too well what would happen. Madame would be fine; she had her alchemy to protect her. But the punishment she'd inflict on Breen would make her recent beating seem like nothing.

The chain slipped again as Breen released her grip with one hand. She grabbed it again, clutching the links with a death grip. Madame was out of sight now, but there was still a long way to go . . .

She felt tremors in the floor and glanced to the side. The boy approached with swift steps, the fear in his face replaced by solemn determination. Breen shook his head at him and spoke aloud, hoping he hadn't lost his hearing already by some other method. "You'll get hurt."

He shrugged and signed back, "You said the pain fades." He placed his hands between hers on the chain, and together they lowered the lift.

This poor boy. No wonder Madame had brought him here; no wonder she was trying to scare him into submission. How long until he was stuck in a tower — or worse — simply because his kindness overwhelmed his sense of self-preservation?

For a fleeting moment, Breen wondered if somehow Josiah could save this boy, even if he couldn't save her. A one-armed boy could survive without blood alchemy. Life might be hard for him, but Josiah might be able to find him work, and that would make things a little easier. It would be better than being trapped like Breen — and while Breen could see how she might deserve this fate, this boy didn't.

The chain went slack as the lift settled onto the ground below. The boy flashed her a frightened smile and dashed towards the steps. He disappeared in a few moments, moving so quickly Breen feared he'd fall.

Though he couldn't see it, Breen signed, "Thank you." Just in case someone was listening, she silently prayed that Madame would be lenient. That she wouldn't hurt him too much for his kindness. She knew there was little chance of that, especially if Madame was already displeased with him. But she could hope.

Now for dinner. Breen crossed to the cupboard and checked what was inside. Madame had left more than she did last week, but Breen doubted that she'd increased her rations so soon. More likely, she wasn't planning to come back for over a week.

That bought Breen some time. It also meant she'd have to be more careful not to fall too often, but she could live with that. She'd take a day or two longer to let her back heal and to work on her lift device. Then, she'd clean every inch of the tower until the gears shone as brightly as the crystals. And then, maybe when Madame returned, she would be pleased, and everything would go back to normal.

Well, normal except for Josiah and Grace and Luis and her plans for the lift device. But if they became normal as well . . . Breen managed a smile. She could live with a new normal.

CHAPTER 27

It was strange, Josiah had often reflected, how the best way to make people take notice of something was to convince them it was a secret. You could make a hundred public speeches, and people would ignore you — or, worse, claim you were lying or putting on an act to win their favor. But as soon as there was conspiracy involved, people paid attention, and they believed what they heard.

That tendency had annoyed Josiah on more than one occasion in the past. But he certainly wasn't above using it to his advantage either. Take today, for instance. To the untrained observer, it would seem that Josiah was doing his best to go out without notice: taking an unmarked carriage through back streets just after dawn. However, those whose job it was to pay attention would notice the details: the horses were unmistakably the type favored by the Royal Stables; Josiah, though in plain clothes, wore no hat and kept his signet ring on his finger; and the early hour meant there were no other carriages on the street that could hide his.

Any spy or informant who happened to be watching would recognize Josiah easily, of course. Most would probably assume that he was just doing a shoddy job of *not* being recognized. The wiser among them might guess his true goal — but they would also know the value of knowing what your opponent wanted you to know along with what they didn't.

The carriage stopped in front of Senator Aaronson's townhouse, and a footman in black scuttled up the stairs to inquire if the senator was at home. Josiah waited in the carriage and laughed to himself. How many people had marked his passage from the palace to the just-barely-genteel neighborhood where Aaronson lived? No doubt in a few hours the leading nobles and senators would be panicking over the fact that the crown prince was meeting in secret with the head of the Workers' party instead of doing so openly as usual.

What reason would they guess for the meeting? The Loyalists would likely fear that the crown's unofficial favor would pass from them to the Workers — and if so, good! Perhaps they'd look for what the Workers' party was doing right. The Progressives — thus far the most vocal supporters of the blood alchemy bill outside of Weston's main following — would panic over the fact that the two biggest opponents of the bill were collaborating.

And Weston himself . . . he was clever enough to guess Josiah's goals. But he was also intelligent enough to recognize the danger to himself. Public preference often followed the crown's favor, and the Workers' party hated Weston almost unanimously.

The footman returned and informed Josiah that Senator Aaronson was indeed here and would be honored to receive him. Josiah nodded and hurried into the house, ducking his head and glancing from side to side in an exaggerated fashion. Halfway up the steps, he wondered if he were laying it on a bit too thick, but he couldn't go back now.

Inside, a butler led Josiah down halls with worn carpeting and sparse decorations. Josiah could read the furnishings like a book: this was the home of a man trying to appear suitably cultured without spending more than the absolute minimum.

They reached a narrow door, which the butler opened with a bow. "His Royal Highness, Prince Josiah."

Senator Aaronson stood as Josiah entered. The man's appearance matched his house: a bit shabby, certainly not elegant, and just this side of genteel. But his face was honest, and his hands were those of a worker, and what he lacked in privilege, he made up for in passion. "Your Highness." He made a short bow. "How can I help you?"

Josiah gestured for Aaronson to sit back down. "How you can help me, Senator, is by telling me how I can help you."

To Senator Aaronson's credit, his only reaction was to raise his eyebrows in surprise. "I beg your pardon, Your Highness?"

"I believe you heard me correctly." Josiah helped himself to Senator Aaronson's second chair as he spoke. "We are not blind to your efforts on behalf of the common man. And while we cannot, of course, give you our official support any more than we can give it to any individual or party, we would be glad to quietly do what we can to further your aims. So, I repeat, how can we help you?"

Senator Aaronson blinked, looking as if he might fall over. Instead, he sat down heavily in his own seat and stared at the papers on his desk as if he'd never seen them before. After several long moments, he recovered. "On behalf of those I represent, thank you, Your Highness. In answer to your question . . ." He relaxed; no doubt this was more familiar territory. "The better question is how can you *not* help? Our resources are spread thin as we try to meet every need, and the bills and petitions proposed by our members and those we represent rarely reach the Senate floor. And, of course, there is the problem of the blood alchemy bill."

"Indeed. Quite a problem that is." Josiah leaned forward slightly. "Tell me, Senator Aaronson, what do you think of the bill? You have argued earnestly against it on the floor, but what do you believe will occur if it is passed? Do you believe good can come of it?"

"Good?" Senator Aaronson shook his head. "Good for some. But ill for more, whatever Lord-Senator Weston says. I'll freely admit, Your Highness, I'm not surprised so many otherwise good men are backing him. I've done research of my own into the matter, and I'd not be surprised if blood alchemy can indeed do all he claims it can. Old accounts record more miracles than monsters, if I'm being honest. Or perhaps they're the same thing, just seen from different sides. There are plenty of stories about men and women who could survive anything short of beheading, or who lived a hundred years or more when the folk around them were lucky to survive to thirty. Good things, Your Highness.

"Good things, indeed." Josiah leaned forward slightly, tilting his head. "Yet you're still concerned."

"Of course I am. Everything has a cost, Your Highness. In blood alchemy, that cost is blood." Aaronson raised an eyebrow. "My question is, who's paying it?"

"Weston claims it will be paid by criminals as their debt to society," Josiah replied. "I take it you have a different answer?"

"I do." Senator Aaronson shuffled through papers on his desk until he found the one he wanted. "It'll start with the criminals, sure enough, and I could almost support that. But it won't end with them. We don't have enough criminals, frankly.

"Weston's already proposed the next step, saying that the people injured or ill to the point of death could choose to die so another could live," Aaronson went on. "And I'll give him this much: it's not the worst idea anyone's proposed in the Senate — as long as it's the person's choice and not the doctor's. And that's my first worry: how long until it's not their decision?"

Josiah nodded slowly, recognizing Aaronson's train of thought. "You're worried that doctors will start pressuring their patients into dying for the greater good?"

"Or worse!" Aaronson exclaimed. "What happens when doctors give up on a man while there's still hope so they can bleed him out for a so-called noble cause? Or the criminals; how long until judges decide a man's blood is more valuable than a fair sentence? It wouldn't happen to the rich and the nobles, no. They can fight back." Aaronson clenched his hands around his papers so tightly that they crumpled, as if he wanted to give those people someone to fight here and now. "But the poor? Those who struggle to be heard at all? That's another thing."

"I see your point. And I share your frustration with how the poor are frequently overlooked." Josiah paused. "But I doubt that the bill will pass at all if we don't place heavy regulations on whose blood can be used. Those regulations would apply to everyone, regardless of social class."

"Can you guarantee that, Your Highness? And can you guarantee that the regulations will stay? You can't, no more than I can." A reddish flush crept over Aaronson's face, and his practiced upper-class accent started to fade into the native accent of the lower middle class. "The regulations will be relaxed eventually. And then? Most of the upper classes already act like the poor are less than human. They enslave people in working conditions that practically guarantee early death.

"Blood alchemy will just make everything worse. The prejudices will grow. Eventually, the blood of the poor will turn into a commodity. Men, women, and children will sell their lives so their families can survive a little longer. Suicide will become acceptable as long as you're giving your blood for the greater good. And on the streets?"

Senator Aaronson took a breath, almost shaking with anger. "Your Highness, you try to keep your finger on what happens in the city, but you don't know the streets like my people do. We see people — children — disappear every week, and no one takes any notice. They know *better* than to notice because they know who takes them: the cursed bleeders! Ask the people on the streets and in the slums. They'll confirm it — but we can't get actual evidence, so we can't do anything about it."

"The blood alchemy bill might stop that," Josiah spoke quickly. "If the blood alchemists have a legal source . . . ?"

"It won't stop them. It'll just make it easier for them to hide what they're doing." Aaronson paused, breathing deep as he tried to calm down. "Blood alchemy could do good, Your Highness, but only in the right hands — and those right hands don't exist in this city. Perhaps not in this whole world."

"I see, and I understand your concerns. I appreciate your honesty. You've given me significantly more clarity in this issue." Josiah kept his tone calm and measured. "How, then, would you have me help with this matter or any other?"

"Make sure everyone knows the risks, Your Highness. *All* the risks. Remind people of the effect this will have on the whole country." Senator Aaronson leaned forward, arms on the desk. "I know you have access to the investigative committee. Raise my points with them. Raise them with other senators — with Caraway and those like him. They won't give me the time of day when protocol doesn't demand it, but they listen to you. And if you can,

[239]

if this madness ever ends, try to point him and others towards the other problems we face — poor education and working and living conditions and everything else. Help them understand that protecting the rights of the poor will benefit them as well."

"I can do that, certainly." Much of it, he would do anyway. "What more?"

"Well . . ." Senator Aaronson paused; clearly, this wasn't a question he got asked often. "Protection for our orators, perhaps. There have been riots in lecture halls when other groups try to stop us from speaking. I understand that you can't officially endorse us, but if you could make sure we have the same chance to spread our message as any other party does, I'd appreciate it."

"I will see to it." Josiah added increased guards in lecture halls to his mental list of things to discuss with his father. "What about monetary needs?"

Senator Aaronson cleared his throat. "The Workers' Party doesn't accept donations. We'd rather people give their money to charities, churches and so on."

"Ah, yes. Focus on the community. I expect you have a list of recommended charities and such that people can give to?" Josiah waited for Aaronson's nod. "Excellent. Have one of your assistants send me a list of those by the end of the day, and I'll see what I can personally do."

Aaronson nodded. "I'll have my secretary do that as soon as possible. Thank you, Your Highness."

"No, senator, thank you for the stand you make and for your time this morning." Josiah stood. "I am sure you have other duties to attend to, so I will take my leave now. Good day, and may Jeros bless your efforts."

"And yours, Your Highness." Senator Aaronson rose as well and bowed. "Thank you for listening."

Josiah nodded and departed. That was one errand down. His other would have to wait — but in the meantime, Aaronson had given him plenty to think about.

CHAPTER 28

Cabs and carriages filled the streets when Josiah again left the palace that afternoon, this time riding in a nondescript hackney cab pulled by a plain brown mare. Josiah grinned as he watched the crowds outside and adjusted his hat and the lapels of his charcoal grey jacket. Good luck to anyone trying to spot him in this crowd! It was the busiest time of day, and he was in a cab just like a hundred others, wearing a suit that made him indistinguishable from any young government clerk. With all that to aid him, he was practically invisible.

The cab took a circuitous route through the streets of Rivenford, stalling occasionally as it was caught in the crush of people trying to get to the next event or duty of the day. Once it crossed the main bridge across the Trevis River, however, the cab moved more quickly. There were fewer vehicles here; the cabs Josiah saw were typically shabby, much-used affairs. They and the dirty streets drew a stark contrast with the occasional carriage that rolled by, all sleek, shiny things of the type preferred by factory bosses drunk on new money.

As the carriage traveled deeper into the slums, Josiah had to force himself to keep watching out the window and not to look away from what he saw. The ragged children; the dead-eyed men; the women, gaunt all over except for occasional pregnant bellies — the fact that people lived in such states made Josiah feel sick. But he had to look, had to see them, to remind himself that each person was an individual and not just part of a great mass of less fortunate. These people were who he fought for: people who had so little and yet could do so much if they were only given the chance . . .

The cab stopped in front of a tenement building. Daubs of hardened river mud covered cracks and chinks in the rough board walls, and many of the cracked windows were tacked over with scraps of wood or layers of newsprint.

Josiah stepped down from the cab, holding a leather portfolio notebook, conscious of eyes watching him from windows and alleys and sidewalks. What did they see when they looked at him? A government man come to collect a debt unpaid? A churchman trying to save souls and offer barely-welcome charity? A mark to be robbed?

No matter. Josiah walked up to the tenement and rapped on the door. It shuddered beneath his knuckles as if a stronger blow would take it off its hinges. After a moment, the door creaked halfway open to reveal a short woman with grey-streaked hair and weary, reddened eyes. Something about her face reminded him of

Breen, or how Breen would look if she were older and worn by a different kind of care.

"Yes, mister?" The woman looked him up and down, eyes narrowed. "We've paid our taxes already."

"I am not here for taxes, Mistress Wellens." Josiah adjusted his grip on the portfolio. "I am an agent of the crown with an important message for you about one of your family members. Is your husband home?"

"He isn't. He'll be at the factory until late tonight." She pressed her lips together into a thin line. "You're welcome to tell me the message."

"Unfortunately, I need to speak to both of you at once. As I said, the message is of considerable importance. So, it would be ideal if your husband could return from work now." Josiah offered what he hoped was a friendly smile. "I am fully prepared to compensate you both for any wages he might lose by doing so."

The woman shook her head. "He'll lose more than wages if he comes home early. He'll lose our whole livelihood. Begging your pardon, but I don't think your message is near that important."

Ah, yes. Josiah had expected something like this. He swore; he had to get the Senate to do something about the way the factories were run. Maybe that could be his next project . . .

But right now, he had other things to focus on. Josiah opened the portfolio and took out of the folded papers he'd tucked inside the front cover. "I assure you that your husband will not lose his job. The Crown will make sure of it." He held up the paper so she

[245]

could see the royal family's seal on the outside. "This is a letter for your husband's employers, informing them that your husband has been called away by a representative of the crown and that there will be consequences if they attempt to penalize him or his family for the time spent away from his work."

Mistress Wellens peered at the seal. "And how do I know that's what it is?"

"You have my word, mistress." Josiah kept his tone carefully polite and even. "Is there someone with whom I could send this letter and a note explaining the situation to your husband?"

Mistress Wellens eyed him a moment longer. Then she nodded sharply, turned, and called into the house, "Tom! Come here!"

The sound of running footsteps came from within, and a dirty-faced boy appeared behind Mistress Wellens. "Yes, Ma?"

"Tom, this man wants you to take a message to your da." Mistress Wellens moved aside so her child could step out the door. "The factory bosses might not let Tom through."

"I have already considered that, mistress. It will not be an issue." Josiah knelt so he was on eye-level with Tom. He handed him the first paper, along with a note he'd written that morning for Mister Wellens. "Take these directly to your father." He removed another sealed envelope from the portfolio. "If anyone tries to stop you at the factory, give him this. Do you understand?"

Tom glanced at his mother for approval. Then he nodded, grabbed both notes, and took off down the street. Josiah stood and faced Mistress Wellens again. "I apologize for the trouble, mistress, but this matter truly cannot wait."

"So you say." Mistress Wellens's voice held a tremor that might've been either fear or anger. "But I want to know what kind of news is so important that you have to tell it now, but you can't tell it just to me and be done with it."

"I will explain everything once your husband arrives, mistress." Josiah smiled again, as disarmingly as he could. "Please, trust me."

"It seems I don't have a choice." Mistress Wellens scowled. Apparently, she was no more disarmed by a smile than was her daughter — no surprise there. He considered trying to continue the conversation, but somehow he suspected that taking even a friendly interest would put Mistress Wellens more on guard.

So, they stood there, Mistress Wellens staring at Josiah and Josiah studying the whole street. He smiled at a few passers-by, but they mostly just looked away.

Finally, Mister Wellens appeared, storming down the street with Tom in tow. He headed straight for Josiah, shoulders tensed and hands balled into fists as if he were ready to take a swing in defense of his family. "What's this about, then? I'm about my work when Tom comes running in with a note telling me to come home hours early. Then when I show the other note to my bosses, he rushes me out of the factory like the world's on fire."

"As I told your wife, Mister Wellens, I have important news for you about one of your family members. In addition, I have a few questions I would like to ask you both." Josiah glanced from one to the other. "May I come inside?"

"Suppose so." Mister Wellens nodded to Mistress Wellens, who stepped back and opened the door slightly more.

"Pardon the mess," she added, stiffly, as Josiah stepped inside.

"What mess, mistress?" Josiah gave her what he hoped was a friendly smile and stepped inside. The room in which he found himself was relatively clean, as much as one could keep a clean house in the slums. A few wobbly chairs sat around a rough wooden table, and a small fire burned in the stove. A much-mended curtain off to one side offered privacy for a sleeping area.

"Thank you." Josiah again faced the couple. "This may take some time. Could we sit?"

"Suppose," Mister Wellens said again. He and his wife sat, pulling their chairs to the same side of the table.

Josiah sat across from them and set his portfolio on the table. Here was the tricky part — the moment that would determine if he'd found the right family or not. "First of all, Miss Breen sends her greetings and misses you considerably."

He'd expected the telltale flinch at Breen's name — but he hadn't expected either Mister or Mistress Wellens to recover so quickly. Mistress Wellens's expression went as flat as her daughter's ever did, while Mister Wellens shook his head. "I don't know who you're talking about."

"I believe you do." Josiah kept his voice calm, quiet. "Your daughter, Breen. She's about twenty, with her mother's face and

[248]

her father's hair. A brilliant young woman who could have a very promising future if she wasn't confined to a clock tower. I admit that it's possible that you're not the family I intended to talk to, but based on your reaction a moment ago, I believe that you are."

A flicker of some emotion that Josiah couldn't identify momentarily broke through Mistress Wellens's flat look. Mister Wellens's brows drew together, and his eyes narrowed. "How do you know all this?"

Confirmation. Excellent. "Because I met Miss Breen just under a month ago," he replied. "I saw her in the clock tower and decided to investigate. She was reluctant to give details of her situation or her past, even after I made my desire to help her clear. However, she is concerned for your safety, so she eventually gave me the information I needed in order to find you."

"What else did she tell you?" Mistress Wellens asked, gripping her husband's hand tight — perhaps reassuring, perhaps seeking reassurance, perhaps both. "Did she say why she thinks we're in trouble?"

"I hoped you might be able to answer some of those questions." Josiah turned to a fresh page in his portfolio. "Miss Breen informed me that she owes someone a life debt and that if she runs away, one of her siblings will have to work in her place. She also told me that her life is somehow tied to the clock tower in which she is held and which she tends. Beyond that, she has revealed relatively little other than the fact that there are others who share her plight. Perhaps you can fill in the details?"

[249]

"We could." Mister Wellens spoke slowly. "But we aren't meant to speak of it either. Why should we trust you?"

"An excellent question." This, too, Josiah had expected. "I am, as I said earlier, a representative of the crown. You saw the seal on the letter to your overseer. I hope that would give some indication of my allegiance. Beyond that, I can say only that Breen trusts me enough to send me to you, and that my aim is to ensure her good — and yours. If you choose not to trust me, I will not hold it against you. But I hope that you will believe me."

Mister and Mistress Wellens looked at each other, almost seeming to converse without words. Then they turned back to Josiah. "Fair enough," Mister Wellens said. "We'll tell you what we know, the little there is. But what do we get from it?"

"The crown's protection and, if you desire it, a better situation." Josiah paused. "To be clear, I am prepared to offer you those things whether or not you share what you know. However, I will be better able to protect you and your family and help Miss Breen if I know what to prepare for."

"That'll do." Mister Wellens took a deep breath. "Well. It happened some ten years ago. Breen and Lily —"

Josiah held up a hand. "A moment. Lily?"

"Another of our daughters. Breen's twin," Mistress Wellens replied, pressing her lips together. "She's . . . no longer with us."

"I see." Josiah inclined his head slightly. "My condolences for your loss."

Mistress Wellens just nodded. Mister Wellens continued. "As I was saying, Breen and Lily'd just started work in one of the weaving factories. Missus Wellens and I were none too happy about it, but we needed the money. So, off they went. Then, not a month in, there's an accident at the factory. One of the machines broke, and Breen and Lily were both near killed.

"Some folks at the factory pulled them out and sent another man to let me know what happened. Our girls were barely hanging on to life when I got there. A few friends and me took them to the free hospital at the edge of the river — you know the place?" Mister Wellens waited for Josiah's nod before going on. "They couldn't do naught, though. Just said they'd make the girls comfortable as they could. And then . . . *they* showed up."

Josiah raised an eyebrow. "'They'? Who do you refer to?"

"Bleeders. Blood alchemists, you'd call 'em." Mister Wellens's fists tightened, and bitterness saturated his tone. "They said they could save one of our girls, maybe even both of them, if the girls would work for them afterward."

"And we said yes." Mistress Wellens let out a shaky breath. "Like fools. We thought it was our only choice."

"It was our only choice if we wanted our girls to live. And we did." Mister Wellens shook his head. "I would've let the bloody criminals cut *me* open if that's what it'd take — if not for the missus and our other children, anyway. As it was, trading a life's work for a life to work in seemed fair enough. So, they took the girls out of the hospital, off to their place, and well . . ."

He trailed off, shaking his head. Mistress Wellens took up the story. "They came back the next day. They had Lily's body. They said she hadn't survived long enough for them to save her. But they brought Breen with them too, lively as if she'd never been hurt."

"They saved her life." Mister Wellens almost whispered the words. "How I don't know, and I don't want to know. I knew what they were; I saw the signs of their guild on 'em. But I wanted my little girl back, and I didn't care. And then I got her back, and I cared even less. But . . ." His expression clouded. "Then, a week after, they came back and took Breen away. They said we'd made a bargain, her life for her work, and that it was none of my business where or what that work was or if I'd get to see her again. As if I didn't have a right to know if my girl was well!"

"They let us see her once, a year after they took her," Mistress Wellens added. "Just for an hour. She looked better fed and clothed than she ever had here, though I hate to say so, and she said they had her serving in their guild-hall on a manor outside the city, and that they were teaching her to read and to talk some special hand-language. And then we thought maybe we'd made the right choice after all.

"But after that year . . . they didn't bring her back. ." Mistress Wellens paused, lost for a moment in memory. "We saw her once again after that. She came alone, said she'd run away. She said they'd moved her, that she was taking care of one of the clock towers, and that she never saw anyone and missed us terribly. She still looked all right then, but her eyes and her spirit were dead."

[252]

"We thought about trying to hide her," Mister Wellens said. "Then *they* came before we could try, and they dragged her off. She didn't fight them either, but not like she wanted to go. More like she was scared of what would happen if she struggled." She shook her head. "That's all either of us can tell you."

"Thank you both. I understand that this is a difficult subject to talk about." Josiah jotted down the last of the notes from their stories. "Mister Wellens, you said you recognized the sign of the blood alchemists. How do you know what it is?"

Mister Wellens shrugged. "It's hardly a secret, this part of the city. The bleeders show up any time there's a bad accident, hover 'round the edges, and watch for anyone almost dead — like they did with Breen and Lily. Sometimes they hunt through the streets too, find anyone weak enough that they can't resist and take them away. After a while, you learn to spot them. They're usually the best-dressed people about, and even if they're trying to blend in, they've always got some fancy jewels on them. Always a red stone, and usually set in gold. It glows a bit if you get a good look at it."

"I see." Josiah hid his disappointment. Of course the blood alchemists wouldn't be foolish enough to put a physical mark on their bodies or even their clothes. But a red stone set in gold was too common an accessory among the nobility — including some who Josiah knew wouldn't be involved in blood alchemy — to be a good identifying feature. "Could you recognize any of the blood alchemists if you saw them again?"

Mister Wellens considered this. "Maybe. Not likely. Odd thing about them; you'll see them near accidents or on the streets, like I said, but you can't get a good look at their faces. Any time you try, they go all shimmery. Some sort of alchemy magic, I'd guess."

Josiah nodded slowly. "Unsurprising." He recalled clearly a discussion with the court alchemists about creating illusions; so far, the best anyone could do was make something look blurry or wavering, as if it were a distant desert mirage. "What about when you interacted with them directly?"

"They wore masks." Mister Wellens paused. "One of them, though, a woman with a foreign accent — I saw her with her mask off. I'd recognize her again. Already have, actually; I saw her in a picture in the papers recently. She was with one of the lords, sort of behind him."

Aha! Here was a lead! If Josiah could trace the practice of blood alchemy back to the household of a specific nobleman . . . "Which noble, do you know?"

Mister Wellens dropped his voice. "Lord-Senator Weston. Most folk know better than to speak ill of that man, at least in public, but I'll say this: at least one of his people dabbles in blood, and I'll wager his hands are no cleaner than hers."

"I can't imagine they are, Mister Wellens." Josiah jotted down more notes. So, here was proof that at least one of his people engaged in blood alchemy. No wonder the man knew so much about it! "And you could pick this woman out of a crowd if you saw her again?"

"Most likely. Wouldn't be much more difficult than spotting her in a picture." Mister Wellens paused. "Not that I'd do it unless I knew my family'd come to no harm, as I said."

"I wouldn't ask you to do it if I believed your family would be in danger. As I said, you have the crown's protection from the blood alchemists." Josiah closed his portfolio. "To that end, I am prepared to offer you and any other members of your family work in the palace, either on the grounds or as part of the staff. What exactly is your trade, Mister Wellens?"

"I'm a factory man now, as I said earlier. Started out as a bricklayer, but the fellow I learned from died just before I finished my training. Someone started a rumor that it was my fault — by accident, but still — and between the two, I could never find work. So, I went to the factories." Mister Wellens lifted his head and straightened up. "I'll do any honest work, though. I'm a quick study at most things."

"I have no doubt you are." Josiah hid a smile, afraid Mister Wellens would take it as laughter. "I'm confident that we'll be able to find a position for you, hopefully in your original trade. No matter where you work, we will pay generous wages and provide room and board for you and your family in the staff quarters of the palace. Is that acceptable?"

Mister Wellens nodded. "More than, sir. Thank you."

"Yes, thank you." Mistress Wellens looked as if a weight had fallen off her shoulders. "And thank you for helping Breen as well and for letting us know she's all right."

"No, thank you for your help." Josiah stood. "I have other business to attend to, but someone else from the palace will arrive in an hour to help you move. Once at the palace, one of the stewards will speak with you and determine where we can best use your skills. Any of your family who wishes to work can, but only one of you is required to do so. I will find you again once you are settled in and arrange a time for you to visit Breen, assuming that is your desire." He picked up his portfolio. "Good day to you both. Thank you once again for your time and your answers."

Mister Wellens stood as well. "And good day to you, sir. We'll be ready to go in an hour, as you said."

"Excellent." Josiah nodded, then headed outside. He climbed quickly into the carriage and instructed the driver to return to the palace. Then, he sat back in his seat.

So, blood alchemy again. Josiah recalled the red spot on her shirt that he'd noticed a little over a week ago. Now that he thought about it, it had looked very like the spot on Stephen's shirt over the gem that powered his lung. He should've put two and two together when he saw that!

What would refusing to pass the blood alchemy bill mean for people like Breen and Stephen? Without something to power their artificial parts, they'd die. No wonder Breen refused to leave the tower! If she left, who would provide the blood alchemy to keep her alive?

And if blood alchemy could save people like Stephen and Breen, should it really remain illegal? Perhaps Weston was right.

How many people would live because of such technology? And yet, Aaronson had a point too. Neither Stephen nor Breen seemed happy to be alive. Blood alchemy had kept them both trapped and forced them to live with the guilt of those who'd died so they could live. Blood alchemy in the wrong hands *was* a terrible thing — not because it was used to make monsters, but because it stole the life and hope even from those it saved.

Would blood alchemy in the right hands do any better? Josiah sighed. Yet another thing to consider. But at least he knew now what he was dealing with.

CHAPTER 29

Breen sat on the edge of a walkway on the fifth level of the clock tower, staring at the beams that crisscrossed the interior machinery. Could she safely go out there now? Or would her body rebel against her like it had yesterday? She shifted her shoulders thoughtfully. The movement still spread pain down her back, but she'd had worse from falling down the tower . . .

She sighed. She *should* rest and give her body a day or two more to heal. She knew that. But doing nothing when she wasn't really in constant pain seemed like such a waste, especially when the memory of Madame's displeasure was all too fresh.

She could work on her lift device more, of course. But she'd worked on it all day, and she'd forgotten how the next parts fit together, and if she stared at the thing for another minute, she thought she would go mad. Then again, who would care if she did go mad? Madame wouldn't. As for herself, who knew? Insanity might be better than her life.

Grace would care, though. And so would Josiah. And if she went mad, she couldn't finish the lift device, and if she didn't finish it, she couldn't sell it to help her family. So much for madness, then.

Breen huffed and contemplated the beams some more. She'd very nearly made up her mind to try when the lift signal in her pocket vibrated. Immediately, she scrambled to her feet. Josiah was back; hopefully, he'd brought Grace with him.

She reached the third floor just in time to see Josiah coming up the stairs with a package under his arm, this one much smaller than the one he'd brought the last time. He gave her a smile and a tip of his hat. Breen nodded back.

Grace appeared behind him, holding up her skirts as she climbed the stairs. As soon as she spotted Breen, however, she let go of one side so she could wave. Breen grinned and returned the gesture.

Once she reached the solid floor, Grace practically ran the rest of the way over to Breen. She paused before reaching her however and signed, "How is your back?"

"Better." Breen rolled her shoulders to demonstrate the fact that she could move with minimal pain. "Thank you for bringing a nurse."

"Of course." Grace fairly bounced on her toes. "Can I hug you? Or will that hurt?"

Breen considered this, then nodded. "Be careful."

Grace gave her a smile that said "Of course!" as clearly as if she'd signed it, then gently squeezed Breen into a hug. Breen gingerly hugged her back. It still felt odd, hugging and being hugged after so long — but not in a bad way.

All the same, she pulled away before Grace let go. Then she turned to Josiah. "Did you find my family?" Her hands trembled slightly as she signed. She'd second-guessed her decision over and over again over the last few days. If he found them, what would he learn? Would they tell him about her heart? About the fact that she was living a stolen, artificial life? *Please, let him not have found them.*

Josiah nodded. "I spoke to them today. I offered your father a job in the palace, and I told them that anyone else in your family who wanted to work there could as well. They'll be living in our servants' quarters until I can be certain they and you are safe." He grinned wryly. "This won't be the first time we've housed an entire family, if you were wondering."

Grace giggled — or, at least, Breen assumed the scrunched-up face and the hand over her mouth accompanied that sound. "Before we were born, our father used to go out and walk around the city in disguise. He would meet people and talk to them every week. Sometimes it was more often. Then, if someone he knew very well needed work, or was in a bad spot, or had a child who was old enough to work, he'd send someone to offer them a job and a place to stay at the palace. Some of them are still with us."

Apparently, the desire to save everyone ran in the family. Breen wondered if she was supposed to laugh at that story. She wasn't sure, so she just nodded and signed, "That was nice of him. I'm sure they appreciated it." It was better than the charity some rich

[261]

people offered — no strings or lost dignity attached! And work at the palace would be more than respectable; even the lowest gardener or kitchen maid was probably better off than many factory workers.

"They seem to." Josiah shrugged. "Your father seemed to as well. I told him that I would bring him to visit you later. I thought about bringing him tonight, but I wanted to tell you in advance so you could prepare."

"Thank you." She smiled. "I look forward to seeing him."

How could Josiah be so casual? Had he in fact not asked about her? Did he not know her secret? Certainly, her parents wouldn't have told if he didn't ask — but he'd been so determined to find out about her past when he first arrived in the clock tower. He'd become less pushy, yes, but she still couldn't believe that he would pass up an opportunity like that. So why did he act as if nothing had changed?

Grace sat down on a crate, arranging her skirts so she wasn't sitting on a lump of fabric. "Josiah, you should show Breen what we brought."

She used the name-sign Breen had taught Josiah. The realization made something inside Breen feel warm. It was nice to have her name used by a friend, rather than as a code to determine who was safe to talk to and who wasn't. She'd missed it.

Had Josiah gone to the other towers yet? Probably not. He hadn't had time to, not if he'd had a senate meeting the other day and then had gone to find her family today, along with whatever else princes did. Breen had a vague idea that they had to be fairly busy — though perhaps not, if Josiah's father had found time to wander the streets and talk to people. She'd have to ask all the same.

Not right now, though, because Josiah had set down his bundle and was now unwrapping it. The cloth came away to reveal several oblong objects, all of them brown, slightly fuzzy, and somewhat damp-looking. A darker, round spot on the end of each resembled the place on a fruit where it had been attached to the stem. Were these some kind of fruit?

"The Royal Botanical Society made a presentation at the palace today." Grace's hands fairly danced through the signs, and her eyes sparkled with excitement. "Several of their members are explorers, and they brought exotic fruits that aren't available in markets yet for us to try."

"It's from Shanfey," Josiah added. "The people there call it a . . ." He paused as if trying to remember the name, then slowly fingerspelled the word. "M-i-h-o-t-a-u. It's a very interesting flavor. Some were left after the presentation, so we brought them for you to try."

"Thank you." Breen bit her lip. "You didn't have to."

"We wanted to." Breen gave Josiah an expectant look. "Enough talking. Did you bring utensils?"

"Yes." Josiah slipped a covered knife and three spoons from one of his pockets. He handed spoons to Breen and Grace, then uncovered the knife.

"The botanists showed us the best way to eat the fruits," Grace added, apparently as explanation. "You cut them in half, then scoop out the inside as if the skin were a bowl."

Josiah nodded agreement as he cut two mihotau in half. He gave two of the cut halves to Breen, one to Grace, and kept one for himself.

Breen looked at the two halves of fruit. "You gave me twice as much as either of you."

Grace wrinkled her nose. "Of course. We had some before. You didn't. So you get more. I can't eat more than half of one anyway; I'm still full from earlier."

What was that like, to be so full you truly couldn't eat anything else? Breen pushed the thought away before she could dwell on it. Instead, she picked up one of the mihotau halves and studied it. Bright green, semi-translucent flesh surrounded an oddly-shaped white core. Tiny black seeds clustered around the core in lines of darker green flesh. Between that and the fuzzy skin, it was certainly an odd-looking fruit, especially compared to the apples and pears that Breen was most familiar with.

Tentatively, she dug her spoon into the fruit. Sticky juice immediately squirted out over her hand, and she ended up with a much larger piece than she anticipated. She eyed it for a moment, then put it in her mouth.

Sweetness flooded her taste buds, then gave way to a hint of tanginess as she chewed. Breen's eyes widened. This was *good*. She

[264]

ate another spoonful, trying to savor it. Most likely, she'd never get another one after today.

Josiah and Grace ate theirs at a leisurely pace, occasionally trading single-handed signs that Breen didn't bother trying to read. Instead, she focused on the fruit, trying to take in every detail of its flavor, of the firm, smooth texture, of the faint citrus smell and the odd feel of its fuzzy skin. Perhaps if she stored a good enough memory, recalling it would be almost as good as eating the mihotau again — if significantly less filling.

She finished the first half and set the spoon aside for the moment, licking the juice off her fingers. It probably wasn't polite — but Josiah and Grace didn't seem to care. "That was good."

Grace grinned. "I thought you would like it." Her spoon and the empty skin of her mihotau sat on the crate beside hers. "We brought more than two. Josiah can leave the rest with you if you want."

Breen hesitated. She certainly wouldn't mind having more of the fruit. But . . . "I shouldn't."

"That means you want it and you don't want to say so. That's what Grace usually means when she says those words like that." Josiah wrapped up the other few mihotau. "I'll leave them. We have more than we need at the palace. You'll do us a favor if you enjoy them."

Breen narrowed her eyes slightly at him. That *had* to be a lie. But arguing with him wasn't worth the energy — not when he was technically right about her meaning. "Do you get fruit like this often?"

"More often than most." Josiah nodded. "The Botanists' Society makes a presentation about once a year. Sometimes foreign visitors bring fruit as gifts as well, and we can afford to import exotic fruits for special occasions."

"That must be nice." Breen busied herself with the other half of her mihotau. Lucky them, to be able to enjoy this sort of thing so often — but that probably came with being royalty, and that was a responsibility she'd never want to bear. And it was nice that they were sharing and attempting to do so without being condescending.

Why was Josiah doing this when he had to know her past? Had he truly not asked her parents what had happened to her? Or had they refused to say? Breen glanced over at Grace. What about her? Did she know whatever Josiah knew?

She could ask. But she wouldn't. She didn't dare; she didn't want to know.

Instead, she finished the other half of her mihotau, watching as Josiah and Grace chatted back and forth about other foods they'd tried from far-off: pomegranates and dates from the deserts to the southeast, papaya from the west, and all manner of strange fruits from Shanfey and its neighbors. Then, once there was a break in the conversation, she asked, "Have you visited the other towers yet?"

Josiah shook his head while Grace perked up. "What about the other towers? Are there people in them too?"

Breen nodded. "Josiah asked me about them. He said he might go look for others like me." Like her in multiple ways — would any of them be willing to give up their secrets? And if they did, would Josiah realize that their secrets were the same as hers? Surely he would; he was intelligent enough.

"I haven't had time." Josiah shrugged. "I hope to start visiting them sometime in the next week. Do you have any idea which ones are probably occupied?"

Breen shook her head. Then, she hesitated, recalling her visitors the day before. Should she say anything?

She had to. That boy, whoever he was, didn't deserve this life, and there was a chance he'd be able to survive outside the blood alchemists' care. "When you do, look for a boy. I don't know his name. He's about this tall —" she indicated height with a hand held the appropriate distance above the ground — "and young. He has a clockwork arm. I don't know if he'll be in one of the towers, but if he is, please, ask if you can free him."

Josiah raised an eyebrow. "He won't die if he leaves his tower?"

"I don't know. He might. He might not." Did that phrasing mean he didn't know why she was here? Or was he trying to be subtle? "Please, ask. He deserves to be free."

"So do you!" Grace's motions were sharp, her eyebrows drawn together. She almost *scowled* as she signed. "Do you think you deserve this?" She paused, took a breath, and relaxed a little. "I'm sorry. I don't mean to be harsh. But no good person deserves to lose their freedom."

Breen winced. What was this vehemence, from Grace of all people? "I don't know." She slumped slightly, glancing down at her hands. "I know that he will be in the tower because he was kind. I'm here because I was stubborn."

"I remember when you told me why you are here. I thought it was because you were brave. Because you clung to your morals." Josiah smiled wryly. "We need more people who do that."

Breen just shrugged. Josiah wasn't wrong. She'd give him that much. But it had still been her stubborn refusal to help Madame and the others with their work that had put her here. "It doesn't matter. I have to stay here. He might not. Will you ask?"

"Of course." Josiah nodded. "I'll tell you if I find him. Even if he can't leave, I'll look after him."

"Thank you." Breen managed a smile. Even if she had to stay here, perhaps he could be free. Of course, if Josiah did find and rescue the boy, he'd probably learn about why Breen was here, if he hadn't already. And then . . . What? Would he and Grace abandon her at last?

Perhaps. But at least someone would be safe, even if it wasn't her. And that would have to be good enough.

CHAPTER 30

Three days later, Josiah sat in one of the small meeting areas off the Senate waiting room. He'd arranged with Weston to have their meeting moved here; now that he knew for a fact that someone connected to Weston actively practiced blood alchemy, he didn't want to spend more time in the man's home than necessary. Besides, if he was going to try to help Stephen . . .

A knock sounded on the door. Then, a servant pushed the door open. "Lord-Senator Weston and his party are here to see you, Your Highness."

"Thank you. Send them in, please." Josiah stood, resting one hand on the closed notebook waiting on the table. He nodded as Weston entered, followed by three servants and Stephen, who looked simultaneously exhausted and terrified. "Thank you for coming, Lord-Senator." He glanced over Weston's group. "I see that Madame Gottling and Doctor Baumann have not accompanied you?"

"Unfortunately, both are focused on their research and will be unable to join us this afternoon." Weston stopped behind a chair, placing both his hands on the back. "However, as you wished to speak with the boy we liberated from the blood alchemists, I made sure that one of my attendants will be able to serve as a translator."

"Thank you for your concern, Lord-Senator, but his services will not be necessary. I am skilled in sign, and, as I said before, I would like to talk to the boy directly. One-on-one, if at all possible." Josiah glanced meaningfully towards the boy. "In fact, perhaps I could do so at once and then speak to you afterward?"

Weston raised an eyebrow. "Are you throwing me out, Your Highness?"

"I am attempting to waste as little of your time as possible by getting straight to the point of this meeting." Josiah met Weston's gaze unflinchingly. "I informed you before that I wished first to interview the boy and second to speak with you and your researchers further on the points you raised in the Senate meeting, and I would prefer to do so in that order. And, in order to make sure that the boy answers as honestly and genuinely as possible, I choose to conduct the interview in a space in which he is exposed to the minimum number of potentially threatening people."

Weston smiled in a way that really wasn't a smile at all. "The boy has me to thank for the fact that he is no longer in the grip of the blood alchemists. You believe he sees me as a threat?"

"Sometimes, even help is a threat if it's unwanted or seems to have strings attached." Breen had made that abundantly clear to

Josiah all those weeks ago. "I will thank you to step out for the time, Lord-Senator, and to take your attendants with you. I assure you that no harm will come to the boy and that I will not keep you waiting longer than necessary."

Weston made a slight bow. "Very well. Have it as you will, Your Highness."

He turned and walked out along with his attendants, leaving the boy, Stephen, alone with Josiah. Josiah pulled out a chair. "You can feel free to sit. I mean you no harm." He sat down, keeping his focus on the boy. "So, tell me: who cut out your tongue?"

Stephen's eyes widened. He signed frantically: "You understood me?"

Josiah nodded. "Yes. I have a sister who's deaf, and I learned how to sign so I could communicate with her. Who taught you?"

"The bleeders." Stephen coughed into his sleeve, then continued, "They teach all of us. They use it in their lab some. And sometimes we get sent other places to work, and it's always loud there, so people go deaf."

Josiah nodded. "And sometimes they cut out your tongue so you can't speak; you can only sign. Is that correct?"

Stephen glanced towards the door as if making sure that Weston wasn't peering in. Then, he nodded. His fingers flew: "I back-talked too much. And then I ran away once and tried to tell someone about what happened. So they cut out my tongue. Then I couldn't talk anymore unless someone knew sign."

[271]

And, as a bonus, that had made him the perfect candidate when they needed a success story for blood alchemy with minimal risk that he'd say something they didn't want others to hear — except, of course, if one of their enemies knew sign as Josiah did. "Was what you said in the Senate true?"

"Yes. Mostly. But I wouldn't have said yes." Stephen screwed up his face and coughed several more times before he could go on: "I wouldn't. I would've rather died."

"Why?" Josiah opened his notebook as subtly as he could. "I promise I won't tell Lord-Senator Weston or any of his people what you say. But will you tell me?"

Stephen nodded. "I'm not a person anymore. The bleeders don't think I am. I'm a test. Or a machine. It's like I really died, but they made my body something else and put me back in it." His hands stumbled through the signs. "I want to be a person again."

"You're still a person. The fact that the blood alchemists don't recognize that doesn't make it false." Josiah leaned forward, meeting Stephen's eyes. "You don't stop being human just because part of you is made of gears and magic instead of flesh."

Stephen shrugged morosely. "It doesn't matter." His fingers formed the start of another word, but before he could say anything, he doubled over in a fit of coughing.

Josiah stood, shoving his chair backward. "Are you all right?" He hurried over to stand by Stephen. Was the boy somehow choking? If so, on what?

Stephen managed to stop coughing long enough to sign a few words. "My chest hurts. Breathing is hard." He coughed again, then took several gasping, desperate breaths.

Up close, Josiah could now see that what he had thought was ink stains on Stephen's fingers was actually dark blue-tinted skin. He put a hand on the boy's shoulder. "Stay calm. Something must be wrong with your lung. Wait here; I'll call for someone."

Stephen shook his head and tapped his sternum. "This. This is the problem. It feels like when they take it out, just worse."

Josiah knelt. "May I?" At Stephen's nod, he undid the button and peered at the crystal. Its depths were dull and clear, without a hint of a glow, red or otherwise. "When was this last charged?"

Stephen held up two fingers, then added a third. Three something? Or . . . no, two and then a *W*. "Two weeks?"

Stephen nodded. His formally red face had gone pale. He grabbed Josiah's arm like a drowning man grabs a rope, shaking.

"It's all right. It's all right." Josiah stretched and just barely managed to grab the bell pull in the corner. He yanked on it firmly, once, twice, thrice. "I'm calling someone, and they'll bring a doctor. You'll be all right."

Stephen shook his head. He managed to unclench his hands and signed swiftly and shakily, "No. I'm dying. I know I am." He trembled, slumping against the chair. His lips had started to go blue. "Please. Make sure the bleeders don't make more people like me. Make them stop."

[273]

"I will. And I'll save you." Josiah put his hands on the boy's shoulders. "Just try to be calm. You'll be all right."

The door swung open, and a servant poked her head in. "Your Highness?"

Josiah looked up. "Call a doctor here! This boy is dying!"

"Yes, sir!" The servant darted back out. Josiah heard her almost run away before the door shut.

Stephen shook, clutching Josiah's arms. His lips moved like he wanted to say something, but no sound came out. Then the boy doubled over, still shaking.

Josiah kept hold of him, not sure what else to do. Nothing had ever prepared him for this. He'd been taught what to do if someone was choking or if someone fainted — not if someone's lung just stopped working. "Just hold on. You'll be fine. I promise."

Stephen didn't respond. Josiah glanced at the door. How much longer would the doctor take? *Hurry* —

Stephen suddenly went limp. Josiah's heart sank. He put his ear against the boy's chest, hoping for the noise of a heartbeat.

There was nothing.

Josiah fell back, reeling. The boy — Stephen, he had a name, he needed to remember that — he was dead. Just like that.

I should have done something. I should have seen something. I should've guessed . . .

The door opened. Doctor Hartford, one of the two resident doctors for the palace, stepped in. "How is he?"

Josiah shook his head numbly. "He is . . . I'm afraid you're too late, Doctor."

"Let me see, Your Highness." Doctor Hartford stepped forward and gently but firmly pulled Josiah away from the body. He knelt in Josiah's place. With careful, precise motions, he felt for a pulse at the boy's wrist and neck and then pulled out a stethoscope. He placed one end of the tube in his ear and the other on the boy's chest and listened.

Then he shook his head gravely and coiled the instrument up again. "I'm afraid you were correct." He gently closed Stephen's eyes and then stood. "I will inform Lord-Senator Weston."

"Thank you, Doctor." Josiah took a deep breath and then rose to his feet as well. "I will come with you."

Josiah took a moment to compose himself, to straighten his shoulders and settle his expression into calm. He couldn't let Weston see him rattled. Had Weston known about Stephen's condition? Probably. Maybe this had been his plan all along.

Will that happen to Breen if the blood alchemy bill doesn't go through?

Josiah squelched the thought as soon as it crossed his mind. He couldn't think about that right now. He had to focus on what was before him. There would be time for regret and reflection and questions later.

Doctor Hartford led the way out. Weston rose as soon as they exited. "Finished so soon, Your Highness?"

Blast the man. Blast him and his mocking tone and his coldness. Josiah was seized with a sudden urge to punch Weston in the face. He took several deep breaths, trying to calm himself. Thankfully, Doctor Hartford responded instead. "Regrettably, his highness's interview was cut short. Were you aware that the boy's lungs were on the verge of failure when you brought him here, Lord-Senator?"

He has a name. Josiah opened his mouth, ready to correct Doctor Hartman. They had to remember that . . .

Weston replied before Josiah could say anything. "I was aware that the boy was at risk. After all, we had no way of knowing how much power his lungs had. But there was, of course, nothing we could legally do to help him even we had known. I take it he is dead, then?"

How could he talk about it so casually? A boy had died, a boy with a name and a story and a life that he could've lived — except Stephen had been living on borrowed time already, but still; with the impetus of a life on the line, someone would have found a solution. Surely, they would have.

Doctor Hartman nodded. "Unfortunately, yes. I am sorry."

Weston merely shrugged. "It was unavoidable." He turned to Josiah. "I regret, Your Highness, that it happened in the middle of your interview. I hope you were still able to speak to your satisfaction?"

Focus. Pull it together. Josiah straightened, forcing himself to pretend like everything was fine, like he hadn't just watched a boy die. "Yes. I was." He cleared his throat. "With your permission, Lord-Senator, may we keep Stephen's body and see to his burial? I would like to see him treated as he deserves."

"If you like. It hardly matters to me." Weston raised an eyebrow. "I believe you had matters you wished to discuss with me as well?"

"Only a few. If it is agreeable to you, I would like to reschedule the remainder of our meeting." Blast the man for making him ask; for forcing him to show that he *had* been disturbed by this. But, then again, so what if Weston knew he cared about Stephen's death? So what if he knew Josiah was a decent person?

"As you wish, Your Highness." Weston bowed his head slightly. "However, I would not dwell too much on the boy's death. I doubt he is the only one who will suffer that fate today."

Breen — but, no, Weston didn't know Josiah knew about Breen. He couldn't know. And Breen's heart couldn't be running out of power already, not if her keeper had visited recently. Unless Madame didn't recharge the crystal every time . . . how frequently did that happen?

Josiah pulled his mind back to the present. "Any life lost is a tragedy, Lord-Senator, even if it is one of many. Thank you for your time. I apologize that it was not as productive for you as you might have hoped. Good day."

"Good day to you, Your Highness." Weston nodded and turned. He strode away, flanked by his attendants.

Josiah took a deep breath. *Breen is fine.* She had to be fine. And he was going to the tower with her father tonight, so he could make sure. He wasn't sure how he could ask about her heart without making things awkward, but perhaps her father would bring it up himself . . .

Yes. Breen was fine. She had to be fine — at least for now. In future, on the other hand . . . would her survival forever depend on her being tied to the tower? On Josiah turning a blind eye to the blood alchemists who sustained her life?

There had to be another way. And somehow, he'd find it.

CHAPTER 31

Breen sat cross-legged atop a crate on the third floor of the clock tower, staring at the steps and waiting. Her whole self seemed to tingle with anticipation. Any minute now, the lift signal would buzz, and then moments later, Josiah would walk up the steps — and with him, her father.

Breen fidgeted, rubbing her fingers along the edges of a gear she'd missed putting away earlier. It had been so long since she'd seen any of her family . . . What if her father wasn't the same as she remembered him? What if he resented her for the trouble she'd brought upon the rest of her family?

She peered upwards, gauging the time by the positions of the machinery and the weights. Josiah should have arrived nearly five minutes ago. What if something had happened to him? What if Madame had found out he was visiting? He was the prince, true, but he wasn't invincible.

What if he found out about my heart?

Breen unconsciously touched the crystal in her chest. Her parents must not have told him her story when he first met them, but what if he'd learned since then? He wouldn't be bringing her father here, nor would he be coming back himself — not unless it was to take her to trial as a criminal or to kill her like an animal. He might even throw her family out of their new positions, or, worse, imprison them for cooperating with the bleeders. They'd be worse off than before, and it would all be Breen's fault.

Breen tried to shake the thoughts away, but they clung to her like a cold sweat. Had she a real heart, it would've sped up with fear. But as it was, the machinery continued to pump at its usual pace, heedless of her feelings.

More time passed. Breen squeezed her eyes shut and pulled her knees up to her chest. They weren't coming. Josiah had found out; he'd never be back; she'd never see her father or the rest of her family or Grace or Luis again . . .

The signal in her pocket vibrated. Breen's eyes flew open. She slipped off the crate but stopped before she ran to the stairs. Better to wait a moment, just in case Josiah really had learned her secret and had come to kill her and not to bring her father . . .

Josiah's head appeared above the floor a few moments later. He didn't seem particularly judgemental; he waved to her when he saw her and signed cheerfully, "Guess who's here?"

Breen couldn't do more than smile in return. *He doesn't know. Thank goodness, he doesn't know.* And that meant that her father . . .

Her father was here. She spotted him coming up the stairs behind Josiah mere seconds after. Still, she hung back, waiting for her uncertainty to subside, waiting for him to see her.

Josiah reached the top of the stairs and said something to her father. He looked up and over. His gaze met Breen's. Then his whole body shook for a moment before he fairly ran over to her. He grabbed her in a hug as if she were still a little girl and held her tight. She could feel his breath on her ear as he whispered something she couldn't hear, but she could guess. She could hope.

She hugged him back, burying her face in his shoulder and trying to memorize this moment. Who knew how long until she'd have another like it, even with Josiah's help? "I missed you," she murmured, or thought she did. "I missed you so much."

He squeezed her tighter, enfolding her as if he never meant to let her go. She almost hoped he wouldn't, that if he didn't, time would stand still and she could feel safe and loved again forever.

But it couldn't last, no more than any other good thing. Eventually, her father let go and stepped back, holding her shoulders as he looked her over. His mouth moved swiftly, too fast for her to guess at any words even if she'd been particularly skilled at lipreading in the first place. So she just waited with a sinking heart for him to realize what she'd forgotten he didn't know: that she couldn't hear him. That she was deaf.

It took longer than she expected for him to finish pouring out all his words and then pause, clearly waiting for an answer. Breen looked at him sadly, then glanced at Josiah for help. She could try to explain, but it was hard when she couldn't hear what she said.

Josiah nodded understandingly to her and tapped her father's arm. He turned, and the two conversed for several minutes. Breen watched them, trying to guess at their words. Josiah gave no clues; he stayed calm, a hand on her father's arm and a sympathetic half-frown on his face. Breen's father, on the other hand, started out with his brow furrowed with confusion, but gradually his eyes narrowed, his fists clenched, and his stance said *shouting* even though Breen couldn't hear his voice. Still, from Josiah's lack of reactions, Breen guessed that any shouting was directed at Madame and her kind, not Josiah or Breen.

After a few more moments in which Breen's father gradually slumped into resignment, Josiah turned to Breen. He signed slowly and clearly, "Your father and I have agreed that I will interpret for you two. Is that acceptable?"

Breen nodded. It would make things more awkward; there were some things she didn't want to ask with Josiah around. But what choice did she have? For the first time in years, she cursed the bells and her deafness for putting up another wall between her and her family. Even the beauty of the striking tower wasn't worth this!

Josiah nodded back and smiled sympathetically. Then he turned to her father and said something before facing her again. Breen's father spoke once more, slowly this time. Josiah waited several moments before starting his translation: "Your mother and siblings and I are well. We miss you too. How are you doing? Have they been treating you well?"

Breen met her father's eyes and saw desperation there, an unspoken prayer that she would say yes, that she would tell him that he hadn't sent his daughter into torment in an effort to save her life. She thought about the beatings, about Madame's habit of cutting her rations and always finding something to criticize —

And then she nodded. "I'm fine." Speaking aloud felt strange, even more than normal. "They aren't kind, but I have what I need."

Her father nodded. Again, Josiah translated his words: "No more any of us can ask for. At least you're alive."

"Yes." Breen stepped back and sat down on one of the crates. She gestured to another in what she hoped was a clear invitation for him and Josiah to sit as well, then asked, "What work are you doing at the palace? How is everyone, really? Do I have any new siblings? I want to know everything."

Breen's father sat. Josiah didn't, but rather stood beside the crate, hands at the ready. Breen's father took a deep breath. Then, with Josiah still translating, he began: "We're all well enough, really. Mary's wed Andrew Smith. You remember him? They're fair happy together. William's married as well, to Linda Topper. He's still at the factory, same as where I was. Henry and Martin both went off and joined the army, and they shipped them off months ago. Ellie's still at home; she and your mother both found work in the palace kitchens. And Jack's just found a spot as a gardener's boy up at the palace. He particularly wants to come see you sometime. New

[283]

siblings, you've got one. Tom's about eight now, a quiet boy. You'll meet him one of these days."

"I look forward to it." There were no real surprises in Breen's father's list. Of course Mary would be married; of course Henry was off having adventures in the army while William made a home and raised a family. And now she had another younger sibling besides Ellie . . . honestly, Breen had half-expected there to be more. Perhaps there had been, and now they were gone, killed like Lily or taken by illness or hunger. If there were, Breen doubted her father would mention them. He probably didn't want to worry her any more than she wanted to worry him.

"What about you?" she added, realizing what he hadn't said. "What are you doing at the palace?"

A smile of sheepish pride crept onto Breen's father's face. It looked odd there, used as Breen had been to seeing him strong and determined and ready to fight on behalf of whoever needed defending. "Seems they needed another bricklayer around the place and on the public works crew. The lead foreman knew my old teacher, said he'd never heard a bad word about me 'til his accident, and gave me a chance."

"I'm glad." Breen only faintly remembered hearing her father talk about his almost-career as a bricklayer; he'd very rarely brought it up when she and her siblings were around. But she remembered one night, only a year or two before her own accident, when she'd laid awake while her siblings slept and listened to her father and mother talking. He'd cursed the fate that had put him in the factory instead of in the more respectable position of a qualified bricklayer; cursed the fact that an accident had wasted so much of his work then, and that all his work since couldn't make up for what he'd lost. But now he had what he'd wanted — and better!

"What about you?" Though Breen couldn't hear her father's voice, could only read his words in Josiah's signs, she could imagine his tone: rough-edged with embarrassment, but still caring and concerned. "You told us when you came home years ago that you kept the clock."

Breen nodded, reading the additional unspoken questions in the statement. "I do. I like it. The clock is beautiful, and I've learned so much about how it works. I . . ." She paused, debating what to say, debating whether or not to tell him about her creations now or if she should wait and surprise him later.

She'd wait. Then she wouldn't get anyone's hopes up if she failed. "I can tell you all about the clock and the machinery if you like. And show you too."

"I'd say you want to show me whether or not I want to see." Breen's father stood and offered her a hand even before Josiah finished translating. "Lucky I do. Let's go, then."

Breen smiled at him, slid off her crate, and took his hand. Then she led him towards the stairs, up through the tower. As they went, she explained the clock and its workings, just as she had for Grace the first evening they'd met. She watched him closely while she spoke, hoping for his approval, hoping to assure him that she was all right, that he hadn't made the wrong choice when he chose to save her.

Not that she knew if it had been the right choice. She often thought it hadn't been. But she didn't want her father to have to live with that guilt.

By the time they finished, the hour was late. They'd had to retreat to lower levels more than once so Josiah and Breen's father could escape the deafening effects of the bells. At last, they returned for the last time so Breen's visitors could depart.

Breen hugged her father one more time. "Thank you for coming. I've missed you."

He held her tightly, his action answer enough. Breen rested her head against his shoulder, wishing she could ask the question that still nagged at her: what had he told Josiah?

But even if she could ask without Josiah hearing, her father couldn't answer without going through him. So she kept her mouth shut and prayed that the answer was *nothing, nothing at all.*

Breen's father let go and stepped back. Josiah grinned at Breen. "I'm glad you two were able to talk," he signed. "I'll try to bring him or some of your other family back next time. But I think Grace has claimed the guest spot next time I visit. Is that all right?"

Breen nodded. No matter how much she'd like to see the rest of her family, she couldn't refuse Grace — and there were other visitors as well she'd like to see. "Will you ask Luis if he wants to come back sometime, as well?"

Josiah raised an eyebrow, still grinning. "I will. I'll tell him you specifically asked for him." He tipped his hat and took a step towards the stairs. "Good night."

"Good night." Breen waved and waited until Josiah and her father were out of sight. Then she headed back to the steps. She knew this peace wouldn't last; eventually, something would happen, Josiah would stop coming, and that would mean no more visits from her family or Luis or Grace. But at least she could enjoy it while it lasted.

CHAPTER 32

The next morning, Josiah found a report on his desk from the royal intelligence forces: one page inside a sealed envelope, covered in odd lines and dots. Josiah checked to see that the shades were drawn, then sorted through a drawer. He removed a tiny alchemical lamp, a single gem set in a silver disk, and tapped the crystal to activate it. Its blue light on the page revealed the real message, written in normal, though coded, script.

With a sigh, Josiah pulled out a single sheet of paper and a pencil and began the laborious task of decoding the message. He had the key for this particular code memorized, but it was still just as difficult as reading a passage in any foreign tongue.

Decoding the short missive, then double-checking his work, took Josiah a solid half-hour. At last, however, he held up the translation.

Two individuals, one male and one female, spotted entering tower not in company of Prince Josiah on Sentesday, 32 Marren at 7:34 P.M; exited at

8:01 P.M. The female individual has been identified as Ms. Klara Gottling, alchemical researcher currently in service to L.S. Frederick Weston. The male individual has yet to be identified, but appeared to be 13 years of age, dark-haired, and fair-skinned, wearing a brown cap, pants, and boots with a white work shirt and brown workman's jacket and gloves. We will continue to keep watch for additional or returning visitors.

So. Gottling had been in the tower just a few days ago. That practically *proved* that she was involved with the blood alchemists — she probably was one herself, given how much she knew about blood alchemy. And if she was connected to blood alchemy, between that and what Josiah had gathered from Stephen's testimony, that likely meant Weston was involved in it as well.

Josiah stood and walked over to one of the gas lamps, carrying the message and its translation. He rolled the two papers into a loose tube, then stuck it into the gas flame. The papers caught almost instantly. He pulled them out, let the flame grow a little more, then tossed both into the cold fireplace and watched and waited until he was satisfied that they were ash.

His previous fields of inquiry were nearly dried up; he'd interviewed every alchemist, every archivist, and every scientist and researcher and learned nothing substantial enough for action. But now — now, with Gottling sighted at the tower and the Wellens's story and the bits and pieces Breen had dropped — now, he had a new path. If he couldn't discredit blood alchemy or the blood alchemy bill themselves, he could expose those who the bill would benefit. And then, even if the bill passed, they'd know how to make sure the power it granted remained in the right hands, assuming there were right hands to hold it.

Smiling in satisfaction, Josiah headed for the door. Now that he had a new aim, there was no time to waste.

Josiah packed the next few weeks full almost to the breaking point. He sent intelligence agents to investigate the clock towers to determine which were inhabited and when he could visit those. He set others on Weston and Gottling, ordering them to learn all they could about what role those two played among other blood alchemists and, if possible, where the main gathering place of the alchemists was.

For his own part, Josiah continued to interview the occasional alchemist or scientist, but he mostly left these to Luis. He sent him out to drink and dine with one alchemist-inventor after another, providing in return enough capital to fund the largest and most complicated invention Luis possibly could've come up with. He instructed Luis to particularly focus on how blood alchemy might connect to the towers, though he didn't provide details about why.

Josiah, on the other hand, switched his own focus. Aided by the Wellenses and the staff of the free hospital by the river, he identified several other families who might have been offered similar deals by the blood alchemists. Of those, two hesitantly recounted stories much like that of the Wellens: a child near death, an offer of salvation, a miracle, a theft.

"They want subjects for their experiments," Luis said when Josiah told him about the search one rainy afternoon in the Kronos workroom. "I've talked to some alchemists trying to apply normal alchemy to medicine. Younger test subjects are better because then you can observe long-term effects more effectively. Of course, the people I talk to use animals, not humans, but the principle's the same."

That had made sense, and it made Josiah itch to pry more details from Breen about her past. But he refrained, despite his thirst for answers. For one thing, he wasn't sure how to broach the subject without putting her on her guard. How did one *say* "Oh, by the way, since you wouldn't give me any answers, I talked to your family and learned that you're kept alive by illegal magic. Would you like to tell me more about how that happened?"

For another thing, it never seemed like the right time. Every time he visited Breen, he did so with a guest: Grace, Luis, or one of the Wellenses. He didn't want to expose Breen's secret in front of Grace or Luis; better to let Breen share it herself. And even if Breen's family already knew, he was so busy translating, and they seemed so happy to see each other that he couldn't bring himself to ask.

And, if he was being honest with himself, he enjoyed the opportunity to relax and put his work aside. The investigation excited him, true, but he frequently thought himself into headaches as he tried to put the pieces together. State affairs and royal events interested him as much as ever, but his every word and action had to be calculated, now more than ever.

And the Senate . . . just the thought of the Senate's current state made Josiah grimace. He'd started meeting with more and more senators, sometimes half a dozen in a single afternoon, trying to gauge their thoughts on the blood alchemy bill and encouraging them to consider it carefully, to not be drawn in by pretty promises when they didn't know the risks. Yet, even many otherwise steadfast Loyalists and Workers seemed to be swaying. *"Perhaps Weston is right,"* many suggested, hesitant and almost embarrassed. *"Perhaps it's not so bad if it's regulated properly. Perhaps . . ."*

Perhaps! Josiah felt as if all his plans teetered on that word. Perhaps Weston would push for a vote at the next Senate meeting, long before Josiah was ready. Perhaps he could build up a case against Weston, the bill, or both in time. Perhaps Weston and the blood alchemists would realize the extent of what Josiah was doing; perhaps Josiah could continue to hide. All Josiah needed was one event that would tip things one way or another.

Then, one afternoon, Josiah received a long-awaited message: *"Important information. Come as soon as possible. -L.K."*

Unfortunately, "as soon as possible" meant that evening after dinner, though not as late as when Josiah usually visited Breen. The clock shop was closed when Josiah arrived, but when he circled around and knocked on the back door, Luis opened it. "Took you long enough, Your Highness. You'd better see this."

Josiah followed Luis to the workroom. "Why the urgency? What's wrong?"

"This." Luis grabbed a sheet of paper and shoved it at Josiah. "Take a look."

Josiah skimmed the page. Large letters at the top of the page read *Submission Review: Compact Lift Engine*. Below them was a small sketch of a familiar device, followed by smaller text. "This looks like Miss Breen's invention, doesn't it?"

"*Exactly*." Luis almost seemed to vibrate with indignation. "It *is* her lift engine. Apparently, one Richard Daniels, a new member of the Inventors' Guild, recently submitted it to be patented. I asked a few questions about the man, and it turns out that he has close ties with Lord-Senator Weston. Daniels does quite a bit of work for Weston, and Weston sponsored the invention that won Daniels's entry into the guild." Luis scowled, throwing himself into his seat. "The snake. It wouldn't surprise me if he'd stolen *that* invention too."

"This is unfortunate, indeed." Josiah frowned at the page. "But what can we do? This is your field of expertise, not mine. And how did you learn of this in the first place?"

"Witsworth told me — another of my friends in the guild. He thought I might want to come to the initial presentation; it's open by invitation to non-guild members, and it's similar to the first stage of the review process for guild applicants." Luis picked up a gear, turning it over and over as he spoke. "I can go with him, then have a word with the review committee before the process begins or something of that sort. But I'd need proof, especially since I'm not the one who invented it and I'm not a member. I don't know exactly what the procedure is for challenging a patent on behalf of someone else, but I'll guess it's complicated."

"I see." Josiah began to pace. The space in front of the workbench wasn't much — three steps one way, turn, three steps the other — but it was enough to help him think. "What kind of proof would you need?"

"Another prototype — identical to the first, perhaps even better. That would be ideal." Luis paused. "Barring that, some kind of question or information about the lift engine that Daniels can't answer but would know if he'd invented it."

"The latter almost sounds harder than the former." Josiah glanced at Luis. "Do you think Miss Breen could recreate her invention, given materials and time?"

"I have no idea." Luis shook his head. "You can ask her next time you see her. But even if she does, there's still the problem of what to do if the Guild asks for the original inventor."

"That is a problem. I doubt they'd believe you if you said it was devised by a girl who lived locked in a clock tower." Josiah paused as another thought occurred to him. "You do realize that this could be a trap? Weston and Gottling may suspect that someone has been sneaking in the clock tower and helping Miss Breen. By protesting, we alert them that we're the ones they're looking for. Or, at the very least, that you are. They may act against you and her both."

"True. But Weston exposes himself too." Luis pointed a screwdriver at Josiah. "This shows that he's connected to Miss Breen and that he's involved in illegally indenturing people. It could be what you need: solid proof that will make people question him, maybe even get him removed from his position. You tell her what's happening and convince her to come challenge the matter herself. From there, the whole story comes out. You just have to protect her until the matter's all over."

That would solve the problem, wouldn't it? All except for one thing . . . "You forget. Weston has plausible deniability. It's this man Daniels who's submitting Miss Breen's invention. Weston can claim he knew nothing of the invention's origin. And . . ." He hesitated, debating how much information he could share. "I learned something of why Miss Breen is so reluctant to leave the tower. I can't provide details, but it will indeed make protecting her . . . difficult."

"Then what do you suggest we do, highness?" Luis shot back. "We can't let them go through with it."

"We may have to." Josiah grimaced, hating the words even as he spoke them. "I'll ask Breen about it tonight and suggest that she start work on a new prototype. But depending on her choice, it may be necessary for this crime to go temporarily unpunished so we can resolve the greater evil."

Luis slumped in his seat. "I still don't like it."

"Neither do I." Josiah sighed. "When is the presentation?"

"A week from now." Luis paused. "You said you'll visit Breen tonight?"

"Yes. She won't be expecting me, but I think this is important enough to warrant it." Josiah managed to grin teasingly. "Care to join me? I expect she'll be happier to see you than me."

"Don't be ridiculous, Your Highness." Luis rolled his eyes, then slumped. "I wish I could come, but we've had a run on clock repairs and orders this week. I thought I'd be done by tonight, but with all the investigations I've been doing for you, I'm going to need tonight to work on them."

"I apologize. If I had known you were so busy, I wouldn't have pushed you so hard." Josiah stopped pacing and faced Luis. "On that note, did you learn anything else about the towers?"

"Oh — yes. I did." Luis sorted through piles of items on his workbench until he found a large, full envelope. "I finally convinced several alchemists and inventors to tell me what they know. I had to more or less commit to trying to create a machine for charging miazen crystals, but at this point, I've talked about it with so many people that I would've done that anyway. I have the full details here, but the short summary is that blood alchemy might be the secret to why the towers have run so well for so long. See, while ordinary people are bad for alchemically-powered devices, people who've been . . . well, they used the word *infected* by blood alchemy are actually good for them."

Josiah raised an eyebrow. "Really? In what way?"

"It's complicated, but . . ." Luis grabbed a pen and started sketching on the envelope. "The energy that the alchemists charge the miazen crystals with comes from living things, people especially. We more or less just radiate it out into the atmosphere somehow — the fellows I talked to couldn't explain how. Then the alchemists pull it out of the air and into the crystals, and the method they use to do that is what determines what the energy can be used for afterward.

"Most people know about the last part; what they don't know is where the energy comes from. But the fact that it comes from living things is part of why miazen crystals lose energy when they're around people. Apparently — and this is what I was told, Your Highness, so don't blame me if it sounds crazy — apparently, people don't just let off this energy; they draw it back in too, though in smaller quantities." Luis made a face. "Turns out, there's a significant debate about why that is. Some alchemists think that we're subconsciously trying to use the energy ourselves; others think that we're trying to make up for the energy we lost. Either way, the energy gets pulled from miazen crystals as well as the 'loose' energy in the air.

"But —" Luis held up a finger — "people who have some kind of blood alchemy connected to them don't pull in energy like most people do, even though they still release the same amount of energy. No one's really sure why except maybe the blood alchemists. And miazen crystals can pull in energy too, just with lesser speed and force. So in a situation like we find in the clock towers, if you send a person in who's connected to blood alchemy, you give the crystals more energy to draw on, which means they won't lose their charge. But if someone with no blood alchemy connections spent too much time in there, the tower crystals might lose their charge and need to be replaced."

He paused, raising an eyebrow at Josiah. "Of course, that does raise an interesting question about Miss Breen, Your Highness . . ."

Josiah took a deep breath. "I am aware of that. I suggest you ask her that question yourself."

"I take it that you already know?" Luis didn't wait for Josiah to reply. "Don't answer. Of course you do. If you didn't know, you'd have speculated with me, not told me to ask her myself."

Josiah raised his hands slightly, an expression of *what-can-I-say?* on his face. "Fair deductions."

"So, I'm right." Luis nodded confidently. "It wasn't a bad idea on their part. Keeping Miss Breen in the tower was a clever way to make sure it lived up to the promises about it, and it gave the blood alchemists a place to hide their test subject. I'd guess the other towers serve the same kind of purpose."

"I believe they do as well." Josiah picked up the packet of information. "Thank you for gathering all this for me, Luis."

Luis nodded. "You're welcome, and my inventions fund thanks you for all the times you thanked me before." He paused. "So, what does this mean?"

Josiah paused, thinking. "I honestly don't know. It may have implications for the future of the towers. It may also mean that the blood alchemists have been keeping people imprisoned in the towers longer than we thought, given how long the towers have lasted without known human intervention. And it certainly means that removing people from the towers could have even more consequences than I expected. But if we want to know more than that, I think we'll simply have to wait and see."

CHAPTER 33

Breen sat on the uppermost level of the clock tower in the light of dozens of tiny crystals. She still didn't dare sit in the clock faces like she used to. Madame seemed to have grown suspicious over the last few weeks. She visited more frequently and at odd hours, and every time, she demanded to know if anyone had come to the clock tower since her last visit.

Breen always told her no, of course, though that was rarely the truth. Josiah visited as often as he could, always bringing someone else with him: usually Grace, but sometimes Luis or one of Breen's family members. Breen enjoyed the company and clung to each moment they were there, all too aware that it could end at any moment. All it would take would be for Madame and Josiah to show up at the same time, and then . . .

Even if Madame didn't find out, Josiah seemed more and more distracted lately. Breen tried to tell herself that he was just worried about the country and the Senate and everything else. He'd told her some about his chief project, fighting a petition to legalize blood alchemy — that would worry anyone. But she couldn't help the fear that he knew her secret; she still hadn't had a chance to ask him or her family about it. And even if he didn't know, how long until he gave her problem up as unsolvable? How long until he found someone who could accept the help he most wanted to give or discovered another project that interested him more? And once he lost interest, Breen lost contact with everyone else.

Breen shook herself, wincing as the movement disturbed recent bruises. Regardless of what Josiah knew or thought, she wasn't about to tell Madame that anyone else had visited the tower. So she covered for them, though Madame struck her more freely than she had ever before and left only the bare minimum of rations. That was another thing that had changed: when Madame replenished Breen's food stocks, she left enough for four days, maybe five, and those with only one small meal a day. If not for the fact that Josiah brought a bundle of food with him every second visit, Breen thought she would've let something slip due to sheer hunger by now.

The signal device vibrated in her pocket. Breen started. Why was someone here *tonight*? Madame had just come the day before, and Josiah and Grace weren't due to visit until tomorrow.

Maybe Madame was back early, trying to catch her doing something wrong. Just to be on the safe side, Breen scrambled to her feet and down the stairs to the next level.

The device remained silent as Breen crossed to the lift in the corner of the room, and when she peered down the shaft, she saw no one at the bottom. So it was Josiah visiting — Madame wouldn't warn her if she were coming up the stairs. But why was Josiah here?

She'd find out soon enough. Breen slipped back up the stairs to her former spot, confident that Josiah would guess where she was. Sure enough, Josiah appeared only a few minutes later. He carried a bundle under his arm, which he set down between them as he sat. "Hello."

"Hello." Breen pulled the bundle to her, wondering what he'd brought. He'd resupplied her with food just the other day. Opening it, she found an assortment of gears and mechanical parts, along with two large miazen crystals. "What's this?"

"Luis says they're the parts for your lift engine, as far as he can remember." Josiah pulled a piece of paper from his pocket and handed it to her, then signed, "This explains."

Breen slowly read the contents of the sheet, occasionally pausing to puzzle out an unfamiliar term. Coldness crept over her heart as its meaning became clear. She stared at the drawing at the top for a few more moments, then looked at Josiah. "This is mine."

Josiah nodded.

Breen blinked, tearless yet ready to cry. Hadn't they done enough? They'd stolen her life, her family, her humanity. And now they took her creation too. *It's not fair.*

But why should it be fair? Nothing in life was, no matter how hard Josiah tried to change things. And why should Madame's people treat her with any kindness? They thought she was nothing but their property, and so anything she created was theirs too. Whether or not it was *right* made no difference to their minds.

Josiah tapped her shoulder. She looked up to see him sign: "Luis wants to challenge them. He hopes if you recreate the device, we can prove it wasn't created by the person trying to claim it." Though his words were hopeful, a frown creased his face. "It would be a risk."

Breen nodded slowly. "I'd have to leave the tower."

"Yes." Josiah nodded. "Maybe Luis could challenge on your behalf, but we'd still reveal that we'd been visiting the tower. You might be hurt if you stay."

Breen pursed her lips, considering. What would happen then? Would Madame move her elsewhere? Back to *their* laboratory? What about the other clock-keepers in the city? *Would she move us? Or just kill us?*

"If we don't challenge it?" Breen asked. "What happens?"

"The patent succeeds. Or doesn't." Josiah signed slowly, more so than usual. "If you chose, we could challenge more than the patent. We could use this as the first step in exposing Madame, her people, and everything they've done to you. Or we could wait until I figure some things, and maybe the situation would be safer."

Breen looked at the page again, at the drawing and the words that taunted her, and she thought about her hopes for the lift device — that perhaps she could use it to help her family more, even if she couldn't leave the tower herself. That would never happen if the patent went unchallenged. But what could she do? If she left, she'd die. If Luis and Josiah challenged on her behalf, Madame would move her or kill her.

Then her mind caught up with everything Josiah had said. Her brow furrowed, and she looked up at him. Her fingers shook as she replied: "What do you mean, everything Madame has done?" *What do you know?*

"I mean everything." Josiah took a deep breath and almost seemed to steel himself. "I know about your heart. I asked when I first found your family. It might have been wrong. But I wanted to understand your problem, and you wouldn't give me any information yourself. So I asked them."

Breen stared at him, eyes wide, hands and lips frozen. He'd *known*. All this time, he'd known what she'd thought would drive him away.

And he came anyway.

He knew she was an empty shell; he knew she lived at the cost of another's life. Still, he came. Still, he cared — or acted like he did. Maybe that was all it was, just an act. Just his attempts to get what he wanted from her before he dropped her and move on.

If it was . . . Something inside her squeezed. Not her heart; wires and gears couldn't feel anything. But the part of her that remembered when she'd had a heart and hoped she could be a person without one. The part that thrilled to life when she was talking with Grace or creating with Luis or hugging her father.

"If you know, why are you still here?" She finally found her words again, her fingers trembling through the signs. "Why did you keep coming back? Why do you act like you care? You know I'm not really worth it, no matter what you say. So why bother with me? You know you can't fix my problem, so why don't you just move on to some other poor girl who you *can* help?"

"Because you are more than a problem to be fixed. You're a person. A friend, even," Josiah signed sharply, his eyes alight with something like flame. He stood up as he were about to start pacing, but instead, he faced her directly. "Not a charity case. Not a political stepping stone. A person whose worth is not dependent on whether her heart is made of flesh or gears. A person who deserves more than what life has given her. And a person who I have come to consider my friend, whom I respect and whom I want to help succeed. That is true now, and it will be true no matter what happens tonight or tomorrow or a year from now."

He paused, his hands slowing. "And as your friend, I am honored that I can remind you of who you are: an intelligent, wonderful young woman, a treasure in the sight of Jeros. Someday soon, Miss Breen, I hope you will no longer doubt that. I hope you will be free to use your talents as you choose and to explore all of Rivenford — all the world — all the places you've only ever seen from above. And if I can do anything to make that hope a reality, I will do it."

Words. Just fancy words, all of them. Easy enough to say, especially for him. But, then, the fact that he *had* kept coming back spoke far more strongly. He'd known for weeks; he could easily have come up with an excuse to stop visiting. He could've said it was too dangerous, or he could have just stopped showing up. And he'd helped her family even after he knew their part in her situation.

Breen fished the tower keys out of her pocket. She'd taken to keeping them on her, just in case anything serious happened. She held it up so Josiah could see, then signed, "If you had known what I was after the first night or second night, would you have given me this?"

Josiah nodded. At last, he sat back down beside her. "I would have."

"And when you brought Luis to help me with the lift device." Breen tilted her head. "Would you still have done that?"

Again, Josiah nodded. "I would have. And I am confident that he still would have come."

Breen hadn't even *thought* of that. If Josiah knew, who else did? Luis? Grace? "Does he know now?"

"He guessed, though not through anything I said about you." Josiah smiled sheepishly. "I asked him to investigate the towers and blood alchemy, and he put the clues together. You should ask him about it sometime. I don't think Grace knows, but I doubt her friendship would change either."

That Breen didn't doubt. "And you're not just coming back and helping me because she wants you to?"

Josiah raised an eyebrow. "Miss Breen, I give a great deal of weight to Grace's advice, and I am happy to carry out her reasonable requests. But if I did things for you simply because she wanted me to, I wouldn't be here tonight. After all, my little sister does not run my life!"

Breen had to laugh at that. Oddly, it lightened the weight in her chest more than any of his speeches had. Then another thought came to mind, and she sobered. "What about the blood alchemy petition?"

Josiah sighed. "I don't know. The more I learn, the more uncertain I am. Blood alchemy does save lives, and you're living proof of that. But you're also proof of how the blood alchemists can hurt people using blood alchemy. How they can cheapen life and cause people to doubt their worth. And there's still the matter of the blood itself and the fact that someone has to die to provide it." He shrugged. "What would you say? If you had a vote in the Senate, would you say yea or nay?"

If I had a vote in the Senate. Wrapping her mind around that impossibility took Breen a solid minute. And then the meat of Josiah's question . . . Breen stared at her hands and touched the crystal in her chest, considering. What would she do?

At last, she made up her mind. "They could do good. The blood alchemists, I mean. They've saved more lives than mine. But they hurt as many people as they help."

She took a deep breath, forcing herself to continue. "They used Lily's blood to start my heart. They could've saved either of us or both of us. They told me later. It was an experiment. They had me and Lily and another boy from the same accident, and they wanted to know if a close relative's blood worked better than a stranger's. So they saved me and the other boy, but they killed Lily.

"They killed her — but there was no point in it." Breen's fingers trembled. She tried to still them, but she couldn't. "I'm trapped here. Living like this. Until you and Grace came, I didn't even know if I *was* alive or if I was just a body that my heart kept going. And now I know I'm alive, but it still hurts."

Tears pricked her eyes, but Breen blinked them away. She had to finish. "Maybe if the right people were in charge of blood alchemy, it would be ok. If no one died who could've been saved, and if the people who were saved knew they were still people and not machines, maybe it would be worth it. But if Madame and the others were still in charge, I would never, *never* vote yes."

"Even if voting against meant you'd die?" Josiah asked, concern written in his face and in the gentle motions of his hands. "I understand that your heart will stop without power."

Breen nodded. "I'd rather die than force someone else to go through the same thing I did."

"I can understand why. Thank you for sharing. Knowing what you think helps. And thank you for trusting me with your story." Josiah smiled. "I appreciate it."

Breen smiled back, a bit shakily. "So what will you vote?"

"If it comes to a vote, I will vote no," Josiah replied. "I've heard good arguments for both sides, but I think you've hit on the heart of the issue. As long as there's a good chance that control of blood alchemy will stay in the hands of the people who use it

[309]

primarily for harm, we can't legalize it — especially not when they misuse it so badly that you're willing to die to make sure no one else suffers the same fate." He paused. "I hope it won't come to a vote, though. At this point, my goal is to expose Weston, the leading advocate for the bill, and his connection to the blood alchemists and what they've done. Then the bill will most likely drop — and if it doesn't, people will know exactly what they're voting for and against."

Breen nodded slowly. "You said something like that earlier. If we challenged the patent on my lift device, you would use that to expose Weston?"

"With your permission, yes." Josiah nodded. "But I would rather wait. I hope that I will be able to gather additional proof linking Weston to the blood alchemists. I know Madame works for him, but I need more. I need enough connections that he can't possibly shake off all of them. However, if you wish to challenge the patent now, we can do so."

Breen studied Josiah for a moment, considering not just his offer but what it meant. He was willing to risk his plans — for her. That wasn't something you'd do for someone you didn't care about, someone you thought was a non-person. That was the type of risk you'd take for a friend.

She recalled what he'd said earlier. He'd called her his friend. And now, at last, she could believe it. Perhaps some of it had been pretty words all the same — but the important part, the part where he said *you are a person* and *you are worth something* and *you are a friend* had been true.

"Thank you," she signed, wishing she had more words to say what she felt. Then she pulled herself back to the issue at hand. "But we can wait to challenge it later like you said. Madame and her people need to be stopped, and your plan sounds like the best way to do that."

"It's the best way I can think of, at least." Josiah smiled. "Thank you. I appreciate your sacrifice. I still recommend working on a new prototype of the lift device, though, so we have it ready when we need it."

"I will. I already started, actually." Breen glanced down towards the bundle of parts. "This will make it easier."

"Good. That was the goal." Josiah straightened, a glint in his eye as if he'd just thought of something brilliant. "I have another question for you, though you don't have to answer immediately. Would you be willing to share your story when I expose Weston? He's already brought one of the blood alchemists' newer captives to promote his side of the argument. If you could come and tell people what the blood alchemists really do, that would help." Hurriedly, he added, "You don't need to answer right now, and you don't need to say yes. I'll do whatever I can for you whether or not you testify. I just thought it might be fitting for someone who's been hurt by them to be involved in exposing them."

Breen pursed her lips, considering the idea. There was a certain appeal in speaking for herself — and she'd probably be safer in the

Senate than in the tower. But at the same time . . . that would mean speaking in front of the most powerful people in the country. It would mean she'd be exposed.

"I'll think about it," she said at last. "I'll let you know what I decide."

"That's fine." Josiah stood. "I should probably go and let you get some rest."

"Thank you. I'd appreciate that." Breen wrapped the bundle of parts back up. "And thank you for telling me about the patent, and for — everything."

Josiah grinned back — a casual grin, like the one he gave to Grace. "Of course. That's what friends do." Then he disappeared down the stairs, leaving Breen with her thoughts.

CHAPTER 34

The key fit the lock. That was something.

Josiah turned the first of the three keys in the door of the tower nearest the main bridge across the Trevis River. The royal intelligence forces had determined that all seven clock towers were inhabited. Or, at the very least, they were all visited weekly by either Madame Gottling or Adam Surland, an alchemist whose only claim to importance was that he had nearly been expelled from the Guild on three separate occasions: twice for misuse of alchemical power and once for almost blowing up a laboratory — the latter by accident, the former probably not.

Josiah tried the second key. It, too, fit. Only one to go. He glanced up towards the top of the tower. What was the inhabitant of this tower like? Would they welcome his presence? Tolerate it out of fear, as Breen had at first? Or would they scream and then tell the blood alchemists about his visit at the first opportunity? He'd tried to think of a way to find out in advance for nearly a week, but in the end, he'd just had to pick a tower at random and hope for the best.

The third key turned as well, and a gentle nudge swung the door open on silent hinges. Josiah stepped inside. He'd expected to feel something like what he'd felt upon entering Breen's tower for the first time, but instead, he just felt uncertain. After all, he knew what was at stake now, and he knew a dozen ways in which everything could go wrong.

He slipped the keys back into his pocket and shut the door behind him. Then, he slid one hand into his pocket and gripped his pistol. He hoped he wouldn't encounter any danger; according to his intelligence agents, Adam Surland, who usually visited this particular tower, had come and gone two days ago, and Josiah wasn't about to shoot whatever poor soul the blood alchemists had imprisoned here. All the same, better safe than sorry.

Like Breen's tower, this one was equipped with a lift in the far corner, visible only by the light of the signal gem. Josiah considered it for a moment. He certainly didn't intend to go up in it, not after Breen had nearly dropped him back down the shaft when she saw who he was. Or, more accurately, who he wasn't. But should he at least warn whoever lived here that someone was coming?

That was probably better than sneaking up on them. He pressed the signal gem and jumped off the platform before anyone could try to pull it up. Then he started up the stairs.

Josiah paused when he reached the third level, looking around in case the tower's inhabitant frequented it as much as Breen did hers. But he saw no one, and he also noted that it was almost as empty as the second level. Only a few crates were lined up against one wall, along with one set of shelves holding what looked like glassware. Spare parts for a blood alchemy lab, perhaps? Or even materials to set up a new lab here in the clock tower?

That was a mystery for later. Josiah continued up the stairs, moving more carefully now and keeping his eyes and ears open for any out-of-place sound. The massive ticking of the clock taunted him; what other noises was it hiding?

He'd almost reached the topmost level of the tower when he heard the voice: "Hello? Is someone there?"

Josiah peered upwards, trying vainly to spot the speaker. Whoever it was, he was male and on the younger side. And he wasn't deaf — if he were, he wouldn't have called out. Josiah recalled Breen's request; maybe this was the boy she'd asked him to look for.

"I'm a friend of a friend," he called back, after a moment. "Can I come up?"

"Can't stop you, can I?" came the reply, tinged with wariness. "Come on."

Josiah took the rest of the steps carefully. He reached the top level to find a boy of about thirteen sitting on a cot much like Breen's. The first thing he noticed was the boy's arm: instead of flesh, it was made of steel rods and brass gears assembled into a delicate mechanism, partially covered by plates of copper. The second thing he noticed was the large wrench the boy held in his lap and gripped with his flesh hand.

Josiah pulled his hands from his pockets and lifted them as he approached. "I mean you no harm. I'm a friend of Breen's." He made the sign, just in case, though he wasn't sure if the boy would know it or not. "The girl in the clock tower nearest the palace."

The boy's brow furrowed. "The one who defied Madame and was beaten for it a month ago?"

Josiah nodded, hoping for multiple reasons that there was only one girl who fit that description. "The same. She said there was a boy with a metal arm who accompanied Madame to her tower and who was kind to her while he was there. Was that you?"

"Yes." The boy raised an eyebrow. "How do you know her? Did she sent you looking for me?"

"I know her because I saw her in the clock face and went to investigate. As for whether or not she sent me . . . yes and no. She did ask me to look for you, but I would have come anyway for my own reasons." Josiah glanced towards the stool. "May I sit?"

The boy nodded, keeping his eyes on Josiah. "Who are you?"

Josiah sat. "My name is Josiah Chambers." He waited, watching for recognition. None. Well, that was all right. "I am a representative of the Crown, and I am trying to expose the blood alchemists and bring them to justice. What is your name?"

"Peter. Ain't got a last name." Peter considered Josiah. "So, you know about . . ." He gestured to his arm.

"What the blood alchemists do to people, yes." Josiah nodded. "Would you be willing to tell me about your experience and what you know about them? Every bit of information helps."

Peter shrugged. "I suppose. Can't hurt. I'm here already, after all, and you don't look like one of them, if you know what I mean, mister. Anything to help." He launched into his own story with much less reluctance than Breen. It resembled Stephen's story more than Breen's: he was an orphan as of five years ago and had lost his arm in a workhouse. He hadn't bled out, but the injury had become infected, and only the intervention of the blood alchemists had saved his life. He'd been in their lab until just three weeks ago.

"They wanted to keep me there," he continued, "wanted me to work in the labs proper, helping with their experiments. But I kept disobeying them to stand up for the younger kids. Then Madame Gottling came and started taking me around to the towers and the pits and everywhere else they stick us when they don't want us nearby. That's how I ran into the girl — Breen. She was hurt, but she still took a minute to encourage me and make me less scared of being alone, so I helped her back." He shrugged. "And now here I am, seeing as I couldn't be scared into behaving."

"I am sorry that you found yourself here, but I am glad you stood up for what you believed. Chania needs more people like you." Josiah leaned forward slightly. "If I offered you a chance to leave the tower, would you take it?"

"Make the offer and find out, mister." Peter grinned. Interesting; apparently the blood alchemists hadn't worn him down as much as they had Breen — though, then again, they'd had Breen for a longer time. "I'd be tempted, for sure. My arm's the only part of me that's mechanical, and I could manage without it, so I'm not as bad off as some. But wouldn't that tip off Madame Gottling and Master Surland and the rest that something was up? The people in the other towers could get hurt."

"Very intelligent; I can see why the blood alchemists wanted you helping in their labs. It would be a risk, yes. But I wanted to give you the option." Josiah flipped to a fresh page in his notebook, which he'd pulled out during Peter's story. "What can you tell me about the location of the blood alchemists' main lab or guild hall? Anything?"

"It was underground," Peter replied promptly, his brow furrowing as he thought. "Any time we left, we always went up. Not too far from the city neither; we never traveled more than a day coming here. Can't say much more than that. I was blindfolded any time we went back and forth."

"I understand." Josiah made a few more notes in his book. "Did you hear anything on the way, particularly when you were leaving the laboratory?"

Peter considered this. "Dunno. I didn't hear city noises. Don't think I heard farm noises either — no animals, anyway. Just birds and . . . trees, maybe? I don't know what trees sound like, but it was kind of all rustley."

"Trees do indeed tend to rustle in the wind." That still didn't narrow the field much. "Could you tell me more specifically how long it took you to travel from there to here?"

"Not exactly, but . . ." Peter frowned. "When I made the trip the last time, we left early, seven maybe, and the clocks were striking twelve not long after we arrived in the city. Sometimes I think it takes less time than that, though."

"Somewhere between four and five hours, then." That would do for an initial estimate. Josiah turned the page in his book. "Did you visit all the towers in the city?"

Peter nodded. "All of 'em. And some places that weren't towers, but I couldn't tell you how to get to 'em."

"Just the towers will do for now." Anywhere else might not be government property and would, therefore, be more difficult to get to. "What can you tell me about the people who live in each tower? Who would be most likely to help me, as you have, and who might tell the blood alchemists I've been here?"

Peter propped his chin on his flesh hand, leaving the mechanical one in his lap. "Hmm. Well, I don't know all the names, but I'll try. You already know the girl in the tower closest to the palace. Then there's the tower in Guilds Square. There's another girl in there, Anna; I knew her in the labs. She's a snitch and a suck-up; only ended up out here because the bleeders got as annoyed with her as we did. I don't know about the Bank Street tower; I only met the boy there the once. The girl in the Wright Avenue tower's all right, though. Her name's Jess; a bit of a mouse, but no snitch.

"That's all the towers this side of the river. On the other side, don't go to the bankside tower." Peter shook his head. "There's another boy there, and he's loony. Got all his gears switched 'round. The other one's probably all right, but I don't really know."

"Thank you." Josiah finished jotting down notes as fast as he could. "Is there anything else I should know about the towers or the blood alchemists or your story?"

Peter shrugged. "I dunno. Tell Jess that I'm alive and all right if you see her. And tell the girl in the palace tower — Breen? right? — Tell her thanks from me. Tell her she was right."

"I will." Josiah slid his notebook into one pocket and dug in another. He pulled out an extra set of keys and a folded and sealed note. "These keys will open the tower doors if you ever need to leave. Keep them secret, keep them safe, and don't use them lightly. If you do leave and you need help, go to the palace gates and show the note to the guards there. They'll know what to do."

"Thanks, mister." Peter tucked the keys and note into a pocket. "I'll remember that."

"Good. I have two more questions for you, then I'll leave you be." Josiah held up a finger. "First, is there any other help you need?"

Peter shook his head. "No. I got all I really need — a roof over my head and enough food to keep me on my feet and now a way out if things get really bad. What's the other question?"

Josiah held up a second finger. "Second — and you can say no to this if you choose — would you be willing to share your story with more people than just me? If, say, you were given the opportunity to speak in front of the Senate . . . ?"

"Me? Speak to all the rich 'n fancy folks?" Peter's eyes widened. "Sure. I guess. Would you really need me to do that?"

"It would help." Josiah smiled. "Thank you for all you've done so far. One of my associates or I will be back sometime fairly soon to check on you and, if the time is right, get you out of this tower. Until then, may Jeros keep you safe."

"Uh. You too, I guess." Peter waved awkwardly, as if not sure what to do. "Wait — one thing. Most everyone I saw in the other towers was deaf from the bells. Is there any way I can keep that from happening to me? I tried moving my stuff down to the ground floor, but Master Surland got mad and made me move it back."

Josiah frowned thoughtfully. "I can do fairly little about that, but I do have a friend who came up with a method of hearing protection. I'll ask him to put something together for you and have it sent over as soon as I can. Until then, I recommend that you try to stay on the lower levels as much as possible, even if it means a less comfortable bed."

"Right. Well, thanks anyway." Peter shrugged resignedly. "Good luck, mister."

"Thank you." With a wave, Josiah headed back down the stairs. He'd been lucky — no, blessed — to find Peter first. Now, not only did he have information on the blood alchemists, but he knew where to go for more.

And so, with Peter's descriptions as a guide, he continued to visit the other clock towers over the next two weeks. Most of his evenings, of course, were occupied with Breen or with royal duties and events. The few that weren't, however, he spent at the other towers. Peter's predictions regarding the tower residents proved accurate — save for what he'd said about the second tower on the far side of the river. The boy there screamed and swung himself down into the midst of the machinery as soon as he saw Josiah, and he didn't stop screaming until Josiah left.

But the others were willing enough to talk — some readily; some after Josiah coaxed them and convinced him that he wasn't with the blood alchemists and he had no intention of hurting them. Here, as in politics, who Josiah knew proved the key; most grew a little less wary at the mention of either Breen or Peter. And, as he drew their stories out of them, he gradually also gathered details about the location of the blood alchemists' main laboratory — enough that he could send messages to local agents and have them look for the place. They narrowed it down to a dozen locations, to five, to three — and, at last, to just one.

CHAPTER 35

If Josiah knew anything, it was that good news was meant to be shared — and so, once he left his meeting with the royal intelligence force agents, his first thought was to find someone to talk to. Tragically, however, Grace, his father, and his mother were all occupied, meeting with various people to discuss various topics — or, in Grace's case, no particular topic. Technically, Josiah was supposed to have another meeting now too, but Senator Frederichs had to cancel due to illness, which left Josiah at a loose end. That left only one option: Kronos Clocks and Gadgetry, where Luis would also be busy — but the nice thing about Luis's brand of busyness was that he could work and talk at the same time. And so, Josiah set off to the Gadgetry.

Luis glanced up for only a moment when Josiah pushed open the door to the back workroom of the shop, having been waved back there by Mr. Kronos. "You look chipper, Your Highness. What's the news? Don't tell me; Lord-Senator Weston has retracted his bill, retired from politics, and intends to donate his entire estate to charity. Is that it?"

"Unfortunately, no." Josiah cleared the extra chair of mechanical parts, transferring them to the nearest shelf, and pulled the seat over to the workbench. There, he sat down in a most un-royal fashion. "We've found it, Luis!"

"Found what, Your Highness?" Luis raised an eyebrow. "Your common sense? I thought that was gone for good."

"Very clever." Josiah resisted the urge to roll his eyes. "No, we've located the main laboratory of the blood alchemists. The head of the royal intelligence force is already putting together a team to infiltrate the facility, investigate, and report back."

"Congratulations. That is good news." Luis looked up properly from the clock he was repairing this time, actually sitting back so he could face Josiah. "Where was it?"

"Ah, that's the best part." Josiah pulled from his pocket the folded map of the southern part of Chania that he'd used in his earlier meeting. "Clear a space, will you?"

"Here." Luis picked up a tray of loose parts and moved it to his lap. "Is that enough for you?"

"It'll do." Josiah spread out the map. The tray hadn't left quite enough space, and the paper tore in one corner when he tried to smooth it over a gear he hadn't noticed. He frowned at the tear, then grabbed a spare screwdriver so he could gesture with it.

Luis plucked the screwdriver from his fingers before he could make a single motion. "No speech-making, Your Highness. Get to the point before my legs fall asleep."

"Very well." Josiah indicated a point on the map in the foothills of the Fluik Mountains, the range that ran from the northernmost tip of the nation almost to the capital city. "The laboratory is here, about five miles outside the town of Kettlingham. And do you know where Kettlingham is?"

"Not particularly, no, but I assume somewhere important?" Luis tilted his head so he could read the writing on the map. "It doesn't look like it's far from Rivenford."

"That depends if you call five hours' travel by carriage far." Josiah tapped the spot again. "Kettlingham is a small city with two very important distinctions. First, of course, is the laboratory. Second, it's the location of Lord-Senator Weston's favorite hunting lodge, *and* it's a mere ten miles from his primary country residence. There is absolutely no chance that he's not aware that they're there, and I would wager quite a bit that my agents will find proof that he's actively involved with them to some degree."

"That's good news." Luis lifted the parts tray. "Now, Your Highness, if you don't mind giving me my workbench back . . . ?"

"Of course." Josiah folded up the map as Luis set down the tray. "If my agents can both get proof of Weston's involvement *and* learn more about what goes on in the blood alchemists' laboratory, we should have a strong case in the Senate." He sighed, tucking the map back in his pocket. "Of course, we'd have a stronger case if the rest of the senators could see whatever the agents see."

"You would." Luis paused, frowning. "I may be able to help with that, come to think of it. One moment." He held up a finger, then ducked under the workbench.

Josiah stood and peered over, watching as Luis dug through baskets and drawers. After a minute of searching, Luis stood, holding what looked like a large pocket watch. He handed it to Josiah. "Take a look at this, Your Highness. It's not finished — I ran out of spending money, and by the time I could afford the parts I needed, I had other projects I was more interested in. But with the funds you've given me these last two months, I could probably finish it."

Josiah picked up the watch and inspected it. It was thicker than a normal watch and had a few extra knobs and small levers along the side. When he opened it, however, he found only an ordinary-looking clock face. "What does it do?"

"It's a hidden camera of sorts. Here." Luis pressed in one of the knobs along the side. A catch inside the watch clicked, and the clock face and hands flipped down against the cover of the watch. What looked like a miniature camera lens sprang out from against the internal workings of the watch. "All you should have to do, once it's finished, is press this knob here —" He indicated another knob on the outside of the case — "and it will take a picture. Then you shut the camera portion — that's the trickiest part — and pull this lever so you can take the back off and switch the plates."

Josiah shook his head in astonishment. "If you can make it work, it'll be ideal. Honestly, if you'd finished this when you came up with it, you could have been in the Inventor's Guild years ago!"

"All I really did was miniaturize a normal camera's mechanism, fit it into the casing, spring-load the lens, and figure out how to easily change the plates." Luis shrugged. "It's not terribly impressive. Nothing that would interest the Guild."

"Well, if that's *all.*" Josiah couldn't help but laugh. He handed the camera-watch back to Luis. "Finish the camera, Luis. Don't worry about funds; the Crown will pay for it and materials for more whether or not you submit it to the Guild. But I think you should apply."

"We'll see." Luis set the watch on his workbench. "I have to finish the thing first."

Within a week, Luis had completed the camera-watch, constructed several more, and trained the agents selected for the mission in how to use them. A few days after that, the agents set out. Their mission was to take just under a week: they'd depart the city heading east, travel for a day in that direction, then make a wide circle around so they could come at Kettlingham from the southwest. Disguised as ordinary travelers, they'd stop in Kettlingham for a few days, investigate the laboratory, and then return to the city a few days before the Senate met again so Josiah would have time to review their findings.

That almost-week seemed one of the longest of Josiah's life. He distracted himself with business as normal — meetings with senators and scientists, evenings with Breen, and the usual assortment of other State functions and social events — but his mind was forty miles away. By the day the team was due back, Josiah felt as if he might burst from anticipation.

Then they didn't arrive.

If Josiah had thought the week before had been bad, this was worse. What could have happened to them? Visions of disaster floated in his mind. The team had been captured; the team had been betrayed; the team had never even made it to the laboratory. As one day turned into two, Josiah met with his father to discuss what they'd do if the agents didn't come back. They came up with no good answers.

Finally, on the day before the Senate meeting, the team returned: burned, bruised, and bloody, but with first-hand reports of the blood alchemists' work. They met with Josiah and the head of the royal intelligence force to debrief and described what they'd seen: strange instruments, countless vials of blood, a whole wing for housing the children on whom the alchemists had experimented. They'd even witnessed and photographed one of the blood alchemists' experiments.

"That was when we were detected," one, a slim, dark woman added, apologetically. "They must have heard the cameras. They called in others to search the room, and we had to run for it. Some of us nearly didn't make it out. The bleeders have strange sorts of weapons and things that neutralized *our* weapons, all powered by their magic."

"We are glad you successfully escaped. Thank you for your service." Josiah stood. "Weston will have heard about your presence by now. I'm sure they'll guess who you were and will move against us soon." He addressed the leader of the team and the head of the intelligence force. "See that the information is compiled into a proper report and delivered to my room along with copies of the photos. I must go inform the king and the captain of the guard of what has occurred and ensure that everyone at risk is kept safe." *Even if I have to carry Breen and the others out of their towers in order to do it.*

Letting the king and the guard know about the potential threat took far longer than Josiah would have liked. Nearly an hour and a half had passed by the time he could head back to his room to fetch his hat and a weapon. But surely, *surely* it would take time for Weston and the blood alchemists to act as well . . .

Josiah reached his rooms only to find a maid there, putting a letter in the tray by his door. She curtsied when she saw him. "Your Highness, a messenger brought this note for you. He said it was important."

It was probably nothing — but Josiah grabbed the letter, broke the seal, and skimmed the contents anyway. The words there sent a sliver of ice into his heart.

Your Highness,
We know you know about us. Well done. We should have guessed it was you from the first day Gottling reported that she thought someone else had found his

way into the clock tower. We hardly expected, however, how far you would go to seek out the truth — or how much you would learn before we realized what you were doing. Again, well done. It is a pity, however, that your curiosity will kill your friend in the tower unless you come here alone, unarmed, and willing to talk.

Josiah sucked in a breath. *I'm too late.* He should have had a message sent to the agents watching Breen's tower at once; he should have gone there first . . .

No. There was no time for *should have.* Now was the time to *do.* He turned back to the maid. "I must respond to this in person. Now, go find the captain of the guard. Tell him to send a squad of soldiers to the nearest clock tower — no, one to each clock tower — immediately. Tell him to come himself to the nearest clock tower and to bring his best men. I'll meet him there."

Without waiting for a reply, he ducked into his room and grabbed his hat and his revolver, pausing only a moment to check that the revolver was loaded. Then, he dashed out the door and down the twisting halls to the castle grounds, startling several servants as he passed. Outside the palace itself, he made for the small east gate.

Then he was out on the crowded streets, still running. People stopped and stared as he passed. Perhaps they recognized him; perhaps they were just wondering why he was in such a hurry. Well, let them wonder. He paid them no heed, pushing his way along to the tower. *Please, Jeros, let me get there in time.*

CHAPTER 36

Breen sat astride a beam, inspecting a gear as mid-afternoon sunlight trickled in through narrow windows and gaps in machinery to create a sort of golden half-light. She wiped away specks of dust with a rag, then glanced upwards, checking the time for what must have been the hundredth time that day.

Josiah and Grace were to visit that night. It might, Grace had told her, be their *last* visit to the tower — not because they were abandoning Breen, as she'd once feared, but because she'd be leaving with them. Though she'd still not made up her mind about speaking to the Senate, Josiah said that he wanted her to be safe in the palace before the Senate meeting tomorrow. There was no telling how Madame and the blood alchemists would react when Josiah exposed them and Weston, after all.

Of course, that would only happen if Josiah's spies came back safely from the lab . . .

The signal in Breen's pocket buzzed. She frowned. Madame had just visited the night before, and Josiah usually came much later. Had something gone wrong?

The signal vibrated again. Breen stiffened. Josiah wouldn't signal twice; this was *Madame*. But why was she here? Had she found out what Josiah was doing?

Breen slid along the beam to the center of the tower and scrambled up the clock chains, leaping from one to another before her weight could pull any of them down. She reached the top of the tower and headed for the lift. But as she grasped the chain, a thought occurred to her. She didn't *have* to pull Madame up. It might be better if she didn't — if she left Madame to walk up the stairs and hid in the midst of the clock machinery. Then she could climb back down while Madame searched for her and run to the palace, where Josiah would protect her.

But what if Madame didn't know? What if this was a false alarm or a test? In that case, running away would prove to Madame that something was wrong. And if Madame *did* know something, wouldn't it be better to find out? Breen had fooled Madame for weeks now; surely she could do it again.

The signal vibrated a third time. Breen steeled herself, then raised the lift.

Madame didn't wait for Breen to pull the lift all the way up. She stepped off as soon as she could reach the floor, then backhanded Breen across the face. Breen stumbled and fell backward, her cheeks stinging. She scrambled back to her feet, signing hastily. "I'm sorry. I was working —"

Madame slapped her again, this time across the other cheek. Breen blinked and let her hands and eyes fall. Madame scowled down at her, eyes narrowed and fingers sharp as she signed, "Do not lie to me. I save your life, and this is how you repay me? You talk to our enemies and tell them all about us and the work we do? How *dare* you?"

Breen curled her fingers against her palms, not quite forming fists, and stood as still as she could. Madame *knew* — or she had guessed and was hoping Breen would confirm it. *What now?*

"What did he promise you?" Madame stepped forward, so close Breen could almost feel her looming. "Did he offer you safety? Freedom? Do you not care about what *we* gave you? Do you want to die?" She touched the crystal in Breen's chest, then added, "If you do, I can give you that easily enough. I can take your life in an instant, and I will. Do you want that?"

Breen didn't have to think twice about shaking her head. She could guess what Madame would say next, and sure enough —

"I thought not." A brief, cold smile flashed across Madame's face. "I will give you an opportunity to earn your continued life. I have ensured that the enemy will arrive soon. When he does, you will pull up the lift and greet him as if nothing is wrong. Then you will stand quietly and obediently as I deal with him. Understood?"

Madame wanted to use her to trap Josiah. Pieces snapped together in Breen's mind like the gears of a clock. Madame would hold her against Josiah just as she'd held Breen's family against Breen herself. And Josiah would fall for it; if he would risk his carefully-laid plans for the sake of her invention, he'd risk more for the sake of her life. And if Grace came too, if Madame threatened *her* . . . if Madame killed her . . .

Breen couldn't let that happen. She had to get out, run to the palace, warn Josiah. *Now.*

Breen turned and dashed towards the machinery in the center of the tower. She'd barely taken three steps, however, before every inch of her exploded with pain. She fell to the ground, red washing her vision. For the briefest of moments, her heart sped up — and then she felt something *crack.*

Madame's riding crop fell before Breen could recover her senses. Madame struck almost wildly, not bothering to aim her weapon where it would hurt the most. Within moments, pain flamed up Breen's arms, across her shoulders and back.

Breen almost let her instincts take over, almost curled into a ball to protect her face and head as she had so often before. But she *couldn't*, not this time. She had to *fight.*

Breen gripped the handle of her largest wrench. Then, she rolled, pushed herself to her feet, and swung at Madame with all her might.

Madame dodged backward. Her ruby pendant and the crystal on her riding crop both glowed brilliant, bloody red as she aimed the crop for Breen's face.

Breen caught it on the wrench, but her limbs felt sluggish. She risked a glance downwards. The crystal's glow flickered beneath her shirt. Why was it flickering? It wasn't supposed to do that.

Madame's next strike caught Breen just beneath her ribs. Breen doubled over, dropping the wrench. Then she grabbed it again and swung wildly upwards.

She missed by a solid six inches. Madame grabbed the wrench and yanked. Breen clung to it with both hands, trying to pull it free. She didn't notice Madame's riding crop until Madame struck her with it again, mere centimeters away from where she'd last hit.

Breen let go of her wrench and stumbled back. Madame's next strike took Breen's legs out from under her. Breen fell forward, smacking her chin on the boards. She felt Madame's knee in her back; felt Madame wrap something around her wrists —

And she felt the signal in her pocket vibrate again.

Josiah! Breen renewed her struggles, trying to wriggle free of Madame's hold, flailing her free arm in the off-chance that she might hit Madame. For a second, she felt the pressure on her back lighten. Then it came down again, twice as hard, and Madame's riding crop struck the side of her head. Breen's vision flashed black; her ears rang.

But when her vision cleared, she saw Josiah dashing up the steps, a gun in his hand. He glanced over the room for only a moment, taking in the situation.

Then he raised his pistol, aimed at Madame, and pulled the trigger.

CHAPTER 37

Josiah's shot rang through the tower, seeming to expand to fill the space. In the same moment, a sphere of glowing red exploded outward from Gottling's pendant. The glow struck the bullet, which immediately stopped and dropped to the ground. Then the light hit Josiah, rushed through him like the shock from one of Luis's inventions, and left him shuddering and holding a red-hot gun. He dropped the revolver with a yell of pain. "How — ?"

"Alchemy has many uses." Gottling dropped her riding crop and drew a pistol. "Recently, we've been testing ways to neutralize weaponry and attackers rather than simply speed-healing the injuries after they occur."

"And how many times will that work?" Josiah bent and grabbed his pistol, gritting his teeth against the pain. In one smooth motion, he stood back up, aimed, and shot again.

Again came the burst of red, the stopped bullet, the shock, the heat. Josiah just barely managed to keep his grip on the revolver this time. He sucked in a breath and shot a third time.

Red light swept over the bullet, the revolver, and Josiah. Josiah yelled in pain as the heat of the gun became unbearable. He dropped it to the ground, where it lay smoking, then fell to his knees, holding his wrist. Angry red burns already covered his palms.

"Are you quite finished?" Gottling's tone suggested nothing so much as intense boredom. She lowered the pistol so it was aimed at Breen's head, gripping the loop that bound Breen's wrists with her free hand. "Now, Your Highness, you have two options. If you ignore all reason and attack me again, I *will* shoot the girl. She is, of course, little more than an intelligent machine at this point, but I am aware that you feel otherwise. Or you can cooperate, and she — and those like her — will live."

"Cooperate with what, Gottling?" Josiah demanded, rubbing his hand. "Do you think I'm the only one who knows about you? No. There are others, and silencing me won't silence them."

"On the contrary, Your Highness, it will." Gottling smiled coldly. "We have watched you; we understand how you work. You investigate and reveal your findings on your own terms. You control what others know and when they reveal what they know. And only you hold all the information, you and whatever record you've made of your discoveries.

"You hold the master copy — and you can make it disappear, along with the original records and any additional replicas. You can tell others to hold their tongues so long that they forget the whole matter. You could even order your people to forget the matter now, but somehow, I doubt you're a good enough liar to do that." She nodded down at Breen. "I'm sure that sabotaging your pet project grates on you, but is your victory worth the life of your friend?"

"This isn't about my victory. This is about justice." Josiah pushed himself to his feet and stepped forward slowly, his eyes on Breen. Was she all right? She lay on the ground under Gottling, bruised and burned, her hands bound. But then she looked up and met his gaze, and he saw the spark burning there.

She trusts me. She believes I can save her. Josiah cleared his throat. "Soldiers will be arriving any minute now, Gottling. You can't fight all of them. Surrender and let Breen go."

"But what soldier will fight me when I threaten both their prince and an innocent bystander?" Gottling let her finger hover over the trigger of her pistol. "And you've already proven that as long as I hold the girl, you'll do whatever I say."

She was right. Blast her, she was right. Josiah stopped where he was. "And what happens when you don't hold Breen? You can't threaten both of us at once. You're only one woman."

"Can't I?" Gottling tapped her pendant with her free hand. The gem's glow brightened. "That pulse earlier seemed to give you a nasty shock, highness. What do you think it would do when its effects aren't dulled by your weapon?"

Josiah hesitated. "You're bluffing." She had to be bluffing. But it *had* hurt earlier, and the agents had been heavily injured when they returned; they'd spoken of strange weapons like this . . .

Gottling just smirked and tapped the pendant again. Its glow exploded into another bubble of red. Josiah scrambled back, but it hit him before he could take more than a step. The sudden electric pain knocked him to the ground and set his arms and legs twitching. He pulled in sharp breaths, trying to reorient himself.

Gottling released Breen, picked up her riding crop in her off-hand, and stalked towards Josiah. "As I thought. I imagine that the effects will wear off in a moment or two, but it should be more than long enough to tie you up as well — *ooof!*"

She fell forwards as Breen scrambled up and threw herself into Gottling. Both women hit the ground with a thump. Breen rolled to the side as Gottling regained her feet. "Blasted wretch —!" She kicked Breen in the ribs, then brought her crop down on Breen's face, leaving a vibrant red welt.

Josiah finally regained control of his limbs and pushed himself back a standing position. "Let her be."

"Why should I?" Gottling struck at Breen again, but Breen rolled away, towards the center of the tower. "She is, after all, my property, and she'll die soon if you don't stand down. Even if you prevent me from shooting her, her crystal will run out sooner than you think. It's cracked, you see, and I'm sure even you know what happens when a charged crystal breaks."

"It leaks more quickly." Josiah hesitated. The memory of Stephen flashed into his mind, only this time it was Breen struggling for breath, clinging to his hands. "You're lying."

"Hardly. And given how injured she currently is, I would give her perhaps two days before her heart stops and she dies." Gottling re-aimed the pistol at Breen. "Her only chance is if you convince me to replace the crystal — assuming I don't simply shoot her."

"You wouldn't." Josiah lunged forward and grabbed for the pistol. Gottling pulled it away and swung her riding crop at the same time, striking him in the gut. He doubled over, gasping. Even through multiple layers of clothing, the blow stung like fire.

Gottling swung at Breen again. Breen rolled onto her stomach and pushed her arms up to intercept the blow. The riding crop hit her wrists, and the cords fell away. Breen rolled again, then pushed herself onto her knees. Not even a foot behind her, the machinery in the center of the tower continued its steady turning.

Gottling swung again. This time, Breen ducked and grabbed Gottling's arm, using the woman to haul herself to her feet.

Gottling stumbled under the force of Breen's pull, but then steadied herself. She dropped her crop and then pointed her pistol again at Breen, who froze. "Enough. Enough. Your Highness, my hands seem to be occupied. Tell the girl that if she doesn't get on her face on the floor, I will shoot her, then kill her friends in the towers one by one until you cooperate. And remember, I can tell what you're saying."

Josiah took a deep breath and raised his hands to sign. But before he could form a word, Breen grabbed the pistol, pushing it out to the side. Madame's finger twitched; a shot rang through the tower. Josiah heard the bullet ricochet off metal multiple times.

Another glowing sphere exploded from Madame's pendant. Josiah dropped to the ground again. He saw Breen do the same, still holding the pistol by the barrel. She met his eyes and smiled — *smiled!* Then, as Gottling reached for her, she twisted and rolled off the edge of the floor into the mass of machinery.

"No!" Josiah pushed himself to his feet and dashed forward, nearly stumbling over himself in his haste. "Breen!"

Gottling grabbed her riding crop and whirled, striking him in the gut before he could reach the edge of the floor. Josiah gasped in pain. *Why would Breen do that?*

He already knew the answer: because she knew the clock well enough that she knew where to fall to avoid getting hurt. And she knew he couldn't focus on the fight with Gottling if he had to worry about her. By removing herself from the fight — and taking Gottling's pistol with her! — she'd given both of them a much better chance.

Gottling sniffed, glancing over her shoulder. "Well. That was inconvenient."

Josiah straightened and lunged again, grabbing for her wrists. "So is your defiance. I'll give you one more chance to surrender, Gottling."

"Why would I surrender? So I can hang or spend my life in prison?" Gottling grimaced and tried to pull away. "You haven't beaten me yet, Your Highness."

She managed to free her crop hand and struck again. Her weapon hit the side of Josiah's head, sending a burst of pain through his skull. Josiah sucked in a yell and twisted her other wrist painfully.

Gottling swung once more, hit, and pulled free. "You can't win this, highness. My lord is no fool. Even if I fail here, even if you ignore our threats and release the information anyway, he'll find a way for our work to continue."

"Not if I can help it." Josiah dodged another blow and threw a punch at her ribs.

"We'll see." With a parting swing, Gottling turned and dashed towards the ladder to the uppermost part of the tower. Josiah charged after her.

CHAPTER 38

Her plan had worked.

Breen lay with her back on a beam, staring up into the machinery. The crystal in her chest burned, and her heartbeat ticked on as if nothing out of the ordinary had happened. As far as it knew, Breen supposed, that was true. She fell often enough as it was.

But never like today. Never on *purpose*.

She hadn't expected to hit a support beam. The edge of a gear, yes. Perhaps even some walkway far below. But not a beam only half a floor from where she'd fallen. And yet here she was.

The fire in the crystal faded — mostly. It was still warmer than usual, and it still flickered strangely. Breen squirmed, fighting through the pain of the beating, until she could sit up. She pulled her shirt away from her chest and peered down at the crystal.

A crack ran from one edge right into the very center of the crystal. Breen sucked in a breath. She'd seen how quickly a damaged crystal could drain. She'd have to be careful not to hurt herself further; if she did, the energy required for healing would probably drain her heart dry.

But she couldn't just sit and do nothing. Josiah wouldn't have to worry about her anymore, and that would give him a slightly better chance against Madame. But Breen intended to give him more than that.

Tremors ran through the tower. Footsteps, somewhere, running. Upstairs, Breen guessed, though she couldn't tell for sure. *Josiah dropped his gun. Did he pick it back up?* Even if he hadn't, Breen knew her largest wrench still lay by her cot, and she had another almost as large on her belt. Either way, she had some kind of weapon. It was too bad she'd dropped Madame's pistol when she fell; that would've been helpful.

She had to get the pendant away from Madame. That and the crop were her main pieces of alchemical magic. And to do that, she would have to stun or distract her. Breen gingerly scooted along the beam until she reached the chains in the center of the clock. *At least stunning her will be easy enough.*

Grabbing the nearest clock chain, she swung herself off the beam, despite her body's protests. Her weight dragged the chain down and the clock mechanism forward. What time had it been when she fell? Just after the hour, Breen guessed. So if she stopped here . . .

She swung herself onto another chain and climbed up it, letting her weight move the clock forward the correct amount as well.

Each clock controlled only one of the four bells, but two bells tolling five o'clock *should* be enough.

Breen swung onto a support beam and slid along it as fast as she could. *Now to get upstairs in time.* Wincing, she pulled herself onto a walkway and, once on the solid floor, took off at the fastest pace she could manage.

One flight of stairs brought her to her living area. No sign of Madame or Josiah; they must have moved higher up. Breen spotted Josiah's revolver on the floor and grabbed it, and then picked up her wrench as well. She tucked both into her belt and scrambled up the ladder.

When Breen cautiously poked her head above the floor of the uppermost level of the tower, she spotted Josiah and Madame immediately. Madame sported a bruise on her jaw, and she wielded her riding crop more stiffly than usual. Either her pendant wasn't enchanted for healing, or it worked much more slowly than Breen's heart did. But Josiah's cheek showed a fiery red welt, and his careful movements suggested that Madame had gotten in several good strikes about his ribs.

Breen climbed the rest of the way up and crouched, hoping neither Madame nor Josiah would spot her. She glanced at the nearest clock face. Only a minute or so left. If she could stay unnoticed until then . . .

Madame glanced towards her and spat a soundless exclamation of shock. Breen pulled out Josiah's revolver. *So much for the element of surprise*. She sprang to her feet, aimed, and pulled the trigger once, twice, four times until she ran out of bullets.

She missed every time.

Her first shot cracked the glass of the clock face. The next three produced a spiderweb of further shatter lines, though the glass held together — for now. Josiah gaped, glancing from Breen to the clock and back. Madame hesitated, shock temporarily overwhelming her fury.

Then the clock struck. Gems flashed red and blue and white. Tiny tremors shook the tower. And both Josiah and Madame stumbled as if shot and clutched their ears.

Breen tossed Josiah's revolver to the side and charged forward at Madame. She slammed her shoulder into the woman's ribcage, forcing her back towards the clock face. Madame stumbled but recovered as the last tremors of the clock chimes died away. She raised her crop and struck at Breen.

As she did, Breen grabbed the pendant and yanked, breaking the chain. The crop stung her back, adding a new welt to the already-painful collection.

Madame snatched at the pendant chain, but she only managed to catch Breen's wrist. Breen pulled against Madame's grip, but she couldn't seem to break free.

Then Josiah recovered and lunged at Madame as well. He didn't bother going for her weapons but instead slammed straight into her. And this time, Madame didn't recover. She fell back into the cracked clock face, which gave way under her weight. Shards of glass hurtled out into the air, glinting golden in the late afternoon sunlight.

Madame toppled after them, pulling Breen with her. Breen stumbled, yelped soundlessly, and fell forward. She felt the brush of Josiah's fingers just missing her other shoulder. Then she was in the air with Madame beneath her.

Wind rushed past her ears; the ground flew towards them at an alarming rate. Madame flailed and grabbed for the pendant that Breen still held. *No. No.* Breen clutched the gem tighter. Could she use it herself? Protect herself from hitting the ground so hard? And if not, did her crystal have enough energy left to heal her from such a fall?

She knew she was about to find out. Breen mentally whispered a silent prayer. *Jeros, if you care, let me survive this.*

Then her body met the ground, and everything went black.

CHAPTER 39

Josiah stumbled forward, catching himself on the edge of the clock frame. He let his hand drop limply to his side as he stared at the spot where Breen had been just a moment ago. *She's gone.* There was no chance she could have survived such a long drop.

He slowly made his way down, down, down to the bottom of the tower. Part of him urged haste, but what was the point? Breen was dead. Of course, Gottling was too, and Josiah now had an abundance of evidence against Weston, but at what cost? Why did his efforts to save lives have to involve others losing theirs?

Josiah stepped out of the tower and glanced around. No one here, but he heard plenty of voices from the other side. He forced himself to stand straight, to walk confidently, to hide his fear and grief. His people needed to see him calm and composed, undaunted by what had occurred, not a panicked mess.

He circled the tower and found a crowd of people gathered a safe distance away, held back by police who didn't seem to know what else to do. Carriages were stopped in the street as their drivers and passengers stared at the wreckage: at the shattered glass and broken bodies and the *blood*. Josiah cringed at the sight. *So much blood . . .* There shouldn't be that much of it anywhere outside the human body. For Breen to have survived would take a miracle.

Please, Jeros. Only You can save her now. Let her live. Let her heal, somehow, no matter what You have to use to do it. Don't let me win this battle only to lose the friend who fought it with me.

The two women lay in the center of the red splattered across the pavement. Gottling was on the bottom, on her back, her body so shattered that it looked barely human. Josiah guessed that she had cushioned Breen's fall somewhat, as Breen lay partially on top of her. She seemed less damaged than Gottling, but she was ominously still.

Please, Jeros. Please, no.

A clamor of new voices from the street heralded the arrival of a squad of soldiers, led by a man in a captain's uniform. He saluted as soon as he saw Josiah. "Your Highness! We came as soon as we could. Are you well?"

As soon as they could — and still too late. Josiah bit back a bitter comment. "I am fine, captain. However, I fear that the person I came to rescue is not." He raised his voice and addressed the crowd. "My soldiers and I have the situation under control. There is no danger to any of you. Return to your business. Officers, see that the area is clear."

The people muttered disappointment, but largely obeyed, save for a few stubborn ones who had to be forced away by the police.

[352]

The guard captain and his men made a circle around the wreckage, and the captain approached Josiah. "If I can ask, Your Highness, what happened?"

Josiah briefly weighed what to say and what the captain didn't need to know. "For the past months, I have been investigating the blood alchemists. One of my main sources of information was Miss Breen, a young woman whom they had trapped in this clock tower. However, the alchemists somehow learned of my investigations and threatened to kill Miss Breen should I not back down. I refused, we fought, and this is the result." He turned and stepped towards the bodies.

The captain cleared his throat. "I wouldn't, Your Highness. The bleeders are tricky folk, you know."

Josiah shook his head. "The dangerous one of the two is clearly dead, captain. I want to see if any hope remains for my friend."

"That would be the girl on top, then? My men will check on her." The captain pointed to two of his squad. "Johnson, Anders, see if there's any life still in the girl. Be gentle."

The two nodded and moved forward. They turned Breen over, and one pressed two fingers to her neck while the other lifted her wrist to check her pulse. "There's something," the one holding her wrist called. "Faint, but it's there."

"Captain, look." The other man touched Breen's shirt just below her collar, where a faint red light flickered weakly beneath the fabric. "There's some kind of crystal here, stuck somehow."

The captain shot Josiah a look. "Your Highness?"

"She is a victim of the blood alchemists' experiments, yes." Josiah kept his voice carefully level. "And she lies here because she chose to risk her life to save mine. You will give her the respect she is due for that."

"Yes, Your Highness," both soldiers said, almost too quickly. "What should we do with her, then?" one added.

Josiah hesitated, running through his options. She needed medical aid, obviously. But he'd heard somewhere that you weren't supposed to move people if they'd broken bones . . .

"Your Highness?" the captain prompted. "Your orders? Should I send one of my men for a doctor?"

Josiah shook himself. "Of course. Yes. Thank you, Captain. Send for one of the doctors from the palace infirmary. Doctor MacFarlane, if he's available."

The captain saluted. "Yes, Your Highness." He turned and called to one of his men, "Run back to the palace and fetch Doctor MacFarlane. Tell him the prince wants him five minutes ago." He faced Josiah again. "What about the other woman, Your Highness?"

"Have her taken to a morgue, but let her identity be kept secret, and see that no one disturbs the body." Josiah paused. "And keep a close watch on it, just in case."

"As you say, highness." The captain sent another soldier running with a message for the nearest morgue.

That left Josiah and the others to wait for his return. Josiah could barely keep from pacing, but he had to stay calm as long as he was in public . . .

Doctor MacFarlane arrived in a carriage ten minutes later, along with two assistants, an assortment of tools and instruments, and a sort of collapsible canopy with canvas curtains on three sides that could be used to keep out both the weather and curious stares of passers-by. He marched up to Josiah. "Came as quick as I could, Your Highness. What's going on, then?"

Josiah indicated the place where Breen lay. "She was a prisoner of the blood alchemists. She fell from the top of the tower. We believe she's still alive, but she's . . ." He couldn't say *dying*. The word stuck in his throat like a stone, choking him.

"Ah." Doctor MacFarlane gave a decisive nod. "Never fear, lad. I've seen men survive worse. I'll do all I can for her." He turned and strode towards Breen, calling orders to his assistants and the soldiers alike, "Hurry up with that cover! You there, bring me my other bag from the carriage. No lagging, you hear!"

Josiah took several deep breaths, trying to calm himself. Doctor MacFarlane was the best of the best when it came to medical matters. If anyone could save Breen, surely he could . . .

Someone grabbed his arm. Josiah startled, whirled — only to find Grace there. She released him and signed furiously, hands moving so quickly that he could barely keep up. "What happened? I heard that the spies had come back, so I went looking for you, but someone said you'd gotten a note and then rushed off. And then the next thing I heard was that you'd called Doctor MacFarlane down here, so I came after as fast as I could. Are you all right? Is Breen all right?"

Josiah shook his head. "No. No, she's not." He explained the whole story, from the agents' arrival onwards. His hands shook far more than usual, especially when he described Breen's fall.

Once he finished, Grace hugged him tightly. Then she stepped back and signed, "Father wants you to hurry back and tell him what's happened as soon as possible. And I want to know: what about the people in the other towers?"

"Oh, blast," Josiah muttered aloud. Then, signing, he added, "You're right. They're likely at risk as well. But . . ." He didn't finish the sentence, instead glancing towards the canopy where Breen was being treated. He needed to know if she'd be all right; needed to be here in case she didn't make it . . .

Grace patted Josiah's arm. "I'll stay with Breen. You need something else to think about. I can tell. Unless you're hurt too?"

Josiah shook his head. "Only bruised." And his hand was burned, but between adrenaline earlier and shock now, he'd barely noticed it since he first received the burn. He flexed his hand. It hurt to move, and the skin was red and blistered, but he'd survive.

"Then go." Grace nudged him. "Take a soldier or two with you as well."

"There are soldiers at the towers already." But she was right, and he *did* need to get away from the tower. He could do next to nothing for Breen by standing outside the makeshift infirmary and worrying. Better for him to go accomplish something useful.

Going from one tower to another and collecting the inhabitants took just under two hours. Thankfully, none of the other tower prisoners had been harmed, and the soldiers stationed at the towers informed him that no one had even attempted to pass. Apparently, Gottling had gone straight for Breen.

When they returned to the palace, Josiah knew he ought to go straight to his father and tell him what had happened. But instead, he made his way to the infirmary and asked one of the nurses on duty if she knew what had happened to Breen. She informed him that Breen had been given one of the guest suites nearest the royal rooms, and so he set off again.

He reached Breen's rooms only to find Grace coming out. Grace raised an eyebrow at him. "You should go tell Father what happened."

Josiah glanced at the door Grace had just exited, as if it would somehow tell him anything about the occupant. "How is Breen?"

"She's resting. Doctor MacFarlane treated her injuries, though some of the things he thought were broken turned out not to be. He says she needs to sleep now." Grace gave him a severe look. "And you need to talk to Father. Don't worry. I'll come with you."

Josiah nodded and reluctantly set off to his father's study. He found not only his father there, but his mother as well. King Stephen and Queen Lillian sat together behind the king's desk, looking at papers and talking in a not-quite focused way. Both looked up with expressions of relief when Josiah entered.

King Stephen spoke first. "Josiah, I am glad to see you here in one piece. We heard about the note that called you away. You should have waited for the guard before rushing into danger, though."

"I apologize, Father." Josiah inclined his head slightly, then crossed the room to kiss his mother's cheek. "And to you as well, Mother."

Queen Lillian rose and embraced him. Josiah winced at the pressure on his sore ribs. "Careful. I'm only mostly unscathed."

The queen stepped back and looked him up and down sharply. "You're injured?"

"Bruised around the ribs, mostly. And here." Josiah touched the welt on his face. "But I came out with the fewest injuries of anyone in the fight."

"Perhaps you should sit down and explain," King Stephen interrupted. He gestured to the chair. "Start from the beginning."

Josiah obeyed, explaining the note and how he'd rushed off and the fight in the tower and what had become of Breen. Grace added her side of the last matter, explaining that Doctor MacFarlane had done all he could and thought Breen would pull through if her heart didn't give out first.

"This won't do Weston any favors," Josiah added, once he finished. "Gottling threatened me and nearly killed me, and she's his main authority on blood alchemy. Even if he claims he had nothing to do with any of it, her involvement on top of everything else I found will reflect badly on him."

King Stephen frowned thoughtfully. "True. Do you still intend to announce your findings at the Senate meeting tomorrow? With this new development, we may have grounds to place Weston and those who directly serve him under house arrest until we can question them."

Josiah shook his head. "Weston makes a statement out of anything he does, and he still has a hold on too much of the Senate. The best way to unseat him will be to make an even bigger statement. If we move silently in the night, people will talk. They'll wonder if the Crown is overstepping its boundaries. They may even think that we see Weston as a threat to us rather than the people and therefore desire to silence him without giving him a chance at a public defense. But if I speak against him publically to his face, in a venue where he does have a chance to respond, my confidence will say as much or more than my actual words."

King Stephen nodded. "Wise words. What say you, my queen?"

Queen Lillian smiled slightly. "I say that Josiah is right. Whispers and rumors spread in secret are powerful, but open truth is more so."

"Very well. We defer to your judgment. Speak well tomorrow." King Stephen sighed. "I wish I could be there. Unfortunately, your mother and I must both meet with the Tollestein ambassadors tomorrow to renegotiate our alliance."

"I don't have to be at the negotiations." Grace glanced from face to face. "And I don't have any other responsibilities. I'll go with Josiah to the Senate. For moral support."

Josiah raised an eyebrow at her. "Moral support?"

Grace nodded. "Moral support. And to see how Weston reacts. And in case you need me." She grinned. "Also, if I come, you have a reason to bring a sign interpreter with you. You still plan to have some of the former tower prisoners speak, don't you?"

"You're suggesting I can catch Weston off-guard? Good idea." Josiah managed a grin. "I would be glad to have you join me at the Senate." He glanced to the king and queen. "Unless you see any reason for her not to?"

"Not at all," Queen Lillian said. "I used to accompany your father to Senate meetings, and my own father and brother before that."

"Good." Josiah took a deep breath. "In that case, I suppose I had better go prepare." He still needed to review the agents' report, speak with Peter and the rest of those rescued from the tower to make sure they understood what to say and how to act, prepare his own speeches . . .

It was going to be a long night.

CHAPTER 40

The first thing Breen noticed when she came to was *softness*. She'd never felt anything so light and comfortable as the cushiony surface beneath her, or the thick pillows under her head and feet, or the satiny-smooth fabric that lay over her. Was this Heaven, then? Had she died falling off the tower and woken in the mansions that the priests claimed Jeros would give His people?

She stretched experimentally and stifled a yelp of pain. Her whole body came alive with familiar aches: the all-over soreness that came after a particularly bad fall and the sting of a slowly-healing beating on her back and shoulders. And several parts of her were wrapped in something that kept them stiffly in place: her torso, her left arm, both legs down to the ankles.

Well, that answered the question of whether or not she was in Heaven. But she didn't think she was in the other place either. The obvious way to answer the question would be to open her eyes — which she did, blinking in the pale, early morning light.

She lay in a massive bed, bigger even than the clock faces in the tower. Clean white sheets and a deep green comforter covered her up to her chin. The room beyond the bed was furnished with the sort of simple elegance that, even to Breen's undiscerning eye, said *rich and respectable* more clearly than any extravagant display, all carved dark wood and green brocade and subtle, shining accents of gold and silver.

After a few minutes of staring, Breen noticed someone sitting in the chair beside her bed. She had to peer at the person before she recognized her. Princess Grace was curled up sideways in the oversized seat, her head resting against the back of the chair. Her hair fell around her shoulders in tangled waves, and she was wrapped in a pink robe. The end of her white nightgown peeked out beneath the robe, just above her bare feet.

As Breen watched, the princess stirred slightly, stretched, leaned back, and then jerked awake as she found nothing behind her but the low armrest. She shook herself, eyes wide as she took in her surroundings. Then her gaze fell to Breen, and she smiled. "Good, you're awake," she signed. "Doctor M said he thought you would recover as long as you hadn't hit your head so badly that you never woke up."

Breen automatically reached up to touch her head but stopped herself before she actually could. She tried to lift her other arm so she could sign, but she found that the wrappings extended all the way down past her wrist, almost to her fingers. She settled for fingerspelling with her free hand: "How?" She gestured around the room, hoping Grace would understand her meaning.

"After you fell, Josiah called for Doctor M. He set your broken bones, then had you brought here to recover. You're in the palace, in one of our guest rooms." Grace stood and peered into Breen's face. "How do you feel?"

"Hurt." Breen tried to wiggle herself up enough that she could see the crystal on her chest. It had been damaged; she remembered that. How much longer did she have?

She couldn't move much without pain, but she managed to lift her head just enough to see the faint flicker beneath her — nightdress? Rather than her usual work clothes, she wore a loose white nightgown of fine muslin. Apparently, someone had lent her their clothes.

"Josiah told me about your heart and your broken crystal," Grace signed. "He said he would call for the best alchemists in the city as soon as you were awake so they could find a way to keep your heart going. I have another idea." She reached into a pocket of her robe and pulled out Madame's pendant, which she set on the bed. "If you just need a crystal, maybe you can use this one."

Breen tilted her head, contemplating the idea. Based on what she recalled from her time in the lab, there were two parts to determining the effects of any crystal: one part in how it was set, and one in how it was created. And this pendant did have the ability to heal; Breen was certain of that much. She'd seen it once, years ago, when she'd accidentally dropped Madame down the lift shaft.

[363]

"Try," she signed. "Now." Who knew how much time she had left? She touched the crystal tentatively, making sure it wouldn't trigger some defense. Nothing happened. She gripped the crystal between her thumb and forefinger.

Grace, apparently guessing what she wanted, took hold of the back of the pendant. Breen twisted, and the crystal popped out. Breen rolled it into her palm, then squirmed again.

Grace helped her into a sitting position and piled pillows behind her to help support her. Breen took a deep breath, then tapped the crystal in her chest with her closed fist.

Grace nodded, then tugged the neckline of the nightgown down enough to expose the broken crystal. She glanced at Breen once for reassurance, then carefully twisted the crystal free.

Breen's heartbeat slowed; her body grew suddenly heavy and clumsy. Breen automatically started counting the seconds as she lifted the pendant crystal to the socket. Her fingers shook, and she nearly dropped it but caught it just in time. She twisted once, twice, three times, pressing in gently.

The crystal snapped into the proper position. Her heartbeat sped up. Warmth rushed through her body — more than warmth; *fire* that made her whole body tingle as if it had been asleep for months, yet didn't burn. Pain burst briefly in her legs, her arm, along her ribs, and up her back and shoulders. But each instance faded far more rapidly than it normally would.

Finally, her body settled back into its normal state. Breen unwrapped her arm, batting away Grace's hands as she tried to stop her. She tested her fingers and felt her arm for broken bones. Nothing. She rolled her shoulders; no pain. Apparently, the pendant crystal was far more potent than the one she'd had.

Grace stared, eyes wide, mouth gaping. Her fingers shook as she signed, "How?"

Breen touched the crystal, then signed, "It doesn't just power my heart. It heals me too." She pushed the covers down so she could undo the wrappings on her legs as well.

Grace stood and pulled a cord by the bed. Then she went to wait by the door, resting one hand on its surface. A few minutes later, she opened it and said something to the maid there.

Grace shut the door and faced Breen again. "I called for Doctor M and breakfast. I'm sure you're hungry."

Breen nodded absently. She didn't feel particularly hungry, but she suspected that was just the crystal's effects. She finished unwrapping one leg, then signed, "Why are you here? You're a princess, waiting on me."

Grace returned to her seat and grinned sheepishly. "I couldn't sleep because I was worried about you. I came here around midnight and told the maid who was watching you to go sleep. I must have dozed off sometime, though."

"Thank you." Breen went back to unwrapping her leg.

The doctor, a short man with greying red hair, a mustache, and the gait of a retired soldier, arrived some time later. He brought Nurse Turner with him as assistant and translator, and Breen smiled and tapped her lips to the woman, thanking her again for her help. Nurse Turner smiled back.

Doctor M insisted on checking Breen all over, and on having Nurse Turner feel what he couldn't. At last, however, he pronounced Breen perfectly healthy, though he commented afterward that he didn't know how such a miracle could have occurred.

Breen thought about explaining, but breakfast arrived just then. The maid had brought two trays full of bacon, eggs, fruit, and scones, with not a big of porridge in sight. That distracted her enough that Doctor M and Nurse Turner slipped away before she could say anything.

Breen and Grace ate without saying anything, both caught up in enjoying their meals. Breen savored every bite; even before the tower, she'd never tasted anything this good.

Only after finishing breakfast did Breen ask the other questions that had been weighing on her mind. "What happened to Madame? Is Josiah all right?"

Grace nodded cheerfully. "Josiah's just bruised." She sobered. "Madame G died. She didn't survive the fall."

Oh. Breen blinked and stared at her hands, processing the idea of a world without Madame in it. She tried out the words mentally: *Madame is dead.* The idea didn't seem quite real.

Long ago, when she'd dreamed of freedom and an end to Madame's control, she'd thought she'd feel triumphant when Madame was gone. Instead, a vague numbness hung over her, as if she were in a dream that she knew was a dream, aware of what was going on but not terribly concerned by it.

She pulled her thoughts away from the matter. "Has Josiah's Senate meeting happened?"

Grace shook her head. "No." She tilted her head, raising an eyebrow. "Did you decide whether or not you'd speak?"

Breen shook her head. She'd pondered the question for weeks now. Could she risk such a thing? Could she risk exposing herself like that? If she stayed quiet, she imagined that she might, just maybe, be able to remain under anyone's notice until her heart ran down. There'd be no one looking at her like she was something *other*, no one to start her wondering again if she were a person or just a shell. She'd be safe.

On the other hand, if her testimony could protect one other person from suffering what she'd suffered — if it could keep one other girl or boy out of the blood alchemists' hands — shouldn't she speak, and speak willingly?

And, beyond that . . . it had always been Madame and the other alchemists who told her that the world would reject her if it found out what she really was. But Josiah hadn't. Grace hadn't. Luis hadn't. They'd accepted her. Loved her, even. Perhaps others would accept her too. But she'd never know if she didn't take the risk.

"You don't have to talk if you don't want to." Grace's signs were gentle, her motions slow and non-threatening. "I understand.

You've done so much already. Josiah has asked others to speak already, and they said yes."

Breen looked up and met Grace's eyes. "Will my story help?"

Grace nodded. "Every story helps. If you or any of the others go into the Senate and tell everyone what happened to you, you help the nobles and senators remember what's really at stake. I know your story helped Josiah figure out what to do. I'm sure other senators will see it the same way." She smiled slightly. "I know it's frightening. Josiah and I will both be there, though."

"I know." Breen took a deep breath. "I'll do it."

"Thank you." Grace stood and hugged Breen.

Breen hugged her back. When they broke apart, she added, "Should you tell Josiah?"

"Yes. No." Grace grinned. "I think we should surprise him. I can help you prepare just as well as he can. And the look on his face when you walk in with the others is something I want to see, and I want everyone else to see it as well. Is that all right with you?"

Breen thought for a moment, weighing the options. Then she nodded. "Yes."

"Good." Grace sat down again, grinning like a kitten who'd found a saucer of milk. "Here's what we do . . ."

CHAPTER 41

The Senate argued.

Of *course* they argued. Josiah tapped his pen in the corner of his page of notes, creating a series of tiny dots. That was human nature. Even the most optimistic idealist couldn't deny that. And when you brought up topics like blood alchemy, you were guaranteed to find that *everyone* had an opinion, even if no one had a *solution*.

Thankfully, Josiah would put a stop to that arguing today — or at least send it in a more productive direction.

He glanced down at his book full of documents, notes, and other evidence, waiting for the right moment to speak. His spare copy was safely locked in his father's safe, just in case anything happened to this one. He was taking no risks, not after last night.

Beside him in the Senate box, Grace fidgeted. Josiah turned towards her. "Are you all right?"

She nodded impatiently, smoothing her dark blue skirts. "What are you waiting for?"

"The right moment." Josiah faced forward again. He was still surprised Grace had insisted on joining him for the Senate meeting. All the same, he appreciated her presence — he knew how much Senate meetings bored her. She always said that if she were going to change the world, she'd much rather do it by going out and helping people directly rather than by arguing concepts and theories and regulation in a stuffy room.

On the floor, Senator Aaronson was once again facing down Lord-Senator Weston. "And how do we know that blood alchemy will do all you promise?" he demanded. "How do we know that it will be worth its price? You say your scientists and alchemists have verified these claims through theoretical research and confiscated notes, but I have spoken with respected alchemists myself, and they do not share your certainty. They agree that there is potential for good, but potential alone is not enough to act, especially not when the potential for evil is so great."

Lord-Senator Weston smiled disarmingly. "If my scientists have happened upon a breakthrough that no one else has, Senator Aaronson, I see no reason to complain. Instead, I might wonder what your people are doing wrong."

"And I might wonder how your scientists came upon that breakthrough," Senator Aaronson shot back. "What details are they not telling us, Lord-Senator."

"Exactly what are you saying, Senator?" Weston's smile suddenly turned icy; his tone smooth as a snake's scales. "Are you suggesting that my alchemists would break the law in order to further scientific progress? And, if so, what proof do you have of this claim?"

Senator Aaronson stood straight, just managing to keep his tone controlled. "I'm asking the questions that need to be asked, Lord-Senator. I don't control the answers."

And here was his opportunity. Josiah stood. Grace tensed. Her interpreter, also seated in the box but with no idea of what Josiah planned, jolted in shock. "Prime Minister, gentlemen of the Senate, I have some information relevant to this topic. If I may speak?"

More than a few senators glanced at Josiah in surprise. Even Lord-Senator Weston seemed shocked. Minister Wentworth, however, nodded. "Your Highness, you have the floor. What says the Crown on this matter?"

"The Crown would like to suggest an answer to Senator Aaronson's question, Minister." Though Josiah theoretically addressed the Prime Minister and the Senate as a whole, he kept his attention fixed on Weston, watching for a reaction. "Over the last weeks, I have performed my own investigation into both the potential effects of legalizing blood alchemy and the ways in which blood alchemy already affects our society.

"During those investigations, I discovered that what we know of illegal blood alchemy is but a taste of the whole truth. Already, blood alchemists prey on the most vulnerable among us. No doubt all of you recall the story recounted by young Stephen some weeks ago. His account is characteristic of many. Worse still, the blood alchemists approach lower-class families, seeking more subjects for their experiments. They prey on those who have no other hope and promise a miracle for loved ones injured seemingly beyond repair. And then they claim a price for every life saved, indenturing the children as slaves in their laboratories and other secret places and as subjects for continued experimentation — even before indenturement was legalized!"

Lord-Senator Weston tightened his grip on his cane slightly, but otherwise, he didn't even twitch. Other senators, however, muttered to each other. Josiah continued, "In the course of these investigations, we have identified multiple practicing blood alchemists. One of them is Ms. Gottling, who has spoken in this very room as Lord-Senator Weston's expert on theoretical blood alchemy research. Gentlemen, she may be an expert, but her research is far from theoretical.

"And she is not the only one of the blood alchemists to be linked to his household! She is merely the most recognized. In addition, interviews with some of the former test subjects of the alchemists, young men and women who were wrongfully imprisoned in our own city's great clock towers, have led us to the laboratory and Guild Hall of the blood alchemists, which is located on Lord-Senator Weston's own land."

Josiah paused. The senators' muttering rose, taking on an angry tone. Senator Aaronson glared at Weston with mingled disgust and triumph. Weston stood at his podium, fingers clenched around the handle of his cane. Josiah suppressed a smile. The man was cornered, and he knew it.

"So, Senators," Josiah concluded, "given how closely blood alchemy seems to be tied to Lord-Senator Weston's own household and dealings, one might wonder about his own motivations for supporting the blood alchemy bill. Is it indeed meant for the good of Chania? Or is it simply a way for the blood alchemists to continue their dirty work without hindrance?"

The muttering of the senators stopped abruptly, replaced with a heavy silence. All stared at Josiah as if wondering, *Did he truly just say that?*

Lord-Senator Weston squared his shoulders and lifted his chin so he could look directly at Josiah. "Are you speculating, Your Highness? Or are you making an accusation?"

"The latter." Josiah stared down at Weston, resting one hand on the edge of his Senate box. "I accuse you of harboring illegal blood alchemists, of supporting them in their endeavors, and of backing this bill primarily so you could benefit openly from their work." Unfortunately, he couldn't outright say that Weston *was* a blood alchemist — he didn't know that for sure. But having helped them was bad enough.

"Bold words, Your Highness. Dangerous words, even." Weston's tone was measured, calm, even, though a hint of anger simmered underneath. "While we are questioning motivations, why do we not question yours? Every person in this room knows that I wield considerable power in this land and in this Senate, power you would like to see returned to the throne. So, do you bring these claims against me because you truly want what is best for Chania?

Or do you simply want to eliminate a threat and claim the ability to mold Chania to your will?"

The Senate broke out in shouts. Grace, reading her interpreter's signs with narrowed eyes, huffed angrily.

Senator Aaronson glared at Weston like he wanted to punch the man in the face. "How dare you accuse Prince Josiah of such a thing? He has always worked within the laws of this country and done the best he can for its people! He would not speak against you without good reason."

"Then let him produce the proof!" Weston shot back. "There are laws in this country against knowingly bringing false charges against another, and even royalty cannot escape them. Has he any proof of his claims?"

How dare — Josiah forcibly tamped down his anger at Weston's accusations and held up the notebook full of evidence. "Indeed, I do. I have here records of interviews with those affected by the blood alchemists, along with photographs of the blood alchemists' Guild Hall and laboratory and statements from various experts that will reveal just how deep this treachery goes. Prime Minister Wentworth, I pass this to you for inspection and temporary safe-keeping." Josiah turned away and handed the notebook to a page waiting outside the Senate box, taking a hard look at the young man to make sure he was indeed the page who was supposed to be there and not some pawn planted by Weston.

"I see." Weston nodded, undaunted. "This is all well and good, Your Highness, but even if you believe what you have in that notebook, secondhand stories can be misinterpreted — or faked altogether. Without firsthand witnesses, one might still question your claims. Have you any of those?"

"I have firsthand witnesses, yes. But I did not wish to bring them into the Senate hall without permission." Josiah turned to address the prime minister. "Minister Wentworth, do I have your permission to bring in witnesses to clarify both my accusations against Lord-Senator Weston and the potential consequences of his proposed bill?"

Prime Minister Wentworth looked up from the notebook, which he had been rapidly flipping through. "By all means. Let them be brought in and speak their piece."

Josiah nodded and turned to another page. "Go. You know who you're looking for?"

The page nodded; Josiah had warned them of this possibility earlier. "Yes, Your Highness. I'll return in a moment."

He disappeared out the door. Josiah waited and listened as whispers spread again through the Senate room. He wished he could hear more clearly what they were saying and what kind of witnesses they expected to walk through those doors. Did any of them guess the truth?

Not ten minutes later, the page returned. "They're here, Your Highness." He held the door open for those who came after him: two young women and two young men, all dressed in rough work clothes. One girl and one boy had arms made of rods and gears, with small crystals at the joints. The boy, Peter, nodded cheerily to

Josiah as they approached. The other boy and girl had no visible defect, but the girl . . .

Josiah stared. *Breen?* The last he'd heard of her, she'd been unconscious in a guest room. But if this girl wasn't her, she was like enough to her to be her twin — and he *knew* Lily was dead.

Then she glanced in his direction, and he had no doubt at all, only wonder. He knew that face, even if he most often saw it in only dim light. How she was here, he didn't know. But he silently thanked Jeros for the miracle all the same.

The page guided the four to the royal box. Josiah moved to the side as they crowded in, silent and staring. Two of them, a girl and a boy, held tight to each other, their uncertainty written plainly across their faces. But Breen and Peter stood straight and bold. Josiah could tell that they were nervous too, but they hid it well.

He nodded to them, resisting the urge to single out Breen and ask her all his questions about how she was here. "Thank you for coming. Will you please tell the Senate who you are and why you're here?" He signed as he spoke, translating his words for the benefit of the four.

There was a hastily signed conference among the four, which then devolved into a minor argument between Breen and Peter. After a moment, Breen stepped to the very edge of the box, clearly steeling herself. She cleared her throat and glanced towards Grace, who nodded encouragingly. Then, she spoke, her voice just a touch louder than necessary. "My name is Breen Wellens. This is Peter, and these are Jess and Jack Atwater. We're here because J — His

Highness said he needed us to tell the Senate what happened to us so it wouldn't happen to others."

The Prime Minister stood and turned around so he could see the four better. "And what is it that happened to you?"

The interpreter passed on the question. Breen shut her eyes for a moment, opened them, and spoke, her voice dropping slightly. "I was ten. There was an accident at the factory where my sister and I worked, and we were both almost killed. Our father took us to the free hospital, but they said we'd die. Then the blood alchemists went to my father and said they could save my sister and me if he promised we'd work for them after. He didn't know what they really meant, and he wanted us to live. So he said yes."

Breen trembled slightly. Peter put his arm around her shoulder from one side, and Grace took her other hand. Breen managed a shaky smile and went on. "The blood alchemists could've saved both of us. They have that power. But they wanted to experiment. They wanted to know if a relative's blood worked better than a stranger's. So they killed Lily and saved me, gave me a mechanical heart to replace my real one."

"Objection." Weston's voice cut through Breen's. The interpreter held up a hand to stop Breen speaking. "This girl appears entirely normal. What proof do we have that she is, in fact, a former experiment of the blood alchemists?"

Josiah stepped forward. "As I recall, Lord-Senator, your own firsthand witness also appeared normal save for the power crystal and socket. And I cannot imagine that you would ask a woman to expose herself so indecently!"

Weston merely shrugged. "You bring weighty accusations against me, Your Highness. I will have full proof, or I will not hear them."

Josiah sputtered, trying to formulate a response. Breen tapped his arm and gave him a look. Then she faced the Senate, said loudly, "Sorry for the indecency," and unbuttoned her shirt low enough to expose the crystal. It shone bold, bloody red against her pale clothes and skin. "Do you believe me now?"

"That is acceptable," Minister Wentworth interjected before Weston could demand more. "Please cover yourself again and continue your account. Any further objections will be held until after you are finished."

Breen waited a moment, reading the interpreter's translation. Then she nodded. "Yes, sir." She buttoned up her shirt again and went on, "The blood alchemists made me work in their lab for the first few years, cleaning things and such. Then they got mad because I disobeyed them, so they sent me to the clock tower instead. I kept the clock ever since, and if I didn't do my work well enough, Madame beat me. Then Prince Josiah came and started asking me why I was there, and he kept coming back. And then Madame found out, and she . . ." Breen hesitated as if trying to pick the right word. "She tried to hurt me and threaten the prince."

Josiah cleared his throat. "I will note that a desire for witnesses today was not my only reason for extricating the blood alchemists' victims from the towers at this time. Last night, I received a message informing me that, if I revealed the results of my investigation, the young men and women in the clock towers would die. Rather than be cowed or allow that to happen, I simply removed them from the reach of their former captors."

On the Senate floor, Lord-Senator Weston was turning a very interesting shade of red. "This is slander. I will not stand for this."

"Then you may sit down, Senator." The Prime Minister fixed him with a hard look. "All scheduled Senate business is hereby postponed while we look into this matter. Those who wish to leave may, with the exceptions of Lord-Senator Weston and his retinue and his highness and his witnesses. They will remain, as I believe we have further questions for all of them."

A few senators left. Most remained. Weston stayed standing, though Aaronson returned to his seat, looking smug. Prime Minister Wentworth picked up a pad of paper and a pen, then called to the Senate recorder, "Make sure you get all of this." Then he faced Josiah and his group again. "Now, my first question . . ."

As the hours passed, Josiah came to a very firm conclusion: Prime Minister Wentworth would be just as good at controlling a courtroom as he was at leading the Senate. He questioned Breen, Peter, Jack, and Jess with all the thoroughness of a lawyer or a judge. First, he had them recount their experiences, and then he picked at those stories until he knew every relevant detail.

From there, he turned his questions to Josiah. Josiah answered readily, beginning with the first night he met Breen, continuing through his investigations and interviews, and ending with the previous night's events. Wentworth's brow rose slightly when he heard about the fight in the clock tower, but he only commented, "That would explain why I heard about a disturbance near the tower. What became of Madame Gottling, Your Highness?"

"She is, I'm afraid, dead, Minister. Falling from a clock tower will have that effect in most cases." Josiah inclined his head slightly. "I had her body sent to the Upper Rivenford Morgue. I intend to see that her next-of-kin is notified as soon as this meeting is over."

"This is an outrage!" Weston's face had gone from red to white. "First you slander me, then you have my leading researcher killed?"

Prime Minister Wentworth turned to face Weston. "From what I understand, Lord Senator, Madame Gottling attempted to kill His Highness and Miss Wellens first. A court would no doubt find that they acted in self-defense and merely saved the hangman a job. But, since you are eager to speak, perhaps you will answer some questions now. When did you first meet Madame Gottling?"

Weston went purple and gripped his cane like it were a lifeline. Josiah sighed and sat down — on the ground, as there weren't enough chairs in the box, nor was there room for any to be added. He looked up at Breen with a weary grin. "I think we've done it, Miss Breen. Thank you for your help, and thank you for saving my life yesterday."

Breen, who'd been leaning on Grace, smiled and sat up. "You're welcome. Thank you for rescuing me."

"I believe it was a joint effort. You rescued yourself as much as I did you." Josiah shifted to a slightly more comfortable position. "How are you doing? You look remarkably well compared to yesterday."

"I'm very well." Breen touched her crystal again. "Grace came up with the idea of switching my broken crystal for the unbroken one from the pendant. Part of the crystal's magic is healing as well as power for my heart."

"Thank Jeros for that." Josiah sighed, leaning his head against the edge of the box and listening to Wentworth's questions and Weston's increasingly slippery answers.

"So what happens now?" Breen asked, her fingers and face sharp with sudden nervousness. "You've won. You exposed Weston. I'm free — we're all free. What do we do next?"

"Weston and the blood alchemists go to court. I imagine you'll be called on as a witness. The Senate and I come to a decision about the blood alchemists. And beyond that?" Josiah smiled — a full smile this time. "As you said, you're free now. You choose your path. And whatever I can do to help you on that road, I will. After all, that's what friends do."

EPILOGUE

Breen had always known the clock tower was beautiful. But she hadn't realized just *how* beautiful until it was no longer her whole world.

Breen sat on a crossbeam in the center of the clock tower as the clock struck two. Around her, the crystals on the machinery glowed, and the tower trembled with the striking bells. Breen trembled too, not from fear but from beauty.

The tower stilled, and the moment passed. Breen sighed happily. Glad as she'd been to finally leave the tower, there were moments she missed. That was half the reason why she'd been so excited when she heard that the towers would still need a keeper, someone to check them once or twice a week and ensure everything remained in working order. She'd offered her services at once, as had Jack Atwater. They split the seven towers between them, and so every other afternoon, Breen traveled to one or another of them and climbed up through the machinery, reveling in the fact that what had been a chore was now her choice.

Breen turned her attention back to her work, inspecting the gears for damage and wiping away the occasional bit of dust, grease, or condensation. She only had this level left to do, then she'd be done for the day.

Breen finished her work, then dropped down onto the third floor, careless of injury. The first few days after she and Grace replaced her crystal, she'd made every move hesitantly, uncertain how long the new crystal would last. But, almost two weeks later, the crystal showed no sign of running out of power. And even if she drained it all the way, Josiah's soldiers had raided the old blood alchemist laboratory and come out with, among other things, a large stock of already-charged crystals suitable for use by Breen and the others. Some of those had been claimed by the alchemists for further study, but most were reserved for keeping the blood alchemists' former captives alive.

On the third floor, Breen fetched her satchel from the shelf where she'd left it. She pulled off her goggles and tool belt and stashed them in the bag, then changed her work pants for the skirt she'd brought with her. Normally, she wouldn't have bothered to change; enough working women wore pants that she only stood out a little on the streets. But today, she needed to look a bit nicer — though even her skirt was more practical than pretty. It was, however, sturdy and comfortable and full of useful pockets, and, most importantly, it was *hers*. And, paired with her work shirt and a fitted brown vest, she looked . . . well, nice enough for the Inventors' Guild, at least.

She took her time transferring the smaller tools from her tool belt into the pockets of her skirt and lacing up her boots. Then she slung her bag over her shoulder and headed down the steps.

On the ground, Breen walked out of the tower and locked the door behind her. She stretched, exulting in the warm sunshine on her face, and then circled around to the main street, skirting the scaffolding that climbed up the sides of the tower. Workmen were still in the process of replacing the clock face that had been broken during the fight in the tower. Breen wished they would hurry up — but, of course, they could only spend a short time each day working on the tower, or they'd risk draining the crystals too much.

It was only a fifteen-minute walk from the tower to the Inventors' Guild Hall. Breen enjoyed every moment of it, pausing along the way to peer in shop windows or watch sparrows pecking at the sidewalks for crumbs left by passersby. Even with her slow pace, she reached the guild hall with time to spare.

Other guild members waved to her as she entered, and a few even signed greetings. Breen waved back but didn't pause to chat. The heads of the guild had been willing enough to transfer the patent from Daniels to her and to grant her membership in the Guild once she explained what had happened and produced her second prototype. One blessing of her imprisonment in the tower: no one could accuse her of having copied someone else's work. Even so, she couldn't yet talk to most of the other guild members without feeling like she didn't deserve to be there.

She spotted Josiah across the entry hall, near the great wooden doors to the lecture hall. She hurried over to him, waving. As soon as she was close enough, she signed, "Are you here for Luis's presentation?"

"Hello, Breen." Josiah grinned at her. "Yes. I promised him I would be in the front row. After all, I am sponsoring his entry. I assume you are here for that as well?"

Breen nodded. "He asked me specifically to come. Are you going inside soon?"

"I am." Josiah nodded towards the doors. "Sit with me?"

"Yes, thank you." Breen followed him inside.

Breen and Josiah claimed seats near the end of the front row. Breen checked the clock at the back of the lecture hall. Ten minutes remained before Luis's presentation. She spotted him in the front row, in the very center of the hall, but he was occupied talking to an older man who she recognized as one of the Guild officials.

The rest of the hall filled quickly. Much of the Guild, it seemed, had made time to see what Luis had to offer. At about five minutes 'til, a woman Breen recognized as one of the Guild members skilled in sign language stepped into place by the stage, just beside the left-side stairs. She nodded to Breen, and Breen nodded back, thankful that the Guild had been able to find someone to interpret. She guessed that Josiah would've done it in a pinch, but it was better that he be able to celebrate Luis's big moment without distraction.

At exactly three o'clock, Sir Kensworth, the senior Head of the guild, opened the presentation by introducing Luis and praying to

Jeros. Then he moved to the side of the stage, where seats had been set for the three Heads, and Luis took center stage. He set his watch-camera prototype on a small table provided for that purpose and took a breath, scanning the audience. Breen grinned at him and gave a little wave. He gave her back the smile of someone running on coffee and adrenaline and turned to address the Heads.

Though Luis stumbled a bit at the beginning of his speech, he quickly seemed to forget his nervousness as he explained how his watch-camera worked, how he'd come up with the ideas, and the challenges he'd overcome to make it. Breen did her best to keep one eye on the stage and one on the translation, but she didn't have to know exactly what was being said to guess how things were going.

After Luis's initial presentation, the Heads and the audience peppered Luis with further questions, which Luis seemed to answer without much trouble. Finally, the Heads nodded and dismissed Luis. Luis bowed and walked off the stage, taking his prototype with him.

Breen stood, tracking Luis's progress as he made his way towards her. Every so often, others stopped him to shake his hand or slap his shoulder and say something. One older gentleman had quite an extended conversation with Luis, from which Luis came away beaming. He was still beaming when he reached Josiah and Breen.

Luis went first to Josiah, exclaiming something. Breen watched them, trying to guess what they were staying, but lip reading remained mostly a mystery, and they were facing partially away from her anyway.

Luis finally ran out of words for Josiah and turned to Breen. "Thank you for coming. I am glad you could be here." He signed slowly and carefully, his furrowed brow and slight frown suggesting frustration — or, more likely, deep concentration. Though he'd picked up more sign around the same time he started visiting her in the tower, and though he'd started learning sign in earnest after Breen accepted his father's offer of a job at Kronos Clocks and Gadgetry, he was far from fluent.

Breen nodded, smiling. "You did well." She signed it slowly too, making sure he could follow what she said. Then, gesturing to the man he'd been talking to, she asked, "Who was that?"

Luis made a few helpless motions, then turned to Josiah. Josiah signed as Luis spoke. "That was the man who invented the camera model I used for my watch-camera. He said he would like to see my watch-camera up close for himself and asked if I would like to collaborate on similar projects in the future."

Luis grinned broadly, fidgeting as if social decorum were the only thing keeping him from actually dancing for joy. "I said yes, of course."

"I'm happy for you." Breen turned to Josiah. "What now? You said a few days ago that you planned something for tonight."

Josiah nodded. He spoke and signed at the same time, as he frequently did. "I do. I thought celebration was in order. Grace will be here with the carriage soon, and then we will go to one of the new cafes that just opened recently. Over dinner, we can decide what we want to do next. The Royal Theater Company is performing in the Crown Park Amphitheater, and I have confirmed that they will have sign interpreters tonight so we could all enjoy the show. In addition, the Rochester Art Gallery has a new collection that just debuted. Or we can simply walk and enjoy the city."

"I like all of those." Any new experience would be welcome, especially with friends. Breen gestured towards the doors, then signed, "Should we wait outside for Grace?"

"Good idea." Josiah led the way outside. Benches flanked the doors to the Guild Hall, but no one sat. Instead, Luis turned and asked Josiah something.

Josiah repeated the question in sign for Breen's benefit. "How is the court case going?" He went on, now both speaking and signing again, "It's going well. I think I told you that Weston is under house arrest and is permanently suspended from the Senate."

Breen nodded. "I was there. Remember?"

"That happened the day you testified. Yes, I'm sorry I forgot." Josiah went on, "Two of Weston's aides have come forward with information about how Weston was supporting the blood alchemists and making a way for them to work openly in return for the first claim on the use of any technology they created. Their story matches what we learned from the blood alchemists who agreed to talk in exchange for a reduced sentence."

Luis asked something else. Josiah shook his head gravely. "Tracking the remaining blood alchemists is going poorly. Not all were present when our soldiers raided the lab. In addition, some blood alchemists weren't connected to Weston. We will simply have to keep looking."

"And the bill?" Breen added. Other than the special provision for her and the other victims of the blood alchemists, she'd heard little about what happened to the blood alchemy bill. "Is it still there?"

"It was voted down yesterday." Josiah seemed far less triumphant than Breen had expected him to; his tight expression suggested concern more than anything. "I expect another bill will be proposed before long. Perhaps a year or two from now. Now that the idea is in people's minds and we know exactly what blood alchemy is capable of, more people will be interested in harnessing it. I hope that next time, it will be in better hands."

Just then, an open-top carriage pulled up by the Guild Hall. Grace bounded out. "You all look glum! What's wrong? Did Luis do poorly?" Her hands fairly danced through the signs.

"We were talking about the blood alchemy bill," Josiah replied, more sedately. "Luis did very well, indeed, and I have no doubt that he will be accepted as a Guild member."

"Good!" Grace grinned. "Then we should celebrate. Politics will wait until tomorrow." She beckoned to Breen. "Come on. You sit by me."

Breen grinned and followed Grace back into the carriage. Grace was right. Weston's trial, the remaining blood alchemists — they were problems for another day. Tonight, she was free, and she was with friends, and she could celebrate without fear. And so she would.

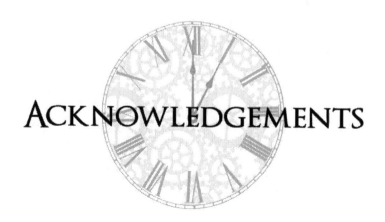

ACKNOWLEDGEMENTS

Like most things worth spending time on, writing this novel would not have been possible without the help and support of quite a lot of people. I'd like to take a moment to recognize a few of those people.

First and foremost, I would like to thank Kendra E. Ardnek, who organized the Golden Braids Arista Challenge and group release. I truly appreciate all the time and effort she puts into helping other authors (myself included) succeed, and her advice and support have been invaluable.

I also want to thank my beta readers: Alina Kanaski, Kathryn McConaughy, Matthew Sampson, Meghan Largent, Marlene Simonette, and Tobia Gemmell. When I sent them *Mechanical Heart*, it was a half-grown, unwieldy story that was trying to say something but couldn't quite figure out how to do it. Their feedback and encouragement helped me grow the book into what it is today.

I also would like to thank Hallie Martin, Michaela Proffitt, and Ashley Stout, who acted as ASL consultants while I was writing this book. Despite being busy people with lives of their own, they were always willing to answer my questions, whether I needed help translating a section of dialogue from English to sign or wanted clarification about a concept I'd found out about in my own research. Without their assistance, I could not have written Breen's story in a way that I felt comfortable sharing.

Of course, it's not just people who directly contributed to this book who deserve thanks. Throughout the long process of writing and publishing *Mechanical Heart*, my parents and sister have been incredibly supportive and encouraging. I am incredibly blessed to be part of such a wonderful family (even if some of them don't quite understand what steampunk is — hopefully, this book cleared it up for them).

I also want to specially thank Alana, who is the best friend and roommate a writer could possibly have. Without her, I would probably *still* be stuck trying to write one of Josiah's Senate scenes (and she knows why). Whether I need a listening ear, a person with whom to talk through my characters' philosophical and ethical dilemmas, a distraction from the frustrations of uncooperative words, or someone to tell me to stop procrastinating and start writing, she's been there through the hardest part of writing this book. Furthermore, Alana acted as Emergency Science Consultant at a few key points in this book, for which I am also very grateful.

In addition, I need to mention two people who currently do not (and probably will never) know that I or my book exist. The first is pop violinist Lindsey Stirling, whose album "Shatter Me" provided both the first sparks of inspiration for *Mechanical Heart* and much of the soundtrack for the book's first draft. The second is Epbot blogger Jen Yates, who first introduced me to the wonders of steampunk (even though she didn't know she was doing it). Admittedly, I probably would've discovered it by other means later on, but that initial impression had quite a bit of influence.

Finally, I give thanks to my God, the Great Author of my story, for giving me this book. As in all things, He has organized my life so I would read the right things, hear the right ideas, and meet the right people at the right time for *Mechanical Heart* to exist. I pray that my writing is, and always will be, glorifying to Him.

ABOUT THE AUTHOR

Sarah Pennington has been writing stories since before she actually knew how to write, and she has no intention of stopping anytime soon. She is perpetually in the middle of writing at least one or two novels, most of which are in the fantasy and fairy tale retelling genres. Sarah's first published work, *Blood in the Snow*, received a perfect score and Special Unicorn status in Rooglewood Press's *Five Poisoned Apples* contest. When she isn't writing, she enjoys knitting, photography, and trying to conquer her massive to-be-read list.

Sarah can be found online at sarahpennington.com. She also blogs at Light and Shadows (tpssarahlightshadows.wordpress.com) and Dreams and Dragons (dreams-dragons.blogspot.com).

OTHER GOLDEN BRAIDS TITLES

This book was published as part of the Golden Braids, a collection of five unique and exciting retellings of *Rapunzel*. Check out these other titles, each showing a side of the tale you've never seen before!

HAIR WE GO AGAIN

Kendra E. Ardnek

Still reeling from recent trauma, Robin and Eric agree to help
some friends. But can healing be found when people refuse to
communicate?

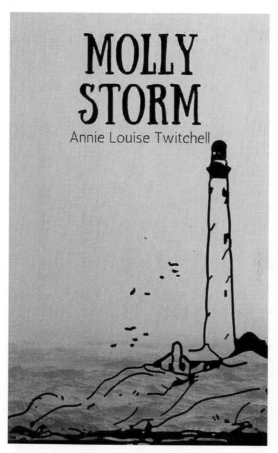

MOLLY STORM

Annie Twitchell

A witch, a pirate, a lighthouse, and . . . seaweed?

REBEKAH'S REFUGE

Meredith Leigh Burton

Above all, never, ever allow your hair to be cut.

THE DRAGON'S FLOWER

Wyn Estelle Owens

Can the imprisoned princess and the exiled samurai save the

Seven Kingdoms from ruin?

Made in the USA
Middletown, DE
04 October 2023

39754810R00243